FIRE
AND
ICE

Volume Two of
The Mountain Trilogy

Edward Myers

A ROC BOOK

ROC

Published by the Penguin Group

Penguin Books USA Inc., 375 Hudson Street,
New York, New York 10014, U.S.A.
Penguin Books Ltd, 27 Wrights Lane,
London W8 5TZ, England
Penguin Books Australia Ltd, Ringwood,
Victoria, Australia
Penguin Books Canada Ltd, 10 Alcorn Avenue,
Toronto, Ontario, Canada M4V 3B2
Penguin Books (N.Z.) Ltd, 182–190 Wairau Road,
Auckland 10, New Zealand

Penguin Books Ltd, Registered Offices:
Harmondsworth, Middlesex, England

First published by Roc, an imprint of New American Library,
a division of Penguin Books USA Inc.

First Printing, December, 1992

10 9 8 7 6 5 4 3 2 1

This one, too, is for Edith

Some say the world will end in fire,
Some say in ice.
From what I've tasted of desire
I hold with those who favor fire.
But if it had to perish twice,
I think I know enough of hate
To say that for destruction ice
Is also great
And would suffice.

—Robert Frost

EDITOR'S NOTE

Is there a city on earth gloomier than Lima? It's overcast nearly all year round; an almost imperceptibly fine drizzle—what the locals call *garúa*—falls month after month; and the heavy cloudcover leaves the whole place dank and chilly despite its proximity to the equator. This is a city so damp you have to leave a light on in the closet just to keep your clothes from rotting.

Yet it's not really the weather I mean. There's something else, something hard to identify but impossible to avoid, that makes the Peruvian capital so ponderous and gray. Is it the pollution billowing forth from innumerable badly tuned cars, buses, and trucks? The gradual crumbling of the city as the Peruvian economy itself deteriorates? The shanty-town slums springing up out of junk lumber, straw mats, even cardboard boxes as millions of peasants wander down from the Andean highlands looking for work? It's all of this but something else as well.

There's a legend I've heard repeatedly during my stays in the Peruvian capital. After Francisco Pizarro conquered the Inca empire in 1532 and toppled its rulers from power, the Spaniards set about establishing their new colony. One of their tasks was to found a capital. At some point they asked their Indian subjects for advice. What would be the best place for a city? The Indians told them to build on the site of what is now present-day Lima. This advice has come to be known as the Incas' Revenge.

* * *

In 1970 I found myself in Lima yet again. Once more I wandered through the perpetually twilit streets; once more I struggled to find what I sought. The *garúa* fell as it always falls—silent except for the slightest hiss. The odors of cooking oil, sauteed onions, and diesel fumes intermingled in the mid-afternoon air. As I passed cheap restaurants and *bodegas*, I heard snatches of the rhythmic tunes that mix Indian with European elements to create *música criolla*. I felt uneasy when the people I crossed paths with stared at me, a gangly *gringo*. Yet I felt resolute in being there regardless of my unease.

I'll admit that despite Lima's gloom I've found myself repeatedly drawn to the place. Never mind that my father did business there during my boyhood, and that I spent several years living in the middle-class suburb of Miraflores. That early experience accounts for my introduction to the city, not my subsequent pull toward it. In fact I've returned as an adult, not once but time and again, searching for something I could sense but not identify. It wasn't Lima itself that drew me. Lima was my port of entry, not my goal; the rest of Peru was the gravitational field I've never successfully resisted. Yet even Lima—cold, gray, drizzly Lima—has served a purpose.

I was late for my appointment. The Peruvians aren't scrupulous about time; in fact, they're pretty casual. If someone invites you to dinner at seven you can arrive at eight and be the first guest present. But I was pushing my luck. I'd convinced a prominent Peruvian scholar to meet with me at noon. Now it was already well past three.

"Señor Myers," he greeted me, smiling with gentle derision, and shook my hand. He was sixtyish but still dark-haired, more Hispanic than Indian in facial features, with a straight nose and a mustache so thin that it might as well have been etched on his lip with a fountain pen. *"Quizás está acomodándose a nuestros costumbres un tantito más rápido de lo prudente."* Perhaps you are adjusting to our ways a little faster than seems prudent.

I offered profuse apologies. *"Perdóneme, Profesor. Las circunstancias—"*

With a grand didactic gesture he motioned for me to sit. He wasn't about to *perdonarme* for *las circunstancias.* All he wanted was to get down to business and be done with this young *gringo.*

I took a chair opposite his massive desk. The office was oppressive—dim and unventilated—but I distracted myself by noting the quality of the pre-Columbian pottery stashed here and there on the bookshelves. These were better pieces than I'd seen in many museums.

"So what serves your purposes?" he asked.

"I'm trying to find information about the *alpinistas cholos,*" I told the professor. "The so-called Indian mountain climbers."

He held off briefly before responding: we heard a knock at the door. When the professor beckoned, someone entered. A cleaning woman, it seemed. An ancient Indian tottered in with a rag and a blue enameled bucket. Her appearance startled me—her face was so purely Indian in its features that she might have been the model for some of the finer Nazca or Chimú pots on the shelves around her—yet she paid no attention to us, and the professor didn't acknowledge her in the least. Without a word she knelt and started scrubbing the floor on hands and knees.

The professor turned to me with the same derisive smile as before. "What were we discussing? Ah, yes—information. The Indian mountain climbers. I would have thought you had already found quite enough about them already."

He was referring (with more than a tinge of academic envy) to a book I'd published some years earlier. *The Mountain Made of Light* had made public the journal of an American anthropologist named Jesse O'Keefe, who, in 1921, discovered a lost civilization deep in the Peruvian Andes. Interwoven with a narrative by Aeslu of Vmatta—the young native woman assigned to Jesse as a translator—this journal portrayed the clash between an ancient and a modern culture. Yet the professor's envy was ironic. O'Keefe's and Aeslu's documents had lain unread and unpublished for fifty years, but not because anyone had so carefully hidden them. I had found them stashed under a pile of old *National Geographic*s at the Biblioteca Pública de Lima. All I'd done was to salvage these documents—documents that everyone else had ignored—from the inexorable march of mildew.

"I don't know if it's really enough information at all," I responded, "but it's certainly enough to whet my appetite."

The professor nodded slowly, never taking his eyes off me, no doubt concurring that some sort of peculiar gluttony was the sin I'd committed.

This wasn't the first time I'd encountered this reaction. The educated Peruvians I was tracking down and interviewing often manifested the same mix of disapproval and exasperation. What was it that disturbed them about me or what I'd done? Did they resent a foreigner finding and publishing an account that Peruvians might consider theirs alone? Did they covet the attention that *The Mountain Made of Light* had received? Did they somehow prefer that the story had never gotten out in the first place? Watching the professor, I couldn't answer these questions now any more than I'd been able to earlier.

I told him, "It seems clear there's more to the story."

"What do you mean by *more*?"

It seemed unlikely that the professor didn't know, but I sketched the situation anyway. *The Mountain Made of Light* portrays a complex sequence of events. It describes how Jesse was unprepared for the complex Rixtir ("Mountain-Drawn") culture he encountered; how the Rixtirra were equally unready for the gentle newcomer in their midst; how Jesse's attraction for Aeslu complicated the situation; and how their crossing paths with a wealthy playboy-mountaineer named Forster Beckwith made matters still more intricate. The book also describes how Rixtir theology predicted that two outsiders would some day enter the Mountain Land—one threatening the people with destruction, the other sparing them from the first—and how Jesse and Forster were prime candidates for these roles of destroyer and savior. And it explains how all these aspects of the situation led to a search for the fabled Mountain Made of Light and, ultimately, to disaster in a city called the Web.

But no matter what these documents reveal, they're also significant for what they don't. Aeslu's narrative, especially, makes clear that she survived the Web disaster. Had O'Keefe and Beckwith survived as well? If not, what became of Aeslu afterward? And if she *did* survive, what further events took place in the Mountain Land?

The professor was unimpressed. "You were lucky the first time around," he noted as he took a Gaulois from his silver case and tapped the cigarette against the crystal of his watch. "And such luck rarely strikes twice."

Of course he was doing everything possible to make sure it didn't. Within a few minutes I'd been shown out of his office and returned once more to the street, the *garúa*, and the waxy evening air.

* * *

So it went with the other interviews I arranged. I had planned to stay in Lima several weeks but had lingered for months. In addition to the good professor, my interview subjects included some historians, anthropologists, and linguists in three local universities; a variety of government bureaucrats; and anyone else I thought might help me. Nothing worked out. Most of these people weren't intentionally rude—they simply didn't see the point of what I was attempting.

My luck was equally bleak at the various libraries and archives I visited. The staff members did their best. Still, no luck. Even the Biblioteca Pública was a dead end. Finding the O'Keefe and Aeslu documents seemed little more than a fluke. No one could remember seeing anything remotely like what I'd stumbled into earlier.

By late August I prepared to leave. My money had run out; besides, I wasn't getting anywhere. I planned to fly back to the United States in early September.

Then, late one evening, I left my room to go get some dinner. I'd been staying at a third-rate hotel near the Plaza de Armas. The place itself was bleak enough—a musty dive—but it had been convenient to many of the places I frequented in that old part of the city. Now I hurried through the drizzly night to find some hot soup and bread to warm myself up a bit.

One of the incidental nuisances of that area was the number of hawkers out and about almost round the clock. The Plaza de Armas attracted vendors selling everything from balloons, candy, and gum to watches and transistor radios. It seemed impossible to go five feet without someone pestering me to purchase a trinket, record, lottery ticket, or toy. Didn't these people ever sleep? It was almost ten already. And beggars: the

Plaza drew more than its share of the lame, the halt, and the blind.

Now without warning a dark figure approached me on the left. Instinctively I eased toward the wall—I wasn't in a mood to be accosted—but too late. Whoever it was began pulling out some sheafs of paper before I could object. Magazines, newspapers? I couldn't tell.

"For you," he said. "For you." He muttered in a low, hoarse voice.

No, it wasn't a man—it was an old woman. When she stepped into a streetlamp's cone of light, I could see her braids, blouse, and shabby cotton skirt. She appeared to be an Indian. I tried to slip past her but she blocked me, and in that moment of standing face-to-face I saw that she was even older than I first thought. Seventy, maybe older: a gray-haired crone. And she was speaking to me again.

"For you, Meester."

Whatever she was shoving toward me wasn't anything I wanted. A piece of cloth: no, paper. Rumpled sheets of paper.

Just what I needed: getting accosted by a half-wit beggar on a half-lit street.

"For you," she said, "Meester Myers."

I stopped abruptly. She had spoken my name as many Peruvians do—*Mee-ers*—as if reading it phonetically in Spanish. But somehow her mispronunciation convinced rather than dissuaded me that she knew who I was. I turned and looked her over. She was a full-blooded Indian—that much I could tell. Then with a jolt I realized that she was the cleaning lady from the professor's office. "Who are you?" I asked.

"No one you know," she said quietly, almost timidly.

"Did the professor send you?"

"Not at all—he knows nothing about me."

"What do you want, then?"

"Just to help you." She spoke good Spanish, though an accent I couldn't identify colored the words. A Quechua dialect, perhaps? Or Aymara?

I glanced around. Surely an old crone like this presented no danger, yet I felt tense with alarm. "I can't talk with you," I told her.

"Please, Meester Myers."

I backed off. Before I could escape, though, she shoved something at me. Enough light from the streetlamp struck it that I caught a glimpse of the writing there.

At once I pulled the paper out of her hands. Stunned, I glanced it over. "Where did you get this?"

"I've always had it," she told me without any air of boasting or apology.

"Had it? What do you mean?"

"I obtained it shortly after it was written. I have had it ever since that time."

I stared at her without believing what she said, yet I couldn't deny her claim. "Why are you showing it to me now?"

"Because you know what to do with it."

Across the street was a café of sorts, one of those unadorned eating places that crop up throughout working class areas of Lima—a few oilcloth-covered tables in a concrete room, a slate on the wall providing the only menu. A few men sat there drinking beer and eating plates of rice and beans. Otherwise it was empty.

"Come with me," I said, helping her across the street.

PART ONE

1

URGENTE—URGENTE—URGENTE
Entregue esta carta inmediatamente a:
Señor Forster Beckwith III
Industrias F. F. Beckwith e Hijos, S.A.
Jirón Unión No. 62
Lima, Perú
12 September 1921

Dear Father,

Rest assured that I have already anticipated your anger in response to my long silence; still, I have high hopes that this effort at renewed communication will at least begin to allay your irritation. Moreover, I have news that will justify whatever patience you can muster while I try to explain myself.

I have made a remarkable discovery. Let me spare you the details just now; soon enough you'll see for yourself. For now let me say simply that I have stumbled into a long-lost civilization, a whole culture packed away in cold storage. In itself this is a remarkable find—so much so, in fact, that the Beckwith name will be all the more famous once I present my discovery to the outside world. Yet the payoff far exceeds whatever name and fame our family will reap. There is something else in the offing, too, a potential accomplishment I find difficult to explain and perilous to reveal under the present circumstances. Hence I must urge you to trust my judgment about the potential benefits no matter how strong your inclination to the contrary; I must withhold certain details out of prudence.

I can, of course, already hear you scoffing. A long-lost civilization? A culture packed away in cold storage? A difficult-to-explain, perilous-to-reveal accomplishment? What's all this bunk! Father, I understand your skepticism. What I am stating now sounds less persuasive than many of the other assertions I have made in the past—assertions to which you have responded with such strenuous disapproval. Even so, I urge you to give me the benefit of the doubt till I can prove myself and win your confidence.

The truth is, I have the whole situation under control. All I need is a little help in taking the solid groundwork I've built to its logical conclusion.

Which brings me to the main point.

I am asking your help. To complete the final phase of this endeavor, I need some supplies and support. Specifically, I need at least twenty men, an appropriate number of horses and pack mules, two months' worth of supplies, guns, ammunition, and mountaineering gear. I realize that whatever else I'm requesting, the mere mention of mountain gear puts my whole request in jeopardy at once. No doubt any effort requiring equipment of this sort is, in your eyes, immediately suspect. Yet I ask that you transcend your own disapproval of the sport in the interests of a higher goal. Please trust what I am trying to accomplish.

Here is what I ask of you. Before you leave Lima for New York, wire Armando Hoyos Montero in Huaraz. Ask him to hire the guides he knows. Send whatever funds he wants to get outfitted with the supplies I need, including

ice-axes, pitons, carabiners, cold weather
clothes, boots, and five dozen coils of rope.
Tell him to head up the Callejón to Olleros,
angle due east over the Punta Llanashallash,
descend through the Quebrada Huachecsa to
Chavín, and from there zigzag northeast to
Lat.—.—S., Long.—.—W.

If you will only suspend judgment on my
actions during the past year long enough for
me to finish the task at hand, I promise you—I
swear to you—I'll do you proud.

Respectfully, I am

> your son,
> Forster

P.S. Please expedite my request to the degree
possible.

*And so it happened that I met Esperanza Martí-
nez, a woman whose ordinary name belied a remarkable history. Although she admitted to having
been a minor player in the events concerning the
Mountain Made of Light, she claimed nonetheless
to have witnessed most of them.*

*My skepticism lingered despite the letter liter-
ally in my hands. "You were there?" I asked.
"There for everything?"*

*She shrugged almost imperceptibly. "Not every-
thing."*

"What, then?"

*"I'll tell you if you want to listen." She said noth-
ing for a while. Seated before me in that stark restaurant, she gazed for a while at the food I'd
bought her. Then she said, "What I wasn't there
for, I still know about."*

"What do you mean—'know about'?"

At this question she leaned over to a bundle be-

side her and lifted it up to the table. It was a woven manta, one of those cloth squares that Andean women of many cultures use for carrying everything from potatoes to babies. This one had a red, yellow, black, and white design I didn't recognize. Without self-consciousness Esperanza Martínez proceeded to unfold and spread it out on the tabletop. Then she eased back slightly, her posture remarkably straight despite her years.

On the manta was a stack of pages. Actually, just some of them were pages; others were scrolls. And though I first thought they must have been paper, even a cursory examination revealed that most were cloth.

I reached out to the stack and picked up one of the scrolls. Without asking permission, I eased a black cloth band off the scroll and unfurled it. Surely this woman would stop me at some point, I thought, but she didn't. The sight of the writing before me left me almost dazed. I knew from having read sections of Aeslu's Chronicle of the Last Days *that this was Rixtir script. But that had been the merest start—just enough to whet my appetite. Here, now, was an entire pile of Rixtir manuscripts.*

For a long time I stared at what lay before me. At some point Esperanza Martínez spoke again: "I can tell you what these say."

"All of them?" I asked, incredulous.

She laughed at me gently. "Some are in your language," she said. "I can read only those in my own."

I still couldn't believe what I heard. "You'd translate for me now?"

"Whenever you want," she said. "I've waited so long."

2

[Message, dated the Twenty-ninth day of the Third Moon-span, Sunrebirth (September 15, 1921.)]*

> From Marhaislu of Qallitti to Loftossotoi of So: Upward to the Summit!

We have proceeded with the current patrol in keeping with your commands. Most of the past Moon-span has been uneventful. During recent days we have witnessed several events that require your immediate awareness, however, and for this reason I am conveying this message to you now.

About ten days ago I ordered our patrol to set up camp at the edge of a glacier. (I am not revealing precisely which, of course, in case this missive falls into benighted hands.) Let me say simply that we felt safer there than in the valleys: the clouds shrouded us. It was also drier: we had to endure only snowfall instead of rain. We hid near the ice and continued to probe for Umbrage activities in the area.

One afternoon the call sounded to warn of strangers approaching. Everyone rallied, scrambled up the boulders ringing our camp, and peered over the tops to see whether it was friend or enemy who sought us.

* I have dated these documents as accurately as possible, given some uncertainties about the exact correlation between the Rixtir and modern calendars. I have also identified the documents' authors when advisable for the sake of clarity. E. M.

What we saw was a far stranger sight than any we had expected. Staggering up the slope were two small figures. At first we couldn't make much sense of them. These shapes were too distant to allow detail. Then, as they drew closer, we could tell a little more. They wore rags, skins, or shreds of leather bound to their bodies with bits of rope. Umbrage? Unlikely—but we had to be careful. Two wretched travelers would be far from the most outlandish disguise the Umbrage have assumed. Yet their wretchedness seemed too genuine to be trickery. One of these two was so close to collapse that he or she needed support from the other, who practically dragged the first one up the slope despite his own difficulties.

A strange sight—more pathetic than frightening. Still, strange enough. These two proceeded as if they knew their exact destination and were intent on reaching it.

At some point someone among us said aloud what I myself had been thinking: that one of the intruders wore a convoluted cap typical of the Bringers. But of course all the Bringers had died long ago. All but one.

We watched. We wanted to ward off these two strangers yet wanted to help them as well. Caution overcame our other impulses. And so we watched—just watched.

They fumbled their way up to the base of our camp. The smaller of the two figures hesitated, gazed upward, raised both hands as if to hail us, then lurched sideways. His companion caught him.

The rags bundling the little man obscured everything but his eyes. But meeting that gaze, I could not have failed to recognize it. At once I abandoned our parapet and rushed down to help the newcomers.

* * *

It was Norroi of Iqtiqqissi, the Bringer—that much I could see right off.

But what a state we found him in! Norroi had always been thin, but never this shadow of a man. His lean body had shrunk to little more than bones, skin, and a calm stare. Welts mottled his face. Later, once some of us had removed his rags to bathe and dress him, we discovered that other marks of the same sort blotched his hands, arms, and legs. Wounds? Burns? We did not learn the truth for another few days. Not that the Bringer himself refused to tell us: he was incapable of speech. All he managed was a hoarse rasping sound and a smile.

And so he failed to explain what had happened to him and his companion. For several days, what little we have learned about them we figured out ourselves.

I should hasten to add that the other man is a Lowlander. He is in fact a young man of startling appearance: tall, narrow, pale. I have seen more than a few Lowlanders in my day, of course, but none like this one. Something makes him different from the others in my experience, but nothing I can easily identify. A weariness, perhaps? Some kind of sadness? All the Lowlanders I have seen had a hunger about them. How they watched. How they coveted what they see. This one is different. He, too, watches; but his stare lacks that old Lowland craving.

The other striking aspect of his appearance is that this man, like the Bringer, has suffered strange wounds. Something harsh has left his pale flesh mottled and raw. My own hunch was that something had burned him: not only his hands, as with the Bringer, but his face as well. Something had burned some of his hair off, too, for one side of his head has a bare patch.

Who is this man? Each time we have asked, he

gives the same answer: Jassikki. But is this possible? Can this really be the man whose arrival in
Makbofissorih I have heard about from some of
the other Masters?

All our questions have brought no response we
can understand—only a scattering of feverish re-
plies, pleas, demands, supplications, some in a
garbled version of our own language, others in a
Lowland dialect that made no sense at all. With
one exception. From time to time, always without
urging, this man stammers like someone calling
out from a dream and blurts a few half-intelligible
words.

Of the two new arrivals, this Jassikki has survived the ordeal better than Norroi has. Yet he,
too, has reached us near the point of collapse and
now finds speaking difficult. Another day or two
passed before we could grasp what has befallen
them.

All we could do was take in these refugees, keep
them warm, feed them, dress their wounds, and
wait.

I shall keep you informed of this situation as it
develops.

Upward to the Summit!

[Message, dated the Fourth Day of the First
Moon-span, Sunreturn (September 19, 1921.)]

From Marhaislu of Qallitti to Loftossotoi of So:
Upward to the Summit!

My earlier message related several events that
have taken place during our current patrol. Let
me now tell you of more recent developments. My
hope is that the runners will not only put my
words in your hands quickly, but that they will
also bring your response to me without mishap or

delay. The significance of what is happening could
not be greater.

For almost a full Moon-span we have been hearing rumors of a catastrophe in Lorssa. What exactly has taken place no one can tell us for sure.
A battle, a fire, an accident? The pattern of these
accounts, however, proves that the Web has been
destroyed.

Here is the evidence. First, shipments of rope
out of the Web have ceased abruptly and totally.
More alarming, however, are the reports from
those few voyagers who have skirted Lorssa in recent days. All of them tell of a terrible sight: the
Web itself has fallen. What little remains of it lies
in charred pieces on the valley floor. Pieces—and
not just pieces of rope. A few travelers, venturing
onto forbidden ground, tell of seeing more broken
bodies than they could count. Yet no one knows
what has happened. The stories are few, sporadic,
contradictory.

What has happened to the Web? An accident?
Sabotage? Have the Umbrage attacked the Ropemaster's citadel? Or has someone else done so?
Whoever destroyed the Web, how many of its people have survived? And is it possible that the
scarred, delirious Bringer and his Lowland companion were present at whatever events befell the
people there? If so, how have they survived?

I would be delighted, Master, if I could answer
these questions. You know that I would do (and
am doing) everything within my power to learn
what has happened. In fact, all we know is that
something terrible took place in the Web, and that
soon afterward two feeble, ragged men reached us
alive—and then just barely.

What we know from these wayfarers themselves has not been much more detailed than we
would have learned without their help. The

Bringer has the words but no strength. The Low-lander has more strength but no words. Thus each of them tells us little more than silence itself.

I should hasten to add that we have enough worries to keep us busy for the moment. Both Norroi and Jassikki have suffered bad injuries and, worse yet, severe chillsickness. The younger man is weak and ill but likely to survive. The Bringer's life, however, is in grave doubt. We have put our best efforts into saving Norroi. Should we proceed in some other manner? Maybe so. Who knows what is right? All I can say is that we are doing the best we can.

Later—Sunabove the day after I began this letter.

We have now begun hoping that both men will survive. The Lowlander grows restless. Norroi has started asking questions. Neither is clear-headed; half our task is convincing them to stay calm and let us indulge them a while longer.

Regarding the younger man: I can see that he distrusts us, yet he makes no effort to leave. He has no choice, really. He would not survive more than a day or two on his own. Whether for his own good or the old man's, he seems unwilling to abandon Norroi.

As for Norroi, he has even less choice than the other. He simply has no strength. He is regaining it fast enough; yet he, too, must depend on us. Hence whatever they might prefer to do, they have stayed put.

Most everyone in the camp takes turn keeping watch. At any given time, two of us look after Norroi and two look after the Lowlander. Last night I myself took a turn to size up the situation firsthand. Not that there is much to do: we just make sure that he stays there; we keep his blankets on; we give him water if he wakes. He sleeps most of

the time. His breathing makes a lot of noise. Now
and then he coughs, fights to sit upright, struggles
with us if we help him, then settles back and falls
asleep again. Sometimes he sounds like a drown-
ing man: full of water. Then, just as fast as he
rouses, he sinks out of sight again and falls silent.

Sometimes he talks—not quietly, but loudly—
all at once, and plainly, as if to someone right before him. But not *to* us: he speaks in another
tongue, some sort of Lowland tongue, a sleeper's
tongue. Thick. Harsh. Abrupt. Words like a fox's
bark and howl. Words like grunts and supplications. At times one or another of us has imagined
hearing what sounds like our own language, and
perhaps it is. But no one can make sense of it.

I myself never heard him say anything intelli-
gible—except once.

Sitting there, I heard the Lowlander begin to
weep. The sound was unmistakable. He was weeping. I drew close, ready to speak with him, to reassure him. To my surprise, though, I saw that he
was still asleep: he lay in curled up with knees
and thighs touching, fists brought close to his face,
his eyes shut tight. Yet he wept.

Then I heard him speak. It was unmistakable:
"Aeslu! Aeslu!"

Thus we suspect much but know little.

Rest assured that further messages will follow
as soon as possible.

Upward to the Summit!

[Message, dated the Sixth Day of the First Moon-
span, Sunreturn (September 21, 1921.)]

From Marhaislu of Qallitti to Loftossotoi of So:
Upward to the Summit!
By the Sun's good graces, the Bringer has re-

covered enough that we can ask him questions. A good thing, too: the Lowlander will soon be up and about. We have no idea what to do with him. And so yesterday we Masters gathered in Norroi's tent to hear his story. I am describing the incident in detail to let you judge for yourself the situation now taking shape.

"Why so grim?" said Norroi, who lay propped up on a bed within his tent. "You look like buzzards waiting for a hare to drop dead at their feet."

I laughed and told him, "Hardly."

"Then cheer up."

Rokovsotoi—the Hookmaster on this patrol—then said, "Nothing could cheer us more than seeing you well again."

The Bringer smiled his ancient babysmile. "Stop this foolishness. I know you better than that, and you know I know. Besides, I am an old man. When my time is over there will be no cause for sadness."

A long silence followed. Norroi lay before us with his eyes closed. Had he dozed off? With a tingle of fear I thought he might even have died. Then, just as I felt the impulse to reach out and make sure he was still alive, Norroi spoke again: "Aeslu is dead."

The silence continued—now a different silence.

"Aeslu," I said. "A lovely child. What a pity."

"More than a pity," said Norroi.

"She served us well, but there are other Wordpathguides as gifted."

"Do you imagine," asked the old man, "that she was just a Wordpathguide?"

Rokovsotoi said, "That is the duty we granted her."

"Perhaps she was more than what you grant. Perhaps far more. Perhaps she was even—" and here the Bringer smiled weakly "—the Moon's Stead."

"Nonsense!" exclaimed one of the other Masters. I can still hear the anger in his voice.

"Is it? Aeslu was Saffiu's daughter. She was the Moon's Stead. And she died just a half Moon-span past," said the Bringer. "Died in the Web."

"How did she die?" I asked, eager to learn of events in the City of Rope.

"At Soffosoiti's behest. Yet the Ropemaster is not fully to blame. He merely acted out of his usual ignorance. He condemned Aeslu to death for crimes she never committed. In fact, the person to blame is a Lowlander."

These words now prompted a hiss of questions from those present. Which Lowlander? The one with us now?

Rokovsotoi cut everyone short. "Him?" he asked, gesturing toward Jassikki's tent.

"Far from it," was Norroi's answer. "Not him. A man named Forssabekkit." The Bringer paused. "The Man of Ignorance. The Man of Darkness. The Cutter of Wounds."

At once the other Masters and I pounced, our questions talon-fast and sharp. How did Norroi know that Forssabekkit was the Man of Darkness? How did he know that Aeslu was the Moon's Stead? What did this mean about the other Lowlander, the one lying just a few manlengths distant? How had they—and Norroi himself—escaped from the Web? This above all: what did his claims imply about the Last Days? Then at last we fell silent, waiting for the old man's response.

Norroi lay there with his eyes closed.

No one spoke. We knew that we could not rush him.

"In time you will learn everything," said the Bringer. "You will learn what happened in the Web. How the Man of Ignorance revealed himself.

How the Ropemaster condemned us all. How Forssabekkit set fire to the City of Rope. How Jassikki slid down one of the ropes into the lake below. How I myself rode another rope down like a boy swinging on a danglevine. But for now—" and here the Bringer took off the knotted fur cap that he always wore "—here is the answer to all your questions."

With those words he opened his cap with an abrupt yank like that of someone skinning a rabbit. A single piece of transparent rock fell onto the rug at our feet.

It was the Mountain Stone. Big as a man's fist, this pointed lump of summer-ice sat glinting before us. Everyone present stared in silence. We had all known of the Mountain Stone since childhood, but few of us had seen it even once and none at all for almost twenty Sun-spans. What could we have done but stare?

"How did you find it?" I asked, reaching out to pick it up. I held it gingerly, as if it might suddenly burst and disappear.

"It was not I who found it," Norroi answered. "The young man did."

I asked, "This Jassikki?"

"The same."

"And where would he find such a thing?"

"Down there—among the pieces of what was once the Web." After a few moments Norroi added, "I only wish that its true owner were also with us today."

When the Bringer fell silent, all of us returned our attention to the Mountain Stone. It borrowed the lamp's light and intensified it: intricate sparkles emanated from a deep, rich glow. For a while it seemed that none of us would ever do anything but stare at this stone.

Then Rokovsotoi said, "What does it matter who found it? The Stone means nothing by itself. By itself it is a note without a melody, a word without a story."

He was right. The Stone by itself would never get us to the Summit; only with the Diadem could we reach the Mountain and begin the climb. Now the sparkles and glow we watched seemed unpleasant—not enticement but mockery.

Only the Bringer smiled.

Several of us noticed him. Soon all stared at Norroi instead of at the Stone.

"Well?" I asked. "What is so amusing?"

"We can find the melody for your notes," said the Bringer, "and the story for your words."

After a long pause Rokovsotoi said, "How do you know? Or have you made this up, too, like so many of your tales?"

"I have made nothing up."

"Do you swear it?"

"I swear. The Diadem is now all in one piece."

"The Diadem still exists?" asked Rokovsotoi, looking even more surprised.

"Of course," replied the Bringer. "Even before we found the Mountain Stone, Aeslu found the Diadem."

Now Rokovsotoi asked, "In pieces? Or put together?"

"In pieces."

"Then what good would it do even if we had it?"

"It would serve our purposes," said the Bringer. "Wherever it lies—whether in the lake or on the grasslands around it—the Diadem is probably still in one piece."

Rokovsotoi sounded angry as well as doubtful when he asked, "How did you put it together? Why would Soffosoiti have let you?"

The Bringer smiled his weak smile. "I did not need to do it," said Norroi. "Soffosoiti did it for me."

"*For* you!"

"Of course. The night before the Web fell, I saw the Ropemaster place the stones in the right order. Or rather, I saw him direct several of his servants to do so. They hooked them together with the little chains."

"He let you watch him?"

"That was part of my punishment. He gazed out over the mountains and matched the Diadem stones to what he saw. All this as I watched."

The other Masters and I listened, waiting.

The Bringer continued: "Soffosoiti hooked them together for his own purposes. No doubt he intended to send some of his own people to find the Mountain. But Forssabekkit thwarted him. The Man of Ignorance set fire to the Web. Poor Soffosoiti! His city fell, and the Diadem fell with it— fell far down to the Valley of Lorssa."

"Where you found the Mountain Stone," I said.

"Where Jassikki himself found it," said the Bringer. He then reached out to the Stone, picked it up, and raised it to his head. He set it carefully on his pate.

Despite his silly appearance, everyone stared in silence.

Norroi said, "No doubt the Diadem, too, fell somewhere below the Web. Jassikki and I looked for it there but never found it. No doubt it lies there still—unless, of course, someone else has reached it first." After falling silent a while, Norroi added, "What a shame that Aeslu could not have worn what was hers to wear."

And so as you yourself will see, Master, Norroi's words have raised far more questions than they answer. He has informed us that Aeslu the Worthpathguide is dead; that this woman was the Moon's Stead; that the Lowlander named Forssabekkit is to blame for killing her; that the man who opposed Forssabekkit is the same Jassikki who now lies recovering among us. We listened. We heard what the old man said. But we hardly know what to believe.

I need not remind you that the Bringer has always caused more than a little trouble in the Mountain Land. Never mind that some of the Heirs—even a few Masters!—consider him the wisest man among us. Far more see him as a tedious old codger who long ago outlived his usefulness. Others like him but have never fully trusted him. Still others have no idea what to make of him. Obviously his arrival half-dead in our midst now intensifies rather than diminishes our uncertainties. I only wish that Rovtoksotoi, the other Masters, and I could benefit from your immediate advice on this situation. In its absence, all we can do is proceed as wisely as our station and experience allow.

Two other situations face us in the meantime.

First, Aeslu of Vmatta is dead. A pity: that young woman has been well-known and well-liked among the Heirs. She distinguished herself early as a Wordpathguide of uncommon gifts. Aeslu's beauty, too, had drawn attention throughout the Realm. Still, she was just a Wordpathguide. She served the Masters well with her skills. So be it. Under other circumstances the death of a cook or a weaver would have caused no more lamentation than Aeslu's. Yet now the Bringer tells us that Aeslu was more than she had appeared—far more even than we could have guessed. The Moon's Stead! No wonder the old man's news not only saddened but baffled and alarmed everyone who heard him. What will be the consequences now of her demise?

And this Jassikki—what are we to make of *him*? Is Norroi implying that this feverish youth is the Man of Knowledge? So it seems. Jassikki the Throw-Pall-of-Gist. The Asker of Questions. The

Scribbler of Words. Some of us have already dealt with him, considered his merits, found him wanting, and came to see him more as a threat than as a benefit to the Realm. Now here he is again, if anything even less auspicious than before. As you can imagine, we find it difficult to decide the proper response to his presence in our midst.

So what are we to do? Believe the Bringer? Gamble that he is telling the truth? Or assume that he has lied to us or (more likely) that his injuries make it impossible for him to distinguish the truth from his own rambling tales?

My deepest hope is that in receiving my accounts of these events, you will guide us at once in making sense of them. Unfortunately the weather is harsh; snow has fallen almost continuously for days; our runners will have more than ordinary troubles in reaching you at the Veil. May the Sun and the Moon guide them and protect them on their journey.

Upward to the Summit!

[Message, dated the Eighth Day of the First Moon-span, Sunreturn (September 23, 1921.)]

From Marhaislu of Qallitti to Loftossotoi of So: Upward to the Summit!

Still no message from you in response to my own. I pray to the Sun and the Moon that neither yours nor mine have gone astray. But for now I consider falling silent far more risky than keeping you posted as events proceed.

The Lowlander, too, has begun recovering—not all at once, but faster than we expected. Perhaps his youth accounts for his strength. Perhaps he was not so badly hurt as we first thought. In any case, he seems stronger and more active by the day—so much so that his recovery has become problematic in its own right.

What are we to do with him? When he was flat on his back, scarcely able to stay awake, all we needed was to keep him warm and fed. Now he is up and about, asking questions, poking around the camp, trying to figure out who we are and what we want from him. His presence worries me and the other Masters as well. In addition to the puzzle that the man himself presents, there is an added difficulty. The rumor is circulating among the lower-ranking members of this patrol that Jassikki is the Man of Knowledge—or at least that Norroi the Bringer makes that claim. It is simply a matter of time before this rumor escapes the confines of our camp and makes its way throughout the entire Mountain Land.

Of course the rumor is true: Norroi indeed claims that Jassikki is the Man of Knowledge. I need not stress to you, however, the risks to the whole High Realm if word of this situation becomes widely known before we establish its truth or falsity.

For this reason, I have advised everyone caring for the Lowlander to feign ignorance of what he says and asks. In fact, we have found as Jassikki regains his senses that he speaks our language remarkably well. Some of it is garbled—a mix of T'taspa and Common dialects—but we can still understand him. Thus all his caretakers have been instructed to play dumb. We will keep him isolated till we can decide what steps to take next.

In truth, he may well be the Man of Knowledge. If so, then everything about our lives will soon change. Our way of life will end. Some of us—many of us—will die. Others will have to leave the places that we have held dear all our lives. At the same time, his arrival will also mean a new life in a new place. Not for all of us, to be sure, but for some. For the remnant. For those who would join Ossonnal and Lissallo at the Summit.

I find it hard to explain how I see these events. As if the world will end, then start over in an eye-blink! The cause of both that end and the new beginning may well sit just a few manlengths from where I am writing now.

If nothing else, the weather has helped us. The wet season began somewhat late this Sun-span but has now hit with full force. Every day dark clouds either fill the sky from first light or else move in fast right after. Down in the valleys, rain falls at least from mid-morning till late afternoon, sometimes all day. Entire days go by without a lull. Up near the ice, snow falls unceasingly. Big storms sweep in, or else a gentler, steadier snowfall sifts over us. It is harsh weather, but it helps at least to keep the Lowlander in our midst.

Just yesterday I shed my Masters' robes, put on a more humble garment, and took another turn looking after him. He is better now and requires almost no care. Since we pretend that we cannot speak with him, however, there is no way to pass the time in conversation. Thus I sat, he sat, and each of us did little more.

He spends all his time watching the snowfall. He sits in the tent with the door-slit pulled partway open. He sits there hunched over, a blanket pulled around his back, and simply stares. The snow comes down. It swirls, sifts, drifts. He watches as if the sight before him is the most compelling anywhere. Perhaps it lulls him. Perhaps it soothes him. Even when it blows in and dusts him, he simply stares. What does he see? Just the snow? Something within the snow? Beyond the snow?

All I know is that the snow keeps him there when nothing else would.

* * *

Master, I know that you will grasp the significance of what is happening. (I refer not just to the situation in our camp, but elsewhere as well.) To avoid worsening the problems that already face us, we will do everything possible to convince Jassikki that traveling to the Veil suits his own as well as the entire Realm's best interests. All signs indicate that this Lowlander is the Man of Knowledge; thus we will not force him. But we will endeavor to persuade him. I trust that the Bringer's influence will be powerful in this regard.

Upward to the Summit!

3

18 October 1921

Dear Father,

It is a month now since I sent my first letter yet still no response. I shall admit to feeling disappointed by your silence, of course, but not altogether surprised; there are plenty of opportunities hereabouts for lapses in communication.

Thus to hedge against the possibility that the letter went astray, I am taking pains to reconstruct it. Enclosed with this note is a copy of my requests and my reasons for making them.

I only hope that this time around the signal gets through, so to speak.

Your son,
Forster

4

[Jesse O'Keefe, journal fragment (undated), probably written around September 24, 1921.]

... and now and then remember what I wish more than anything I could forget.

It's hard to believe she's gone. For months I watched her, listened to her. Just a few weeks ago I touched her, held her, made love with her. Now she's gone. She no longer exists.

How is this possible? How is it possible that someone so strenuously alive can now be dead? That such warmth and energy can fade to nothing?

I'd give anything to have her back. I'd leave the Mountain Land, or stay. I'd climb the Mountain any way I could, or I'd relinquish it forever. I'd join the Heirs or Umbrage. I'd do anything. Anything at all.

But of course this is pointless conjecture. Aeslu is dead.

At least Forster is, too. Small consolation—but it's a start. Damn the bastard! Everything that's gone wrong here has been his fault. How he sneaked into Xirrixir. How he tried turning Aeslu against me. How he stole the Mountain Stone. How he killed the Woman of the Wood. How he lied and got us into trouble at the City of Rope. How—this above all—he put the whole place to the torch. If he'd never come here, hundreds of people now dead would still be alive.

Can people really have been so blind not to see

what he intended? Can *I* have been so blind? It's
not that I didn't have my suspicions; I knew he
was up to no good. I did everything possible to
block him without jeopardizing my own position.
What else could I have done? With someone that
powerful and headstrong, there wouldn't have
been many choices. I couldn't exactly have dissuaded him from pursuing his own dark goals. I
couldn't have threatened him persuasively. Every
effort I made to alert the Rixtirra to the danger
of his presence simply backfired. What alternatives did that leave me? Killing him? I didn't
want to kill him—didn't want to kill anyone. But
perhaps I should have. In the long run it would
have spared many lives, not least among them
Aeslu's.

If only they'd understood. If only they'd listened.

Now Aeslu is dead, and so many others with her.

Forster, too. At least he got a dose of what he
dished out. I saw him plunge through the fabric
platform beneath us at the time of our execution.
After that, who knows? Did he burn alive? Fall to
his death? It hardly matters.

The only consolation is that this strange, dangerous moth flew too close to the flame and was
himself consumed.

5

28 October 1921

Dear Father,
    I'm hoping that your silence indicates you
have agreed to my requests, have arranged

everything, and have sent Armando on his way. These are not, however, events that I feel like taking for granted. Other possibilities explain your silence better than the one I find most appealing.

Perhaps my previous letters are lost somewhere between us. Perhaps you have received my letters and believe my claims yet equivocate in taking the actions I have urged upon you. Perhaps—as seems most likely—you have received the letters but find my claims incredible, my requests devoid of merit.

None of these alternatives will help much in my present situation.

What can I say to reassure you that my words are the truth? That my requests are urgent? That your delays put my efforts in jeopardy and quite possibly risk my life as well?

I should mention, however, that knowing as I do how slim the odds are of my receiving your assistance, I have made a few other arrangements just in case. Not ideal arrangements, I'll admit, but arrangements all the same. Before venturing into the Andean backwoods some months ago, I dismantled my initial base camp, hired some local Indians to help me move the resulting crates and duffles, and bribed them sufficiently to guarantee the safety of my climbing gear, provisions, amenities, and various other goods that hold only minimal interest to these people but far more to me. I have now dispatched some of the local folk to retrieve what I cached in less obscure precincts. Whether this *matériel* is sufficient for my present purposes remains, of course, to be seen. But it's certainly more help than what I have received from you to date.

As for my earlier requests—enclosed here

yet again, just in case you missed them the first and second times—all I can do is urge you once again to help me out. I know you would prefer that I address other matters than the ones I persist in broaching; still, I continue to maintain that what I have undertaken is not without merit.

What of our other commitments, you ask? Well, they certainly exist. Yet by all appearances they will continue to exist regardless of my attentions. No matter what you say, the family businesses are not idiot children that need minding every instant of the day. The seagulls will keep making their priceless deposits on the guano islands off Pisco and Paracas. The miners at Tingo Maria and La Oroya will keep dragging baskets of tin- and silver-laced dirt out of the earth. The rubber trees at the plantations near Iquitos will keep oozing their precious goo. Meanwhile, time's a-wasting. So is the best opportunity of my life.

Please rise to the occasion.

                                        Forster

6

[Aeslu of Vmatta, *Chronicle of the Last Days.*]

It makes little difference how I survived what took place at the Web, still less how I fell in with the Umbrage afterwards. In some ways it hardly matters even that I lived to tell the tale. What matters is the Sun and the Moon, Ossonnal and Lis-

sallo, and the Mountain-Drawn. But I serve the
Sun and the Moon; I serve Ossonnal and Lissallo;
I serve the Mountain-Drawn. If I had died along
with so many other people at the Web, the story
of the High Realm would be far different. A sad-
der one? Happier? All I can say is that I endured
the Web disaster, then strove to serve my gods
and the people who worship them. For this reason
(if none other) my survival did not lack meaning.

Something else mattered, too. Forssabekkit survived. Not just survived: he emerged from the disaster so nearly spotless that he came to my own
aid as well.

How? I have no idea. What did he do to escape
unscathed from the Web? There, too, I am uncertain. For a long time after the calamity I knew
little of what went on around me, having floated
not only in the lake that fills Lorssa but also on
the surface of that other, greater, deeper pool. All
I perceived at first was an unbroken calm and a
silence ruffled only by the most distant murmurs.

Since then I have learned that the Man of Ignorance found me where I had crawled out of the
lake; that he warmed my chilled body with his
own; that he carried me from the desolation that
lay all around; that he found a less windswept
place; that he waited with me there. I have
learned, too, that Forssabekkit succeeded soon after that in spotting some travelers en route to
Lorssa—travelers who turned out to be Umbrage.
He signaled to them; they approached us; they
took us in. By this means I ended up once again
among my sworn enemies.

Later, Forssabekkit scolded me more than once
for complaining about their attentions. Would I
have preferred to lie among the seared corpses
littering the Valley of Lorssa? He never understood that the answer was yes. I would have preferred anything but to serve the Umbrage.

Anything. Even death would have delighted me compared to advancing their cause even the width of a single hair.

My fate, though, was not to die, not to evade the Umbrage, not to find a quick or easy escape from my duties. Ossonnal and Lissallo had other plans for me.

[Aeslu of Vmatta, *Chronicle of the Last Days*.]

Like shadows, the Umbrage were everywhere yet impossible to grasp. They came and went with the shifting light: welled up out of nowhere, revealed themselves briefly, then melted away. How did they live their shadow-lives? Within the great cities of the Mountain Land, they no doubt lived outwardly like everyone else—working, eating, sleeping, loving, raising children—all the while somehow hiding the secret of their Umbrage ways. In the villages and farmlands they must have had an easier time: less closely watched, thus freer. And high above the valleys, where the hillsides tilt toward the clouds and the Realm turns to ice, the Umbrage surely went about their business altogether unconstrained. They lived off the land. They slept in the open. They grazed their pathbeasts without any but the slightest fear of detection. They gathered together, amassed their equipment, and plotted the Heirs' downfall.

For most of my life I had wondered about the Umbrage, yet I could never have located them anywhere within the Mountain Land. Now, without trying, I found myself in their midst.

The Umbrage! If nothing else, they always live up to their name. Tucked away at the base of a mountain—which mountain, exactly, I had no idea—they had cloaked themselves in its shadow. More than shadow: in the ice sheathing its slopes.

Who but the Umbrage would have been so brazen as to make the ice their camp? They hid not so much behind the ice as in it. They stored their supplies in some of the shallower ice-fissures. They penned their pathbeasts in corrals made from blocks of ice. They pitched their tents on the glacier itself. Small wonder that we Heirs so rarely succeeded in finding our enemy! Even as I followed the Umbrage onto the glacier's surface and worked my way into the maze that these people now inhabited, I found it hard to believe that this was a camp.

Since then I have often wondered why I made no greater effort to resist following these birds of prey right into their nest. They were not coercing me; on the contrary, both Forssabekkit and the others made it clear that I could proceed elsewhere if I so desired. Did they speak truthfully? Perhaps. If so, then my will-weakness made me a virtual partner to their actions. If not, then I should probably have resisted anyway. But I did nothing of the sort. They led; I followed.

I have reassured myself since then that I was, after all, in less than the best of health. Never mind the burns. Never mind the bruises, cuts, welts. These injuries were the least of my problems. Battered as I was, what left me docile was deeper and less conspicuous. I had eaten nothing for almost five days. I had slept little. I could scarcely walk. I had grown so weak that for half our journey, the Umbrage carried me in a blanket slung under a pole like a dead deer! How could I have plunged alone into the Realm in such a state?

In fact, something quite different from mere bodily fatigue left me willing, almost eager, to see where they would take me. I find it difficult to name what I sensed then and remember now. Some sort of curiosity: perhaps not the curiosity of amusement, but something deeper, more intense. Do ferrets wonder about the owl's nest? Do hares crave a glimpse of the puma's den? Perhaps I went along because of a need, however inexplicable, to see full-face the danger confronting my people. No, that explains it no better than my hunger and wounds.

This, then: I felt an urgency beyond my own thought, my own effort, my own purposes. Stumbling as I did into the Umbrage camp, I knew I was there by necessity, not by desire.

[Aeslu of Vmatta, *Chronicle of the Last Days*.]

Rise and shine.

The voice startled me. I forced myself up, then fell back again: I was that weak. I lay there a while, light and dark whirling all around, wondering what was real and what still a dream. A man's voice had said Rise and shine; had spoken as if addressing *me*. But what rises and shines but the Sun himself?

Once again I tried sitting. This time I succeeded. The room, the tent, whatever it was—spun and tilted, then slowed and stopped.

A man crouched before me. Light poured in through the tentflap at his back so that its intensity surrounded rather than illuminated him; I could see his outline but not his features. The light set his wheat-colored hair afire. Against my will I raised a hand to protect my eyes, for the days of walking through the snow had left me so dazzled that the slightest glare made me wince. Then I took down my hand. I would not let him think himself the source of my dazzlement.

He asked, Are you feeling better?

Was I feeling better . . . Was I feeling better . . . The question made no sense. The words did, but not the question. Not from *him*.

I brought you something, he said.

He reached forward with both hands, offered me what they held: two bowls. I could smell something without knowing what it was. Food? Drink? My nose was too swollen, too bloody, for me to detect more than the vaguest scent. But even the possibility of food was more than I could tolerate. I snatched one of the bowls from his grasp, and gobbled the contents: some sort of gruel. I grabbed the other bowl and did the same, then wiped the inside of each bowl with my hands and licked them.

Quel apetit! he exclaimed.

I threw the bowls at his feet and flopped back onto the blankets.

He sat near the bed.

I would have pulled away, evaded him, fled from that tent altogether if I had found the strength. I lay there incapable of moving.

Wearily I said, You killed him. You killed Jassikki. First you killed my mother. Then you killed my beloved—

With someone like him, said Forssabekkit, what's the difference? He'd been dead a long time before I met him. The war killed his mind even if it spared his body.

By this point I could no longer control myself. Although unable to sit, I felt some sort of force well up within me. *Mind?* I blurted. How dare you imply—

It's nothing personal, he told me. I'm not picking on poor old Jassi. He wasn't a bad chap. He certainly meant well enough. But lots of soldiers suffered the same fate. Shell shock, they call it. Scrambled brains, loss of nerve, all sorts of lamentable symptoms.

Not true.

Of course it's true. If you set him on fire, he'd

have wondered all day whether to put out the flames.

I almost spat at him in rage. It wasn't Jassikki who set the fire!

That's not the point. He was defective.

Far less so than *you*, I sputtered.

For a moment he fell silent. He squinted at me almost imperceptibly. Then he said, Believe what you wish. The fact remains: Jassi is dead.

He was the Man of Knowledge! The Man of Light! The Healer of Wounds!

Jassi? laughed Forssabekkit. Come now.

You are the Man of Ignorance!

Instead of responding with the anger I expected, Forssabekkit smiled. He reached over just then and picked up a small flat object roughly the length and width of his hand; he removed the shiny Sunmetal-colored paper that had enclosed it; he took a bite from the mudlike substance within; he chewed slowly. Forssabekkit held out what remained. Care for some? he asked, then used a Lowland word I had never heard before: chocolate.

No, thank you.

It's the best. You'll like it.

How could he offer me food, I wondered, while relating the details of my beloved's death? I shook my head but glanced at the paper he held forth as if to prove his point:

CÔTE D'OR
Chocolatiers
Bruxelles, Belgique

When I made no response, he continued: All right, then. Suppose I *am* the Man of Ignorance—whatever that means. Suppose my mind is empty of the slightest insight, perception, or wisdom. Where does that leave you? I'll tell you where.

Even if Jassi were alive, you're still better off with my ignorance than with his knowledge. You wouldn't have gotten far with him, believe me. Climbing the Mountain requires someone else altogether. I'm afraid Jassi wasn't up to snuff. Besides, he now has the added handicap of being dead. No, you won't get much help from Jassi.

Forssabekkit's words weighed heavily as I listened, yet I could only protest what I heard. Perhaps what you say is true, I said, but it makes no difference. Jassikki was the Man of Knowledge. You are the Man of Ignorance. Even dead he is more help than you are alive.

Now, now—that seems rather an overstatement.

Better to be reckless serving Ossonnal and Lissallo than careful serving their enemies.

But *are* you? asked Forssabekkit. What makes you so sure *who* you're serving?

I told him, Please go now. Please—

But *who* are you serving?

I know whom I serve. Now go.

Your confidence impresses me. He stood slowly, stretching. What a shame, though, if you pass up the opportunity to climb the Mountain, he said. To lead your people upward. To save them.

Please go.

As you wish. Perhaps you'll understand better once you've rested.

[Aeslu of Vmatta, *Chronicle of the Last Days*.]

Over the next several days I regained much of my strength. The speed of my recovery surprised me: having come so close to death just a short while earlier, I now found myself not only alive but restless, pent up, eager to be out of the Umbrage camp at all costs. I attributed the speed and the fullness of my recuperation to the gods I served. By day, the Sun's radiance fell upon us with unusual generosity for that time of year. The warmth eased the chill in my bones; the light cleared the shadows from my soul. By night the Moon's glow soothed my wounds and eased my worries. Every day I felt stronger, angrier, more resolute. Of course in the time since then (I am an old woman now) I have come to see that my youth itself was the chief source of my quick recovery. I was little more than twenty Sun-spans in age. Yet my youth itself and the strength that youth bestowed were the Sun's and Moon's gifts; I could not have found the will to continue if they had not healed me first.

Forssabekkit spared me his company, too, and his absence proved to be strong medicine. Of course I wondered what he was doing, what he was scheming among the Umbrage, and how I could deal with him. But not having to see or listen to him did wonders for me. If nothing else, the time alone gave me a chance to strengthen myself against him.

Thus I lay in bed, ate the food that boys and girls brought me, accepted the attentions that healers provided, slept or pretended to sleep, and struggled to devise some sort of plan.

Where was I? Peering through a slit I tore in the tent, I saw nothing familiar. Often as not I saw nothing at all. Snow filled the air. Cloaked men and women passed through its flurries, vague as spirits, appearing and disappearing.

Who were they? Umbrage. But which Umbrage? Survivors from the disaster at Leqsiffaltho? Some other gathering? I had no idea.

And what were they doing? Preparing another foray on the Mountain? Waiting to communicate with a larger force? Doing something else altogether? Here again I did not know.

All I knew was that I wanted to get away from them. Not that they held me captive: from the start Forssabekkit had reassured me that no one here would restrain me if I chose to leave. Unfortunately I was still not yet strong enough to wander through unknown territory in hopes of finding my own people. That left me to do what I was doing already: to heal my wounds, to regain my strength, to wait, to decide upon my next step.

[Aeslu of Vmatta, *Chronicle of the Last Days.*]

Only my own weakness restrained me—that, and the weather. Snow had been falling for days. I decided to leave when the storm's decline and my strength's return coincided.

Yet at once I saw the risk in this plan. Even if the Umbrage allowed me to leave, they would surely trace my path and follow me to wherever I sought refuge among the Heirs. How much better, then, to leave undetected; to leave when the storm itself was my ally.

Snow was the door I walked through. Snow was the path I followed from the Umbrage camp. Snow was the broom that swept my footsteps after me.

Easing out of my tent, I worked my way upwind. In this way anyone following me would have to face the blast; would have to see past all the snow billowing forth; and would have to struggle into the same wind that I myself did. No one bothered. The Umbrage may have been infidels but they were no fools. Most of them had sought refuge from the storm. The guards on watch (there were several of them at their posts) hunkered down as best they could, bundling themselves against the cold, and their clothes and postures limited even their best intentions. None of them so much as spotted me.

I headed uphill for a long time. Then I made a wide arc, traversing the glacier as well as possible, before moving downhill. What I did was a double risk. First, because I might have returned by accident to the Umbrage camp itself, having swung too little to one side. Second, because every instant on the glacier left me in great peril of stumbling into an ice-fissure, those gaping mouths that lay open to devour me at the slightest misstep. The sooner I got off the ice altogether, the better.

By the Sun's and Moon's good graces I survived. Within a short while I knew that I could descend without fear of pursuit. The wind whirled so fast over the ice that any sign of my passage would have disappeared almost as fast as I could walk.

Little could have pleased me more than what I had accomplished just then. I had escaped the Umbrage! Not I alone, of course: the Sun and the Moon had made this possible. I felt their guidance in my bones; I felt their presence. It was all I could do not to stop, kneel, and do obeisance to them. But I knew even at the time that such piety would have insulted more than honored them. What mattered now was getting free and locating the nearest encampment of Heirs.

I raced downward. Two forces aided my flight. One was the mountain's slope, which pulled me forward much faster and more easily than I could have run on the level. The other was the wind, which pushed me hard from behind. Together, these forces tempted me to hurry down almost faster than my legs could carry me. Like someone drunk on cornbeer, I thought myself invincible, light as the snow itself, and I bounded ahead scarcely able to contain my delight, as if with just a little more speed I could take wing and soar to safety.

At some point I began to grasp my peril. I could feel the ground beneath me but without any confidence in what the next step would bring. My feet had vanished below me, my hands before me. Flakes matted against my face, clogged my nostrils, blinded me, choked me.

I slowed and stopped. I looked this way and that, trying to see past the storm. Flakes moved all around me, not so much falling as roaming, an infinity of white bees swarming over an infinity of white flowers. There were no mountains, no glaciers, no waterfalls, no ground underfoot. Only snow. I stood there a while longer, then took a few more steps. Something tripped me at once. I fell forward, grazing the side of my face against a rock or a lump of ice. I sat there clutching my cheek. When I pulled my hand back, it was bloody.

At other times in my life I had been caught in blizzards, but never while alone in unfamiliar territory. How long would I survive under these conditions? Half a day? A day? Already the snow had coated me, had worked its way through the gaps in my clothing. The wind was even worse: claws that tore into even the thickest fabric.

Struggling with my pack, I removed the nightlair blanket I had taken from the Umbrage camp. The wind snatched it from my grasp at once. I pulled out the raincloak I had also taken. This, too, the wind stole. A cap, the waterbag, my food: everything blew away. Then the pack itself.

I stood there without fully grasping the situation.

Then I sat, pulled my knees up, clutched them, and forced my head down. I would diminish myself; I would leave the storm as little as possible to find. I would wait till the snow eased and the wind subsided. Then I would be on my way again.

But the snow did not ease. The wind did not subside. The storm howled and shrieked.

Soon I began to tremble. No matter how hard I tried, I could not keep the cold out. Within a short while I was shaking so hard that I saw my fate.

So be it, I told myself. I shall die here, frozen by the storm. When the snow eases, Forssabekkit and his Umbrage minions will find me hard and white as a statue not half a morning's walk from their camp. But I will not relent. I will not go crawling back, will not ask his help, will not beg his mercy. I will succumb—yet precisely by succumbing I will deny him what he wants.

I rolled over, threw my arms open, waited for the cold to possess me.

The wails I heard! The wind's endless wail! Like a thousand people dying: worse than dying: waiting in terror to meet their deaths. Listening, all I could think about was the Mountain-Drawn, how they would suffer when Forssabekkit held sway over them. Man of Ignorance, Man of Darkness, Cutter of Wounds: how lucky that I would be long dead by then! How lucky to escape his dominion!

It was then that I understood the cowardice of what I had chosen. Dying now, I would abandon the people who depended upon me. I would be casting them to their fate. They were not helpless; I knew well enough how hard many of the Mountain-Drawn would fight against their coming servitude. Yet whoever faced Forssabekkit needed any help available. How could I surrender to the storm knowing full well what would happen afterwards?

Lying there, I realized that I had three choices.

I could join the Umbrage.

I could try to reach the Heirs and probably die trying.

Or I could attempt one last gambit. Having betrayed Jassikki earlier through my darksighted alliance with Forssabekkit, I could now make up to him (if nothing else, I would make up to his memory) by means of another betrayal: not of Jassikki, but of Forssabekkit himself. At once I realized that this was the necessary course of action.

I had come this far through the storm with the wind at my back. If the storm had held steady, then perhaps I could find my way back by walking straight into the wind. Whether I could make it to the Umbrage camp was uncertain. But I would at least have to try.

Forcing myself up, knocking the snow loose from my clothes, I stumbled off again, heading upward.

[Aeslu of Vmatta, *Chronicle of the Last Days.*]

Forgive me, I blurted, staggering toward Forssabekkit and collapsing at his feet.

If my words were false, at least my fall was genuine. The effort of returning to the Umbrage camp had depleted me; I felt no sensation either in my hands or feet; I could scarcely walk. But I was not disappointed. So much the better if the Man of Ignorance mistook my weakness for obeisance!

Now, now, he said. I thought you'd come around. He stooped, put an arm around me, and tried to help me up.

I lay there before him. In fact I could scarcely breathe, much less move.

I heard Forssabekkit ordering the Umbrage to assist me in various ways—to lift me carefully, to bring warm blankets, to settle me into a bed they prepared in his tent. I neither cooperated with them nor resisted. I saved my strength for those same two words:

Forgive me.

[Aeslu of Vmatta, *Chronicle of the Last Days.*]

Later, once I had slept a while and the Umbrage had brought poultices to take the chill from my flesh, Forssabekkit said, Did that really accomplish anything? You could easily have died. You'll be lucky if you don't lose a couple of fingers and toes.

Better to lose all of them, I said, than to risk losing what matters.

He did not grasp my meaning. All he said was, Go on.

The truth.

What exactly are you driving at?

Perhaps you should tell *me*.

Forssabekkit gazed at me then with one of his careful expressions: simply waiting. He made me more uncomfortable at such times than if he had taken hold of me, shaken me, and shouted *What do you mean!*

You claim to be the Man of Knowledge, I told him. I have doubted you. In some ways I still doubt you. But at some point in the storm I started doubting my own doubts, and I saw the risk of being wrong.

He smiled his calm, tight-lipped smile. Ah. I see. You wandered off and heard a voice crying in the wilderness. And what precisely did it say?

Nothing in words.

An ineffable insight, then.

Simply this: whether you are the Man of Knowledge, the Man of Ignorance, or someone else, do what my people need done. Find the Mountain. Climb it. Lead us to the Summit.

Nothing about his demeanor suggested a change in how he saw me. So much the better. A more dramatic gesture on his part would have concerned me—would have suggested the same trickery that I now attempted. But he scarcely responded. He merely watched.

He watched a long time, then said, All right:
have it your way.

7

2 November 1921

Dear Father,
   I now mostly despair of hearing from you at
all. Of course, *despair* is overstating it: one can
hardly despair in what inspired no hope in the
first place. You may yet decide to help me. The
stones may also rise up and sing hosannas in
polyphonic harmony. Let's just say I'm no
longer counting on your assistance.
   Why, then, am I writing? A good question.
It's not as if there's nothing for me to do just
now. True, I'm free to do as I please, and a
remarkable assemblage of men and women
here seem willing, even eager, to look after me
in any way I request. Yet I have better things
to do than write letters I don't expect you to
receive. Thus I'm hard put to explain the
repeated urge to send you these missives.
Whim? Habit? Something to pass the time of
day? Let me say simply that I feel a need to relate
to you what appears to be transpiring; and I wish
to indulge the need no matter how pointless.

   Whether for your edification or for my own
amusement, let me describe my situation.
   Imagine the surface of the moon. Great
crests, pinnacles, and spires of ice rise out of a
frozen sea. Some of these formations have
toppled or lean precariously; others remain

largely intact; overall the vista is that of an otherworldly desolation. What you see is gray, white, gray-white, white-gray, with the occasional tinge of blue. Everything you see all around is ice.

I resort to lunar hyperbole because you have never experienced a glacial landscape; you know nothing of the technical vocabulary— icefall, bergschrund, serac, crevasse, moraine—for such scenes; and, most exasperating of all, you would find both the sight itself and my descriptions of it so alarming that you would avert your gaze and deafen your ears to what you were obliged to see and hear. Perhaps I can bribe you with the baubles of my words. The frozen sea stretches outward in all directions. It is calm, in fact motionless: Sea of Tranquillity. The fissures that have opened its surface seem eternal despite the ramshackle appearance of their highest reaches. You are at risk here from occasional perturbations of the ice but otherwise safe. No one on earth can find you.

Now imagine what I have described as an *inhabited* landscape. Moonmen dwell among the icy towers and battlements. Not moonmen out of H. G. Wells or Jules Verne—green midgets or deadly octopi—but people of a still stranger sort. They live as if in the glacier itself: chilly snow-encrusted hummocks. These are tents but resemble nothing so much as the wind-eroded blocks of ice that have toppled over the years. The moonmen dress not in unearthly garb but in garments to camouflage their dark skin and hair in a pale place: white-gray tunics and leggings; woolen helmets; gloves, boots, and masks. I concede that the overall effect is unsettling, but not really because of what one sees—rather, because of what one doesn't. The outfits are unpleasantly effective. It's hard to keep track of these people as they move about in their landscape, their attire is so fully effective in obscuring them. At times—notably when it's snowing—all I can see is their dark eyes shifting before me.

These moonmen call themselves Umbrages. Never mind who Umbrages are—I'll tell you more later. For now let me say simply that they are long-time enemies of the Heirs. And who (you now ask) are the Heirs? It makes no difference. There's no point in your getting caught in their cross fire; all that matters at the moment is how much they hate each other. Think of them simply as indigenous Crusaders and Saracens, Guelphs and Ghibellines, Roundheads and Royalists—still another variation on the ancient cutthroat tune of mutual enmity. What are they fighting over? Who cares! I'm not one to split hairs. In any case it's little more than happenstance that I've fallen in with one group rather than the other. With one small exception, I couldn't care which is which or who believes what.

The only other details warranting the ink I use to write about them are these:

First, both parties are hot to climb a peak they call the Mountain Made of Light. Why? Your guess is as good as mine. Lord knows it's the first time I've come across Indians who evince so much as the slightest interest in alpine pursuits. Too, they lack anything remotely resembling modern mountaineering technique. Why should they bother? Well, it seems less out of a gentlemanly sporting attitude than out of a more basic, even

primordial, need. In their eyes, the object of
their quest isn't just another mountain so
much as the ur-Mountain, the meta-Mountain,
the Alpha and Omega Mountain. They see it as
Mt. Olympus, Mt. Sinai, and Mt. Meru all
rolled into one. Hooey? Of course. I'm not
arguing their case—I'm just telling you what
they believe. If they want to believe they've
found the staircase from Earth to Heaven,
that's their business; I have no obligation to
carry the same bulky load of nonsense on my
back.

At the same time, the nonsense they carry
doesn't mean there's no mountain. Not a
mountain made of light, but a mountain.
Mountains aren't exactly in short supply
hereabouts. Is it possible that something
special lurks undiscovered in the Andes? I've
tended to scoff. Still, it's worth considering.
British colonists posted in India scoffed for a
hundred years at rumors of Chomolungma,
Mother Goddess of the World, lost somewhere
in the back alleys of the Himalaya, until
English surveyors confirmed that the mountain
we now know as Mt. Everest existed not just
in fancy but in fact. A similar presumption
would make it easy to rule out an unknown
peak in Peru. One must be careful. One can't
go chasing after each and every wisp of native
mythology. Still, still . . . There's always the off
chance that locals know something even if they
misinterpret its significance.

What am I driving at? Simply this: that both
the Heirs and the Umbrages are sufficiently
desperate to climb this mountain that their
eagerness, once properly harnessed, might serve
good purposes. Keep in mind, too, that an
outsider's attempt to climb the peak without
having first received the local benediction (so to

speak) might not be smiled upon. Father, even you can grasp the implications.

I mentioned one other matter worth considering. To wit: of the two rival factions, the Heirs are the more legalistic; the Umbrages, the more practical.

The Heirs spend their days chanting mumbo-jumbo at the sun, then half the night all but baying at the moon. Their idea of climbing mountains bears as much resemblance to real mountaineering as girls playing dolls resembles living in a real house. It's amazing that they get about at all; they almost never leave their aeries, and even then most often merely to proffer sacred knickknacks to the waning sun. True, in recent days they've shaken off some dust and stretched out a bit. Lord knows they need the exercise. But I wouldn't count on the Heirs for the most dynamic response to the matter at hand.

By contrast, the Umbrages don't hesitate to apply a little elbow grease if necessary. They're not sophisticated climbers; they rely too much on brute strength; their equipment is a joke; but unlike the Heirs, the Umbrages at least have some notion of how to get what they want. Climb a mountain? Well, then—climb it! Find a lost peak? Go round up some equipment, train some climbers, get moving! No, the Umbrages needn't worry much about competition. It's been clear to me from the start on whose favor to curry.

Speaking of curry, I have to run. The food is a bit too spicy here for my tastes—smacks of what I ate rather to excess in the Karakoram—but there's not much choice in the matter. All the more reason to get my provisions out of cold storage where I left them.

And, of course, anything you send wouldn't hurt, either, if you deign to do so.

Your son,
Forster

8

[Jesse O'Keefe, journal entry (undated), probably written around September 26, 1921.]

This morning I went to Norroi's tent and found it empty. My alarm eased when some of the Heirs, smiling, gestured toward the south edge of the camp. *"Or la'aftakki osa,"* they told me: You will find him there.

And I did.

Over the past few months I've noticed thermal springs boiling up out of the ground here and there in the Mountain Land. Norroi now sat with three of his young attendants near—or rather *above*—one of these springs: his rump on the grotto's stone rim, his feet dangling just five or six inches above the water. Vapors wafted from the surface. Even as I approached him I could feel the pall of humid heat. "Upward to the Summit," I said, greeting him in Rixtir.

He smiled and greeted me in return. "Upward to the Summit, good friend Jassikki."

"Are you feeling well now?"

"Much better. You, too, it seems."

"I'm on the mend."

He nodded toward the youths who were looking after him. They seemed uneasy with my presence but not unfriendly—perhaps just taken aback by a Lowlander's company. Or did they know more about me than I thought? Yet I saw no hostility in their responses.

Norroi, meanwhile, sat there twisting and turning a piece of string. With little more than a few knots he formed a cuplike net no bigger than a sparrow's nest. He placed four small speckled eggs in the web. Norroi tied a few more knots to form a pouch out of the web, then extended a line from the pouch. He tested the line for strength. At last he lowered the line, pouch, and eggs into the bubbling steamy water. He leaned back, guiding the line with his foot toward its proper place below.

Stalling, I spoke in English: "A clever method."

He nodded once. "It works."

"How long does it take?"

"Till the eggs are done."

I know the Tirno well enough by now to understand that he was testing me. As well he might.

I watched bubbles rise toward us from below, then said, "I've decided—" and I faltered a moment before finishing: "I've decided to leave."

No response. Norroi kicked gently at the air with his right foot, tugging at the string that passed between his toes.

Had he heard me? "I don't belong here," I went on. "Maybe I never did. Maybe I shouldn't have come here in the first place. It's better for everyone if I go."

Still no response. Not a word, glance, or twitch.

"Norroi?"

He nodded: again just once.

"Do you understand what I'm saying?"

He ignored me, peering toward his rootlike feet and the simmering broth beneath them.

"I must go."

"The Mountain," was all he said.

"The Mountain has no use for me, and I have no use for the Mountain."

"The Mountain awaits you."

"The Mountain awaits Aeslu and me together.

Aeslu is dead. I can't climb the Mountain without her."

"How do you know?"

My impulse was to cut the conversation short and leave. Instead I sat beside Norroi on the stone rim. With my feet nearly touching the steamy water, the warmth went straight up into my bones. I told him, "It's not what *I* know. Isn't it what everyone here knows, too?"

"Of course. But what about you?"

"Norroi, I'm sorry. I don't know what I know. I'm not sure if I know anything anymore. All I know is that Aeslu—"

"You are not the only one who lost her," said the Tirno. "You are not the only one who loved her."

He fell silent, his head bowed slightly as he gazed into the pool.

I gazed there, too, as my reflection repeatedly distorted, disintegrated, and reassembled itself when bits of air burst forth from below.

Norroi stared a while, then resumed. "I was just her friend. An old, old friend. But that will never keep me from wanting what she wanted. Do you understand?"

For a while I said nothing. If the Tirno had pressed the issue, I would have left. Instead he let me sit in silence. "I understand. But I can't be what I'm not."

"You are the Sun's Stead."

"I don't know what that means."

"Find out, then."

"Not possible."

"It is just possible, but certain if you do your duty."

"I don't know what my duty *is*!" I cried out.

"To climb the Mountain Made of Light."

Now I got angry. "It's all rather easy for you to say, isn't it? I should do my duty. I should climb the Mountain. And where will *you* be, meanwhile?"

"Here. Helping you."

I faltered.

"Helping you," he repeated. "Whatever you need to know, I will help you learn."

"Norroi, I'm so *tired*."

"Then rest a while."

"I feel so weak."

"Then strengthen yourself."

I couldn't help laughing at the old man's words. Strengthen myself? For what? For the Mountain? Who cares about mountains—about the Mountain Made of Light or any other? If the Rixtirra are correct, I've lost the partner I need to reach the summit anyway. Why bother even thinking about the Mountain?

Shaking my head, I told him, "Norroi—I'm sorry. I'm sorry. I have to go."

"Then go!" he said abruptly. "Leave the Realm. Go back to the Lowland. You can always go back to the Lowland. The Lowlanders will be there with their green paper, their machines, their Lowland things. Perhaps you can find another war to keep you busy."

"Enough," I said.

Norroi huffed at me. "Enough? Is that enough?"

"You know what I mean."

"But do *you*? I am not so sure. Please understand: you are not the first person to wear out, give up, and go back to the Lowland. Go ahead. Do your work, take part in the Lowland festivals, find a wife, do everything else that people do in the Lowland. But you will never *be* there. You will be back in the Mountain Land. You will think about the mountains and remember the Mountain. You will wonder about the Mountain all day long."

"When I leave I'll stop thinking about it."

"You will think about the Mountain awake and asleep. All night long you will dream of the Mountain, and you will rise from your bed still weary."

"I don't believe you." Not that there wasn't some truth to the old man's words. Even as we spoke I kept remembering that last night in the Web. I'd seen the Mountain with my own eyes. I'd seen the great glaciers leading upward to its walls, the walls angling to its ridges, the ridges converging toward the summit. And the summit? Had I seen the summit, too? I don't know. Perhaps I had; perhaps not. I couldn't be sure from there with the perspective distorted, the distances foreshortened. But this much I know: I'd seen the Mountain.

"Believe me or not as you wish," said Norroi. "Yet I promise you this: you will long for the Mountain till the day you die. You will long for it as a blind man longs for light. As a mute singer longs for a melody. As a barren woman longs for a child. But your longing will be worse. You had the object of your longing, but you left it. You abandoned it. You fled from it."

"Let me explain," I protested.

"There is nothing to explain. Go if you must."

"It's not that I want to."

Norroi now grasped his string and, guiding it with his toes, reeled in the little net and the eggs caught there. The eggs twirled and dripped till the Tirno reached forward and grabbed them.

"Please understand."

"I already do."

"No—I mean understand *what I'm telling you.*"

"Would you like an egg?" he asked me just then, holding out the whole bundle.

"Thank you—no, I'll pass."

"Take them."

"I'm not hungry."

"You will need them," he said. "Put them in

your pocket. They will keep you warm as you set off for the Lowland."

[Jesse O'Keefe, journal entry (undated), probably written around September 27, 1921.]

I'm letting him down, of course, and I know it. No one else around here seems to be making any bones about it, either.

What had been a relaxed mood about the place has changed in just a few hours. People will scarcely talk to me. There's no anger—just an air of sadness dense enough to put a barrier between us. People come and go, sometimes within a few feet of my tent, always in a great hurry, everyone doing what they can do to avoid any contact with me. I watch, dismayed with what I see but convinced I'm doing what I need to do.

Norroi himself is nowhere to be seen. I stepped over to his tent at one point: empty.

The shoulder is cold indeed.

Somewhat later.

I'd leave tonight if I could—things are that tense. Better to stay briefly, though.

Preparations tonight. Then tomorrow I'll be off.

"If you insist on going, then by all means go," said Marhaislu, one of the Masters, when I told her.

This wasn't the response I'd expected—far from it, given how these Masters have reacted in the past—but I could hardly complain. "I appreciate your understanding."

"Not understanding. Acceptance."

"But you won't stop me?"

"If this is what you want, we shall do everything possible to help you."

* * *

[Jesse O'Keefe, journal entry (undated), probably written around October 2, 1921.]

I emerged from my tent around two or three this morning and met up with my guides at once: Norroi, Marhaislu, and others I didn't know or couldn't recognize. Did it matter who led me when all I wanted was to leave? I didn't quibble when we started working our way down the slope, half-walking, half-sliding down the packed snow; jumping over narrow crevasses that appeared as big black gashes on the moonlit skin of the glacier; angling hard right to avoid descending onto the moraine; then skirting the granite rubble and runoff where the ice ended. We made good progress.

By now the Tirno and the others have guided me half the length of Leqsiffaltho—nearly to the place where Norroi, Aeslu, Forster, and I climbed the Hermit's peak and captured the Diadem. I can see the peak even as I sit here writing. In such a place it's been hard not to think about what's happened since then—how much has been gained and how much irrevocably lost.

Am I right to be leaving? There's no alternative. I serve no purpose in the Mountain Land, nor does the place serve my own purposes any longer. Quite the contrary: it rubs salt into the wound.

Just a short while ago, before we stopped to rest, our group passed through a fissure in a vast granite slab that had dropped from the overhanging cliffs some years back and now blocked the narrow canyon. The way would have been impassable except for that corridor-like crack. I remembered it from having eased through it going the other direction. A claustrophobe's nightmare: rock walls just nine or ten inches apart. We had to ease sideways for at least ten or fifteen yards to reach the other side. Now, awaiting my own turn, I watched one of my guides try to work his way through.

Standing there, not paying much attention, I noticed something on the slab's surface to my right. A spiderweb? A bit of thread? I reached out, tried grasping it, and caught hold on my third or fourth try.

A hair. A black hair almost six feet long.

Of course almost all the Rixtirra have black hair, and some as long as this. But while standing there I remembered not only this place and Norroi's effort to get us through it, but also Aeslu's own difficulty at the time. Her pack had snagged on a stony protuberance; she'd had to twist hard to ease through. In so doing she'd caught her hair on a sharp place, struggled a moment, and tugged free.

It was impossible to believe that the filament I now held was anything but hers. I held it for a moment, letting it whip sideways before tossing it gently upward and letting the wind carry it away.

Aeslu's hair wasn't all we've found in our path.

Today, just before the sun went down over the ridge between Leqsiffaltho and Makb, dousing the whole valley in shadow, we saw smoke ahead. In itself this was unremarkable. We knew that a village lay ahead; we'd caught sight of it earlier. Families would be firing their hearths at that time of day. But the quantity! A thick rope of smoke angled up out of the woods before us, unravelled as it rose, and hung over that part of the valley in a pall. Even in the changing light we could see how much smoke wafted overhead. We couldn't smell it—we were upwind—but the sight was plain enough.

"The town is Hashifa," said Marhaislu, "and the

people here are often careless when they harvest brush."

No one else took her bait. She herself and everyone else knew that kindling wouldn't cause that sort of fire.

We walked in silence. The only sound was the crunch of gravel underfoot.

The sound of footsteps intensified. Without anyone speaking to the rest or signaling in any manner I could detect, the whole band of Heirs walked gradually faster and faster—loping, trotting, sprinting—until we all but raced each other down that path.

Then, abruptly, Norroi stopped us: *"Wait."*

The Tirno's voice is high and weak, yet everyone heard it. Even before the old man's second utterance, everyone had stopped, crouched, and taken cover.

What we saw through the brush was an ordinary Rixtir village. Stone huts with thatched roofs. An outlying corral for llamas and alpacas. A low stone water tank. Two hutch-like structures—perhaps for coneys or other domestic rodents—set on stilts. That was it. No people. No animals. Just the place itself.

One of the roofs was on fire.

We watched the smoke roll upward for a while. No one spoke. The only sound was the stutter of the flames.

Then, without a word, Marhaislu stood and walked forth toward the village itself. The rest of us watched as she reached the settlement, disappeared briefly into a hut, emerged a few seconds later, disappeared again, reemerged, and repeated these actions several times without mishap. At last she made the raking motion—fingers curved downward—that the Rixtirra use to beckon one another.

The rest of us got up and followed.

That village was empty. Nobody in sight. We checked the place from top to bottom: looked into each hut, peered into the cistern, opened the two hutches. Empty. Even the animals were gone.

Yet, except for the one burning roof, the place was undamaged, almost untouched. In some ways the lack of damage bothered me more than the fire. Blankets lay folded in the huts. Corn, potatoes, and meat sat undisturbed on the drying racks. The place looked like a diorama in an ethnological exhibit. I kept expecting to see an informational plaque mounted on one of the dwellings: "Typical habitation, Rixtir Culture ('Mountain-Drawn'), Leqsiffaltho Tribe, North-Central Peru."

"Perhaps they went hunting," said one of the men.

"Hunting!" exclaimed a young woman. "Since when have the Hashifara been hunters?"

Others joked about the first speaker's words.

Marhaislu shot back: "Then *you* explain where they went."

"Climbing," someone said.

This remark triggered even more commotion: hoots, hollers, shouts, laughter.

Another voice muttered, "Climbing? In the middle of Sunrebirth?"

For the next several minutes the Heirs strayed about, talking and examining the village in a state of uneasy curiosity. I couldn't follow everything they said; couldn't even hear everyone. Perhaps my own confusion got the best of me. I backed off and looked around.

Something caught my attention just then, something that Norroi and I spotted simultaneously: a flash of light on the path leading out of the village.

The Tirno and I walked over to it. Norroi squatted to pick it up. He tilted it back and forth, clearly baffled, then gave it to me.

It was a piece of paper, gold in hue and burnished in texture, with black lettering:

CÔTE D'OR
Chocolatiers
Bruxelles, Belgique

9

4 November 1921

Hail, dear Father!

The vagaries of Andean weather provide the only hope that you've received my earlier letters after all, that you've given them the credence they deserve, and that you've dispatched Armando through the maze of the *cordilleras* with the equipment and supplies I so desperately require. Or perhaps I'm kidding myself. Perhaps the wet season is merely icing the cake of my current troubles.

In any event, here I am writing to you again. Why, precisely, I'm still not sure. But why not? If nothing else, my dispatching these periodic missives gives the Umbrages the illusion that I'm taking action on their behalf.

Ah, yes: I was telling you about the Umbrages.

Of course, I wouldn't really give two hoots either way about these Heirs and Umbrages if it weren't for a certain complication. Complication, you ask: what kind of complication? Wake up, Dad. You're not quite so naive as that. *Cherchez la femme.* In this case, *cherchez* till you find a lovely Indian *femme* named Aeslu. Aeslu is by all appearances the focal point of much activity hereabouts. As with so many other aspects of what the Rixtirs believe, I find it hard to care why they do what they do. What difference does it make if the Heirs find the peak before the Umbrage do? It's all a lot of aboriginal mumbo-jumbo. Aoogah boogah! Frankly, I'd just as soon have concluded my business here by simpler means. I'd have happily found the mountain, climbed it, planted the family colors, snapped a few pictures, and called it a day. Needless to say, the task wasn't going to be quite so simple as that.

Seems this gal is some sort of princess. What kind, exactly, I'm hard put to tell you. I tend to get my princesses all mixed up. She's daughter of the moon—or maybe that's granddaughter of the moon, Mom and Pop themselves being the celestial offspring, Sonnol and Lissal. Got that? You figure it out. In any case, she gets a lot of attention here, even from people who don't care for her personally. The local myth has it that Aeslu will be the bride of whomever proves himself son of the sun (or was that grandson?)—at which point the happy couple will go off to a honeymoon atop the highest peak of 'em all.

Before you scoff, Father, let me assure you that she's one tasty dish. She's about nineteen or twenty and in the full flower of womanhood. A sweet tomato! A hot potato! A real peach who's plump, soft, and ripe for the picking. But there's more than sugar beneath that tawny skin. I've touched her and felt the fire. Aeslu is bright, impatient, quick to rage. Why? It's not just her temperament. She knows what she wants and plans to get it: not just what suits her, but what she feels her people deserve.

Of course by now I can hear you badgering me. Forster mooning for this moon-child! A native, yet! After all these years spent wandering from table to table at the great banquet that Eros has thrown to amuse the male of our species, why should I start hungering for this exotic but humble fare? Why these inexplicable appetites?

Spare me your amusement, Dad. You simply don't understand. Never mind the girl herself: in some respects Aeslu herself is beside the point. What matters isn't who she is, but who the people here—the Rixtirs—think she is. This gal is the moon. Rather, the moon's assistant, if you will. Once again I hear you huffing and puffing. Balderdash! Hooey! Rubbish! Nothing but a lot of superstition! As usual, you miss the point. It's precisely the Rixtirs' superstition that makes this chickadee so powerful.

This in turn is why she's worth the time and attention I've been giving her. Whoever wins her loyalty wins the whole place. Or—to put it in words these folks understand—whoever proves himself to be the sun's offspring also proves himself the moon's beloved. Something like that. Got it? Sun-moon, day-night, hot-cold? I'm hoping the subtle imagery doesn't totally evade your grasp.

For a while I was prime suitor for the lady's hand. I really had her bowled over. She knew it—knew it in her heart, her bones, her loins. She is the moon, I am the sun, and by our own melded light we would find the long-lost peak and climb it to the top. Why not? As I said, what matters isn't the truth so much as what the people here take it to be. If they want to declare me the sun incarnate, I won't quibble. Fine and dandy. It beats what I've gotten stuck doing at F. F. Beckwith & Sons. Regrettably,

though, I bungled it. I overplayed my hand.
Aeslu called me down, called my bluff, called it
off. A nasty row ensued. I ended up with no
choice but to make a hasty exit and see if I
could undo the damage at a later date.

I should mention that this eclipse wasn't
wholly my own doing. The anthropologist I
mentioned earlier—an addle-brained doughboy
by the name of Jesse O'Keefe—caused most of
the trouble. I won't squander your time or
mine going into detail about him. Let me say
simply that this chap had caught a few too
many whiffs of mustard gas, knocked heads
excessively with German artillery shells, got
his gray matter rattled by all those machine
guns—in short, he lost rather more of his wits
than he could spare. It was bad enough that he
turned up hereabouts. Worse yet, he decided
that he was the long-awaited lover for the
moon-child. Him, of all people! Somehow he
prevailed, though, and managed to cast
aspersions on my character. The Rixtirs took
his slander at face value. I lost my cool and
made a few false moves. Then this Jesse fellow
overstepped himself, too, and his fortunes took
a rapid decline. *Quelle domage*—but no
surprise. People like that live on borrowed
time; he merely got his loan recalled.

About the girl, though: we crossed paths not
long ago. She's still touchy about what
happened earlier. What a spitfire! After all the
demure lap-cats back home, it's hard to deal
calmly with a puma cub on a short leash.
I've been mauled more than once. Still, it's
worth the effort—at least as a long-term
investment. Whatever else, she's not a gold
digger. (My descriptions of the family fortune
elicit no more reaction than if I had boasted
about owning sand or sea water.) Neither is

she drawn to my looks. (If anything, she finds
me alarming—too big, too strong, too
unfamiliar in my yellow-haired, pink-skinned
foreign cast.) Let the New York debutantes
glance demurely and the Southern belles bat
their eyelashes; this wench watches with
something less complimentary but more
intense in her gaze. What, precisely? I'd be
hard put to tell you, but all the same there's
something there. She's not impressed. She's
not amused. She's not bowled over, run down,
hooked, snookered, taken for a ride. Quite the
contrary: she's scared of me, on guard, and
hostile. Small wonder. I've not acted with my
usual aplomb. But the tale's not fully told yet.
I'm sure of it—whether she is or not.

I could go on, but holding off makes more
sense for now. This is enough of a bedtime
story for you, Dad.
Sleep tight.

                                        Forster

PART TWO

Esperanza Martínez ended up loaning me a whole batch of the documents she had brought with her the night of our first encounter. She turned them over without demanding compensation of any sort and without requesting any assurances of what use I might make of them. All she wanted was that I read them.

And I did. I stayed up what remained of that night and most of the next day; I read and reread them; I found a serviceable office supply store and arranged to have the originals photocopied. Then I took the entire pile back to my hotel. After sleeping half a day, I started reading everything all over again.

At least I read what was in English. Yet even the documents written in one or another of the Rixtir languages turned out to be far more accessible than if I'd acquired them by some other means, for Esperanza herself insisted on translating them for me. That first conversation—our late night's talk in a dumpy restaurant—was just the first of what became a long series. For five or six weeks after that, we met every few days to sort through Esperanza's private archive, render what was Rixtir into Spanish, and answer my almost interminable questions.

"I still don't understand how you got all this stuff," I told her one afternoon.

She sat in a chair before me, resting her lightly closed hands on her thighs. Her eyes drifted shut as we talked, but I never sensed that she was dozing off; instead, she seemed to be screening out the *present simply to summon the past more easily or fully.*

"Some of what I'm showing you came by one means, some by another," she said after a while. "Most of these writings came to me directly. I was a Keeper of Records. Looking after documents was my duty at the time."

"You were a tolliafassitirno?" I asked, using the Rixtir word for a linguistic expert.

"No, that was something different. My responsibility was to keep track of what the Masters sent and received."

"Sort of a scribe."

"Not quite, but that's closer." She now fell silent long enough that I worried I'd disrupted her train of thought. After another pause, though, she continued. "What I mean to say is that some of these documents fell into my hands as a matter of course. Some I acquired later. Some—" and here she opened her eyes and gazed straight at me "—I obtained against the owners' will."

"You stole them?"

"Not I myself. Let's just say I arranged to acquire them."

"Jassikki's journal?"

"You should decide for yourself." Before I could discuss what she was telling me, however, Esperanza said simply, "There are more."

"More? More letters? Journal entries?"

"More of everything."

I rambled a while: how grateful I was for her help, how eager I felt to see anything she cared to show me . . .

Esperanza cut me short. "Please understand. No matter what I show you, no matter what you read, you must hear what I have to say as well. Otherwise the letters, journals, and all the rest will not make sense."

"I hope you understand how pleased I am to

hear anything you have to tell me. I'd be delighted to interview you."

She didn't seem altogether impressed by my eagerness. "Others too," she said.

"What? Other people I can interview?"

Now she nodded just once, and curtly.

1

[Jesse O'Keefe, journal fragment (undated), probably written October 24, 1921.]

. . . then they led me due north into a progressively narrower box canyon. On each side, sheer cliffs at least a thousand feet high. Ahead and above, an asymmetrical pyramid-peak of ice. Before us, a lake of eerie blue-green hue filling the entire canyon. And angling down from the peak to the lake, a vast snowfield.

Where in such a tight, steep valley would we go? The great glacial lake filled almost the entire canyon. The cliffs dropped almost vertically to the water. I saw no sign of a path anywhere, no sign of a settlement. The only way out would be up the snowfield—and I found it hard to imagine my guides going anywhere that used that great ramp of ice as our route. They intended just that, however, and proceeded at once.

Working our way around the lake, we scrambled up a rubble-strewn slope to where the snowfield began. We climbed up onto the ice. We headed up. I was relieved to find this a true snowfield—not so severely angled as a glacier, thus lacking the chasms in the ice that make glaciers so deadly—but our ascent turned out to be exhausting anyway. Marhaislu and the others pushed ahead without hesitation. No one showed any need for rest or even for a more moderate pace. Luckily the snowpack underfoot was dense enough, so I didn't skitter about as awkwardly as I might have on icier terrain. But the push upward winded me; within a few hours we must have reached a height of 16,000 or 17,000 feet.

Then, without warning, we approached a ridge. I didn't see it till we'd almost arrived: its snowy color and texture precisely matched both the foreground and background. Another instance of Rixtir camouflage: this ridge, like so many others in the Mountain Land, harbored a city. I could see it only as we literally walked into it. Gray-white, radiant as the snowfield itself, this place reflected so much glare from the Andean sky that I almost couldn't bear to gaze toward it at all. I shielded my eyes with both hands and tried to make sense of the walls rising from the ridge.

"What is it?" I asked Norroi.

"*S'sapassi,*" replied the old man. "The Veil."

All the snow and the light cast from it distorted my sense of distance and perspective. First I nearly missed this city of ice altogether; then, abruptly, we were there.

[Esperanza Martínez, formerly Issapalasai of Mtoffli, interviewed August 28, 1970.]

We had learned that he would soon arrive: a runner had brought the news to us several days earlier. For this reason we should have felt no surprise when he stood among us. We already knew that Jassikki planned to leave the Mountain Land; that the Masters at the high camp near Lorssa had consented to let him go; that their consent served chiefly to buy time while the Masters decided what steps to take next; and that Jassikki himself then somehow changed his mind and, confounding all our expectations, chose to seek us by his own free will. This much we knew.

Of course we knew other things about this man, too, before he reached the Veil. We knew everything that the Masters elsewhere had already learned over the course of almost four full Moonspans. We knew what he looked like. We knew what brought him to the Realm. We knew what had happened to him since he first set foot among us. We knew what these events meant about his presence in the Mountain Land. Why, then, should we have felt such shock when the guards helped him through the gates, up the stairs, and into the gray light of our city?

Everything about Jassikki had boded ill. The Masters elsewhere had already expressed their doubts about him. Others throughout the Realm had done the same. What chance was there, really, that he was the Man of Knowledge? What chance that he was the man who would defeat the Man of Ignorance, find the Mountain, and lead us to its Summit?

Yet as he walked past us—past the warriors who lined the way, past the citizens of the Veil who had gathered to greet him, past all of the Masters, Adepts, and Aspirants as we watched the procession below from our balconies—we saw someone who wasn't who we had expected. I don't mean simply his features. True, he was taller than almost all of our men, and thinner as well; he was pale, his pink skin blotched red with scars; he was hairy about the jowls and upper lip. I mean something else—something beyond how his flesh, hair, skin, and clothing looked as he walked by. Everyone who ever told us anything about this man had described him as broken, baffled, unsure of what to do or think. Whatever his intentions, he had always seemed incapable of acting on them. He had lacked the will.

This was not the man we now saw entering our midst.

He was weary; yes. He appeared as well to have suffered grave injuries: burns, scrapes, bruises that even now showed signs of only partial healing. Yet he strode among us as if sure of his precise intentions. He looked odd, this Lowlander dressed in our attire—sandals and leggings, woolbeast cloak, cowl, and pathpack—but he showed no concern about his oddness. All he wanted was to be here. True, his motions were abrupt. Yet the abruptness was not indecision. It was impatience.

[Jesse O'Keefe, journal entry (undated), probably written October 24, 1921.]

So this is S'sapassi—the Veil. Like other cities in Xirrixir, it's built into a mountainside; unlike all the rest, however, this one is carved in ice. The Heirs have chosen a snowfield angling up against a peak, they've tunneled into it, they've built a honeycomb of rooms and passageways in its icy depths. Concentric rings of ice walls surround a central plaza. In the center—as in so many other Rixtir cities—is a mountain monument. But unlike the others, this one is made of ice. A glistening white pyramid rises from the city's central point, a pyramid whose summit is the highest place in the Veil.

My hosts have settled me into a room that gazes out directly onto the glacier. It's a precarious place. Even moving around inside the room is tricky, though the Heirs have eased the dangers by embedding gravel in the floor. Yet I feel as if I've taken up quarters inside an iceberg. Between the uneasiness I feel and the chill this place induces, it's hard to think straight, hard to think at all—yet I know why I'm here and what I must do next.

* * *

[Esperanza Martínez, formerly Issapalasai of Mtoffli, interviewed August 28, 1970.]

There was one other reason for us to assume that Jassikki was the Man of Knowledge: the Man of Ignorance had appeared.

Over a full Moon-span earlier we had learned that the Lowlander known as Forssabekkit had cast his lot with the Umbrage. We would have had good reason to suspect his intentions even without knowledge of this alliance. What had taken place in the City of Rope remained unclear, but all evidence suggested that Forssabekkit was to blame for its destruction. The Masters and everyone else trying to make sense of the situation recalled words from *The Summit:*

. . . and when the Spider burns the Web
To escape the trap he himself has set:
Then shall you know Darkness from Light.

So not only did we suspect that Forssabekkit had destroyed the City of Rope, but also that he sought the Umbrage afterwards; and not only sought them, but joined forces with them; and not only joined forces with them, but offered himself as their leader. As their leader! What our spies told us revealed that Forssabekkit was striving hard to help the Umbrage scheme their shadow plots and accomplish their shadow deeds.

How, then, could we doubt that Forssabekkit was the Man of Darkness—he who would snuff out all light in the Realm? What else could he have been doing among those who are themselves steeped in darkness?

Our spies' sketchy reports weren't our only source of information about the Man of Ignorance. We had another, deeper well to draw from: Forssabekkit himself.

For the better part of two Moon-spans, he had been attempting to sneak wordscrolls out of the Realm, and for that whole time we Heirs had intercepted his letters. Every one of them fell into our hands. How did we know that we caught them all? Because the runner who carried them out of the Umbrage camp wasn't the paragon of Umbrage loyalty his masters had imagined. He was, in fact, an Heir. He carried each missive not to the Umbrage runners' station but to our own, and thus the Man of Ignorance had put his deepest thoughts into the minds he would have least wished to know them.

But there was a problem. Worse yet, two problems.

One was that we had not succeeded in making sense of all the man's words. Even the Wordpathguides most adept at delving into the Lowlanders' script failed to figure out much of its significance. Forssabekkit's writing itself caused part of the difficulty. As if ink-dipped spiders had danced over the wordcloth, all sorts of lines lay entangled there. But even what the Wordpathguides succeeded in translating told us little of what their author meant. Perhaps we could have known more if Aeslu of Vmatta had been among us to help, for she had understood the Lowland script better than anyone in a long time. Her death, however, kept us almost as fully in the dark as if these letters had never reached us in the first place.

The other problem was that after a while, the letters stopped coming. We intercepted four of them altogether. Then nothing. We heard nothing from the Man of Ignorance after that. Worse yet, we heard nothing from the runner who had been bringing his letters out of the Umbrage camp.

It wasn't hard to imagine what had befallen him.

Thus the letters whetted our appetites more than they satisfied them.

But we learned this if nothing else: that Forssabekkit was alive; that he was conspiring with the Umbrage; that together they planned to gather a large force to seek, find, and climb the Mountain Made of Light.

We learned something else as well. If Forssabekkit was the Man of Ignorance, what did that make Jassikki? The Man of Knowledge. Of that we soon felt little doubt.

Of course we wanted to hear from him directly: to hear answers to the questions that would settle our fate once and for all.

[Jesse O'Keefe, journal entry (undated), probably written around October 24, 1921.]

It's as simple as this: if they'll have me, I'm theirs.

If not—well, I'll face that if it happens.

[Esperanza Martínez, formerly Issapalasai of Mtoffli, interviewed August 28, 1970.]

We had already finished our Sunrising Obeisance by the time of Jassikki's arrival at the Rend Hall. All the Masters and many Adepts were present and seated on the rug. When the door opened, letting in ice-glare and a brief view of sky through the Rend, we saw a lean shape enter, hesitate a moment, then stand among us.

Once again his appearance took us by surprise. He looked taller, stronger, healthier. No doubt his attendants had bathed him and dressed his wounds; he had rested overnight; he had eaten

well that morning. Even so, his air of confidence
went beyond anything we could attribute to mere
hospitality and rest. Jassikki seemed ready for
anything. More than ready: eager. Clad in a pale
brown woolbeast robe, he showed little of the
alarm, discomfort, worry, or fear that we had observed in him at earlier stages of his journey into
our midst.

I mentioned already that we had finished our
obeisance and prayers. We had also exchanged our
few words about Jassikki's imminent arrival and
what we anticipated of the visit. Despite our outward calm, however, there was a tension beneath
the surface that any of us could detect. Could Jassikki detect it, too? Perhaps the reason we forced
ourselves into silence was precisely to find out
what he could sense about us, what he knew, what
he expected.

The Man of Knowledge! Was it possible?

What better way to find out than to wait, letting
him reveal himself by whatever means he found
most important.

When he spoke, his voice was quieter and
calmer than any of us had expected; or perhaps it
only seemed so, since Lowlanders more often
shout than speak. But the man's words surprised
us most of all. Jassikki spoke our language! Not
very well—but he spoke it. Sometimes he faltered,
lapsing at once into Lowland; but then the Wordpathguide present started translating the words
from that foreign tongue into our own. Jassikki
would then return to the Common Dialect (sometimes mixed with phrases from T'taspa) and re-
sume telling us what he had come to say.

He said, "My name is Jassikki. In my time here
your people have called me many things—Asker
of Questions, Scribbler of Words, Throw-Pall-of-
Gist . . . Call me what you will. I am not here to
tell you what to think of me."

Of course, he spoke less smoothly than this. There were pauses, hesitations, even occasions when he struggled to find a word or to confer with the Wordpathguide. Yet he spoke, and we understood him.

He said, "I have already met some of you. You have watched, listened, and passed judgment upon me. I have no complaint against what you have done. You are right to distrust all Lowlanders and to fear for the safety of the Mountain Land. You were right to distrust me as well, for I, too, am a Lowlander. But not all Lowlanders mean to harm you. From the start I have meant well. Even so you should listen closely, watch carefully, and decide for yourselves who is your friend and who is your enemy."

All of us listened to these words without commenting or asking questions. This was according to our plan. But it happened as much in response to something else: our own astonishment that a Lowlander would say such things.

He said, "Here is what you must know. A man who has entered the High Realm—the man you call Forssabekkit—now endangers the whole place, its people, and everything you do, cherish, and hold sacred. How do I know? Because I have seen signs of him in your land. For a while I thought this man had been killed like so many others in the calamity at the City of Rope—a calamity that he himself caused. I was wrong. He is alive. And it now appears that he is preparing to cause another calamity, one so terrible that it will leave the City of Rope forgotten in its shadow.

"Perhaps you know everything I am telling you now. You may well know more than I do: where he is, what he is doing. But I assure you that I, too, know much about this man—much that you Masters, for all your knowledge and wisdom, cannot know. For however much you know, the Lowland ways are strange to you. The actions of a Lowlander, too, will be strange. Please do not misunderstand me: I respect your knowledge and wisdom. For precisely this reason I ask you to hear me out."

By this time there was no sound in the room but Jassikki's voice.

"This Forssabekkit is different from what you imagine. He is more intelligent, more dangerous, more deadly. He is far more evil than you can imagine. He is a skunk reeking of his own stench. He is a snake dripping with venom. He is a cinder smouldering with fire. He is a pox, a plague, a one-man pestilence.

"Let me tell you a story. Long ago, in the Lowland, people like the Mountain-Drawn lived much as you do. Some of them even lived in the mountains. They were called Indians. They were your kin—your long-lost relatives. They lived in the Lowland, but they were not Lowlanders as you think of them. Then white men came to steal their land, just as Forssabekkit would steal the High Realm. And like the white bearded slavemasters who came here long ago, these men tried to kill the Indians. One of the ways they killed them was by giving them deadly gifts—the blankets of woolbeasts whose wool the Lowlanders had fouled with sickness. The Indians accepted the gifts, then fell sick and died. Died in droves.

"This is what Forssabekkit, too, has done. Not because he has given you animal skins: that is not what I mean. Not because he has brought you a real sickness. The sickness he brings is not a sickness of the body, but of the mind—his ideas, desires, and intentions. The gift he brings is not an animal skin, but Forssabekkit himself. He is at once the Lowlander, the robe, and the disease."

No sound marred the silence following Jassikki's words.

Jassikki said, "I would like nothing more than to tell you that I am the Man of Knowledge your people await. Until just a few days ago, I thought I could serve you best simply by leaving the High Realm. Then I learned that Forssabekkit—who I thought was dead—is in fact alive. And so all I can do is offer what I know to stop him. Am I the Man of Knowledge? Perhaps I am. Perhaps not."

He stood there a long time. Then, reaching into the folds of his robe, he removed an object that he held forth to us on the palm of his outstretched hand. It was a chunk of the transparent stone we used to call summer-ice. I'd never seen anything like this but knew at once what it was: the Mountain Stone.

Jassikki said, "You decide."

[Jesse O'Keefe, journal entry (undated), probably written around October 25, 1921.]

I've just finished speaking to the Masters' council—twenty or twenty-five of the highest-ranking Heirs in all the Land. I told them what I know about Forster Beckwith and his intentions; I explained the threat he brings to this place; I offered to do anything within my power to counteract him.

The Masters listened. By the time we finished, they understood what I've told them, and they accepted my offer to help. More than that: they welcomed me, cheered me, hailed my arrival in their midst.

So I now know why I've come to the Mountain Land after all. Having been through the war, I know what Lowlanders can do. I know what could happen to this place, too—what the damage could be. It's clear that Forster Beckwith brings to the High Realm everything that's wrong with the

Lowland. Someone must stop him. Is he the dreaded Man of Ignorance? That's almost beside the point. Forster brings quite enough ignorance of his own devising. Whether I'm the long-expected Man of Knowledge is also ultimately irrelevant. What matters is stopping Forster. And if I'm not the one who stops him, who is?

Forster Beckwith: you won't read these words, but be forewarned. Since you threaten the Mountain Land, I'll counteract the threat. I'll work against you in every imaginable way—allying myself with your enemies, planning the strategy against you, organizing the campaign to defeat you. I'll lead the Heirs against you and your Umbrage minions. I'll find you, confront you, and fight you. I'll purge the High Realm of your presence.

And to purge the High Realm, I'll purge myself as well—purge myself of everything that resembles you, however inadvertently, in my own beliefs and actions. Thus whatever you believe, I shall believe the opposite. Whatever you do, I shall do the opposite. Whatever you say, I shall say the opposite. Whatever you want, I shall want its opposite. Whatever you are, I shall be the opposite.

[Esperanza Martínez, formerly Issapalasai of Mtoffli, interviewed August 28, 1970.]

In time we figured out something else from the letters we intercepted from Forssabekkit. Not only was Forssabekkit alive: so was Aeslu of Vmatta. That Wordpathguide—now the Moon's Stead—had somehow survived. We were all astonished that such a thing could have happened, especially because Forssabekkit himself had rescued her following the Web disaster. Aeslu now kept the company of the Man of Ignorance.

What did that mean? I can't even guess how

much time the Masters spent debating the situation—whole days and nights, certainly. They wondered, they worried, they argued. Why was Aeslu the Wordpathguide with Forssabekkit? Had she cast her lot with him? Or was she there against her will? Either way, what threat did she present? Or did her proximity to the Man of Ignorance perhaps diminish the threat he presented to the Mountain Land and its people?

I can imagine what you're thinking: that we could have eased our concerns by reading the letters. And we did. But only to the degree possible. Remember what I told you earlier: Forssabekkit's writing baffled us. Few among our Wordpathguides possessed anything like Aeslu's own facility with the Lowland languages, whether spoken or written. Fewer still could read a Lowlander's handwriting. Forssabekkit's was even more difficult than most. Ah, then why not show the letters to Jassikki? Surely the Man of Knowledge could tell us more than the bits and pieces of information that we gleaned from them.

We decided against this course of action for two reasons.

First, because Aeslu herself was the focus of intense disagreement among the Masters. She was not the Moon's Stead we had expected. True, she was the old Stead's daughter, and all honors ensuing were her rights. But the old Moon's Stead had been Saffiu—the Woman of the Wood. Aeslu was tainted as well as honored by her inheritance. Too, Aeslu herself was a Wordpathguide. She was in fact the most gifted Wordpathguide of our time; all the same, she was a Wordpathguide. But to think that someone of her lowly rank should become the Moon's Stead. . . . This was hard for many people to accept.

The second reason concerned Jassikki more than Aeslu herself. We knew he loved this woman.

As the Sun's Stead, this was his right. More than his right: his duty. Ultimately we wanted what was ordained to come of this love: that together they should find the Mountain Made of Light and lead our people to the Summit. Yet doubts lingered in our minds—doubts I find hard to explain now but which were strong, even persuasive, at the time. How would Jassikki respond to this news? Would he regard Aeslu's presence with Forssabekkit as all the more reason to destroy the Man of Ignorance? Would he strive even harder to defend the Mountain Land? If so, would he strive with the necessary steadiness of purpose? Or would he lose his nerve? Would he grow angry or demoralized? Would he rage against his nemesis even to the point of losing the advantage he held against him? In short, would his own anger jeopardize our common goal?

It was so hard to tell with Lowlanders. Believe me: though we knew Jassikki was the Man of Knowledge, he was still a Lowlander. We worried most of all that he might take Aeslu's presence in the Umbrage camp as a betrayal. How would a Lowlander react to that news—especially since the nature of things might be what they seemed?

No, it made more sense to keep the Man of Knowledge ignorant. To keep the Man of Light in the dark. We couldn't take any chances.

There would be time enough to find out what Aeslu was doing, and why.

2

Dear Father (sort of)—
   When talking with you—and with everyone else in our family, for that matter—I often get the feeling I'm shouting at a stone wall. Maybe this is why I feel so at home among mountains. I've developed a taste for my own voice echoing off granite. Likewise when I write. These several letters I've sent you have been no exception. Was I really so foolish as to expect an *answer*?
   In fact, however, what I've been hearing is another sort of silence. You never responded because my letters never reached you. The courier entrusted with my epistles—a courier whom my hosts had assured me would prove reliable to the utmost—turned out to number himself among the enemy. He was an Heir, not an Umbrage. (Note the past tense. What the Umbrages have done with him, exactly, I have no idea; I just let them go about their business, as seems politic when dealing with tribal imbroglios of this nature.) In short, you never got my letters. Lord knows who did. This is certainly a legitimate concern but not one I'll address at the moment. What's most evident right now is that once again my audience may as well be the granite surrounding me on all sides.
   Why, then, am I still writing? Why start yet another letter when I know not only that it's

never going to reach you, but that I don't even intend to send it? Well, simply because there's no reason not to. When the other party in a conversation is an echo, one grows comfortable with the sound of one's own voice.

Much has happened since I wrote last. It's now almost the end of November—deep into the Andean rainy season in more ways than one. Down in the valleys, there's a heavy downpour each day; up here on the ice it's nearly constant snow. A messy business: one storm after another, slush between times, a perpetual process of digging out. Yet these Umbrages, whatever their limitations, seem a Spartan tribe adept at dealing cheerfully with harsh weather. Their stalwart air is one of their more attractive features. Meanwhile, the glacier cloaks the veritable army amassed here. Anyone venturing from below to within a hundred feet of our camp would be hard put to detect us; anyone foolish enough to venture onto the ice during a storm could walk virtually among us without even imagining our presence here. I can think of no better place to hatch a plot.

Which is precisely what we're doing.

In my previous letters, I described not only these Umbrages but also the much-celebrated Mountain Made of Light that provides the focal point for their obsessions. The Umbrages, having endured the Heirs' dithering for almost half a millennium, want nothing more than to find and climb this mountain. Never mind why; they have their reasons. What matters is simply that their desire coincides with mine, and that our intentions and abilities are mutually beneficial. Of course I haven't stated the situation quite so baldly to

my hosts, but the practicalities involved can't
be lost on such straightforward people. They
won't get halfway up a big peak without
someone disabusing them of their earnest but
mostly ineffectual notions and, to the degree
possible, without someone training them in a
more flexible and forthright technique. At the
same time, I won't reach the goal without
logistical support. Thus a marriage of
convenience. With any luck, we'll locate this
mountain and climb it without the difficulties
that would burden our separate efforts. Their
knowledge of the local terrain plus my
knowledge of modern mountaineering gear
and methods add up to the perfect match.

Of course, I was hoping to simplify the
situation still further by obtaining the equipment
I requested in my first several letters. What a pity
that the local postal service is so rudimentary.
The gear I listed could have made this climb not
much more difficult than a three-weeks' stint in
the Alps. Lamentably, I'll have to make do
without what you would have sent. So be it. No
doubt I'll muddle through regardless. More than
that: I'll excel. Half the fun of these expeditions is
overcoming constraints. Besides, the interception
of my letters ultimately spares me the trouble of
flying into a rage when you refused my request.
Perhaps this is all for the best.

The truth is, I always have an ace in my
boot. I know better than to trust my fate to
one course of action. For this reason (among
others) I'm not wholly without access to useful
equipment. I have a secret cache. Months
ago—just as I ventured into this peculiar place
to see what amusements it might offer—I
abandoned my first base camp northeast of
Chavín. Not exactly abandoned: I packed it up.

I left it in the safekeeping of some local peasants who, by means of both a carrot dangled before them and a stick held overhead, showed every signs of fulfilling their part of the bargain. By means of the same Umbrages who have become my partners in the current endeavor, I'll now retrieve what I left behind. It's not everything I'd have liked: a dozen ice-axes; coils of rope numbering perhaps two score; pitons, carabiners, and other sorts of ironmongery; five or six canvas tents; wool coats, caps, mittens, and other sorts of cold weather garb; no more than four Swiss-made eiderdown bedrolls; three Primus stoves; assorted cookpots, canteens, and utensils; bush food of various half-palatable sorts, mostly dehydrated; and—last but most certainly not least—miscellaneous items which, though hardly crucial, will nevertheless do much to make my stay here more comfortable and entertaining in otherwise spare accommodations. It's hard to say how far this scattering of supplies will take me. Still, I can assume the answer is more optimistic than if I lacked it altogether.

I should mention, Dad, that my cache of supplies isn't limited to mountaineering gear. You know me well enough to realize that I wouldn't paint myself into a corner. And since it's hard to know what sorts of corners may present themselves, I've always assumed it's best to be prepared for anything. I don't mean to sound melodramatic; I'm not referring only to threats or dangers. Boredom is as great a risk in the bush as wild animals or savages. The long wait for clear weather has doomed as many expeditions as have brigands, disease, or avalanches. The solution? You know me well enough to know the answer: wine, women, and

song! Back in Chavín I stashed enough
supplies to guarantee a good time not only for
myself but for whomever I'd care to entertain
as I prepare for the task at hand.

If you were reading this letter, you would
raise an eyebrow at this point, for even you,
dear Father, would have grasped the notion of
precisely whom I have in mind. But of course
you aren't reading this, so I've spared your
eyebrow the exertion.

This is all beside the point. My point is
simply that I won't be at a loss as I seek the
goal before me.

I will attain it.

                                        Forster

3

[Official Heir communiqué, dated the Nineteenth
Day of the Second Moon-span, Sunreturn (November 2, 1921).]

From the Masters of the Veil to the Masters of
each valley in the Mountain Land:

Upward to the Summit!

In the Sun's and Moon's names, by orders of the
Man of Knowledge, and with the authority that
Ossonnal and Lissallo invested in us as their representatives in the world, we command you to undertake the following actions at once.

First: select from among the families under your
jurisdiction whichever ninety-nine have manifested the greatest piety toward the Sun and the
Moon, the greatest love of the Founders, the great-

est loyalty to the High Realm, and the greatest obedience to the Masters.

Second: question every member of every family as necessary to verify their own and each others' piety, love, loyalty, and obedience; and assess every member for any signs of sympathy toward Umbrage beliefs or practices.

Third: reject from consideration any family in which even a single member manifests the slightest sign of impiety, hatred, disloyalty, or disobedience; and any family in which even a single member shows the merest flicker of Umbrage sympathies.

Fourth: of those families remaining, assess all members for strength, stamina, and health, rejecting those who suggest any manner of weakness, frailty, or unusually small physique for that person's age; unhealed injury or uncured disease; dissipation, laziness, lassitude, or vice; and age younger than five Sun-spans.

Fifth: of those families remaining, select thirty-three whose members seem most likely to survive the trials that all Mountain-Drawn long for, but which not all can attain, in striving for the Summit.

Sixth: send these families at once to the Veil escorted by an equal number of warriors.

Seventh: confine all other Mountain-Drawn to their cities and villages until further notice.

Eighth: observe closely any persons known to have Umbrage sympathies.

Ninth: await further communications.

Upward to the Summit!

[Marcelino Hondero Huamán, formerly Marsalai S'safta, interviewed September 8, 1970.]

I was born in the village of Panli, near the pass between Iqtiqqissi and So. I lived my whole life there up to my thirty-eighth Sun-span. I would have lived there the rest of my days—it had never occurred to me to go anywhere else—but one rainy season the Masters came to Panli.

Sometimes that happened, but not often. Panli was a slingers' village. I was one of the *s'saftara*, or slingers. That part of the valley was good grazing land for woolbeasts of the best kind for weaving slings. My duty, like most everyone's in Panli, was to raise woolbeasts and weave their wool into slings. We also hunted with the slings—hunted birds, wild pigs, foxes, and deer—and we turned over our bounty to the Masters. We never boasted about our skill either as weavers or hunters, but word got around that our slings were the best in the Mountain Land. The Masters seemed to think so, too, for they had always arranged for these slings to be distributed throughout the High Realm, and once or twice each Sun-span one of them would stop by and check up on us. They wanted to make sure everything was all right— that we were taking good care of the woolbeasts, maintaining the looms, weaving the slings properly, hunting neither too much nor too little, and training our children to be good slingers. That was fine. The Masters treated us well. They did what they were supposed to do; we did what we were supposed to do. As I said, we were slingers. Making slings and hunting with them were simply our duties among the Mountain-Drawn.

It was unusual for the Masters to show up during Sunrebirth. Ordinarily they came only during late Sundemise, when the weather was clear. The only people we ever saw during the wet season were the porters, who showed up twice each Moon-span to load bundles of slings onto their pathbeasts and carry them away.

But here they were: not just the usual lone Master, but two. Two Masters! And they showed up with Adepts as well—five, six, maybe seven of them. Never in anyone's memory had Panli seen this sort of visit. All the people in our village came out when they arrived.

I remember my wife asking, "What's wrong?" She was afraid.

I told her, "It's the Masters."

"I can see that well enough—but *why*?"

"That's not ours to say."

"It's fair to ask, though."

"Hush up—here they come!"

The Masters and their Adepts ignored everyone but the village elders. They went into one of the elders' huts and stayed there a long time. The rest of us watched at first, then went back to work. But all day long we wondered about the Masters' arrival and wondered, too, what it meant.

At Sunfalling we learned. The elders asked everyone to show up in the village common. One of the Adepts read the Masters' pronouncement: "The following families must prepare immediately to depart from Panli and accompany the Masters." She then read the names of several husbands and wives. My wife and I were among them.

My wife began crying at once. "What have we done wrong?" she called out. "We've always performed our duty!"

Before I could hush her, the Adept answered, "You are to come with us for just that reason."

That didn't really calm her. All evening she wept. Yet we had no choice. We gathered our few possessions, we bundled them in cloth, we loaded them onto the waiting pathbeasts. When we went to say goodbye to everyone else in the village, however, some of the Adepts prevented us from visiting them. "There is no time," one of them told us.

"Besides," said another, "you aren't finished yet."

I asked, "Finished with what?"

"Finished getting ready."

"We have all our things."

The Adepts motioned toward the sheds where we stored our handiwork. "Bring lamps and come with us," they said. "You must bring a big load of slings, too."

Only after bundling up enough slings for ten pathbeasts' burdens did they let us leave. Only after we left did they tell us that the Last Days had arrived, that the Man of Knowledge walked among the Mountain-Drawn, and that my wife and I had been chosen to join him on a voyage to the Mountain Made of Light.

[Anonymous broadside, posted or circulated in Makbofissorih; dated Twentieth day of the Second Moon-span, Sunreturn (November 5, 1921).]

The Few are chosen; the Many are rejected.
   Which are which?
   Ask the Masters!

The Chosen hurry upward; the Rejected fall behind.
   Who is saved and who is lost?
   Ask the Masters!

The Mountain looms; the Lowland waits.
   Who shall reach the Summit—and who fall prey to the white-bearded hordes?
   Ask the Masters!

[Juana Méndez de Mariátegui, formerly Hunatau Mantassi of Va'atafissorih, interviewed September 8, 1970.]

I had always hated the Masters. I had always hated how they told us what to do and what not to do, what to say and what not to say, what to believe and what not to believe. They told us everything. Worse, they expected us to do as they said, do it at once, do it without question.

That was what I hated most of all: we couldn't even ask them *why*.

Not long before the time we're talking about, my husband had asked a question. I never even found out what it was. All anyone ever told me was that he had asked a question. Perhaps he asked why one of the Adepts had ordered him to do something. Perhaps he asked why the Adepts, the Masters, or anyone else should order him about at all. Perhaps he asked why the Sun and the Moon should have granted them the right to hold sway over the Mountain-Drawn. Yes, I'll admit he asked something. He was always asking one thing or another. Now it seemed that he asked one thing too many.

One of the Aspirants came to my house. "Here are your husband's clothes," she said, and gave them to me.

"What happened?" I asked. "Where is he?"

"There has been an accident."

"What accident? Where is my husband?"

"There has been an accident."

She left without explaining further. No one else ever explained to me, either.

I never saw my husband again.

Not more than a few days later, though, a child in the marketplace rushed over, gave me a loaf of bread, and ran away. I didn't know what to do, so I did nothing. Later, at home, I ate the bread. Inside was a piece of paper. On one side of the paper were these words: "He asked a question." And on the other side: "Who will answer it—the Heirs or the Umbrage?"

A short while later, I learned that the Last Days were upon us. The Masters of our city—Va'atafissorih, the City of the Lake—made their selection of people who would be saved. Of course they didn't put it like that, but that's what they did. They chose some people to seek refuge on the Mountain Made of Light; they denied the rest of us the right to join them. Of course, they didn't choose anyone in a way that made the choosing clear except to those actually making the trip. You either got to go or you didn't. Aspirants and Adepts showed up at odd hours; neighbors wept loudly or cried out in exaltation; and people left clutching bundles in the middle of the night.

No one came to visit me. No one told me I was chosen. My life went on as before.

Except for one thing: when I tried to leave Va'atafissorih by one of the causeways that cross the lake from our island-city to the shore, guards stopped me—guards in full battle regalia.

You can imagine my despair. Rumors had already begun to fly: the Man of Knowledge had arrived. . . . The Last Days were upon us. . . . A few people would set off to find the Mountain. . . . But no one knew just what they meant. All I knew was that a few people were leaving Va'atafissorih in haste. And I wasn't among them.

You can well understand how I felt soon after that when the same child approached me once more in the marketplace and gave me another loaf of bread. The bread kept my hope alive! For in the loaf was another message: "Some wait to be chosen; some choose themselves. Which are you?

Meet us near the Shadow Spring at Moonabove tonight."

Was this the chance I awaited—or a trap? Would I find friends there—or a squad of the Masters' Guards? I couldn't take the risk. Yet how could I pass up the opportunity?

Once the Moon had risen overhead that night, I left my house with a few belongings and made my way to the Shadow Spring. The spring has that name because the houses clustered all around leave it continually in shadow. The Shadow Spring is rather out of the way; most people take their water from other wells. All the more reason to use this one: it wasn't water I sought. I brought a pottery jug just in case. If someone stopped me, I'd explain that my cistern had run dry.

At first I couldn't see anyone there—too dark. Then, as my eyes adjusted, I saw someone else filling a jug from where the spout stuck out of the rock. I watched a while, then drew near.

He didn't notice me next to him at first. When he did, he turned, looked me over, then went back to filling his jug. Maybe this man hadn't been expecting me after all. He was just going about his business. I felt disappointed—and relieved. It wasn't such a good idea being here, anyway. No doubt the Masters held me in suspicion already. I'd just leave. I'd go back home. I'd—

"Is it too dark a night to seek more shadows?" asked the man.

What a silly thing to say. The night wasn't dark—on the contrary, the moon overhead made it bright. True, we stood in deep shadow. But that puzzled me further. Had he said "to seek more shadows" or "to seek to be shadowed"? The words in the Common Dialect were almost the same.

"Better shadows," I said, "than what others claim is the light."

Now the man stood straight to look me over. I

couldn't see his face, for he wore his hood up, the cowl masking his whole head in darkness. The sight terrified me. Now I'd done it. I'd exposed myself for all to see.

Just as I felt the impulse to run, this man said, "Come with me."

Fear choked me; I couldn't respond.

"Come with me."

"But please explain," I blurted, "*where* you are taking me."

"You should know by now."

"Should—but don't."

"Then perhaps you shouldn't come at all."

I couldn't decide what to say or do. All I wanted was to flee. I managed to blurt, "Why should I trust you?"

"You shouldn't."

"How do I know who you are?"

"You don't."

"Why, then, should I go with you?"

He lifted his jug from the spring. I saw then that it wasn't a jug at all, but a pathpack. He handed it to me. "If you don't choose yourself, when will you be chosen?"

We left Va'atafissorih that night: worked our way through the city, reached the Shore Wall, and, with at least ten other people awaiting us there, plunged into the lake, swam through icy water to the shore, and fled the Masters' Guards stationed on the other side.

4

26 November 1921

Dear Dad,

The Umbrages are ready for action in more
ways than one. Hundreds of the common folk
mill around when the weather permits; my
lieutenants alternately exhort and calm them;
and I'm busy figuring out what to do next.

I should relate some interesting
developments since I wrote last. Remember
Aeslu, the luscious peasant lass I mentioned a
few letters back? The princess? The Sun's
bride, or whatever? Well, I've had a lively time
with her. Not quite as lively as I'd like—but at
least things are heading in the right direction.
To wit: she's had a change of heart. We had a
little spat and she stormed off, as princesses
are wont to do; but (speaking of storms) she
got caught in a blizzard, suffered a bad chill,
and came to her senses. Somehow she made it
back to the Umbrage camp and recovered from
what could easily have been a fatal case of
thermic exposure. She admitted her
wrongheadedness and even asked me to
forgive her for such impetuous behavior. Far
be it from me to hold a grudge. It was actually
quite touching: once my sworn enemy, she now
confessed to seeing no sensible alternative to
cooperation with me. She has joined the
Umbrage camp. A good thing, too. We can't get
far without her. (More on this point shortly.)

Of course if you were reading this letter,

Dad, you would fancy that you detect a
possibility somehow eluding me. Perhaps (you
would suggest) the sweet young thing is
dissimulating. Perhaps her change of heart
masks another, more devious intent.

Spare me the dazzle of your insights. These
same thoughts have already crossed my mind.

In fact, I feel confident that there's no cause
for alarm. Aeslu herself admits that she
remains less than totally enthralled with me
and what I'm doing here. She doesn't feign
that I'm the long-awaited Man of Knowledge.
Quite the contrary: she still considers me the
Man of Ignorance. Yet she's thrown her lot
with me simply because she knows I'll get the
job done. Forget all this hooey about the Man
of This or That! Just find whoever can locate
the peak these people want, get them to it, and
reach the top. All else is silliness. She knows
that—and she makes no bones about it.

Hence a refreshing lack of pretense. It's
rather appealing, this practical turn of mind.
Quite regardless of who I am, I have what she
wants. I should add that in the meantime, she
has what *I* want. I refer not to what you might
imagine (though the young woman's physical
attributes are obvious enough) but rather to
her understanding of the so-called Diadem.

The Diadem is a bulky jumble of transparent
quartz points and some silver fittings that link
them together. For lack of a better word, it's a
kind of jewelry. Certainly the Rixtirs have
used this Diadem for decorative purposes; it
serves to represent the local potentate's
authority. Never mind the specifics. The crux
of the matter is that each quartz point
resembles a particular mountain in the area,
and together they resemble the central portion
of the Rixtirs' domain. Thus the person

wearing this Diadem on her head symbolically wears the place itself. Clever, eh? In fact, this symbolic meaning is only one of two that the Diadem possesses.

The Diadem is also a map. Those little quartz peaks represent the real ones more precisely than anyone first imagined. Properly hooked up, this Diadem becomes a kind of topographic map of the area, one that potentially shows the way through a maze of valleys, gorges, and passes.

Why *potentially*? Because one of the stones is missing. This gap in the crown, this blank space in the map, brings me to the question of the Mountain Stone.

Ah yes, the Mountain Stone. This is the big daddy of 'em all: the crest jewel, so to speak, the simulacrum of the Mountain Made of Light itself. How do I know? Not just because I've heard it from the people here. It was obvious from the start. For this Mountain Stone corresponds to the Mountain itself just as the rest of the Diadem does to the surrounding area. It's a talisman that the local folk consider radiant with power and authority, much as medieval pilgrims perceived their holy relics; thus the Rixtirs worship, reverence, and fear the Mountain Stone for much the same reasons. Yet it's more than that, too, something more tangible and practical: nothing less than a three-dimensional route map of the mountain.

How do I know? Again, not just because I've been told, though the Rixtirs' comments confirm what I'd already divined myself. One glance at this object would tell anyone with the slightest knowledge of mountaineering that it's more than a paperweight. First of all, it looks like a real mountain. It's stylized, I'll admit, its shape determined as much by the crystalline structure of quartz as by the artisan's hand, but the angle of the ridges and the texture of the cliffs do more than just suggest the contours of an Andean peak. I can look upon this piece of stone and imagine ice fields, cols, ridges, cornices, and cliffs. I can grasp at once what the symbolic mountain says about the real one. That's just the beginning. This Mountain Stone—just big enough to sit comfortably on the palm of my hand—bears a series of etchings unquestionably intended to indicate a path up the peak it represents: some etchings that show the route itself, others that by all appearances explain the route. I can't claim to understand what any of this means; the markings might as well be in Tibetan or Chinese. Yet their import is clear. It's clear, too, that I need the stone to climb the mountain.

Unfortunately, though I've regained the Diadem, I still lack the Mountain Stone. Who has it? I wish I knew. Maybe no one. It dropped out of that overgrown spider's nest along with everything else—but that's another tale, Dad, one irrelevant to the present circumstances. My point is simply that the Mountain Stone fell from my grasp a while back and either landed in the wrong hands or else got lost. Maybe it's at the bottom of the lake. Maybe it's imbedded in the tundra surrounding the lake. Who knows. The Umbrages have searched everywhere to the degree possible without making themselves too conspicuous, yet even *they* don't know. All I know is that it's not here. And I know I need it.

Where does this leave me?

It wouldn't be hard even for you to imagine. I don't have the Mountain Stone, but I have the Diadem. Perhaps I can't find my way up the mountain itself, but I should at least be able to make my way to its base. Perhaps I can work out something between now and then. In keeping with one of your favorite bromides: nothing ventured, nothing gained.

One further complication: the Diadem is heavily inscribed with symbols in an unknown language—symbols that no doubt pertain to finding the Mountain Made of Light. How can I make sense of them?

That, Father, is where Aeslu enters the scene.

Forster

5

[Aeslu of Vmatta, *Chronicle of the Last Days.*]

Thus by all appearances I put my heart and soul into helping the Umbrage while in fact I did everything possible to hinder them. I told them what I knew about the Heirs: all lies. I explained the nature of their intentions: still more lies. I revealed secrets about their plans and methods: nothing but lies. And while I spoke I watched them, listened to their questions, noted gestures of surprise or bewilderment, and committed to memory even the least bit of news that might some day work against them.

What would I do? I had no idea. Yet not more than ten days earlier I had descended from the Web into an icy lake and, without knowing either where I was or how to swim, had thrashed my way out. A few days later I had floundered through a snowstorm to safety. To what could I attribute my survival—not once, but twice? To my own cleverness? To my careful plans? To my own strength? To my limitless ability to overcome obstacles?

No, there was some other reason, some other guiding force. What guided me was a light (*two* lights) far brighter than whatever illumination my own mind could cast.

Yet the task before me had never seemed more urgent and difficult. The Umbrage showed every intention of entering the Inner Realm. Of course I wondered how they would enter it and (assuming they succeeded) how they would find their way about once they got there. The Inner Realm had been sealed for almost four hundred Sun-spans. No map of this place existed but one. Once mine, that map was now lost along with everything else that fell from the Web.

Or was it?

Was it possible that Forssabekkit had acquired the Diadem? After all, if he and I had survived our separate descents from the City of Rope, why should that cluster of stones have not landed intact? Somehow he might have found it, salvaged it. . . . That the Man of Ignorance now possessed the map to the Inner Realm was a thought too sickening to contemplate.

[Aeslu of Vmatta, *Chronicle of the Last Days.*]

Since you're with us now, said Forssabekkit when he entered my tent one morning, I thought you should be in on our little secret.

I watched him as he knelt before me. His right hand clutched a leather bag. As he stared, waiting for my reply, I remember thinking: This man's every word is a baited trap. Why should I grant him the pleasure of watching me spring the snares he sets?

He sprang it for me. Look, he said. Forssabekkit untied the bag with both hands, pulled it open, and dumped its contents onto the blanket. A mass of transparent stones flopped out between us.

I could not restrain my astonishment: The Diadem!

Indeed.

But how—?

It makes no difference. A combination of cleverness and good luck, as usual. What matters is that we have it.

I reached out, prodding the stones with my fingers. What I saw was not just the Diadem stones but the Diadem itself: the stones reconnected; the miniature mountains arrayed into a mountain range. Once separated from one another, they were now connected. Once jumbled together in a leather bag, they were now placed and joined in a clear pattern. Who had assembled them? I could only guess. Norroi the Tirno? Soffosoiti the Ropemaster? Forssabekkit himself?

One is missing, I said. The Mountain Stone.

We're still looking for it.

Below the Web?

To the degree that seems prudent.

Imagining the Heirs who would be keeping close watch over the valley, I asked him, And the lake?

If it's in the lake there's no hope. We found the Diadem itself some distance from the lake, though, which gives me a *little* hope.

I faltered, then said, Unless someone else—

The thought has already crossed my mind.

These words encouraged me more than anything I had heard in days. What if the Heirs had captured the Mountain Stone? Nothing else would so fully hold the Umbrage in check. Did the Man of Ignorance grasp the implications?

Of course if the Heirs have the Mountain Stone, he went on, it won't do them much good without the others. They can't climb a mountain they haven't found yet.

I said, Yet even if *we* find the Mountain, we cannot climb it without the Mountain Stone.

That long gaze: weighing, probing, judging. He asked, Are you sure?

It is impossible.

No chance at all?

None whatever.

Mm. Just as I feared.

For a long time Forssabekkit stared at the Diadem. The light in my tent was not bright; even so, the little peaks glittered and glinted. I stared at them, too, waiting for his next move at precisely the same time that the Man of Ignorance awaited mine. The Diadem itself was now the trap between us.

When neither of us spoke, he reached forward and lifted the whole mass off the blanket like the pelt of a furbeast. The Diadem swayed, clicking and creaking. The stones shot needles of light in every direction.

What are you doing? I asked.

Here.

I do not understand.

Bow.

Confused, I gestured uncertainly.

Lower your head.

Unsure what else to do, I obeyed. The Man of Ignorance then reached toward me, raised the Diadem, and rested it on my head. Its weight startled me.

Its proper place, said Forssabekkit.

I beg your pardon?

He huffed at me. As if you didn't know.

I laughed at him in puzzlement.

Now don't tell me you won't wear it! Not after

all we've been through. Smiling, he watched me glancing up past my eyebrows to catch a glimpse of the stones above.

I cannot *wear* this, I told him.

Don't be silly. You're the Moon's Stead, right? Isn't that the whole point?

His words hit hard. I was the Moon's Stead, and I had the right—the duty—to wear the Diadem. But his actions baffled me. Did he now entrust it to me?

Before I could speak again, Forssabekkit handed me the leather bag, stood, and walked toward the door. Take good care of it, he said. You look absolutely smashing with that on, but we'll need it to do more than just adorn your body. He stared at me for a long time. Now if you'll excuse me, he added, I have a few little errands to run.

[Aeslu of Vmatta, *Chronicle of the Last Days*.]

What took place two days later was typical of what Forssabekkit referred to as his little errands. Leaving the previous night's camp well before dawn, a band of about forty Umbrage descended with their leaders into the valley below. They were women as well as men, most of them my own age or not much older, all healthy and strong. The Umbrage customarily fought only with knives, hatchets, and slings; thus their weapons offered no impediments to speed. They carried almost nothing on their backs: just a small pack apiece. Angling steeply into whatever terrain their path presented, they moved with an ease revealing not just their youth, prowess, and zeal but also their knowledge of whatever destination Forssabekkit had chosen for them.

I was a good walker in those days; even so, these Umbrage ran me ragged from the start. Never mind that I still felt weary from my Web injuries and from my brush with death in the snowstorm; I would have been hard-pressed to maintain the Umbrage pace under any circumstances. Yet I had no choice but to keep up with them. More than that: to precede them, to rally them, to show them the way. For the Man of Ignorance and I were, after all, their leaders.

What complicated my situation further was the weather. In the Umbrage camp, sleet had fallen for days (not hard, but steadily) and this downpour cloaked our departure almost as fully as it had cloaked my solitary escape not long before. The sleet also made our footing treacherous. More than once I slipped and fell to the ground; I lost my balance more often than I had time or presence of mind to count. Here, too, the Umbrage seemed more agile and confident than I had expected—certainly more so than I would have liked. Yet my main concern was neither my own clumsiness nor my followers' skill; rather, it was how fully the weather confounded any efforts to determine our whereabouts. Lost, I would be all the more helpless if I tried alerting my fellow-Heirs to the dangers confronting us.

The Umbrage had been silent throughout our descent; now, abruptly, they began signaling to one another with a sequence of whistles. They had traveled together all along; now they spread out, vanishing on my right and left into the mist.

Alone with Forssabekkit I asked, Where are we now?

See for yourself.

Without warning I found myself entering a village. Stone walls, thatched roofs, muddy paths: a typical settlement for this part of the Realm. Nothing about it suggested any particular place in the Mountain Land. Most of our villages were simply farming towns; this one was no exception.

If I could only have known something about it! If I could only have guessed its inhabitants' allegiance to the Heirs or the Umbrage! Under the right conditions, I might then have conveyed a message to someone capable of passing it to the Masters. Yet I could scarcely see the place, much less decide whether its people were friend or enemy, for the sleet came down so hard that everything around me diminished to the vagueness of a dream.

Forssabekkit and I entered the village. The place was unprotected; we simply walked in. Of course, even small villages like that are always on guard; I knew that someone there would be observing every step of our approach. No doubt a hundred eyes watched us through slits, slats, peepholes . . . yet we saw no one.

All right, said Forssabekkit. Let's begin.

We stopped in the muddy mess that was this town's communal square. We hesitated briefly, then spoke—Forssabekkit first in Lowland, I myself in the Common Dialect.

Listen, all you Mountain-Drawn: the Last Days have arrived. It makes no difference whether you are Heirs or Umbrage. Either way the old era is almost over; the new will soon begin. For we are the Sun's and the Moon's Steads. We are here to lead you to the Summit. Come with us and seek refuge in the place that Ossonnal and Lissallo have prepared for you on the Mountain Made of Light.

These are the words we said—shouted, really, to make ourselves heard over the rain. Of course, we never uttered them together. Forssabekkit made the speech in his own Lowland tongue; I translated. But in some ways we spoke with one voice. Nothing I said in the Common Dialect violated the spirit of Forssabekkit's words in Lowland.

Or did it? All in all I could utter my own

version of the speech with a pure heart. The Last Days had indeed arrived; I was indeed the Moon's Stead; I had indeed come to lead these people to the Summit. If the inhabitants of this village had come forth and followed me alone, I would have been doing no less and no more than my duty. Yet I spoke these words among the Umbrage. I could imagine no greater way of betraying myself, the Mountain-Drawn, and the Sun and Moon we worshipped.

For a long time we heard no sound but that of the falling rain. Forssabekkit and I stood in the center of that village and waited. Then the Man of Ignorance said, Show them your crown.

Till then I had worn my raincloak's hood up. Now I pulled it back, revealing the Diadem I wore. At once I heard our unseen observers' exclamations.

Heed us well, you Mountain-Drawn, we said, each of us in turn, speaking our respective languages. The Last Days have arrived. Flee with those who would give you refuge.

Again no response. Somewhere close by I heard low voices begin to argue; then a woman's voice, a man's, and another man's exchange quick questions and answers; then a wail abruptly stifled.

Forssabekkit spoke without turning my way. Just a few minutes more, he said. Then we call in the troops.

The town is insignificant, I told him with growing alarm. We should leave it alone.

He huffed in derision. Insignificant? I never said otherwise. But these things add up. We need what they have. Besides, we've already made our presence known. We can't just say it's all a mistake and tiptoe away.

It is just a poor farming village.

Fine. Let them toss in their two cents' worth.

I could not protest much more. Anything else I

said would begin to work against me. After all, had I not come forth to call the faithful to their duty? It made no sense for me to make excuses now.

Yet to subject these people to the Umbrage yoke. . . . Surely I could find some way to warn them. For a moment I nearly blurted what first came to mind: Run for your lives! The Last Days have arrived, for this is the Man of Ignorance! Flee for your lives!

I held off. All around this town stood Umbrage waiting to attack. Anything I shouted would reach their own ears as well as the villagers'. What little I might gain for the moment I would lose in the long run.

Just then a man's voice called out: Who are you to call us forth to the Summit?

I am Aeslu the Moon's Stead, I answered.

And who comes with you? asked the same voice.

He is Forssabekkit the Sun's Stead.

A long silence followed, a silence interrupted only by more arguments and lamentations.

Then another voice, this time a woman's: Then you are Umbrage—traitors and infidels!

I said, We are they who will lead a remnant of the Mountain-Drawn to their refuge.

Several voices now: Traitors! Infidels!

Forssabekkit turned to me. What's the problem?

What I feared, I told him. They are defying us.

Oh, they *are*? And with those words (an utterance more of exasperation than surprise or anger) the Man of Ignorance shouted, Now listen—I don't have time for this nonsense! Come out by choice or come out by force.

I translated.

Before he could speak again, however, a shadow emerged from the rain just a few manlengths away, pulled itself together into a human form as it sprinted closer, and lunged toward us; yet at once a second form, then a third and a fourth, emerged abruptly from the rain to intercept the first. They collided with a grunt so loud that it sounded like timbers splintering. At once three of the man-forms pummeled the first with clubs or hatchets.

The sequence of events brought forth more shapes from their huts. I could see men wearing the sorts of attire I would have expected of them (farmers' sandals, deerskin britches, dusky woven raincloaks) but raising their planting sticks and hoes like weapons.

Forssabekkit surveyed this scene for just a moment: a man lying face down in the mud; his three assailants getting up from where he lay; an uncertain number of other men and women watching from all around. He whistled twice. And at once, as if pulling themselves out of the rain itself, the other Umbrage appeared suddenly among the villagers' dwellings, each holding an ice hatchet in one hand, a knife in the other.

These Umbrage were outnumbered, of course; a village like that must have had a hundred inhabitants, maybe more. But the villagers looked so stunned by our presence that they made no effort to fight. They simply stared. Perhaps they never understood how few Umbrage had descended on their settlement. Perhaps they simply failed to grasp that this calamity could befall them in the first place. The Umbrage were in control from the moment they showed up. The only resistance I detected came in the sound of a few frantic splashing footsteps that faded quickly or else ended abruptly in a sequence of thuds, grunts, and stifled screams.

Tell them it's pointless to fight, said Forssabekkit. All they have to do is hand over the goods.

Reluctantly I translated.

He added, Of course the Umbrage among them are free to join us.

I almost cried out what my heart was screaming: Death to the Umbrage! Long live the Heirs! Rise up against the infidels and join the faithful on their voyage upward to the Summit!

Yet again I realized that no matter how valiantly these peasants rose up against the Umbrage, their efforts would come to nothing. And my secret, if revealed too soon, would likewise come to grief.

For this reason I translated Forssabekkit's words just as he shouted them at the villagers cowering before us.

One by one the town's chief men and women came forth, relinquished the stone seals of their authority, and led us through the rain to the storehouse full of the bounty that the Umbrage sought.

[Aeslu of Vmatta, *Chronicle of the Last Days.*]

That raid was just one of many in which I participated. Within a few days after that, I joined the Umbrage in sacking two other towns—one of them another farming village, the other a weavers' community. In both cases, the Umbrage seemed less intent on harming the inhabitants than on plundering their supplies; all the same, many people ended up hurt, and several killed, regardless of the plunderers' intentions. A shadow does not intend to spread darkness; darkness is simply its nature. So also with the Umbrage. Thus they went about their shadow business, acquiring whatever goods they coveted and swelling their ranks with men, women, and children who shared their shadow sympathies. Despite the revulsion I felt, I collaborated with them in hopes that by some means I would dispell their darkness with whatever light I might succeed in casting.

I was not unaware of the quandary that my situation presented. Precisely by appearing to help the Umbrage, I worked most earnestly to defeat them; yet the appearance of my actions would console my enemies and anger my friends. Appearance and action were not so easy to keep apart. At what point did the appearance of my actions become an action in its own right? At what point did my good intentions breed terrible deeds? I did not know. All I knew is that a great anguish devoured me as I followed the path before me, yet following some other path seemed impossible. Even so, I worried about how I appeared to those watching me at the time, and to those who (perhaps many Sun-spans later) might hear of Aeslu the Wordpathguide, an Heir whose piety toward the Sun and the Moon fell away like a gown to reveal the sickly flesh of heresy and treason.

How much simpler to have screamed: I worship the Sun and the Moon, and I revile you Umbrage for your apostasy against them!

How much easier to have dared them: Kill me if you will, for I shall never do your bidding!

How much more tempting to have made my own anguish clear no matter what the consequences. Yet in many ways my anguish did not matter. What mattered was the Mountain Land. What mattered were the Mountain-Drawn. My task did not allow for an easy appearance: simply doing what needed to be done regardless of how I looked in doing it. My task required a more treacherous mix of what I did and what I seemed to do.

I was the liar whose lie was itself the truth. I was the thief whose theft itself returned stolen goods to the owner. I was the traitor whose treason itself sought to honor my land and its people.

Yet however much the appearance of my actions differed from their true nature, what I seemed to do affected people as much or more than what I did.

Word of our raids soon preceded us. Villagers fled their settlements long before we ever reached them (fled, or else flocked to join us) and Forssabekkit's minions gained both whatever booty the departing Heirs abandoned and what the newly arrived Umbrage brought with them.

This is all rather encouraging, said the Man of Ignorance one afternoon after an especially brazen daytime raid. He stood surveying the captured goods now piled in the Umbrage camp: bales of wool, great bolts of cloth, animal hides, pelts of fur, and countless spools of yarn; bags of grain and potatoes; heaps of squash, corn, berries, peppers, roots; woven cages full of scamperbeasts, tundra hens, and wild piglets. He added, The quality may be crude, but the quantity allows room for real logistics.

I did not understand the words. *Low gist*—?

Logistics. Having what we need when we need it.

On the mountain, I said.

Indeed, said Forssabekkit, running his hand over a bolt of woolbeast cloth. On the mountain.

I asked, Soon?

As soon as possible, he answered. It's all well and good to indulge these Umbrages in their propensity for plunder, but it won't keep them occupied for long. Nor should it. Soon enough they'll want to get down to business.

I must have stared at him with a perplexed gaze, for he reached out and shook me gently, as one might waken someone from a nap. He said, They'll want the real payoff.

* * *

I realized just then how quickly I needed to act in thwarting the Umbrage. I realized, too, that the solution was identical to the problem itself: the Diadem. For just as the Diadem provided Forssabekkit with a means of reaching the Mountain, so also did it provide me with a means to throw him off course.

The Diadem had first fallen into our hands as a jumble of disconnected stones. Jassikki, Norroi, Forssabekkit, and I stole it from the Hermit in his aerie; we carried it ourselves through Leqsiffaltho till the Umbrage captured us; we lost it, then regained it, when the Umbrage and the Heirs fought one another in the rain; and we lost it yet again when Soffosoiti held us captive in the Web. During all that time the stones were not so much the Diadem itself as pieces of it. Then, after the Web disaster, the Diadem turned up once more—now intact. Who had decided on the pattern of its stones? Who had connected the little chains that dangled from each of them? Did the pattern reflect someone's desire of how the Inner Realm should look, or did it reveal a true knowledge of its geography?

I could not answer these questions, yet I had my hunches.

Soffosoiti the Ropemaster was the only person I knew—indeed, the only person I had heard of— who claimed to have reached the Mountain Made of Light. He claimed in fact to have climbed partway up the Mountain before suffering the injuries that had crippled him. Soffosoiti might well have been lying about what he knew and what he had done. He might well have received his injuries by other means. Yet I doubted it. A man might lose his arms, his legs, even his ears and lips and nose in some sort of accident other than failing at the Ropemaster's quest; he might even survive the accident and live out his days attended by whomever might take pity on him; but he would not have received the respect (no, the worship) that his people lavished on him unless he had indeed attempted what he claimed to have done. In short, I believed that Soffosoiti had sought, reached, and begun to climb the Mountain before he suffered his injuries. If my belief were true, then the Ropemaster knew the way to the Mountain Made of Light.

Why did this matter? It mattered because Soffosoiti was probably the person who put the Diadem back together. Not Soffosoiti himself: the man had no hands. Yet one of his attendants might have positioned the stones at the Ropemaster's bidding, connected the hooks and chains once again, and thus returned this odd stone map to a semblance of the Inner Realm. Soffosoiti himself had told me that his greatest pain was to gaze out and see the Mountain rise before him. What else could that man have seen from his vantage? The paths; the rivers, lakes, and waterfalls; the valleys; the passes between them; the glaciers and icefalls; the lesser peaks around the greater one; and, rising beyond, the Mountain itself. What better place to size up the terrain and note the correspondence between the mountains themselves and the stones representing them? And who else but Soffosoiti to do so?

This is precisely what frightened me about the Diadem: that it might well show Forssabekkit the way to the Mountain. Never mind that he lacked the Mountain Stone, which was at once the Diadem's crown jewel and the key to climbing the peak itself. I could not take any chances. The Diadem in Forssabekkit's hands was a deadly thing.

Please—I must speak with you at once, I told Forssabekkit that afternoon. Something terrible has happened.

What is it? he asked, looking more concerned than I would have expected.

We must speak alone.

He smiled at my words and said, No one here can understand us anyway.

It is not just what I will say, I told him, but what I will show you.

Forssabekkit motioned for some of the Umbrage to vacate a nearby tent. They did so quickly, almost eagerly, though not without long glances to discern our purposes. He went in first; I followed. Upon entering I knelt, opened the Diadem's leather bag, and eased the stones onto a woolbeast blanket. Forssabekkit remained standing beside me, then knelt suddenly as he saw the Diadem itself.

Some of the stones hung together in clusters of five or six; others rested on the blanket in pairs; a few lay altogether separated from the rest.

Please forgive me, I blurted. Earlier today I put it on, but on entering my tent I brushed against the crossbeam. The Diadem dropped to the floor and fell apart.

Nudging the stones this way and that, he looked uneasy, even alarmed—paler than usual.

Please forgive me, I said again. I have worried—

It's not a problem, he told me.

What did you say?

He turned toward me and smiled. It's not a problem.

I laughed as if in relief but shook my head. Fallen to pieces like this, it will be useless—

Forssabekkit put his arm around me, pulled me closer. Don't worry, he said. I plan for everything. That little artifact has seemed all too delicate from the start. I've assumed it might get some rough treatment now and then, so I sketched its layout for future reference. A map of the map, so to speak.

You know where the stones go? I asked, hearing the words as if they came from a voice other than my own. You know how they fit together?

Just in case. It's a necessary precaution.

I tried to stand but felt so dizzy that I almost fell.

Forssabekkit stood then reached down to pull me up. Rest easy, he told me. All is well.

[Aeslu of Vmatta, *Chronicle of the Last Days.*]

And so my plan to scramble the Diadem came to nothing. Forssabekkit had indeed sketched the stones in their proper places; putting them back together took only a little more time than I had needed to disconnect them in the first place. Then the Diadem once again became what I had tried to prevent it from being: a map of the Inner Realm.

I considered doing more substantial damage, of course. I could have thrown some of the stones away and claimed to have lost them. I could have smashed a few and claimed to have dropped them. I could have destroyed the whole thing and claimed any of a thousand reasons for the mishap. Yet the more severely I harmed the Diadem, the more suspect my actions. I might thwart the Man of Ignorance for the moment only to reveal my intentions, thus defeating myself in the longer run.

No, I had to proceed by other means. I needed to contrive some other way to stop Forssabekkit and the Umbrage.

[Aeslu of Vmatta, *Chronicle of the Last Days.*]

I could not be sure, of course, but I sensed that Forssabekkit trusted me. How deeply? I did not know. Yet somehow his actions suggested a degree of confidence, a willingness to leave me to myself and to my own devices, precisely at the time when my solitude most endangered his purposes. His decision to commit the Diadem to my safekeeping was only the most obvious sign of this trust. In addition, I had complete freedom throughout the Umbrage camp: I went about my business as I wished; I carried on my little masquerade.

Yet the masquerade took so much effort to maintain, and its appearance required me to seem so fully other than myself, that what appeared as my serenity could only have been weariness. I had to listen closely not just to what others said but also to each word I spoke. I had to watch not only their gestures and expressions but also my own. I had to step carefully in every way I could imagine. I dreaded sleep for fear that I might call out unwittingly.

If only I could have shared the burden! I felt no regret in opposing the Umbrage; on the contrary, I did so eagerly. But alone? Part of my duty as the Moon's Stead was to risk my life confronting all my people's enemies. Yet I longed to do so with my proper companion: Jassikki. That was a pointless longing. Yet even its pointlessness did not prevent it from causing my greatest troubles.

What sort of intelligence do you obtain about our enemies? Forssabekkit asked me one morning.

I echoed his final word: Intelligence?

Knowledge by whatever means. Surely the Umbrage have spies.

Spies?

You may be the Moon's Stead, he told me, but you still have a few things to learn about the world.

In fact I knew what he intended. Even though the Heirs almost never knew what the Umbrage were doing, the Umbrage have always kept a close eye on the Heirs.

The Man of Ignorance went on: Surely if something important happens in the Realm, the Umbrage will know about it.

Such as—?

Such as something I thought we shouldn't have to worry about: Whether Jassikki survived the Web.

No change came over his face when he spoke these words. Did any change come over mine? The mere mention of Jassikki stirred more feeling in me than I thought I could mask. Jassikki? I asked. The Throw-Pall-of-Gist?

It's unlikely but possible, he said. After all, both you and I somehow got away unscathed. Perhaps he did, too.

I could not help wondering why the Man of Ignorance brought up this subject now. Was he truly worried that Jassikki might have survived? Did he know the answer—an answer that I had never hoped could be true? Or was he simply broaching the possibility to check my response? I fell silent for longer than I intended, then broke my silence by force of will. If he were alive, I told him, we would know. We might not know right away—the Mountain Land is a big place, and news travels slowly—but in time we would know.

And you feel that the Umbrage are reliable?

Here I could no longer restrain a smile. The Umbrage are *your* people, I said. You tell *me* if they are reliable.

That's not what I meant. I trust them. But messengers might get caught. Messages might get intercepted.

It would be easier to catch a shadow.

Perhaps, said Forssabekkit. All the same, they

might run into problems. The Heirs have us out-numbered, and they have no qualms about playing rough.

He began to look more concerned. I could see it in his eyes. Forssabekkit was never one to avoid my gaze; on the contrary, his own always bored into me without hesitation. Yet now he seemed to be looking elsewhere: past the camp, past the glacier, past the peaks.

Before he could speak I said, Do not misunderstand my words. I am not accusing anyone—not blaming anyone. All I mean is that the word might not have reached us. Or else the Heirs may be so careful that even the Umbrage among them missed what has happened.

Sounding weary, he asked, So what should we do?

If you feel concerned, I told him, then we should find out—

—if Jassikki is alive, said the Man of Ignorance.

[Aeslu of Vmatta, *Chronicle of the Last Days*.]

If Jassikki is alive! The very thought was almost more than I could tolerate. How could I so much as begin to hope for something that had seemed impossible for a long, long time? Yet how could I do anything but hope?

The Man of Ignorance was not one to waste time fretting over imaginary risks; if he worried, then his worry cannot have been groundless. What, however, prompted him to wonder about Jassikki's survival? I had no idea. But Forssabekkit's concern itself—his fear that Jassikki had not perished when the Web fell—was ultimately what saved me from despair.

All the same, this turn of events confused me to the point that even the ground I stood on felt unsteady. I did not know what to believe. I did not know what to do. I began to doubt whether my course of action—trying to sabotage my enemies from within their midst—was so wise after all. Thus despite Forssabekkit's seeming trust, I found it hard not to withdraw, to spend more time alone, if only to keep my head from spinning.

As a child, living in a village near the great glacier in Vmatta, I had seen insects of a sort that I now noticed from time to time near the Umbrage camp. Starbugs, I had called them, for they twinkled like stars. To amuse ourselves, we children had watched for them, chased them, tried to catch them. We believed them to be real stars who had sneaked away from their duties in attending the Moon; and who, in a fit of mischief, had wandered down to visit us mere mortals below. If we could only capture a few (we imagined) they might tell us secrets about life up there with the goddess we worshipped. But they were impossible to catch: no sooner did we spot one by its flickering light than it went dark again; and when we reached the place where we had first seen it, the starbug was already somewhere else.

Of course I learned when I was older that these strange little lights were not stars at all, but only bugs, and I ceased to spend time chasing them. But now I saw them again, and, as I walked alone each evening at the glacier's edge, I found consolation in their unexpected glimmers even though (or perhaps because) they were so gentle and brief. It was not that they reminded me of my childhood, however: the recollection they spurred was of another time.

During a long voyage many Moon-spans earlier—a voyage that Jassikki, Norroi, and I had taken from the Mountain Land's edge into its heart—my companions and I had camped every night. The campfires we built had provided warmth not just for the flesh, but for the spirit as well. The sparks spiraling upward from the fire gave us a magnificent sight, a sight like that of glowing starbugs, a sight that now reminded me of the man I loved and could almost dare to hope was still alive.

[Aeslu of Vmatta, *Chronicle of the Last Days*.]

The Diadem was not the only thing that Forssabekkit had acquired. By means that escaped my understanding, the Man of Ignorance had somehow obtained all sorts of Lowland things. Great packs and bundles lay stacked near his tent within the Umbrage camp. Some of these packs and bundles remained intact, but others had been pulled open to reveal their contents: strange garments, footgear, handgear, headgear; lumpy cloth bags full of assorted goods; shiny metal containers; wooden boxes encasing rows of green or brown bottles; gadgets of sorts I had never seen before; and mountaincraft equipment.

Mountaincraft equipment! Already the Man of Ignorance had demonstrated his prowess as a climber; here now was the equipment that accounted for at least part of his strength and skill. Huge coils of rope. Stacks of long-handled, black-headed ice hatchets. Packs. Footclaws. All manner of hooks. Other things, too—things I could not identify but recognized as devices intended for climbing.

Where had Forssabekkit acquired these things? Had other Lowlanders joined the Umbrage? Had the Man of Ignorance brought his bundles from elsewhere? Either prospect worried me. Most of all, however, I worried about what the presence of his equipment meant for the future.

Before I could speculate further, I heard a voice address me: Admiring my trinkets?

I turned to find Forssabekkit standing near the entrance to his tent.

They will help us reach the Mountain, I said lamely.

True, he answered. And help us have a good time getting there, too.

I gestured in puzzlement toward the bundles.

He said, Let me show you. Forssabekkit turned from me and pulled open one of three large Lowland path-packs resting on the ground near where he stood. First business, he told me, then pleasure. With those words he revealed the pack's contents.

It was full of rope: tight coils of pale Lowland rope. He opened the other two packs as well: more rope.

Where did you get all these things? I asked.

I brought them with me. Or rather, I had them brought. Not all at once, of course. I left them quite a ways back when I first came to the mountains, then arranged to have them transported here.

Yes, but how?

By the same means that you people transport everything else—on your backs.

I could not fully grasp what he meant. I watched in wonderment as he pulled open several of his bundles to expose clusters of Lowland-style ice hatchets, hammers, and other pieces of equipment. At the sight of all this gear, I exclaimed, But for so many people!

Forssabekkit said, I usually climb alone. It's simpler that way. Over the years, though, I've found there's no harm in preparing for collaborative efforts. One never knows who one might encounter in the backwoods. Even here (and he motioned toward the Umbrage all around) one never knows.

Before I could respond, Forssabekkit reached over to one of the larger stacks nearby. So much for business, he said. Now pleasure.

Atop the packs and bundles were two large, smooth brown blocks of stone. At least I assumed they were stone, for they looked so shiny that I could see my shape reflected in their surface; yet when the Man of Ignorance reached out to them, he lifted one almost without effort. Then he opened it up: simply tilted the top off. It was a wooden box so finely polished that it looked like stone. A black disc about the size and shape of a potter's wheel rested inside. Near it were several pieces of stone or metal: one long, the other round. I could not make sense of what I saw. Forssabekkit removed a bent piece of metal from the lid and poked it into the side of the box. Then, opening a second box next to the first, he lifted another disc (this one thin, black, and shiny) and placed it on the potter's wheel.

Are you going to make a pot? I asked.

No, he said. Some music.

Though his words made no sense, I kept watching. I should mention that by this time, others were watching as well: members of the Umbrage who had drawn near to see what was happening. The children came first: two boys, a girl, two more girls, then a whole cluster of boys. Soon some adults approached: three young men, an old man, two women. No one spoke.

They all looked as puzzled as I felt, none at all sure of what the Man of Ignorance was doing. Yet they looked curious, too, intent on being part of whatever happened next. Though I felt curious as well, I resented their curiosity. They waited and watched so eagerly; they trusted him; they let themselves walk so willingly into his trap!

For a few moments nothing happened. Then Forssabekkit started turning the bent piece of metal that protruded from the box. The black disc on top spun around and around. Then he moved the long bar from where it rested onto the disc—

How can I explain what happened? All I can say is that the box began to shriek like a wounded animal; the gathered Umbrage let loose at once with their own cries of bewilderment and fear; and everyone ran off.

Everyone but me.

I would like to claim that I remained there because I felt no fear, but the opposite was true. I was terrified. I felt so afraid that I could no more have run than leap into the air and fly away. All I could do was stand there, frozen. Surely the tortuous screams that deafened me as I stood near that box were nothing less than evil ghosts that would rush forth and possess me.

Then another sound caught my attention. I managed to crack free of the ice that bound my soul and glance over to Forssabekkit.

He was laughing.

[Aeslu of Vmatta, *Chronicle of the Last Days.*]

It was just a little before Sunabove. Thick clouds rolled overhead, yet the Sun's warmth had already turned the previous night's snowfall to mush. The Umbrage camp was wet and splashy. The midday ice-rain only added to the mess. Everyone was soaked: men and women going about their tasks; old people wringing out their blankets or cooking food; children playing. Yet as Forssabekkit and I strode through the camp, I saw no signs of discomfort and heard no complaints. Everyone was busy. Everyone was ready for whatever happened next. Some people even called out to us as we passed, asking what we wanted them to do.

Translate for me, said Forssabekkit, and without warning he turned on his heels and addressed the crowd gathering behind him. He shouted, Listen! We need new gear, new things to help us reach the mountain. If you want to succeed, we need to get ready.

I did as he asked and translated his words from Lowland into Rixtir.

He said, You need better clothing. You can't go up that mountain dressed in nightgowns. It's going to be windy up there. What you wear has to be warm and strong.

Then he asked the weavers to come forth, and they did so. Forssabekkit told them what he wanted: tighter cloth, smoother cloth, something to keep out the cold and the wind. The weavers listened and spoke in low voices among themselves. Now and then one of them asked a question. What color should the cloth be? What sort of design should it show? And Forssabekkit heard them out, thought a while, and responded. White, he said, or gray—the lighter the better—but color makes less difference than the weave itself. Above all, the cloth must be tightly woven.

Once finished with the weavers, the Man of Ignorance called for the tailors. Here's what you must do, he told them. Take these pants (and here he handed the tailors one of the long forked garments that Lowland men wear over their legs) and pull it apart. That's right: dismantle it. Use the pieces as a pattern. Cut the new cloth according to the old. Then put all the pieces you've cut together into new pants. Do you understand?

He asked for the leathercrafters next. The Man of Ignorance showed them a pair of Lowland boots (big and swollen, like an infected foot) and asked them to duplicate it. The craftsmen were unsure;

no one within the Mountain Land had ever made anything like these boots. The leather resembled wood more than animal hide. The sole was stiff and studded with small metal pegs. Speaking among themselves, the leathercrafters looked uncertain of how to accomplish their task.

Look, said Forssabekkit, even a rough copy will do. Anything that protects the foot better than these sandals you wear.

And so it went, from one item to another, until the Man of Ignorance had told the crafters what the Umbrage forthsetting required.

Some of the people now glanced about as if anticipating the end of Forssabekkit's instructions. Not that they seemed eager to leave: on the contrary, I have rarely seen such delight in followers of any leader. They awaited his every word.

Regarding rope, he went on. Forget everything the Heirs ever taught you about rope. If any of you brought that stuff with you—that frilly, lacy, elaborate stuff—just throw it away.

These words brought mixed sounds of shock and amusement. However much they hated the Heirs and held the Heirs' rituals in contempt, the Umbrage seemed to have difficulty shaking the notion of rope as sacred.

Forssabekkit pulled a coil of Lowland rope from his small pack. Now *this* is rope, he said. Manila hemp, to be specific. This can get you up a mountain—and down, too, if that's your fancy.

As he spoke, he held the coil out to his listeners, tempting them to touch it, take it, heft it, stroke it. Some of them did so, although reluctantly at first; others then grasped it more openly, smiling and laughing; soon the Umbrage tugged at the rope, unwound it, and entangled themselves in it with nearly childish delight.

What I want you to do, said Forssabekkit, is come up with whatever most nearly duplicates

this rope. I don't care how you do it: just do it.
Use whatever material you want. Use your own
hair, as far as I'm concerned, like those rope people. Use *theirs*, if it comes to that—there's certainly enough of it scattered around in the valley.
Just make lots of it, and make it good.

Taking Forssabekkit's coil, the ropecrafters left
to begin their work.

One last matter, he told everyone else, and with
those words Forssabekkit removed his ice hatchet
from the small pack before him. He held up the
hatchet for everyone to see. It bore little resemblance to any device I had ever seen among the
Mountain-Drawn. The wooden shaft was longer,
the head was narrower, and (this most remarkably) the metal looked as shiny and sharp as a
Lowland knife. Held before us, this ice hatchet
caught everyone's attention at once. He said,
Someone bring me one of your axes.

Once I had translated, a young Umbrage woman
stepped forth at once with a hatchet typical of our
people: short-handled, heavy-headed, reddish-
brown in color.

Forssabekkit extended his own hatchet toward
the woman with the head in her direction. He said,
Now strike metal against metal.

At first she did nothing but stare, so alarming
did she find his request. To strike her own leader?

Go ahead.

I translated his command.

She stalled another eyeblink or two. Then, gazing toward the Man of Ignorance, she swung with
her hatchet and struck his own.

The clank jolted everyone. People jerked back
in alarm. The head of this woman's hatchet
(Sunrise-metal, the strongest in the Mountain
Land) simply snapped in two. The tip spun off
sideways and fell to the ground.

Forssabekkit watched what happened and huffed

in amusement. You call this *metal?* he shouted. This isn't metal—it's putty, clay, mud! If you want metal, I'll show you metal.

Storming off, he motioned for everyone to follow. The Umbrage did so reluctantly. They looked like children being led away by an angry father.

Forssabekkit stopped short, turned, and beckoned to me as well. I want you to tell them something, he said.

He went on to explain that down in the Lowland, Forssabekkit and his family were accomplished metalmasters. They knew everything about mines, about extracting ore from the ground, about smelting the ore into metal. He himself knew so much that all the Mountain-Drawn metalmasters' knowledge was pitiable by comparison. He knew so much that he refused to make even those metals that we considered most valuable. Sunset-metal, we called it—what Forssabekkit called *bronze*. But there were better metals, he told us: stronger, harder, sharper metals. Metals that could cut bronze like wood. Metals that could dig deep into ice. Metals that could even crack some kinds of stone.

Tell them this, said Forssabekkit. Tell them about *iron*. Call it what you like. Shadowmetal, nightmetal—something that gets the point across and catches their fancy.

At some point, hearing my translation, one of the Umbrage metalcrafters interrupted him with a question. Where will we find this metal? she asked. How will we make it?

That's simple, he said, striding over to some boxes on his right. When you know what I know, everything falls right into place.

These boxes resembled others among his cache of Lowland things: wood of pale hue. Using a black metal stick, Forssabekkit pried one open. The lid came off easily. Inside were neatly packed rods.

At first I thought they were distancelookers, for each was about the same length and thickness as that device for making objects appear closer. Then I realized they were something else. What, exactly, I did not know, but they were red in color, waxy in texture, and two handlengths long.

The Man of Ignorance reached inside and picked one out, then held it up for all to see. *Voilà!* he said. My magic wands. Where I place even one of these, the earth shakes and opens to my touch. Then we'll dig out the special dirt we need, we'll melt it, and we'll make metal worthy of the name.

[Aeslu of Vmatta, *Chronicle of the Last Days.*]

Certain parties are at work on our request, Forssabekkit told me just a day later. Soon we'll know.

And the sooner we know, I said, the sooner we shall know how to proceed.

He gazed at me closely. Then abruptly he said, I can't believe you don't care if he's alive or dead.

I struggled to speak, well aware that silence would reveal my emotions as plainly as the wrong words. You do not understand me, I told him. It is not that I do not care. But I care above all for my people. I want whatever serves their destiny. What serves their destiny is reaching the Mountain—something that you alone can accomplish. If Jassikki has died, then the Heirs can never stop us. If he is alive (and here I faltered a moment)—then the Heirs will become a far greater threat. And we must take action against them.

Indeed, said the Man of Ignorance, still staring at me, but with a less cautious expression on his face. Indeed we must.

[Aeslu of Vmatta, *Chronicle of the Last Days.*]

One afternoon Forssabekkit found me near my tent and said, I want to show you something.

I accompanied him to the camp's central area. A scattering of Umbrage had already gathered there; others soon approached. As we stood there, six or seven people emerged from a nearby tent.

I almost panicked. Lowlanders! Big-booted, coat-clad, pack-burdened Lowlanders! I saw their long ice hatchets and hammers, their coils of pale Lowland rope—

At once I understood my mistake. These weren't Lowlanders at all, but Umbrage dressed as Lowlanders. Four men and three women had put on the garments and gear that Forssabekkit had asked the crafters to make; here they were now, costumed for everyone to stare at. And stare we did. At least thirty Umbrage had gathered all around to see the other seven in their new regalia. They looked, pointed, commented, and laughed. The seven wearing Lowland attire stood there awkwardly, at once uneasy and amused, reveling in all the attention. Some of them smiled. One looked much too serious, as if embarrassed. One— a woman—danced about as she might have during the Festival of Masks. Soon enough the tension eased: something to laugh about, though not a joke. As more people came over, the mood grew more and more relaxed, till at last the Umbrage wearing Lowland garb mingled with the others, and members of the crowd took turns examining the new clothes and commenting on how good they looked.

Well, what do you think?

I turned to Forssabekkit. Impressive, I said. (I did not tell him why I felt impressed: how easily the Umbrage had turned themselves into Lowlanders.)

Wait till you see them in action.

I have my hopes. (I did not tell him which hopes.)

We watched as the seven false Lowlanders stomped about in their boots.

Then Forssabekkit said, Actually, this isn't the whole fashion show.

I waited awkwardly, unsure what he meant.

The rest of it, he went on, is for my eyes only. Then he beckoned for me to follow him.

We walked to my tent.

Just go inside, he said with a smile.

Entering, I saw something on my bed at once. I walked over and picked it up: a folded garment.

Forssabekkit stood in the doorway and watched me.

What is it?

Try it on. Then you tell *me*.

A single touch told me that it was woven from wild woolbeast yarn—the finest in the Mountain Land. There was nothing softer. And among the soft fibers were threads of Sunmetal imparting a delicate shimmer to the cloth.

For me?

Who else.

This, too, is Lowland mountain garb?

He laughed gently. No, not mountain garb. It's party garb. Something to wear when you have a night on the town.

His words confused me. I just stood there holding the folded garment.

Where did you get this? I asked him. Did you bring it with you from the Lowland?

Again he laughed. Do you suppose I pack ladies' finery on my mountain expeditions? No, it's the Umbrage tailors you can thank for such splendid work. The same ones who made the coats and trousers.

The Umbrage know of no such attire—

Not till someone shows them the light. As he

spoke, Forssabekkit crossed over to my bed and picked up the only other item resting there. It looked somewhat like a Lowland book—not rolled up but flat, with leaves that turn—but larger and flatter. On the front I saw the word *Collier's* and, below, a man and a woman, both clearly Lowlanders, both dressed in strange attire. The man's clothes were black except for a band of white extending down his chest from the neck downward. A pure black butterfly had alighted on his throat. The woman's clothes were much different—pale, soft, gentle: identical to those I now held in my hand. I glanced at the flat book, at the garment, at Forssabekkit.

These Umbrages are clever folk, he said. Even the tailors. I just showed them the magazine, told them to copy that dress, and they did it. To your measurements, yet. At least that's the hope. But of course you'll have to try it on. If it's not right the first time, they can always make alterations.

I let this garment unfold from where it hung in my hands. When I held it against my body, the gown reached only to my knees, though a fringe dangled slightly lower.

Where is the rest of it? I asked.

That's it, said Forssabekkit. That's all you need.

Not all *I* need, I told him. No Rixtir woman would wear such scant attire except in shame.

Forssabekkit huffed in amusement. Shame!

It is beautiful, I admitted, but how could the Moon's Stead, of all people, reveal herself so easily?

Given what I've seen so far, you have nothing to hide. Think of it as your royal garb. Your raiment.

I tried another approach. When Lowland women wear such wispy attire, how do they manage to stay warm?

They don't—but the modern woman shivers in style.

Would a Lowland woman wear this gown in a camp like ours? I asked, motioning toward the Umbrage tents and the jumble of ice surrounding them.

Not unless she was the Moon's Stead, he replied.

It is not possible.

Not only possible—necessary. You'll see why.

Unable to convince him otherwise, I consented to wear the robe just briefly. I would prove to the Man of Ignorance what I meant.

[Aeslu of Vmatta, *Chronicle of the Last Days.*]

I was wrong: wrong not just that wearing such attire was a mistake; wrong also because Forssabekkit was clearly right. The Umbrage stared in astonishment. Men and women alike stopped whatever they were doing to watch me pass. No one spoke at first; then, as I walked by, everyone erupted into a frenzy of whispers. None of the responses that I feared took place. I heard no laughter; no shouts of derision or contempt; no hoots, hollers, insults, curses. Quite the contrary: they were dumbstruck in awe.

Was it awe of me that silenced them—or of what I wore? Both, perhaps? The robe sparkled and shimmered as I moved, for the Sunmetal threads woven into its cloth caught the light around me and sent it back in every direction. My wearing the Diadem no doubt intensified the effect.

Thus I went ahead and did what Forssabekkit had requested; I wore the robe; I put up with the chill that such a cold place forced on me; I walked among the Umbrage, let their greedy eyes feast on my flesh; I went about my business; and, however unintentionally, however unexpectedly, I tightened my hold over the very people I held most fully in contempt.

Later that day, I received this message:

> From The Spinner to Aeslu the Moon's Stead: Upward to the Summit!
> In keeping with your request, I have pursued several rumors to their source and have arrived at the Veil. There, as you anticipated, I have found the object of your search: Jassikki.
> He is not only alive—he is hard at work rousing the Heirs from their habitual sloth, inspiring them to overcome their own nature, and preparing them to set forth in search of the Mountain Made of Light.
> Further intelligence follows soon.
> Upward to the Summit!

What does it say? asked Forssabekkit just then.

I did not know what to do. If I refused to explain, the Man of Ignorance would eventually have found out anyway, and my refusal would have revealed more than the news itself. But I wanted to shriek in delight. Jassikki! What I could not allow myself to hope for had come to pass. My beloved—alive! Yet how could I defile his name by speaking it among these Umbrage, most of all before the Man of Ignorance himself? My throat felt as if it would explode.

For a long moment I felt so dizzy that I squeezed my eyes shut. Then, without having fully chosen to do so, I crumpled the scroll into a wad.

Forssabekkit put his arm around me, pulled me close, stroked my hair. What's the matter? he asked. What is it?

I choked out the words: "Jassikki—is—*alive.*"

The Man of Ignorance muttered something under his breath.

When I felt tears well up in my eyes, I turned away before Forssabekkit could see them.

[Aeslu of Vmatta, *Chronicle of the Last Days.*]

Never in my life had I felt more conspicuous, more exposed. It had been one thing to walk among the Umbrage with ill intentions; it was quite another to walk among them feeling jubilant, exhilarated, exalted. My designs against the Umbrage now had a purpose far beyond even what I imagined earlier. The slightest tear I shed in full view of Forssabekkit would have revealed my true feelings. How much less could I afford a laugh or exclamation of joy?

Of course, in some ways what pleased me most was knowing simply that I no longer opposed Forssabekkit alone. The Man of Knowledge would confront the Man of Ignorance; Jassikki would lead the Heirs against the Umbrage. For the first time in more than a Moon-span, I felt that my hopes were something other than a trick I played on myself. Somehow the Mountain Land would endure Forssabekkit's scourge. The Mountain-Drawn would survive his presence. Together Jassikki and I would defeat the forces arrayed against us and, finding the Mountain, would join forces in guiding our people to the Summit.

Yet another feeling welled up in me at the news that Jassikki was alive. Simply this: Jassikki! My Jassikki, my friend and lover, alive! After so long believing him dead, I would have thought it difficult to shift abruptly and accept the possibility of his survival. Yet it took no effort—none at all. Within an eyeblink I believed and rejoiced. In another eyeblink I was ready to celebrate the past hardships we had experienced already and to embrace any new ones now confronting us: anything to be together.

Thus I redoubled my efforts to fool the Umbrage, to make myself persuasive among them, to stall for time, to figure out a way of stopping the Man of Ignorance once and for all. No struggle would be too great. No deception would be too difficult. No lie would be too subtle. No risk would be too dangerous. All I wanted was to prevent Forssabekkit and his followers from finding the Mountain Made of Light.

Forssabekkit's distribution of Lowland garments among the Umbrage only began the changes that he wrought on them. At his bidding, Umbrage porters left the encampment and returned soon after with bundles of supplies pillaged from settlements in nearby valleys; under his guidance, local crafters then transformed these supplies into Lowland climbing gear. Slabs of firetree wood diminished to a thousand handles for ice hatchets. Bundles of hides turned into boots. Pathbeast wool became all manner of cold weather garments: handgarb, footgarb, bodygarb, facegarb. Cloth became pathpacks, trousers, raincloaks, boots, and tents. Dried danglevines became baskets and pallets. Great skeins of hair—human hair—vanished into the ropecrafters' tents and emerged as big black coils of rope.

Rope! The sight of those coils brought home to me what was happening. Everything else that Forssabekkit taught the Umbrage to make could have been used for many purposes, but such a vast quantity of rope could serve only one. Of course, from the start I had known of this man's intentions. The sight of so much rope, however, was what made them undeniable. Rope. More rope than I had ever seen in my life. Lowland rope—if not *from* the Lowland, then at least *of* the Low-

land. The Man of Ignorance would take all these
things, not least of them the rope that the Umbrage made, and would find the Mountain Made
of Light.

Now listen to me! he shouted to the assembled
Umbrage, and I translated. Here's what you need
to do. Get rid of all your old clothes and equipment—all of it! These things no longer serve our
purposes. What you need instead is something
more practical. More adaptable. So gather round,
take what you need, and get ready!

His voice carried over the crowd: confident, eager, relaxed. The Man of Ignorance clearly enjoyed distributing the trappings of folly to his
people. They, too, looked confident and eager: taking what this big Lowlander gave them, laughing
as they put things on, asking questions of one another as they tried making sense of these odd garments and pieces of gear.

Take your time, he called out amiably. There's
plenty for everyone. We share and share alike in
this outfit—unlike those stingy Masters, who keep
all their secrets to themselves. Take it slow! No
grabbing! I've made sure that no one gets over-
looked.

I translated his words. I helped out with the
distribution. I did everything I could to feign full
cooperation with the effort. And while translating,
helping out, and feigning cooperation with the
Man of Ignorance and his lackeys, I smiled and
laughed as much as anyone else. I did whatever
seemed necessary to bide my time and figure out
how to thwart Forssabekkit's intentions.

[Aeslu of Vmatta, *Chronicle of the Last Days*.]

Let's get down to business, said Forssabekkit
the next morning. We had just reached a rocky

canyon near the Umbrage camp. The Man of Ignorance set down his pack; all the Umbrage who had accompanied us there did the same with their own. Among these packs were items that Forssabekkit had selected from his cache of Lowland things. The Man of Ignorance now rummaged intently through his belongings. From one pouch Forssabekkit then removed several of the long red tubes I had seen earlier among his belongings back at the camp. He held them up and spoke again, now in the loud tone he used when expecting me to translate for everyone else.

The other day I said we'll dig up some special rocks for making metal. Well—the time has come.

Forssabekkit stepped closer to his pack, stooped, and took some smaller tubes out of a pocket. From each small tube extended a bit of stiff string. The Man of Ignorance inserted a small tube into each of the bigger ones, allowing the strings to dangle. He then tied the bundle of big tubes with yarn, twisted the strings together, and held the whole device up for everyone to see.

I had no idea what it was or what purpose it served. Forssabekkit's words some days earlier had alarmed me: *Where I place even one of these, the earth shakes and opens to my touch.* Yet the sight of that bundled tube made no sense; my fear churned about within me but soon subsided.

Now watch closely, said Forssabekkit. I'll explain this so you can't fail to understand.

The Man of Ignorance had no need to demand attention; the Umbrage followed his every move.

He said, There's a crack in this slab of stone. The stone is hard, right? Solid rock. To be specific, a rock called hematite. Don't trouble yourselves with the details, though—leave all that to me.

I translated his words.

The Man of Ignorance then attached still more

yarn to his bundle of red tubes: this time a piece far longer than the previous. He held one end of the yarn and dropped the bundle into the fissure in the rock slab at his feet.

Now let me show you, he continued, what happens when I summon the powers at my command. At this point Forssabekkit raised his right hand, held it over the yarn in his left, and chanted in loud, solemn tones: This is the night that shrouds our lives in mystery and fear.

He made me want to laugh. With someone like him around, it wasn't the night who filled our lives with mystery and fear! I translated, however, and the Umbrage grew restless when they heard my words.

Then Forssabekkit said, This is the Moon that fills our lives with longing and hope.

What blasphemy—as if the Man of Ignorance knew anything about longing and hope! Yet I translated once more, and again the Umbrage stirred—some drawing close for a better look, some easing back.

At last Forssabekkit intoned, This is the Sun, who fills our lives with passion.

Now at least half of the Umbrage present backed away: some just a few manlengths, some as far back as they could go without falling into the river to our right. A hush of low whispers started up and ceased almost at once, though a few small children sensed their elders' concern and began to cry.

The Man of Ignorance turned to me and smiled. He said, All right. This is what happens when the night, the Moon, and the Sun join forces against their enemies. Everyone stand back.

Even as I started translating, the Umbrage fled from precisely the spot around which some of them had clustered till just a few eyeblinks earlier. They already knew that something terrible would soon happen; no words in any language were necessary to warn them.

From his pants pocket Forssabekkit removed his fire-tube (the same one with which he had set fire to the Web) and brought forth its flame with a little clicking noise. He hesitated a moment. He held the flame up for everyone to see. Then he touched it to the yarn dangling from his left hand.

I saw nothing but a few sparks. I heard nothing but a brief hiss.

Against my will I laughed: this was the sound of an angry cat!

Abruptly the Man of Ignorance said, All right—let's get out of here.

Grasping my arm just above the elbow, he rushed me away from that fissure and the bundle of tubes he had dropped into it. I half-ran, half-stumbled to where the Umbrage waited; I turned; I waited in bafflement as Forssabekkit and everyone else stared back at the place we had fled.

What happened next lasted only an eyeblink but is sealed into my memory forever. Without warning, stones leaped into the air, pulling themselves apart as they rose, abrupt as a flock of brush-hens panicked into flight; a flash of light blinded us; a great pall of dust blossomed, then wilted at once, crumbled, and blew away; and chunks of rock thudded down from the sky like the biggest hailstones anyone had ever seen.

Something else: the noise. This was the loudest noise I had ever heard. Perhaps some avalanches are louder (and in fact what happened then sounded just like an avalanche) but none I had ever witnessed before came near to what the Man of Ignorance had caused to happen. Anything else would have seemed silent by comparison. Yet silence was not what I heard afterwards. Quite the contrary: a terrible ringing noise lingered in my ears. The Umbrage seemed to have been similarly afflicted, for they glanced around in a daze. More than a few cupped hands over their ears in puzzlement or dismay.

Forssabekkit now turned to them again. Smiling, he said, The Sun, the Moon, and the night have given us these rocks to suit our purposes. Now gather them up, take them back to our camp, and I'll teach you how to make the tools we need.

No one was listening. Everyone paid attention to something else instead.

I noticed it then, a noise reached me past the ringing in my ears. An echo? Thunder?

One of the Umbrage, glancing upward, pointed toward the glacier above us and slightly to the left. Others among the Umbrage did so as well, some with loud exclamations of alarm. For a mass of ice and snow had started down, a great wave that grew larger and moved faster with every passing moment of its descent.

We all stared in astonishment. That wave was coming right toward us. Some of the Umbrage began to flee: running down the slope or sideways across the mountainside. Others sank to their knees and began pleading with the Sun and the Moon to spare them. Others just kept staring.

I was among those who simply stared. I felt no surprise. On the contrary, this calamity was just what I had anticipated all along. What else could anyone have expected from the Man of Ignorance, the Man of Darkness, the Cutter of Wounds? What else could have come forth from the folly of his tearing open the earth and pulling out strange rocks? I would never claim that I felt no fear: I was terrified. But surprise? None at all. What else but a calamity could follow Forssabekkit's deeds?

My only satisfaction was that if this avalanche would now sweep me away, it would sweep away all the Umbrage as well. So much the better that this great white blade would descend, cut us down, harvest us all—

Then the avalanche veered, passed to our left, spread out below us, and expended its force in the valley below.

A great cheer rose from among the Umbrage. They danced, they shouted, they wept, they shrieked in delight and thanksgiving.

Gazing upward, I tried to determine what had taken place. A curve in the glacier that deflected the avalanche? Enough ice-fissures to absorb its force? I couldn't tell. All I knew was that something had spared us.

At some point I turned toward the Man of Ignorance and found him watching me. He showed no signs of fear, of dismay, of shame, of relief. His smile showed a kind of calm delight revealing his thoughts: Look at me, at what I can do, at what I won't hesitate to do.

[Aeslu of Vmatta, *Chronicle of the Last Days.*]

That evening, as the Sun set, the Umbrage remained in high spirits. Laughter floated over the camp as they completed their labors; shouts and cries of delight intermingled with the rumble of distant avalanches on the peaks around us. The work soon done, everyone settled down for the late-day meal and quickly grew festive.

Foodmasters brought forth huge clay jars and platters of the foods that the Man of Ignorance had taught them to prepare: great slabs of roasted antlerbeasts, bread in the shape of strange bloated loaves, pots of vegetables that had been boiled till reduced to slime, and—worst of all—kettles of white grain that resembled nothing so much as a pile of maggots. The Umbrage, though understandably reluctant at first, grabbed at their food and ate with well-earned hunger. I myself felt no eagerness to eat, for my revulsion toward this food, my alarm at what had happened earlier, and my fears about what might yet happen all combined to steal my appetite. I ate anyway, intent on fostering the illusion of enthusiasm. I forced myself to partake of the Umbrage gaiety as well. I did whatever it took to convince these people, and Forssabekkit above all, that I was something other than a worm nestled in the bloom of their endeavor.

As before, the Man of Ignorance lingered among the Umbrage (I could see him no matter where he stood, given his great height), and his people clamored like children around their father. Surely one reason for their eagerness to draw close was their confidence in him and their excitement over what they felt he would make possible. Something else, however, drew them forth: Forssabekkit's music box.

The device itself was the same that I described earlier: what I first mistook for stone in fact turned out to be wood. What made it work? I had no idea. Yet somehow it did. Now Forssabekkit placed one of the thin black discs in the box, turned a bent piece of metal several times, and set a metal bar on the disc.

As before, a great clatter of noise burst forth from the box: howls, shrieks, stutters, wails. It sounded as if someone had dropped an armload of metal pots down a staircase onto a gathering of cats and foxes, who then fled, barking and yowling in terror. The first time the Umbrage had heard this machine, many of them had fled; this time, however, only a few did so, and a few others added their cries and shouts to the racket. I could tell that many of them would have liked to flee: how their eyes bulged, how their hands reached up to protect themselves. Even so, most people remained where they stood. They watched. They listened. They glanced about to see what the rest were doing. Most of all they looked at Forssabekkit, who, arms folded across his chest, stared only at the music machine as it blared its wild noise.

With a smile on his face he called out, There's no cause for alarm. None at all. You'll enjoy these pieces if you give them a chance.

He listened a while longer, tapping his right foot quickly against the ground. Then he smiled and told me, Let's show the hillbillies how we boogie at the Ritz.

Boogie . . . I repeated. Ritz . . .

You'd put all those flappers to shame.

I had no idea what he meant; before I could ask or protest, however, Forssabekkit approached me, grasped my hands, tilted my arms at odd angles, and began to move with peculiar, erratic motions: motions that moved me with him.

What are you doing? I asked uneasily, tempted to pull back but not wanting to reveal my unease. Whatever he wanted me to do at this strange feast, I would do. Any means necessary to prove myself his ally would be acceptable.

It should be obvious, he said. Dancing!

By this time the Umbrage began looking less alarmed. In fact, they soon showed no fear; some of them even appeared to enjoy the commotion. A few even ventured to dance in the manner that Forssabekkit now demonstrated: first children or young men and women, soon others as well. It was a wild sight. It grew even wilder when Forssabekkit told one of the Umbrage how to use the music device. Stepping aside, he allowed this youth to put on a disc till it expended its noise; the boy then replaced it with another, then another, stopping only now and then to turn the bent piece of metal that brought forth the music. While the Umbrage danced, Forssabekkit walked over to his tent and watched from where he sat on a sitting device made of wood and cloth.

Nice, isn't it? he said. It's high time these folks let off a little steam.

Puzzled, I said, *Steam*.

Who wouldn't be boiling with the Heirs' lid on all these years?

To silence my outrage, I spoke the opposite of what I felt: It is time to celebrate.

Forssabekkit smiled. Damn right! he told me, then reached over to squeeze my thigh. He added, I have just the thing to help us.

Among his supplies were five large boxes. Unlike the music machine, these were simply what they appeared to be: wooden boxes. Someone had removed the top from one, revealing twelve bottles within, their spouts either made of Moonmetal or else wrapped with thin sheets of the same substance. They were beautiful but less mysterious than most of this man's possessions: clearly just bottles.

The Man of Ignorance now pulled out one of them. He examined it briefly, tore away the metal sheathing its top, and removed a small cage that constrained a stopper jammed into the spout. Forssabekkit then wrapped a white cloth around the bottle, eased it back and forth, and, with a small but abrupt thumping noise, removed the stopper. White foam spilled out of the bottle onto the ground. Startled, I backed off from this sight, but Forssabekkit showed neither surprise nor dismay; on the contrary, he smiled with great delight.

Ah, he exclaimed, the elixir of life!

A potion?

One might put it that way. One might indeed.

While I watched, he looked around, then walked purposefully to his tent. He entered it, emerging at once with two small pottery drinking bowls. Not exactly crystal stemware, he told me, but it's adequate under the circumstances. Forssabekkit then poured a pale liquid into each of the bowls, gave me one, and kept the other himself. He raised his bowl as if in obeisance. He said, Cheers.

What would this liquid do to me, I wondered. I could not help but think of what the Masters often did to people whose motives they questioned: stunning them with poison till their fate could be determined.

As if reading my thoughts, the Man of Ignorance laughed at my hesitance. Don't worry, he said. It's quite harmless. To reassure me, Forssabekkit took a sip from his bowl, gazed up toward the sky, and swallowed. Good. Very good. It hasn't suffered in transit.

I gazed into my own bowl at the tiny bubbles rising toward me from out of nowhere. Never in my life had I seen anything like this liquid.

Go ahead, said Forssabekkit. I promise you'll like it. Unlike the music, it's not an acquired taste.

Drinking was risky, refusing to drink still more so. To convince this man of my trust, I could not show more than the slightest doubt. I raised my bowl and drank.

At first the sensation was so intense that my tongue seemed wrapped in flames; then I thought it might have frozen; then at once I felt something else altogether, something more complex and gentle—a tickle, a soothing stroke, a caress. I swallowed. The same sensations proceeded down my throat. Although startled, even frightened, I could not constrain myself from laughing.

The Man of Ignorance laughed, too.

What *is* the potion? I asked.

It's called *sham pain*.

In Forssabekkit's Lowland dialect, *sham* means false; *pain* means discomfort or suffering. An odd name, I told him, but a good one.

You could call it guttermuck for all I care, said

Forssabekkit. What matters is the stuff itself. He took another drink.

I did as well. The bubbles seemed to rise from my mouth through my nose straight into my brain.

You have a lot of things, I told him. More things than I thought existed. They are so *strange*! Some of them are frightening, some amusing, some just—*strange*! I rattled on like this for a while, the words gushing forth.

He asked, Don't you like my amusements?

No— Yes— I mean, sometimes yes and sometimes no. But I find it difficult to make sense of them. They confuse me. They baffle me.

All rather unnecessary, he responded, taking a sip from his bowl. Perhaps they can dispell your confusion and dissipate your bafflement. Perhaps the confusion you feel is like clouds lifting, like clear light coming through the fog that has bound you till just now.

What clouds? What fog?

I could venture an opinion, but that's almost irrelevant. You should decide for yourself.

My head spun. I felt I might suddenly fall over.

Forssabekkit then stood, walked a few paces to one side, and returned to where I sat. I was unsure where he had gone or what he had done; now he was back.

. . . and show you something, he was saying. Another device, I'm afraid, but one that illustrates what I'm trying to tell you.

He handed me his distancelooker: the metal tube that somehow made things look closer than they were: the device that Forssabekkit had first used in Leqsiffaltho to locate the Hermit of the Stones.

Glancing up at him, I felt puzzled. What could he hope to see? Night had fallen; the valley lay in deep darkness. Although the Moon had risen earlier, it was a melonseed Moon—one-third light, two-thirds dark—and gave little illumination.

Forssabekkit extended the tube and raised it high. Then I saw his purpose: he gazed directly at the Moon.

Bon soir, he said, speaking in one of the other Lowland languages. *Quel plaisir de vous revoir.* He laughed a hearty laugh. Forssabekkit then handed me the distancelooker.

I took it but just held it.

Go ahead.

Why did I hesitate? What did I fear would happen?

He stood there waiting.

I raised the tube and looked through it. The brightness made me squint. Averting my gaze, I squeezed my eyes shut, opened them, looked again.

I did not know what I was seeing. Light and darkness . . . Textures both rough and smooth . . . A great mass of something—rock? ice?—suspended in the middle of nowhere. . . .

Forssabekkit said, There you are.

Forssa—

It's not your Queen of the Night.

I looked this way and that. Great expanses of white— Deep shadows— When I turned to Forssabekkit, what I saw unnerved me: that calm smile.

Raising the distancelooker again, I peered into it again despite my dread of doing so.

Forssabekkit said, Move toward the right-hand side. See the jagged edge? The little protrusions jutting off into the darkness? Those are mountains. Dry, dead mountains. Empty, lifeless mountains.

At first I understood nothing of his words, as if he spoke of one thing while something altogether different took place before us. Mountains? What mountains? He was showing me one of the two great lights that lit our lives. What do you mean—*mountains*?

Just that: mountains. Stone. Dust. Ice. It's not your goddess—just a lot of ice and rock.

At some point, as he spoke, I looked through the distancelooker again, blinked, and at once saw what he meant. Spires of rock rose from around the glary plain and jutted into the blackness curving around the Moon. They were small—little more than the merest protrusions—yet as my eyes adjusted to their scale, I realized that the sight before me seemed small only because of its distance. I stared for a long time, moving this way and that. The longer I stared, the sicker I felt.

Welcome to the twentieth century, said Forssabekkit.

I kept struggling to make sense of what I saw. The Masters had told me that the Moon was the goddess watching over us, guarding us, guiding our every move. . . . Had they lied? Was I a fool to have believed them? I asked him, Why are you doing this to me?

Sooner or later you have to face facts.

I looked at the crescent of light before me till my eyes welled up and I could no longer see.

[Aeslu of Vmatta, *Chronicle of the Last Days*.]

What the Man of Ignorance did to make stones fly out of the ground frightened me only a little more than what he did to all those chunks and chips afterwards. The Umbrage gathered them; they carried them back to their camp in baskets; they set to work following Forssabekkit's instructions to smelt them into metal. I am not a metalcrafter. I know nothing of this art. What I know, however, is that the big Lowlander did something far different with these stones than what our own artisans would have—or could have.

First he directed the Umbrage to build a great stone oven. Then they constructed a huge device from wood and leather that, when forced repeatedly open and closed, forced air into the oven's chamber. Then they stoked the oven with firewood, fanned the flames, and created a heat so intense that only a few of the Umbrage crafters could tolerate being nearer than a few manlengths to its source. Their preparations complete, Forssabekkit and the Umbrage then dumped great quantities of their special rock into the oven and waited for the fire within to do its work.

What they did, precisely, escaped me. All I knew was that they worked hard for many days to separate the metal from the dross. Did they succeed? I have no idea. And after labors so intense that even the metalcrafters were soon overwhelmed by their exertions, Forssabekkit allowed a stream of yellowish molten metal to pour from the side of his oven; he tested it by prodding repeatedly with some pokers of our own metal that the Umbrage crafters provided; and he announced without asking me to translate that the fruit of his exertions was now ready to be worked into the proper shape.

I watched the Man of Knowledge and his Umbrage attendants struggle with what they had created. The pool of liquid metal they had created was so hot that only the Lowlander himself seemed able to handle it. After a few meager efforts, the Umbrage crafters relinquished any claim to their art and left the work to Forssabekkit alone. He worked most of that afternoon hammering a piece of his new metal—what he called *iron*—into shape.

Why should what I saw have alarmed me? This was far from my first time watching metalsmiths at work; neither was I new to the sight of the fires, the tools, and the efforts of their trade. But this was no ordinary fire; these were no ordinary tools; above all, this was no ordinary metalsmith.

How he toiled! Stripped to the waist, Forssabekkit held a great hammer in his right hand, a pair of metal tongs in his left; and with the hammer he struck an ingot pinched within the tongs' grip. The tools themselves were odd enough: larger, blacker than what our own metalsmiths would have used. The ingot was odder still: the color of the Sun sinking out of sight at day's end. What roused fear in my flesh, however, was the man's exertion. Forssabekkit, though bigger than any man I had ever seen, fought hard to keep control over his tools. The hammer rose like a great stone hurled into the air; it hung there a moment; it fell; it struck the ingot with a blow that shot sparks in every direction and shook every one of us who watched. With each blow the Man of Ignorance grunted the same grunt that the ingot grunted on being struck; then at once he raised the hammer again to strike another blow. How could any metal withstand such battering? Sunmetal would long ago have crumbled under Forssabekkit's attack. Moonmetal, the same. Sunrise-metal, the same. But this ingot, so hot that Forssabekkit streamed with sweat from being close to it, took whatever beating this man provided.

Soon that little stab of metal dimmed: embers to ashes. Forssabekkit raised it in his tongs, tilted it this way and that, examined it, then shoved it back into the furnace. He averted his gaze while holding the tongs in place: the heat welling out of that fiery maw shoved his face away. A long time passed. The Umbrage watching grew restless, glanced from one to another, spoke in whispers. Then at last Forssabekkit withdrew the ingot, lifted it radiant from the fire, set it on his work stone, and (his slick torso, arms, hands, and face all molten orange) let loose again with his hammer.

Later, once the work was done, I was surprised (no—astonished) to hear his opinion of the effort. We gave it a good try, he told me, and the axeheads I've made aren't half bad. But I'm not sure they're quite up to standards.

They are not good? I asked.

Not good enough. I don't risk using anything short of the best.

But you said that anything would be better than what our own people produce.

True. But that's not the whole point. On a climb like what we're undertaking, they still have to be almost perfect. He gazed out over the Umbrage camp for a few eyeblinks. Then he said, Perhaps with some practice we can refine our technique.

Is there time enough?

My question made him pause. I hope so, he told me. Frankly, I'm not so sure.

I felt pleased, of course, that his efforts had fallen short; I felt delighted that the fruits of his labor might serve no good purpose. Yet there was no cause for rejoicing. If nothing else, the Man of Ignorance had impressed the Umbrage in yet another way, had stunned them with his prowess, had tightened the net of delusion that he had already thrown over them.

[Aeslu of Vmatta, *Chronicle of the Last Days*.]

Forssabekkit's festivities and his work among the metalworkers are linked in my mind forever. As different as the two events may seem, they had almost identical effects. Both occurrences shoved me deeper into despair; both delighted the Umbrage. I could not believe that my authority could withstand many more such events.

It was not just that the Man of Ignorance had succeeded in diminishing my authority over the Umbrage; he had diminished my authority in my own eyes as well. The Umbrage went about their revels with an air of exhilaration that embraced everyone present but me. It felt like an intruder at the feast. Was this a legacy of my association with the Heirs? Was it Forssabekkit's doing? Or my own? I was unsure, thus uneasy.

Although nothing went wrong in any outward sense, something had happened: something so substantial that I could not deny it, something so subtle that I felt helpless to identify it, something altogether beyond my grasp.

I could sense the unfolding of other events hidden within the revelry that Forssabekkit's feast had occasioned. The Umbrage themselves were not to blame for my state of mind; if anything, I felt a growing pity for how easily and eagerly they succumbed to the Man of Ignorance. They were Umbrage, thus my enemies. Yet they were Mountain-Drawn, thus my people. How to resolve the discord between these two impulses? I had no idea. I felt sure, however, that whatever ability I possessed to thwart Forssabekkit and to free these people from the burden of his ignorance, it was fragile: the merest ember whose warmth a burden of ice could effortlessly quench.

That ice was Forssabekkit himself. Within a few days (less, perhaps) I would end up helpless before him; my power among the Umbrage would vanish; my efforts to stop their quest would fail.

Yet the same day that I watched Forssabekkit crafting metal, as I saw his great hammer send swarms of sparks shooting outward, I understood what to do. Forssabekkit's Lowland gadgets were not the only way to hold sway over the hearts and minds of these Umbrage. His fire was not the only fire.

[Aeslu of Vmatta, *Chronicle of the Last Days*.]

That night, while the Umbrage slept, I left my tent and walked from their camp down the glacier's slope. Guards were up and about, of course, and they challenged me. But once they cast their feeble torchlight on my face, they bowed and begged forgiveness for their presumption.

I am the Moon's Stead, I told them. Let me pass.

They did nothing to obstruct me.

Earlier I mentioned starbugs—those insects that flit about, flickering, on the cool nights of the rainy season. As it so happens, there is a berry called sweetstone that the starbugs love. However humble in appearance (it looks like a little brown pebble) the sweetstone berry is the starbugs' favorite food. Yet sweetstones have a thick skin that the starbugs cannot break. One reason that so few starbugs hovered about the Umbrage encampment was that the Umbrage themselves seemed not to have discovered the sweetstones in their vicinity, thus had not picked them, thus in turn had not spilled the juice that would have attracted the insects. (The Umbrage are ignorant about so many things, perhaps they were ignorant as well both about sweetstones and starbugs.)

The night was cold but still: perfect for my purposes. Within a short while the ice tapered away beneath my feet and diminished into soggy turf crisscrossed with rivulets; soon after that I found some sweetstone berries—a whole thicket—and grabbed them by the fistful. Heavy, tough brown berries! At once I crushed berries in my hands, then wiped my hands all over my clothes.

Then I stopped short. What would the Umbrage

find so scary about the sight I was about to present to them? What would be so scary about a woman dressed in robes?

I faltered briefly, then tried a more desperate plan. I took off my clothes. Squeezing berries in both hands, I smeared my whole body with their juice.

Nothing happened. I stood there, already cold and frightened. I sat on a rock. What a fool I was to think that some silly ploy might scare the Umbrage! Of course the berry juice worked in one respect: lots of insects came to me. Stingflies, fleshnippers, all manner of tiny creatures. But no starbugs. Soon I was shivering hard: not just from the cold but from all those insects hovering about me. I hunched forward, covering my face and chest.

I wept.

Then I looked at my hands. They were glowing. Fingers, palms, wrists. I looked up. My knees glowed also. My belly and breasts. My whole body turned radiant.

Starbugs now flitted about me, alighting and taking off again. At every moment more and more of them appeared out of the darkness and swarmed around me. Soon hundreds, even thousands covered my skin; hovered close; came and went, touching me just long enough to taste my sweet flesh, depart, and return again for another taste. Just as a firebrand snaps and pops while burning in a hearth, my body sent forth innumerable sparks into the night.

I could hardly constrain my delight.

I got up and began walking; I worked my way back to the Umbrage camp; I hid, waiting, at the edge. I did not want to hurry—any sudden motions might scare off the bugs. By then I was lit up like a bonfire: sparks flying everywhere.

I heard screams. Great commotion from the tents. Shouts, supplications.

I walked forth into their midst.

I am the Moon's Stead, I cried out in a steady voice, almost a drone, so loud that the words seemed to come from around me rather than within me. Look upon me, O Umbrage, for I am the Moon's Stead!

Men, women, and children stumbled out of their tents as I walked among them. People stood motionless at first, still dazed with sleep; then, realizing that they were not dreaming, but already awake, they staggered back in confusion and alarm. Of course they could see me better than I saw them, for most of the light was what I brought with me. Yet all the same I caught glimpses of the growing crowd by the flicker of my own light, and what I saw pleased me even better than I had expected.

Some of these people tripped over one another, blundered backwards against their tents, or simply fell over. Some dropped to their knees and pleaded for mercy. Some crawled backwards on all fours. Some simply stared, trembling.

I opened my arms as if both to embrace and trap them. By the grace of Ossonnal and Lissallo I am the Moon's Stead, I shouted, and they have invested in me all their power and authority. I shall lead a remnant of the Mountain-Drawn to their refuge at the Summit. Whoever doubts me, mocks me, disobeys me, or works against me falls by the wayside and will be lost to the Lowlanders soon to ravage our land. Whoever believes me, trusts me, obeys me, and works with me finds safety, peace, and justice. Do as you will, O Umbrage. But ignore my warning at your own risk.

I remained there with my arms open for a long time. The effort took almost more strength and patience than I could muster. Starbugs swarmed all over me, tickling and itching. It was all I could do not to sweep my hands over my body, to rid myself of their countless kisses. Yet I forced myself to hold off. I stood before the Umbrage in that defiant posture; I stared at them; I turned slightly this way and that.

Then, stepping carefully within a cloud of sparks, I walked away.

I dreaded that they would come after me. I dreaded that the starbugs might suddenly take flight and depart, leaving me far less visible and far more naked than I was already. I worried that one of the Umbrage, doubting the sight before him (for the Umbrage had doubted so much already) might chase after me, hit me with his fist, even strike out with a mace, a hatchet, a stone to see whether I was indeed the goddess I seemed rather than the mere woman I was. I feared that warriors might follow me. I wondered even if Forssabekkit might render the blow himself. No one did anything of the sort. What they did, exactly, I have no idea, for during the brief eternity of my departure I heard nothing from the crowd. Perhaps they maintained the same postures in which the sight of me had frozen them. I would have liked nothing more than to see the Umbrage struck silent—they who have filled the Mountain Land with so many pointless dares, threats, curses, taunts, and insults!

Yet I had no choice but to continue down the ice onto the marshy turf below. There I scrubbed myself with handfuls of grass, then splashed myself with the water that streamed everywhere around me, and removed the sweetstone berry juice from my skin. I dressed in my robes again as fast as I could. I walked up the slope once more to the camp where the commotion of Umbrage greeted me as I approached (first a mere rush, then a rumble, then a roar, as if I had been approach-

ing a waterfall) only to lapse into silence once I
stood again in their midst.

[Aeslu of Vmatta, *Chronicle of the Last Days*.]

You're a smart cookie, said a voice as I entered
my dark tent. That was quite a stunt you pulled.

These Lowland words did not startle me; I had
been expecting Forssabekkit from the moment I
returned to the Umbrage camp. The words themselves made no sense to me, yet I grasped their
significance. I pretended otherwise. Cookie? I
asked. Stunt?

Don't play dumb. You were brilliant. You know
it, too. I only wish I could have been there to ice
the cake.

Cake, I said.

He stepped over to me from the tent's far side.
He grasped my shoulders in his big hands, pulled
me closer, nuzzled his face against my neck, in-
haled the scent of my hair. He said, You're sticky.
Was it treacle? Syrup?

I have other means, I told him.

The Man of Ignorance said nothing for an
eyeblink or two. He was a mass of shadow steeped
in the night. Dull light from the guards' torches
flickered on the tent walls, and I caught the muffled noises of the Umbrage trying to settle down
around us; otherwise I saw little and heard even
less. People must have been whispering in their
tents (each man, woman, and child comparing
what he or she had seen when I appeared before
them) or else they just listened to Forssabekkit
and me. Then, quietly, he said, I understood the
ruse the moment you showed up. Fireflies! You
were brilliant! If you'd risen from the grave you
couldn't have terrified the Umbrage more than
you did.

I laughed in exhilaration. The Umbrage, terrified!

No, he went on, reaching out to me once more, taking me now by the waist, pulling me close again: It wasn't fear *I* felt. Not with you standing before me like that. Etched in fire. God, you were beautiful!

Please stop.

He kissed me, pulled me tight against him. I shoved myself back till he relented.

You can't be serious, he said. You show up like that and now you expect me to *stop*?

To console him I bowed my forehead against his chest. I told him, In the interests of our cause. There will be time later.

No one else has to know—

Later. Otherwise all is lost.

[Aeslu of Vmatta, *Chronicle of the Last Days*.]

It was then that I first tasted power—or rather, when I first identified what I had been tasting and found savory all along. The Umbrage would do my bidding! Forssabekkit would dance to my tune! I found it hard not to delight in how easily I moved toward reaching my goal and, too, how eagerly the Man of Ignorance and his lackeys helped me to reach it.

Whatever I wanted, the Umbrage now brought. Whatever I asked, they now did. No request struck them as difficult, silly, or unfair. Quite the contrary: the more challenging my demands, the more earnest their attempts to fulfill them; the more inexplicable my whims, the more willing their efforts to indulge them. If I asked someone to bring me soup, they cooked five kinds for me to choose from. If I complained of feeling cool, they brought me enough cloaks, shawls, and robes to garb fif-

teen or twenty women. If I complimented them on
their tents, they all offered to give me their own.
The merest hint prompted such a flurry of efforts
that I could have asked the impossible and
watched ten, twenty, a hundred people stumble
over one another to accomplish the task. Bring me
cakes made of air! Build me a house from thistle-
down! Catch a bird in a net woven from shadows!
Teach a chunk of ice to sing! They would have
gladly attempted these tasks, or any others. All
they wanted was to serve me well.

And Forssabekkit? In his expression I saw not
only new eagerness but new longing. He wanted
not just to please me; he wanted *me*. I found it
hard to believe that I could not persuade him by
some means to do my bidding.

This was what I wanted. However startling I
found this new obedience, I wanted the Man of
Ignorance and his followers to do as I wished. I
wanted them to obey my whims. I wanted them to
meet my desires. I wanted them to do this and
more—to do everything, anything—without the
slightest hesitation.

It was not that I delighted in their subservience
in its own right, not that I enjoyed ordering them
around, simply that I wanted them to do what I
needed done.

Which was, of course, to defeat Forssabekkit
and the Umbrage before they reached (much less
climbed) the Mountain Made of Light.

Both the power I wielded and my delight in
wielding it were unfamiliar. Trained as a Wordpathguide, I had been accustomed to receiving orders, not giving them. Even when I learned of my
role as the Moon's Stead, I never imagined that
whole legions of the Mountain-Drawn would wait
breathlessly for the vaguest expression of my
wants or needs. I admit that I found the situation
uncomfortable. The newness of ordering these

people about was the least of my discomfort. There was something else, something more intense. Like a butcher leading a dumb beast to the slaughter, I felt a tension between the act of doing what I needed to do and the awareness of the act itself. If only these Umbrage had been less eager: that would at least have left me more at ease with my own duplicity.

Still, they were Umbrage. They fell far short in worshipping the Sun and Moon. They made few efforts—almost none—to follow the path that Ossonnal and Lissallo set forth in *The Summit*. They resisted the Masters' will. They sought the Mountain without permission and, worse yet, went about seeking it in the wrong way. What choice did I have but to counter them by any means— every means?

Thus I knew that I could delight in my power over the Umbrage without suffering any harm. No matter how uneasy I felt about finding myself at the head of their forthsetting, my intentions were good. I was not who I claimed to be; I was not doing what I claimed to do. An Heir, I pretended to be an Umbrage. Enemy of Forssabekkit, I pretended to be his friend and lover. Yet I was neither. Appearances ceased to interest me. Only the goal mattered. The goal itself—confounding the Umbrage in their quest—could never have inspired anything within me but just that same pleasure that I now felt with such intensity.

6

Dear Father,

Of course I've never assumed that I can reach the mountain, much less climb it, simply on the basis of these Indians' odd little crystalline map. The Diadem and its wayward Mountain Stone may be the *sine qua non* for reaching the summit, but I've understood all along that these trinkets are just a start. Hence the cache of mountaineering gear I mentioned earlier. Hence my requests for similar supplies in greater quantities. Hence my exasperation at the events that have prevented me from acquiring what I've needed. Climbing the mountain will involve a logistical effort far greater than anything else in my experience.

Where does this leave me? Obviously in something of a bind. I can't proceed without amassing the necessary supplies.

Yet the impasse doesn't leave me stuck at the end of the road. I may not have huge quantities of good Swiss and English alpinists' equipment, but I have more than enough for my own use. As for everyone else—I'm always ready for a little improvisation.

As it turns out, this hasn't been difficult. These Umbrages are a clever lot. With the proper guidance, they have risen to the occasion and have jerry-rigged enough gear to provide the basics for everyone involved. The items in question—wool knickers, sweaters,

jackets, and other items of European-style
bush-garb—look as comical on these people as
if they'd gussied themselves up in swallowtails
for the men, evening gowns for the women.
They strut around looking self-impressed and
amused, yet the attire in question serves good
purposes. Let them have their fun; it's a small
price to pay for their collaboration. Likewise
regarding the ersatz tools they've devised
under my tutelage. Ice-axes, crampons, ropes,
packs, and whatnot: all the climbing regalia
they'll need if we're to track down the errant
peak. The Umbrages remind me of natives
anywhere. Give them the white man's gadgets
and they get so puffed up they could walk to
the moon. No harm done. What we'll
undertake won't be much easier.

I should mention that I've had a little more
help in accomplishing these tasks than I first
expected. I don't mean help from the rank-and-
file Umbrages themselves; I'm referring
instead to a collaborator of more nearly equal
status. Whatever Aeslu's reservations toward
me, she's been nothing if not cooperative.
She's a princess, true, but practical at heart. It
makes no difference how much she likes or
dislikes me just now; she perceives my ability
to get things done. So be it.
Better yet, she isn't quite so standoffish as
she herself imagines. Aeslu claims indifference
to me as a person; she admits only to a
utilitarian attitude toward my forthrightness
and organizational skills. Even if I'm the
much-dreaded Man of Ignorance, she finds me
useful. Fine. But over the past few weeks I've
sensed that Aeslu's disinterest is less
persuasive than I thought. In the valleys below
us grow cacti whose prickly pears lie within a

tangle of thorns, yet once properly coaxed
from this protective armor, their fruit exudes
a taste like the intermingled flavors of mango
and persimmon. Who knows what tenderness
ripens beneath this young woman's testy
manner?

I've proceeded slowly, carefully,
deliberately. Her problem, I'm convinced, isn't
in her nature as a woman so much as in her
beliefs as a Rixtir. Never mind the Heirs'
mumbo-jumbo; that's only the start. I mean
something deeper and more fundamental. Even
if Aeslu weren't an Heir, she would still be
prey to half the delusions that these people
suffer. She might celebrate rather than merely
tolerate my presence as an outsider who
doesn't fit her people's expectations for the
long-awaited conquering hero; yet she
wouldn't be open to me as a man. She would
hold off. She would find me strange, even
repugnant, because she doesn't understand
me. What's the answer? Quite simply this: to
help her shed the Rixtir ways. To purge her of
the misunderstandings, confusions, fears,
muddle-headedness, and pointless longings
that cloud her sight. To shake her out of the
ancient daze in which Aeslu herself and all the
rest of these people are submerged. In short,
to rouse her into full awareness.

Yesterday evening, latish, I visited Aeslu's
tent to have further words with the young
lady. I didn't much like how our last
interchange had ended; some sort of odd
aftertaste lingered, and I'm not one to miss a
chance for clearing things up. Hence the urge
to stop by for a little chat.

I stood outside the tent and spoke her name.
No answer.

I called out again.

Again no answer.

Then I pushed past the tent flap, which was untied, and said the sort of words one says on barging into someone's room unannounced.

Aeslu was asleep on the floor. Poor thing—still exhausted from a recent nocturnal stroll. These Rixtirras tend to be early-to-bed-early-to-rise types, I'm afraid, so there she lay, curled up in a heap of blankets. I couldn't see her well at first—these people have only the most rudimentary oil lamps, and none happened to be lit just then—but her slow deep breaths told me she was out cold. I stood near the doorway a minute or two, just listening. In addition to her exhalations I could hear the sounds of other Rixtirs in the vicinity: laughter and occasional flurries of conversation as everyone else settled down for the night. Now and then came the rumble of the glacier shifting beneath us. Otherwise silence.

I waited a short while longer, then switched on my flashlight. The batteries were low; it didn't cast much of a beam. This will be a problem shortly—I have only two batteries left—but at the moment the dim light suited me well. I could look around without making myself conspicuous. Even directing the beam this way and that revealed my surroundings discretely.

Her cold-weather robes lay neatly folded near the door. Three empty ceramic bowls rested next to the robes. Otherwise all I saw were the tent walls themselves, the thin staves supporting them and, before me, Aeslu herself.

She rested on her left side, her back slightly curved, the left leg bent, the right extended. Both arms lay before her, both bent, with the hands reaching up toward her face as if to shield it from a blow. Her head floated in a great swirling black pool of hair. Despite the cold, her covers amounted to little more than a few homespun woolen blankets, and those few had fallen away to expose much of her torso.

This wasn't what I'd expected. This wasn't even what I'd sought. Still, there she was, and you know me well enough, Dad, to understand that I don't easily avert my gaze from display of female beauty.

Of which she was a fine specimen. Not like what you might anticipate; not like what people of our ilk have tended to appreciate; yet beauty nonetheless. This is a swarthy race, their skin dark as earthenware pots. The features we admire in our women—eyes of Wedgwood blue, hair of summer cornsilk, skin of fresh cream, and so forth—are not what one finds here. Still, beauty is beauty. I've resisted the notion; the women have generally seemed not quite to my liking. Yet Aeslu makes the alternative compelling. At least she did so now, curled up and mostly uncovered.

I should stress that I had no intentions at first of taking liberties, however harmless; this was simply the state in which I found her. Quite the contrary: my first impulse was just the opposite. Even in the dim light I could see her shivering. These Rixtirs are a hardy lot, but anyone would have been cold half-covered in a flimsy tent pitched right there on the ice. The temperature was frigid; small wonder that the chill air disturbed her. This and nothing else prompted me to draw close, kneel beside her bed, and pull the blankets up again.

Yet temptation got the best of me. She was a splendid sight: smooth-skinned and full-fleshed. I could feel her warmth even from several inches away. I could smell her scent, at once sweet and tart, like the juice of some wild mountain berry. Only a fool or a eunuch would have hesitated to draw back the covers and savor this woman's loveliness. All the more so in my case, since for a while—a longer while than I cared to remind myself— Aeslu and I were once regarded as the perfect match for each other's embrace. No doubt the Umbrages still held the same opinion. She is the Moon's daughter; I am the Sun's son! What more could either of us want than one another? Yet Aeslu's is the dissenting vote. Or is it? She had returned to me; she had confessed that I am the man capable ultimately of leading her and her people to the mountain they covet. Why does she hold herself back?

I'll admit that my thoughts soon grew unruly. Here she was; here I was too. She was lovely almost beyond toleration. Her body was a pool I'd dive into. By the time she knew what was happening, she would be incapable of resisting. Would anyone hear the first scream of bewilderment and fear? Perhaps. But the Umbrages had heard our arguments before and paid no attention to Aeslu's exclamations. More to the point, they consider us the sacred couple; what we do is our business alone. Or do they believe otherwise? It's hard to tell with these people—probably good not to take any chances.

Still, this wasn't really what restrained me. There was something else. I've prided myself on never having resorted to force—of never having needed to—with any woman. I've always made myself persuasive in other ways. More than persuasive: desired. This has never been difficult before, so why should it be now? For some reason Aeslu has proved resistant to

whatever magnetic pull I exert. At least so far.
What a shame to press the issue and lose the
chance for subtler means.

This, then: I reached out to stroke her thigh.
The warmth of her skin kept my hand there
against my will. I touched her again. Then
again.

She stirred slightly; I drew back. She did not
wake.

Best to leave, I told myself. Now.

Before I could, however, Aeslu shifted, eased
back gently, then forward again. With her own
right hand she brushed against the flesh of her
left arm. She began to moan.

Moan indeed! I'd give her something to
moan about.

Moments later I heard another sound. She
had begun to talk. *Talk* is too strong a word: it
was a mutter, a mumble. Speaking in her
native Rixtir—a language that under the best
of circumstances sounds like people talking in
their sleep—she went on for a long time. Of
course I didn't understand a word, as I've
never been able to make sense of these
people's gobbledegook; but I listened anyway,
wondering at what point her mind would come
to the surface and, abruptly aware of my
presence not more than a foot away, she would
begin to scream.

No screams. Just those mush-mouthed
words, their tone somewhere between a
lament and a plea. If only I could make a little
sense of them!

Then I did. I understood a single word.

"—Jassikki—"

PART THREE

In Lince, a working-class suburb of Lima, Esperanza had introduced me to Marcelino Huamán and, later, to Juana de Mariátegui. Both seemed about Esperanza's age—I'd guess seventy or seventy-five—but more heavily burdened by the passage of time. Marcelino, especially: a stooped old man, half-blind and frail, whose hands were knotted with arthritis. I found it hard to imagine him weaving slings, much less wielding them as weapons. Juana, by contrast, looked weary but less damaged by the years. Stocky, buxom, round-shouldered—a great haystack of a woman—she consented at once to speak with me. Marcelino did, too, though at first more reluctantly. In itself their cooperation didn't surprise me. What did was that all four of us were to get together at the same time.

And so we met at Juana's granddaughter's house—a plain, boxy dwelling not far from the Lima airport, with whitewashed concrete rooms surrounding a courtyard—and we talked for each of several consecutive afternoons. A scattering of Juana's relatives came and went: a son, several grown grandchildren, and three great-grandchildren who chased a single panicky hen about the courtyard. Juana, Marcelino, and Esperanza sat uncomfortably in ladder-backed chairs and listened to one another with an attentiveness I couldn't quite identify but would have hesitated to call affection.

1

[Esperanza Martínez, formerly Issapalasai of Mtof-fli, interviewed September 8, 1970.]

When they heard about what Forssabekkit was doing, many of the Masters changed their minds about Jassikki. Forssabekkit had allied himself with the Umbrage. That in itself marked him as the Man of Ignorance. Worse yet, he had begun attacking villages throughout the Realm, laying them waste, plundering their supplies, welcoming the Umbrage among their inhabitants, and scattering the Heirs. If Forssabekkit was who he seemed, then what did that make Jassikki but the Man of Knowledge?

But we had other reasons to regard Jassikki as the Guide we had all so long expected. Never mind that he fit the description offered in *The Summit:* he was a Lowlander who despised the Lowland, a warrior who hated war, and so forth. I mean something else. He ended up *seeming* more like the Man of Knowledge than we first thought. He began acting like the Man of Knowledge. He started behaving like the Man of Knowledge. When Jassikki came to the Veil, he seemed different from the man we had seen before. He looked stronger, healthier, more confident—this despite all his wounds. Hesitance had left his manner. He knew what he wanted and knew how to get it.

Soon he even started looking like the Man of Knowledge. Not that Ossonnal and Lissallo had ever stated how the Man of Knowledge would look; let's just say that he seemed intent on changing his Lowland features. He shaved off his face-hair. He tied back his hair in the style of our men. He discarded his old clothes and dressed in the attire that we Masters had sent him—attire befitting his new role among us. Of course, there was nothing he could do about the color of his skin or his height; even so, he seemed far less a Lowlander than before. He almost looked like one of us. The one who mattered most.

That brings us around to your first question again.

How did we know he was the Man of Knowledge? We just knew. We knew he was because *he* knew.

2

December 20, 1921

Dad:

Is it possible that Aeslu still pines for Jesse O'Keefe? The ex-doughboy? The addle-pated anthropologist? What a sordid thought. After having considered him so neatly out of the picture these past few months, now I have to tolerate his influence on her yet again!

Better to have him the object of her wistfulness, however—someone who haunts her dreams on cold nights—than something more substantial. I can't stop the fair maid from longing for him; I can't prevent her from reaching out to his memory in her sleep; I can't dissuade her from mistaking my caress for Jesse's. Why Aeslu feels wistful for the likes of him, I have no idea, and I can't take much solace in what she's feeling. Yet all in all I'm not terribly concerned. There's no accounting for taste, eh? Especially among Indian princesses. Contrary to my most immediate impulses, though, I'm inclined to trust the tide of what she does rather than worry about the undercurrents of what she feels. Aeslu may be an Heir, but she's still a practical woman at heart. She has already made the right moves lately in shifting her alliance to the Umbrage—and to me.

So does it matter if she longs for Jesse O'Keefe, weeps at the thought of him, and cries out to him in her sleep? Of course it does. It's foolish of her and, worse yet, a slap in *my* face even as I knock myself out trying to show Aeslu something better. Even so, I'm not worried. I'm still confident that she'll make the right choices. She knows that I, not Jesse, will get her to the goal she craves.

Where actions lead, dreams will follow.

Forster

3

[Marcelino Hondero Huamán, formerly Marsalai S'safta, interviewed September 8, 1970.]

After the Masters came to our village, they led me, my wife, and three other families to Saftofissorih, a town across the pass joining the valleys of Iqtiqqissi and So. It took three days to get there.

We were afraid. Only two of those among us had ever been outside our own valley—I'd never been farther than a half-day's walk from Panli—and we didn't know what to expect. The trip itself was hard. Two of the families traveled with children, most of them under ten Sun-spans in age, one little more than five. The trip took place during the rainy season, too, so we were wet almost the whole time. We didn't really walk there—we slipped and skidded the whole way there. The Masters still hadn't explained how we would make this trip in the first place. You can imagine how we felt on reaching Saftofissorih: such a big town—a walled city of towers, domes, and great stone houses—with hordes of people watching us when we arrived.

The Masters led our group and others to a big open area. There must have been a hundred people there, maybe more. We waited a long time—I don't know how long, maybe half a day—while some Masters decorated a huge pointed stone with ropes, garlands, food, and all sorts of things I couldn't identify. The rain started up, stopped, started up again. People huddled close to keep warm. Babies cried. Children clung to their parents. Everyone watched, listened, whispered to one another, milled around.

Then at last the Masters told us what was happening. I don't remember the exact words. . . . Mind you, this took place almost fifty Sun-spans back. But I could never forget how the words struck us, how they came crashing down, as if the Masters had let loose an avalanche and we were right there beneath it.

The Man of Knowledge had arrived. The Last Days were upon us. The Mountain Land would cease to exist as the place we had always known; the Mountain-Drawn would cease to exist as the people we had always been. Everything that made up our lives would now change. Many of the people we loved would die.

All this, said the Masters, we have known would happen some day, for Ossonnal and Lissallo warned us in *The Summit*. Now the Founders' prophecies have come to pass. Yet whatever the suffering and loss they threatened, they offered promises as well. The Last Days will bring not just darkness but also light. The Man of Knowledge will lead a remnant to the refuge that the Founders prepared long ago on the Mountain Made of Light. You, said the Masters (and here they motioned toward all of us gathered before them), are a part of that remnant.

That's what they said, and we listened. Even the children had fallen silent—they somehow understood what was at stake. *You are a part of that remnant.*

Do you imagine that we felt relieved? Pleased? Delighted, even? Well, we were. To survive the Last Days! To be part of the Remnant! To seek the Founders' refuge at the Summit! This was what each Mountain-Drawn longed for from the time when he or she first understood our beliefs. More than that: it was what we had longed for together from the time that we first became the Mountain-Drawn. To seek and climb the Mountain Made of Light!

But imagine, too, what else we felt. We would never again see our homelands. We would never live as we had before. We would never walk the paths, smell the air, drink the water, taste the foods, hear the words, or practice the customs of our towns and villages. We would never be with the people whose lives we had always shared. You are the Chosen, said the Masters. You will join the Remnant. The Sun and the Moon had granted us this gift, and we accepted it. Yet to leave behind our relatives and friends? Sometimes the Masters chose one family but not their kin, or they chose certain members of a family but not the others.

Usually they chose both the husband and wife, or else neither; they didn't split them up. Young children either went along with their parents or else stayed behind with them. But this didn't suit everyone's hopes. Parents and grown brothers or sisters often got left by the wayside. Young lovers parted company when one was chosen, the other not. Even those who left with their own spouse and children knew that they would never again see their other kinfolk—ever.

You are the Chosen, said the Masters. And as we watched, listened, and waited, Aspirants and Adepts moved into the crowd, eased us in groups toward the outer edges of that gathering place, and gave us the proper equipment—packs, food, clothing—to make the journey ahead.

[Juana Méndez de Mariátegui, formerly Hunatau Mantassi of Va'atafissorih, interviewed September 8, 1970.]

I could tell you how I made my way from the place I'd escaped to the place I'd sought—the journey from the people I detested to the people I longed for—but I won't. Not that I can't remember. Not that I couldn't or shouldn't tell you what happened. Simply this: in some ways it doesn't matter. Traveling from Va'atafissorih to the Umbrage camp near the Inner Realm was little more than a faster, more harrowing trip than the one I'd already traveled my whole life long. I strove hard to reach my destination. I passed every moment in fear of being found out. I tried as hard as possible to avoid the Heirs and, especially, the Masters who held sway over them. I kept going even when the effort seemed pointless. I just kept living as the Umbrage have always lived among Heirs. The only difference was that things happened faster—and that I had more to gain and more to lose along the way.

I was not alone. Fifteen or twenty of us fled the lake's far shore as soon as we reached it that morning. I don't know precisely how many: five or six fell at once under the storm of sling-stones that the Heir warriors unleashed against us. Anyone who turned back for a last look risked the same fate. Our only hope was outrunning the warriors from the start. That wasn't difficult—they wore the usual ungainly tunics, robes, ponchos, and cloaks that the Heirs had always favored, and their weapons slowed them further. Any among us who survived the first attack had little trouble making good headway after that.

How many were left? For several days we numbered twelve. Three soon faltered, overcome by the ceaseless effort of our flight. That left nine: five men, four women. None was a friend, much less kin, to the others. Yet within a few days we felt a bond stronger than any of us had ever felt before. We fed, clothed, and protected one another. We would have done anything in our effort to attain our goal. What united us was the knowledge that we were all Umbrage, that the Heirs hated us and would do anything to stop us, and that only constant attention to one another would ever see us to our destination.

Even so, we realized how great were the forces arrayed against us. Each day brought new reminders. One afternoon, as we hid in a cornfield waiting for nightfall, a young man traveling among us suffered a snake bite, writhed half the night, and died in my arms. (This boy never once cried out, despite his agony, to avoid revealing our location.) Two days later, another of the men accidentally caught the attention of two warriors on a hillside, then sacrificed himself in a skirmish so that the rest of us could escape. Two of the women ended up caught when some other Heirs spotted us near the pass between Vmatta and Mtoffli. We suffered other losses as well. As always, the Heirs seemed to be everywhere. Before long only three of us remained.

I'll admit it: I soon despaired of our situation. We had walked nearly half a Moon-span, much of that without food, all of it without more than the bits of sleep we caught while hiding each day. I was tired, hungry, sore, and afraid. "This is hopeless," I told my companions—a man and a woman, both older than I. "We may as well give ourselves up."

"To the Heirs? asked Loruqtu, the woman.

"To the Masters?" asked Ottai, the man.

"I'd deny them the pleasure," I said, "but I can't keep going like this."

Ottai hooted at me. "Would you rather have the Masters catch you?"

"Of course not."

"Then you have no choice but to keep going."

When I protested, Loruqtu suggested a plan. "There's a city not far from here," she said, "called Ye'affissorih. Till now I've thought we should avoid all cities, but perhaps we should go there."

"Like hares visiting a fox's den," said Ottai.

Loruqtu brushed him off: "It's not quite so simple. In this den the foxes and hares live together."

"Don't we all! What choice have the Umbrage ever had but to live among Heirs?"

Loruqtu pressed her point. "Ye'affissorih is different. Nowhere else in the Mountain Land are there so many Umbrage. This much I know. Believe me or not as you wish. We can surely find someone to take us in."

What she said sounded too good to be true. "How will we ever get past the Heirs?" I asked.

Loruqtu smiled. "Tell me—what day is tomorrow?"

I couldn't remember, but Ottai said, "The Tenth Day of the First Moon-span, Sundecline."

"Which is?"

Neither of us could answer at first. Then I realized her intention. "The Festival of Masks!" I exclaimed.

"Just so. The Festival of Masks."

Thus we made our way toward Ye'affissorih, a place unfamiliar to all of us, with intent to arrive precisely on the one day—a holy day—when even the Masters would have to let down their guard and allow Heir and Umbrage alike free passage in, out, and everywhere within the city.

[Marcelino Hondero Huamán, formerly Marsalai S'safta, interviewed September 8, 1970.]

The Aspirants and Adepts gave us what we needed for the voyage, we left Saftofissorih, and the Masters led us off to join the Man of Knowledge and his forthsetting.

How many of us? I don't know. Hundreds at least, maybe thousands. I didn't count—didn't even have a chance. I was too busy keeping up with the others. My pathpack wasn't much bigger than the rest, but it was full of the slings I'd brought from Panli. Imagine: a pack full of slings! At first I felt angry about shouldering such a heavy burden. Slings! On a forthsetting! Then I thought things through. We would need these slings. At some point we might have to hunt for deer, rabbit, or other animals. Slings wear out after a while. We would have to replace them at some point. It made sense to bring a slinger and some slings: me—and what I carried.

The trip was difficult. We worked our way

through the valley of Iqtiqqissi for several days. That was hard enough but nothing like what followed. Angling up onto high grasslands was far worse: steep trails awash in mud. The rain poured down all day. Then another two or three days toward the pass to So.

The trip weighed heavily upon us. Even the least inattention meant a slip or a fall. My wife and I managed to keep up with the rest. If we faltered, we might not be able to join the forthsetting itself. That's what we had to keep in mind. That's what really mattered. This trip, we told each other, was only the start.

You must realize that no matter how severe the hardships, no matter how deep our sadness, no matter how great our fears, we *wanted* to make this trip. How many of the Mountain-Drawn had waited for just this opportunity? Every one of us throughout the ages had been born to seek the Mountain and the Summit. By the Sun's and Moon's grace, the honor had fallen to us who now plodded upward through the rain. I won't lie: it was difficult. But the difficulty made no difference. Our discomfort made no difference. Our exhaustion made no difference. The rain, the mud, the wind, the cold made no difference. All we cared about was reaching the Man of Knowledge, his forthsetting, and the Mountain Made of Light. No hardship could have stopped us.

What troubled us, though—terrified us—was something we saw from near the pass between So and Lorssa. For several days the Masters' route had led us around the valley about halfway up from the bottomlands. Heavy clouds capped the valley itself. We couldn't see much: half the time we were *in* the clouds. Then, around the eighth or ninth day since our departure, the cloud cover lifted, revealing the valley below.

Great cones of smoke slanted up from near the

river in two or three places. At the tip of one cone we could see the flames causing all that smoke. It must have been a huge fire: houses, maybe a whole town.

"What's happening?" my wife asked.

I answered, "I don't know."

"Tomorrow is the Festival of Masks. Perhaps this is part of the celebration."

"This is no celebration."

We proceeded upward. There was little time for talk.

In fact we knew what the smoke meant. This was no celebration. This was, after all, the Last Days.

[Juana Méndez de Mariátegui, formerly Hunatau Mantassi of Va'atafissorih, interviewed September 8, 1970.]

The Festival of Masks was one of the two most important holy days among the Mountain-Drawn each year. It fell that year on the Tenth Day of the First Moon-span, Sundecline—what we now call the summer solstice—that day when the Sun, having grown strong and splendid, starts dwindling all over again. The Festival of Masks celebrated the Sun's presence in our midst and offered our entreaties that he return to his people.

But this holy day also commemorated a human event: a slave rebellion that Ossonnal and Lissallo had incited at the fringes of the Lowland not long after their founding of the High Realm. The Founders had sneaked back into the Lowland to help some slaves escape their captors and find refuge in the Mountain Land. Here's how they did it. Ossonnal and Lissallo released several hundred slaves from bondage, then disguised them in stolen clothes that allowed them to elude the slave-

masters' gaze. Not everyone made it safely to the
Realm, but enough did that the numbers of the
Mountain-Drawn swelled greatly, and from then
on our people have celebrated this victory over
the Lowlanders—proof that the Sun would never
betray us, proof also that even his departure leads
in time to his return.

I should mention that this holy day changed
over the course of so many Sun-spans. Trust the
Heirs to take something simple and make it complicated! What started out as a day of gratitude
for the slaves' escape soon became much more
elaborate, with some of the Mountain-Drawn
wearing masks to imitate those who had fled to
safety. This in turn eventually grew into a festival
in which all the Mountain-Drawn put on costumes, wigs, masks, face-paint, false armor, fake
weapons, and whatever else they could contrive
to reenact the long-past events. The ex-slaves
pranced about pretending to be slavemasters! It
could get pretty wild. People ate from dawn to
dusk, drank too much cornbeer, and held great
revelries day after day. The masks didn't simplify
things. Enemies settled old scores, lovers trysted,
and mischief-makers caused trouble—all without
fear of punishment. No one could recognize anyone else. Of course the Masters, having permitted
so much commotion in the first place, soon condemned it as excessive. The Festival of Masks violated the dignity that the Sun and the Moon
expected of their people. Such upheaval was an
insult to the Founders who had brought the
Mountain-Drawn to safety in the first place. The
festival exceeded the bounds of decorum. But you
get the idea. The Masters went on and on. Despite
all their objections, though, even the Masters
couldn't keep anyone from celebrating this holy
day. Like the passage from Sunrebirth to Sunde-

cline, the Festival of Masks just came and went as
if of its own accord.

Now, as my companions and I approached
Ye'affissorih, here it was again.

Ottai, Loruqtu, and I first needed some masks.
More than masks, if possible: entire costumes.
That wasn't too difficult. We hid in a cornfield near
the city and, when three revelers passed, took
them by surprise. We stole their clothes, tied them
up, put on their holiday regalia, and left our vic-
tims near the path. From there we reached our
destination quickly and without anyone having
stopped us even once. If anything, other people
were scared of *us*. We'd ambushed people whose
costumes included the scariest masks, the bushi-
est beards, the shiniest armor, and the sharpest
swords I'd ever seen. Even real white bearded
slavemasters couldn't have looked much more
dangerous than we ourselves did when we passed
through the gates of Ye'affissorih.

The city was in upheaval. As if the Lowlanders
had already invaded and taken over, each person
in the crowd wore big black boots, puffy panta-
loons, a Moon-metal breastplate, and one of those
helmets whose crests look like nothing so much
as the blade of an axe. Each person's mask left his
or her skin deathly white. Each person wore a
beard. (Even the women!) Some of these outfits
looked more impressive than others, but with everyone decked out the same it was quite a sight.
If anything, attire was the least of it. People
ran, staggered, and danced in the streets. They ate,
drank, laughed, sang. The noise was deafening.
Now and then we heard shouts or screams, but no
one paid attention because the surrounding commotion rolled everything into one big noise. Children ran every which way underfoot. Long snakes
of hand-linked men and women writhed down

staircases and through alleyways. So much happened at once that I would have found it fearsome if the confusion and noise themselves hadn't served our purposes so well.

Ottai, Loruqtu, and I gripped each other's hands tightly as we worked our way into Ye'affissorih. Getting separated would have been our doom. I felt timid at first—no, terrified. I feared that everyone could spot me at once as an Umbrage. Yet I wore what everyone else wore; I did what everyone else did. I looked so much like everyone else that only fear could have marked me as an imposter.

"Where should we go?" I asked Loruqtu.

"We need to find other Umbrage," she answered. "They can tell us where to find the Umbrage forthsetting."

Ottai told us, "Let's get some food first—otherwise we'll never have the strength to keep going."

He was right. We were so exhausted that nothing else made sense. We could have used some sleep as well, but it seemed too risky. Food, though: that was urgent.

It was easy, too. The whole city was awash in food. Some vendors sat alongside the streets cooking at little braziers; others sold the goods they had spread out on squares of cloth. The air hung heavy with smoke and food-smells. Baked earthnodes. Roasted scamperbeasts. Meat and fruit stews. Cauldrons of tea and hot vegetable juices. Broiled cliffgoat. Antlerbread, mossbread, clothbread, all kinds of bread. It was almost more than I could stand, this feast laid out all around me.

Luckily the Masters had seen fit to require at least one sensible rule during the Festival of Masks: all food is free. Just as Ossonnal and Lissallo fed the slaves who sought refuge with them in the High Realm, so also must the Mountain-Drawn feed each other on these holy days. Thus my companions and I wandered from one stall to another taking our fill—so great a fill, in fact, that we might well have stuffed ourselves too fat to finish our voyage!

At one stall, a baker's, Loruqtu and Ottai made their next move to find the Umbrage forthsetting. "Tasty bread," Ottai told the baker after he took a little loaf, tore it up, and poked some pieces through his mask's mouth hole. "My belly is full at last."

The baker thanked him for the compliment.

Ottai said: "But one kind could have filled me better."

Did Umbrage everywhere pass messages back and forth by this means? I didn't know.

The baker looked up from his goods for little more than an eyeblink. Then he reached into his basket, pulled out a stunted-looking loaf, and handed it over. "Despite their looks," he said, "these are the heartiest."

Loruqtu took the loaf.

As we left the baker added, "Especially for a long voyage."

The loaf contained what Ottai and Loruqtu had hoped for: directions to Umbrage in Ye'affissorih— Umbrage who guided us out of town in the commotion that reigned everywhere that night.

[Esperanza Martínez, formerly Issapalasai of Mtoffli, interviewed September 8, 1970.]

It's hard for you to understand our situation at the depths of the rainy season that year. It was hard for *us* to understand. Our only means of communication at the time was a system of runners who carried messages throughout the Mountain Land. These runners were pretty reliable, but getting the news from one corner of the Realm to another took time even under the best of circumstances. They carried every scroll on foot—young women and men dashing through forests, across tundra, up glaciers, over passes—as if running a great relay race from one way station to the next. Of course the time you're asking about wasn't the best of circumstances. Never mind the rainy season. The problem was storms of another sort.

You see, the Mountain Land hadn't always been the Mountain Land. Before Ossonnal and Lissallo founded the Realm, it had been little more than a patchwork of valleys with the great peaks between them. The tribes living in each valley had gone about their business largely unaware of whomever lived over the next pass. Not all these tribes had gotten along. Before the white bearded slavemasters arrived, other potentates—what we now call the Incas—had reigned a long time over our lands. We had detested them only a little less than we detested the Lowlanders. We hadn't much cared for one another, either, if you want to know the truth. Ossonnal and Lissallo united us into the Mountain-Drawn because we all feared the white bearded slavemasters, dreaded their return, and believed the Founders' entreaties to stand together till the Last Days. Still, the members of each tribe had always felt the strongest allegiance to their own kind. The cloth of each patch proved stronger than the thread sewing us together.

Who could have predicted how easily the Mountain Land would tear apart? Who could have known that the Mountain itself would be the blade that did the cutting?

The Heirs claimed that the Umbrage were to blame: except for the Umbrage heresies (said the Heirs) the Realm would have held together. The Umbrage in turn cast blame on the Heirs: the sheer weight of the Masters' folderol ripped the Realm apart. Who knows which side was

right? One or the other? Both? Neither? I wish
I knew.

All I can tell you is that things got out of hand.
Once started, the tug-of-war was hard to stop. We
ourselves soon tore the Realm to shreds. Learning
of what had happened—first the Web disaster,
then the two Lowlanders' forthsettings—people
responded with astonishment and fear. Each tribe
aligned itself not only with its old allies, but with
the Heirs or the Umbrage as well. Each tribe thus
also found itself opposing some of the others. The
Ussuffira cut off contact from the Zuara, and
Zuara from the Ussuffira. The Nakkixora reviled
the Leqsiffalthora, Larora, and Qallittira. The
Mtofflira shunned the Nakkixora and the Sora. The
Vmattara put their whole population on alert
against the Ussuffira, T'taspara, X'shaffara, and
Iqtiqqissira. The Makbora sent warnings to the
Vmattara. The Larora made threats to the Qallit-
tira. The Sora withdrew their emissaries from
Iqtiqqissi. The X'shaffara closed the pass to Makb.
On and on, tribe against tribe. Of course the con-
tours of the land made these separations possible.
Each tribe inhabits a valley. Each valley is walled
off by mountains. Ossonnal and Lissallo had once
united all the tribes; now there was no Mountain
Land—just the tribes, the valleys, and the moun-
tains between.

The truth is, we didn't really know what was
happening. Only this: that the Man of Knowledge
and the Man of Ignorance walked among us, and
that the Last Days had come.

4

Dad:

There's another possibility, of course—one I first dismissed as out of the question, but perhaps too eagerly.

Is it possible that Aeslu and Jesse are in touch? That they are somehow communicating despite the sorry state of postal service hereabouts? That they are conspiring against me behind my back?

Not likely. I can't believe that Aeslu would try anything so reckless. More to the point, I can't believe she'd try anything so certain to jeopardize what we're accomplishing together.

Still, still . . . My own early letters went astray when a turncoat messenger delivered them into enemy hands. Who knows whether Aeslu might have been responsible for their waywardness?

I don't know what to think.

The easiest response, of course, would be to dispense with her altogether—toss her out, leave her behind, or let the Umbrages take care of her. Maybe I should do precisely that. Yet somehow taking that kind of approach seems too easy, too unimaginative—not just bad form, but simple-minded.

Is Aeslu plotting with Jesse O'Keefe? Perhaps. Or is she not yet plotting with him, but only for lack of the proper means? That seems more likely. Either way, though, it

would be rather weak-kneed to jettison the
lass simply because of a conspiratorial bent.
How much more amusing instead to win her
over regardless of what she feels for the
anthropologist!

Let her scheme, then, if that's what she's
doing. Let her see how far she gets from
stealthy dealings with the doughboy.
Meantime, I'll do what I can to sway Aeslu, to
win her over, to convince her that there's
someone else to set her heart on.

Forster

5

[Jesse O'Keefe, journal entry, dated the Twelfth
Day of the Second Moon-span, Sunreturn (October 26, 1921).]

And so I've offered my help to the Heirs, they've
accepted me as their leader, and the city around
me now hums with activity as its inhabitants mo-
bilize to undertake the tasks ahead. For the Heirs
want what I want: to stop Forster Beckwith from
his depredations, to find the Mountain Made of
Light, to climb it, to lead the Rixtirra to their refuge before any other harm can befall them.

I've never claimed to be the Man of Knowledge, yet
the Heirs respond to my offer as if I provide just what
they need. Knowledge? Maybe so. Or if not precisely
knowledge, then at least a new angle on their situation. If what I'm doing suits them, that's fine with me.
If they want to call me the Man of Knowledge, I have
no objection. If assuming this name and its duties

helps defeat Forster, so much the better. All I want is to stop him before it's too late.

By their definition, I suppose I *am* the Man of Knowledge.

So be it.

[Jesse O'Keefe, journal entry, dated the Thirteenth Day of the Second Moon-span, Sunreturn (October 27, 1921).]

Norroi showed up again this morning: I found him seated on the bed when I entered my tent.

"Where have you been?" I asked, sounding more accusatory than I'd intended.

"Here and there," he said. "First here, then there, now here once more."

"So it seems. I was wondering. I could have used your help, you know."

The old man yawned. "Perhaps you already did."

"I mean here."

"So do I."

I grew impatient. "Look, Norroi—a lot's been happening. The Masters have decided once and for all that I'm the Man of Knowledge—"

"I heard the news."

"—and we're heading off to stop Forster Beckwith."

Norroi nodded, then started patting his woolen cloak, first in one place, then in another, as if trying to locate a lost object somewhere among the folds. After fumbling around like this for a while, he extracted a small cloth bag.

I watched intently. No doubt the Tirno's attention had strayed on purpose; he was about to show me something important.

I should have known better. What he pulled from the bag was nothing more than lumps of dirt-colored sugar. He popped a lump into his mouth and closed his eyes in delight.

"Don't you *care*?" I shouted. "They've decided I'm the Man of Knowledge. Isn't that what we've been wanting all along?"

He forced his eyes open as if with great effort. "Maybe yes. Maybe no."

"*Maybe*? After all we've been through?"

No response.

"After all our waiting?"

His eyes drifted shut.

I wasn't about to let him doze off. "After all your prodding me to stay here and help the Mountain-Drawn?"

Sucking on his earthy sweet without even raising his eyelids, Norroi said only this: "Maybe so."

[Jesse O'Keefe, journal entry, dated the Sixteenth Day of the Second Moon-span, Sunreturn (October 30, 1921).]

Dreams plague me each night.

Just a short while ago I awoke from one in which, having found the Mountain, I began to climb it. A vast cliff rose before me into the clouds. I ascended alone, picking my way up its frozen surface with crampons and ice-axe. The cliff grew slicker, harder, steeper. Soon it was so shiny that I could see my own reflection there, as if the cliff had become a crude mirror. In this surface, the shadow-Jassikki mimicked my every motion. My axe rose; his did, too. My axe struck; his did, too. My body shifted; his did, too.

Suddenly I realized that it wasn't my own reflection I saw there but something else. Someone else. Another figure. Its motions were mine, yet its shape was different. Shorter. Darker. More feminine. Baffled and alarmed, I peered closer—shoved my face against the cliff as if to peer into a dim window.

Aeslu's face peered back.

I jolted in astonishment, then called out, clawed at the surface, and awoke.

Leaving my quarters shortly afterward, I crossed paths with Loftossotoi the Icemaster. He's the Master in charge of the Veil—a solemn middle-aged man attired in grayish-white ceremonial robes so massive and so heavily decorated with crystal amulets that the combined weight leaves him almost helpless to walk unassisted. Now he greeted me with the Upward-to-the-Summit salute and exclaimed something I could only half follow. I caught the words *issi, ha'ata, noq-baissa:* "glad," "your presence," "us-among." Fair enough: "We are glad to have you present among us." The feeling was mutual, so I returned the compliment.

The Icemaster's retinue included a Wordpath-guide—a thin boy half Aeslu's age and less than half as skillful—whose presence nonetheless simplified the situation. The boy translated Loftosso-toi's next utterance: "He tells you that through your survival, the Mountain-Drawn, too, will survive."

Somehow it wasn't his reassurance or his implicit thanks that struck home; something else nagged at me. "But are you sure I survived alone?" I asked. "That is, are you sure I alone survived?" I grappled for words—scarcely managed the question in Rixtir at all, much less with the subtlety I intended. The wordpath boy made his own attempt. All I could do was hope that my intention got across.

Loftossotoi nodded and spoke. Between my own efforts and the boy's, I understood his words. "This is what the Sun and the Moon have ordained. Otherwise something else would have happened."

I pressed the issue. "Of course. But are we sure that what seems to have happened really did?" Again the linguistic hurdles; again the sense that I was stumbling over every one.

The answer: "This is not ours to doubt."

I could barely constrain myself. "I'm not doubting—just wondering."

"Trust what the Sun and the Moon have granted you." Gesturing in some sort of benediction, Loftossotoi tottered off, his myriad crystal amulets tinkling like Chinese wind-chimes in a breeze.

I let him go. What's the point in alienating him? What's the point of risking what I've achieved just to press an issue that makes no sense to him anyway?

It's frustrating, though. If I only knew. If only someone here could prove to me that Aeslu is dead. What could be worse news? Yet what else would cure the anguish festering within me?

Only one other thing would put me at rest: precisely what I don't dare hope for.

[Jesse O'Keefe, journal entry, dated the Twenty-second Day of the Second Moon-span, Sunreturn (November 5, 1921).]

Where is the Mountain? For months now we've been close; over the past few weeks we've drawn still closer. Yet there's no sign of it. Not a glimmer, not a hint, not a glance. It couldn't be less evident if it never existed at all.

Perhaps we're *too* close: the lower peaks between us and the Mountain intervene and block our view. Once we've crossed into the Inner Realm, we'll see our goal at last.

Perhaps this blasted rainy season is the culprit.

The Mountain could be right across the valley and we'd never see it for all the clouds settling over the Andes. What a pity that we couldn't have approached the Mountain earlier, when the air was dry and crisp and the ridges were so finely etched that I could almost reach across the distances and touch them.

Yet surely the Mountain is there. I can sense it. I can feel its presence. It awaits us. Before long we'll see it, reach it, climb it.

[Jesse O'Keefe, journal entry, dated the Twenty-fifth Day of the Second Moon-span, Sunreturn (November 8, 1921).]

A council today. At least two dozen Masters conferred to plan what happens next. Some of these are Masters I've already met; others have just arrived. More of them are arriving at the Veil each day.

Not just Masters, though. Not more than a half-hour into our deliberations, guards sounded their clacking alarm to indicate the approach of strangers. We all abandoned our tent and stepped outside to see what was happening.

A band of travelers was working its way awkwardly up the snowfield. Tiny dark figures flailed against the snow's white background. How many? I couldn't tell. At least a score, maybe half again that number. Coming over the slope's curve, more appeared all the time. What seemed more obvious than their number was their debilitated state. Some wandered alone, straying about, as if in a daze; some assisted each other, bracing or even carrying their fellows; a few collapsed now and then into the snow, then forced themselves to continue.

The Masters watched for a long time. I kept ex-

pecting them to intervene, to send forth a guard
to investigate, even to call out.

Soon I couldn't take it any longer. "Go help
them." At these words many of the Heirs closest
to me looked in my direction, but none responded.
"T'tifsi'a," I repeated in the Common Dialect.

The word brought astonishment rather than
obedience. They simply stared.

"T'tifsi'a."

Loftossotoi stared, too. Then he nodded and, after a moment's hesitation, shouted a phrase that
contained that same command. A handful of warriors set off at once down the snowfield, moving
fast.

"Who are they?" I asked Norroi when the first
of the derelict band reached the camp.

Guards had helped them up the final approach,
in some instances offering a shoulder's support, in
others hoisting the refugees onto their backs.
Weak and injured, wounded, bound in rags—these
people looked helpless, famished, sick, lost.

The Tirno watched them while his toothless
jaws worked against each other: the only gesture
of anxiety this old man ever exhibits. Then, as
more and more of these people entered our midst,
Norroi said, "Heirs. Heirs from Zua."

"What happened to them?"

He eased away from me and moved closer to the
refugees themselves.

Abruptly, one of them staggered forth and collapsed at my feet. Weeping and muttering, he
clutched me so hard around the ankles that he
almost knocked me off balance. He hunched there,
a quivering mass of rags. The Icemaster motioned
to the guards, who moved at once to pry this man
loose from me, but I motioned for them to desist.
They backed off. I stood there feeling awkward
but intent on not adding humiliation to this per-

son's woes. I rested one hand against his shoulder
by way of reassurance.

All the while, other new arrivals stood watching. Their expressions—what little I could see of
them past layers of caked dirt and blood—showed
no emotion. Most of them seemed too stunned to
speak. The man at my feet, however, reared up
just then and beseeched me in a nasal, declama-
tory tone. I couldn't follow a word he said.

Spontaneously the Tirno began translating.
"Umbrage attacked their village. The Man of Ignorance came and took all into his company who
believed like the Umbrage. Of the rest, some died
and others fled. These have traveled almost a full
Moon-span to reach us here."

"Forster Beckwith," I said.

The guards now helped this man up, eased him
away, and motioned for the others to come as well.

So he's doing what I feared—what I suspected
and dreaded but couldn't quite believe he'd have
the nerve to do. As if destroying the City of Rope
wasn't enough, now he's plundering the whole
High Realm.

"We've got to get rid of him," I told Norroi.

"Get?" asked the old man. "Rid?"

"Stop him. Eliminate him. Otherwise he'll ruin
everything. He'll destroy the Mountain Land."

"Maybe he will."

"He's the Man of Ignorance."

"I know that."

The Tirno's diffidence started to get on my
nerves. Something else as well. "You always *did*
know, too."

"Of course." He just sat there smiling.

"Then why didn't you say so? You could have
saved me a lot of trouble. You could have per-
suaded the Masters far quicker than I did."

Norroi said nothing. He simply balanced his

mountain-shaped lodestone on the back of his right hand.

"All right, then—they had to figure it out themselves. Now they know. At least the Heirs do. So now we have to stop him."

"What about the Mountain?" asked Norroi.

"What about it?"

I felt more and more impatient. Wouldn't anything rouse this geezer to action?

"I thought you wanted to climb it."

"That's the whole point!" I shouted.

"It is," said Norroi. Now he took his lodestone and dropped it into the inner pocket of his robe. "So go climb the Mountain."

"Damn right I will! Right after I stop the Man of Ignorance."

Norroi stood and meticulously rearranged the folds of his robe. No matter how hard he tried, the Tirno's emaciated limbs got lost in all that cloth. As he fumbled about, Norroi asked, "Why not forget Forssabekkit? Just go climb the Mountain."

"You know why. We have to stop him—otherwise he'll beat us to the top."

"Let the Mountain decide who gets there."

I wouldn't argue with him further.

What makes Forster do what he's done? What prompts him to plunder villages and kill their inhabitants?

From the moment I met him, I regarded Forster as a one-man walking minefield, but I never thought he'd detonate quite like this. Of course he revealed his nature in the City of Rope, and its cinders fluttered down for days afterwards; yet even that disaster didn't fully anticipate the damage he's now working throughout the Mountain Land.

So what explains what he's doing? Is it a desire

for wealth? Forster shows signs of avarice, and
by all accounts his followers often confiscate the
gold, silver, and precious stones amassed in local
treasuries. Yet Forster has sometimes ignored
these riches in favor of humbler goods: food, tex-
tiles, animal hides, even lumber.

Lust for power? According to some of the refugees, Forster revels in the attention bestowed
upon him; he orders his followers around like servants. Yet here, too, he stops short precisely when
most likely to run rampant. He seems less inter-
ested in adulation than collaboration; he turns
away more people than he allows into his company.

No, something else is at work here. Forster
Beckwith wants more than wealth or power—
more even than wealth and power combined. He
wants what wealth and power will bring him. He
wants the quest itself. He wants what the quest
will lead to.

He wants the Mountain.

[Jesse O'Keefe, journal entry, dated the Third Day
of the Third Moon-span, Sunreturn (November 15,
1921).]

"These are the means that Ossonnal and Lissallo have given us to reach our goal," said Loftossotoi, his voice loud and nasal, the words more
chanted than stated, as he held up Rixtir climbing
implements for all to see. The Icemaster seemed
to be reciting half of an ancient litany—a litany in
which the other Masters present provided the
other half—and the objects of their declamation
seemed equally as ancient. Hatchets, picks, and
hammers ... Hooks of all shapes and sizes ...
Rope in all its wild variety ... Loftossotoi held up

the sacred tools one item at a time for us to venerate.

"With what the Founders have given us," responded the other Masters, "we shall honor the givers themselves."

Although I understood most of the words, and though Norroi's translation filled in what few gaps remained, I still couldn't shake the sense that I was missing the real significance. I watched the Masters pass their holy gear around the circle; I took these items myself, examined them, nodded toward them in respect; I passed them on to the others, who received them reverentially; and I gestured when everyone else gestured, chanted when they chanted, cheered when they cheered. Even so, I couldn't grasp what they found so moving, much less feel moved myself.

A great mass of equipment lay before us. All of it was the ritual gear I'd seen time after time in the Mountain Land. The axe- and pick-heads seemed to be fashioned from silver and gold, some with incrustations of jewels. A few weren't even metal—they were ceramic instead. Ceramic! I'll admit they were beautiful, with complex striations beneath a creamy glaze. Yet what kind of climb could we undertake with ceramic-headed ice-axes? Likewise for the hooks. I recognized talon-hooks, tassle-hooks, and hoof-hooks; thorn-hooks and needle-hooks; beak-hooks and claw-hooks—all the many kinds that Aeslu had showed me on our way through Leqsiffaltho. Again, beautiful. Hooks made of painted seed pods. Hooks made of eucalyptus twigs. Hooks made of llama and alpaca bones so intricately etched that they would have made a New England scrimshaw-carver proud. But how would we trust our lives to these trinkets? How much of even one person's weight would they support, much less a whole expedition of Rixtirra heading up the Mountain

Made of Light? And the rope, the rope! Rope made of braided condor feathers, of tundra grass, of bread, of wax. They could have spun rope out of dreams and I would trust it to support my weight more than I trusted these wisps. Yet the Masters passed each item my way, waited for my approval, watched as I examined the fruits of their people's labor, and smiled in delight, confidence, and relief when I nodded my approval.

What should I have told them? "I am the Man of Knowledge, but I don't know what to make of all this stuff." "I am the Man of Light, but I still feel I'm groping in the dark." "I am the Man of Climbing, but I'm not sure if I can use this gear to get us anywhere near the summit."

I am the Man of Knowledge. Now all I have to do is figure out what to do with the fanciful technology on which these Masters hang the whole weight of their expectations.

[Jesse O'Keefe, journal entry, dated the Sixth Day of the Third Moon-span, Sunreturn (November 18, 1921).]

Later now.

I'm seated at the base of the mountain monument that rises from the Veil's public meeting place. The sky is overcast—big clouds massing everywhere—but so far today we've been spared a storm. No doubt the snow will start falling soon. Till then, it's a relief to be outside in a city whose very nature makes it a perpetual icebox.

No one is attending to me right now, yet I'm not alone in any sense of the word. Five or six of the Masters stand a few paces off, loitering in their intricately woven robes and pretending to confer about one thing or another; several dozen of their attendants linger at a respectful distance; scores of ordinary Heirs watch at the fringes of this meeting place. These concentric circles of people observing me are a great distraction. Yet in some ways everyone is leaving me alone. I'm able to sit here and write more or less undisturbed.

A peak similar to this mountain monument rises from every other city in Xirrixir, but none quite like this one. It's not simply that it's bigger, taller, more imposing. Unlike all the others I've seen in the Mountain Land, this one is made of ice. It's a great icy sculpture—forty, perhaps fifty feet high—and it rises over the gathering place in the same way as all the others. Yet the nature of its substance makes it altogether different from the rest.

Another mountain rests in my hands: the Mountain Stone. The crest jewel of the Leqsiffaltho Diadem. The emblem, carved in quartz, of the Mountain Made of Light. The image, the symbol, and—if my earlier hunch is correct—the map showing an actual route up the peak itself.

It's a hexagonal pyramid of quartz about three inches tall. It weighs perhaps a pound. It is colorless, translucent and, when viewed up close, almost entirely transparent. The base alone shows signs of polishing; all other surfaces reveal intricate accretions of the crystalline mineral which provide the stone's glittery effect. Six triangular planes meet at slightly less than right angles to form a point. Of these planes, three slant toward the base without interruption, while the other three end abruptly in vertical "cliffs" that drop straight down, truncating the stone's slopes. The mineral accretions I've described line up on these three facets to form parallel lines that intensify the impression of eroded cliffs.

One night not long ago—and far too long ago— I saw Sifithirix itself: the Mountain Made of Light. Watching from the City of Rope, I saw the Mountain just briefly but long enough to seal an image of its shape and features into my mind. What I now see in the Stone bears a remarkable resemblance to the real peak. Of course I saw only one side, and in moonlight, yet the Mountain's features are so striking as to defy all possibility of forgetfulness. Its glaciers, cliffs, ridges, promontories, cols, and cornices rose before me in the night; now I see them again, in miniature, right in the palm of my own hand.

And so this Mountain Stone hints at the goal the people here long for. No, more than hints—states, declares, promises, explains. For not only is the Stone a perfect image of the Mountain Made of Light, it also reveals a series of marks whose appearance suggests nothing less than the way up the Mountain itself. How do I know? I don't. But the evidence is overwhelming. Just as the Diadem is a map revealing a path through the Inner Realm to the Mountain, this Stone is a map revealing a path up the Mountain to the Summit. Finely etched lines trace what must be the route. I can follow this route uninterrupted with my eyes; I can even trace most of it with my fingertips.

But that line, however obvious, is only half the story. Other marks are engraved here: smaller, less obvious, more delicate. Some are evident without much effort; some are almost invisible unless I work hard to find them. If I tilt the Stone just so, sunlight throws them into relief, but at the least quiver of my hand they disappear. Sometimes I can see them all. At times half of them vanish, leaving me to wonder if I haven't imagined them in the first place.

What do they mean? I can't even start to speculate. They bear little resemblance to anything I've seen among the Rixtirra's several scripts; the Masters themselves admit to profound ignorance of their meaning.

Could Aeslu have read these marks? Could she
have at least figured out some way of deciphering
them? Surely she would have grasped the nature
of the Stone's hieroglyphs, and she might well
have cracked the code altogether.

But of course that's now all beside the point.

Thus in more ways than one we have the path
without the means of following it, the end without
the means, the promise without the fulfillment.

[Jesse O'Keefe, journal entry, dated the Elev-
enth Day of the Third Moon-span, Sunreturn (November 23, 1921).]

Heirs keep pouring into our camp. Most of them
arrive in groups of twenty or thirty, with axe-
wielding guards fore and aft as an escort. The
members of these groups appear to be healthy and
well-fed, though clearly tired from their travels.
I've seen men, women, and children alike. Many
of them wear the complex attire I associate with
the higher echelons of Rixtir society; others are
working people in more simply-patterned garments. Entering the Heirs' camp at all hours of
the day, these people look alert despite their fatigue—curious, even eager, to see what happens
next. They know they belong here.

But these new arrivals aren't the only ones. Others of less official status straggle into the camp as
well. Showing up in bands of five or ten people, a
few, or even alone, they are much more debilitated than the others: always haggard, sometimes
wounded, occasionally so weak and sick that they
arrive on pallets, on their companions' backs, or,
in one instance, dragged up the snowfield on a
blanket. They look awful. They sound even worse,
their moans and supplications drifting over the

camp. Yet the Masters keep them at a distance; they aren't allowed to enter the camp itself.

Scores of them arrive each day.

"Who are these people," I asked Loftossotoi with a nod toward the refugees, "and what do they want?"

"They are Heirs. They want what all of us want."

The Icemaster hadn't glanced my way as I spoke; he hadn't seen the direction of my gesture. "I don't mean the ones in our camp," I went on. "I mean the others. Those." Now I pointed beyond the last row of tents, beyond the cordon of warriors who stood guard there, to the people waiting silently on the snowfield's edge.

Loftossotoi still didn't look at me. "All Mountain-Drawn seek the Summit, but not all can reach it."

"They won't be coming along?"

"As Ossonnal and Lissallo wrote in *The Summit*—" and he then quoted a verse from the Rixtir holy book:

A remnant shall set forth for the Mountain,
But only a remnant of the remnant
Shall ever reach it. And of that remnant—

"I've heard the words," I said, cutting him short. "That still doesn't explain why all these people are huddled out there on the ice."

"They have not been chosen."

"Chosen by whom?"

The Icemaster turned to me now with a look of mixed astonishment and confusion. "By the Masters," he said.

"On what basis?"

"Piety, loyalty, and obedience. Strength, stamina, and health. Desire to reach the Summit."

"You can't mean that all these others will simply be left behind," I blurted. "Left simply because they don't meet your expectations."

I could see that Loftossotoi was attempting to retain his composure. "Not *my* expectations—all the Masters'."

"But these are Heirs—all Heirs."

"Are they?"

His question caught me short. I felt a surge of exasperation. What right did he have—? Then at once the feeling dissipated. Of course. How could I have been so foolish! Most of these refugees were probably as loyal as the rest, and many of them had suffered terrible hardships at Forster Beckwith's behest. There would be exceptions, however: at best opportunists, at worst something far more dangerous. Thus the dilemma. How could we risk letting in a few wolves with the sheep? Yet how could we ignore the sheep's suffering no matter how many wolves lurk among them?

"You speak wisely when you say that the remnant must be chosen," I told Loftossotoi. "But since I am the Man of Knowledge, let me do the choosing."

The process has already begun. From time to time, the Heirs just recently admitted into our camp have stepped away from their tents and, however timidly, have approached me. Mostly they stare. A few have spoken—at times intelligibly, at times in dialects I find incomprehensible—and I have tried to answer. More than once people have offered me gifts: food, clothing, jewelry, talismans, and tokens I can't even identify. Most of them simply stare.

What do they see? A man? A god? A spirit or ghost? I can't tell from their expressions, which show complex interminglings of fear, longing, delight, and sadness. Yet whatever they see, it's hard for me to exclude anyone automatically from the task we've undertaken. As they press close, as I step more confidently among them, I want to find out what I can, to figure out what needs to be done, to include all those who ought to be included.

[Jesse O'Keefe, journal entry, dated the Twenty-fourth Day of the Third Moon-span, Sunreturn (December 6, 1921).]

"So what you're telling me is that the Mountain-Drawn have always used this sort of equipment? These sorts of hooks, axes, picks? These kinds of rope?"

The Masters listened in silence while I spoke; they remained silent afterward. Except for Norroi, who sat dozing across from me in the council room, everyone present had a look of entrapment on his or her face.

Then I heard Loftossotoi's voice: "Always."

"There has never been some other sort?" I asked. "Something different? Perhaps something no longer used, but used long ago?"

"Never."

"Then tell me this: How do you climb? Not you personally—you the Heirs. Climb at all, climb anything?"

"We have worshipped the Sun and the Moon," said Marhaislu the Stonemaster abruptly. "We have honored Ossonnal and Lissallo."

As if on cue the others began chanting: "They who have honored us, we shall honor; for they revealed the path to our refuge, and both the Sun's radiance and the Moon's glow will illuminate our voyage into their presence."

"That still doesn't answer my question."

The Masters stared at me as I spoke. Now and

then one of them glanced toward another; otherwise the fixity of their collective gaze continued unbroken.

Since my words didn't seem to make any progress, I tried another approach.

Piles of Rixtir climbing equipment lay before us on the rug. Coils of rope, mounds of hooks, stacks of picks and hatchets—the usual. I reached over to the ropes and pulled a length closer. It was weft rain-rope, woven from tundra grasses and tufted with hawk feathers. Even as I uncoiled it the rope hissed a brittle hiss; bits of grass sifted down; a few feathers came loose. I extended the rope's end to Loftossotoi, who took it reluctantly.

"Hold tight," I told him.

He wound the end around his palm several times.

I did the same.

"Now pull."

The Icemaster hesitated.

"*Pull.*"

When he obeyed, the rope snapped at once.

The jolt made the crystal amulets sewed onto his robe tinkle furiously.

Next I picked up one of the hooks—*thagossifaqtsa,* the hawk talon-hook—which is a sharpened hawk's rib attached to a loop of copper wire. Its long white curve was lovely, but nothing could have seemed much more delicate. I held the bone in my right hand, caught its tip against the raised palm of my left, and pulled. The hook bent as I increased the pressure. Then abruptly it snapped, flinging its upper half sideways against the wall and falling to the floor.

The Masters merely watched, though by now a few of them cast their eyes downward and would not look up.

Next I picked up one of the ice-hatchets from the pile. It was a tool of exquisite craftsmanship:

the handle of polished hardwood, the head of matte-finish black pottery. Under any other circumstances I would have treasured it as a priceless artifact. Yet without hesitation I stepped over to the wall at my back, raised it over my right shoulder, and, with a single blow, struck at the ice. The pottery point shattered instantly. Black shards scattered around me.

Whether the noise startled the Masters, I have no idea. I know it jolted Norroi from his nap, however, for the old man snorted once, looked up, and watched the rest of us as if trying to make sense of our presence there.

I asked, "Have I made my point?"

No response.

Then Loftossotoi broke the silence: "You have. But *our* point is that Ossonnal and Lissallo gave us all this gear to climb the Mountain Made of Light."

"Did they?"

"Of course."

"How do you know?"

The Stonemaster gestured quizzically, both hands raised. "Because this is what we have."

"What if there's something else?"

At these words Loftossotoi's gaze grew hard. "There is. Something dangerous, something evil: what the Man of Ignorance has brought and now provides to the Umbrage."

I could sense that my questions were getting nowhere. "Look," I said, returning to the circle where everyone else sat. "I know you reject him and his Lowland ways. So do I. You are right to insist that we find the Mountain by using Rixtir tools." Here I paused. Picking up an ice-hatchet identical to the one I'd shattered, I asked, "But are you positive that these are the only tools?"

"Positive."

"There are no others?"

"None at all."

"There never have been?"

"Never."

We all sat without speaking for a long time. The only sound came from Norroi, who yawned loudly, then set to work rummaging through the folds of his cloak.

"Well," I told the assembled Masters, "then I don't see how we'll ever find the Mountain, much less—"

"Once I heard of something."

Everyone turned to the old man. Extracting what looked like a small woven bag, Norroi plunged a gnarled hand into its depths and groped for something within. The Masters watched intently, as if the old man would pull out the solution to our dilemma. I watched, too.

"Heard of what?" I asked.

Norroi removed something that looked like an old teabag. He dangled it before his eyes, smiled at the sight, then lowered it carefully to his mouth and began nipping at it like a cat with an unexpected morsel. The smell was loamy: some kind of root.

The Masters stared with growing impatience.

I repeated my question.

At the sound of these words, the Tirno glanced up, clearly surprised by our presence around him. "Eh?"

"You said you once heard of something. What was it?"

"Oh. Something. Tools. Climbing tools."

Loftossotoi now interjected some abrupt words in a Rixtir dialect I couldn't follow, though I caught the word *t'nosthi*, "explain."

"Once, when I was little more than a boy, I heard of other climbing tools. Tools that the Mountain-Drawn once used. Tools," said the Tirno with a shooing motion toward the tangle of equipment before us, "other than these."

"A mere tale," said Loftossotoi.

"A Bringer's tale," added one of the other Masters.

Some of the other Masters joined in with their own dismissive remarks.

"Be quiet," I told them. "Let Norroi speak."

Even as the old man resumed, Loftossotoi cut him short. "The Bringers were full of tales. Now there is only one Bringer left, and soon enough all his tales—"

"I said *be quiet*!"

The Icemaster glared at me but fell silent.

I told Norroi, "Go ahead."

The Tirno shrugged. "That is all. Just a tale about how the Mountain-Drawn once used other tools."

"They must have been Umbrage!" exclaimed one of the younger Masters with a snort.

"No, Heirs."

"Impossible!"

"What is impossible now," said Norroi, "was not impossible then."

"This is Bringer nonsense," muttered Loftossotoi, "and I weary both of Bringers and their nonsense."

The Masters' voices soon rose into a babble of jibes and insults. Seemingly oblivious, Norroi resumed nibbling his rooty snack.

I shouted, "Stop—all of you!"

The cacophony ceased at once.

"Just stop. I don't care if it's nonsense or not. Norroi's words are the first hope we've had for reaching the Mountain."

"Lies!" cried a woman who had interrupted earlier. "Bringer lies!"

I ignored her and continued: "Listen to me. We all want to reach the Mountain. We want to reach it by the proper means. No Lowland gear, no Umbrage gear. But can we do it with these things—these here before us?"

One of the others interrupted: "They are what Ossonnal and Lissallo have given the Mountain-Drawn."

"What if they're not?" I asked. "What if Ossonnal and Lissallo gave you other tools—other ropes, hooks, hatchets, all the rest—and what if the Mountain-Drawn used those tools from one Sun-span to the next? What if the Mountain-Drawn made more tools, passed the knowledge of making them from one generation to the next, made still more tools, and once again passed the knowledge on? But what if the knowledge changed? What if the Mountain-Drawn forgot how to make the tools exactly as the Founders did? What if the tools you see before you—" and here I picked up one of the pottery-headed hatchets "—are the descendents of the original tools, just as you are descendants of the Founders?"

For the first time since Norroi roused from his nap, everyone gazed in my direction.

"What if?" I asked.

[Jesse O'Keefe, journal entry, dated the Fifth Day of the First Moon-span, Sundecline (December 16, 1921).]

How many Heirs have arrived at the Veil? I can't even guess. Three thousand? Four? All I know is that each day more and more arrive. They just keep coming.

More to the point, how can this raggle-taggle band survive here? And how can they survive, much less prevail, on a voyage to find and climb the Mountain? The terrain, the weather, and the rigors of a long march seem sufficient to do them in. Add the presence of a treacherous enemy, and I feel great dread about everyone's well-being.

[Jesse O'Keefe, journal entry, dated the Twelfth Day of the First Moon-span, Sundecline (December 23, 1921).]

The Mountain Stone rests before me. Though set on a jet-black alpaca blanket, the Stone seems immune to the dark hues beneath; its cliffs and slopes still glint and sparkle. If anything, the black wool intensifies the Stone's luster, making the marks etched into its facets all the more conspicuous. They stand out, they flaunt themselves, they dare me to make sense of them. I know what this Stone is, but I don't know what to do with it.

Even if we could solve the puzzle, how far will it get us? To proceed into the Inner Realm, we need the Diadem as guidance. We don't have it; Forster Beckwith does. Hence, the urgency of stopping him before he reaches the Mountain. But there's a catch. Even if Forster finds the object of his search, he'll be helpless to do more than approach it. He has the Diadem, but I have the Mountain Stone. He'll never climb the Mountain because he lacks what now lies before me. Thus a double dilemma: Forster Beckwith has the way to the Mountain but not the way up it; I have the way up the Mountain but not the way to it.

Where does this leave us? Maybe Norroi is right—I shouldn't worry about Forster at all. Let him wend his way to the Mountain. He'll get no further. Even if we followed him there, we couldn't proceed without figuring out the Mountain Stone. Better to wait. Better to let Forster bog down, fail, and alienate his followers. By then I may have cracked the code. Why deplete ourselves when we can't attempt a climb in the first place?

Perhaps my speculation doesn't give Forster enough credit. Using the Diadem to reach the Mountain, perhaps he'll figure out some way up on his own. He's resourceful; he's experienced. I dread the possibility of what he might improvise if left unchecked.

No, I can't let that happen. He may be the Man of Ignorance, but I can't count on him to fail.

Odd marks on the Stone's base:

I've noted already that the inscriptions here look different from any of the Rixtirra's several forms of writing; what I see on the base differs in turn from anything else on the Stone. These marks seem less like words than pictograms. But pictograms of *what*?

[Jesse O'Keefe, journal entry, dated the Twenty-fifth Day of the First Moon-span, Sundecline (January 5, 1922).]

Another dream.

I have reached the Mountain. As I begin the climb, I find it's made of ice. Not ice like what covers most big mountains—blue-gray ice coating a granite peak in vast, broken layers. Instead it's ice so nearly transparent that it may as well be glass.

I shove my face up against the mountain. I peer within. I stare far into its depths, far enough that I can see all the way to its center. Inside, piled there so high that it seems another mountain, a mountain within the mountain, is—

At once I awake.

[Jesse O'Keefe, journal entry, dated the Twenty-sixth Day of the First Moon-span, Sundecline (January 5, 1922).]

The Masters were not amused to be roused from their slumber. One by one Norroi and I woke them; one by one they joined our procession through the Veil; one by one they followed me up into the city's open gathering place and toward the icy mountain monument at its center. But I didn't care how annoyed or baffled they felt. All I cared about was getting them conscious and co-operative.

Our arrival at the gathering place woke scores of the people camped there, most of them low-ranking Heirs. The first to notice us were the multitude who lay, crouched, and slumped around campfires on the open snow. Merely staring at first, some of them soon stood to watch as we passed. Others, bedded down in woolen tents, emerged only as their fellows' noise drew them out. Soon a huge entourage followed me: first Norroi, then Loftossotoi, then the other Masters, then the Masters' Adepts and their retinue, then a rabble of every other rank and origin.

Once we reached the ice-mountain monument I stood there with my back against it, the Masters lined up facing me, and I shouted: "We're going to melt this now!"

No one spoke. I heard plenty of noise—all those Heirs milling about—but not one of the Masters responded.

Perhaps I'd not made myself clear. I'd not said the words right. "Translate for me," I told Norroi.

He did so.

The only noise was the wind whistling over the Veil.

"We're going to melt the mountain monument," I called out, and once again the Tirno translated. "We're going to build bonfires, you understand? The heat will melt the ice. We'll boil water in big pots, too, so that we can pour it and melt the ice—"

"The Founders built this monument." That was Loftossotoi's voice—a near-shout—interrupting me.

"All the better," I said. "All the more reason to melt it."

"We should never destroy what the Founders created."

A few of the Masters nodded at these words. One or two echoed him: "Never!"

The Icemaster's resistance didn't surprise me. I'd assumed that my intentions would stir up trouble. "Listen to me," I shouted. "We won't destroy anything. We'll just do what Ossonnal and Lissallo intended."

Loftossotoi looked more and more irate as I spoke. "Every Moon-span we add ice to this mountain," he said, "for the wind and warmth continually diminish it. Who would melt what the Founders would have us replenish?"

I could see some of the Masters now clustering in groups of two or three and conversing frantically. Within a few minutes I'd lose them altogether.

Hundreds of ordinary Heirs had gathered beyond the Masters during this increasingly tense exchange. None of them spoke. Yet here they were, looking attentive and far more numerous than the Masters. I soon saw that they were my sole way out.

Stepping backwards, working my way up onto a kind of ledge that formed the mountain monument's first tier, I looked out over the Masters' heads and addressed the crowd beyond. "Listen, all of you! Listen, you Mountain-Drawn! Who will go to find the Mountain Made of Light?"

No sooner had Norroi translated than a shout rose from five or six places in the crowd: "We will!"

"Who will?" I called back, this time in Rixtir.

"We will!"

"Who?"

"*We will!*" Sporadic at first, this cry soon grew stronger, more rhythmic: "We will! We will! We will!"

"And who will climb the Mountain Made of Light?"

Now the words came forth at once, overpowering even the wind: "We will! We will! We will!"

Loftossotoi turned to the crowd, raised his hands, and shouted to them repeatedly. No one seemed to notice.

"And who," I shouted, "will lead you to the Mountain Made of Light?"

"The Man of Knowledge!" came the answer at once. "The Man of Light!"

"Who will lead you up the Mountain to the Summit?"

"The Man of Knowledge! The Man of Light! The Healer of Wounds!"

I paused a moment, watching the sea of faces shift before me in the moonlight, before continuing. "Then do what I say. Bring wood, any kind of wood, all the firewood you have. Put it in piles around this monument of ice. Set it afire. Bring kettles, too. Fill them with snow and set them to heat on the fires. Do as I say—then come with me upward to the Summit!"

"Upward to the Summit!"

As the people rushed forth, many of them clutching bundles of sticks, the Masters had to scramble just to avoid getting crushed.

We made great piles of wood near the icy pyramid; we set fires; we watched the flames rise toward the black sky; we waited for the heat of the fires to work its transformation on the artificial mountain. The wind could have hindered us but helped us instead: stoking the firebrands, fanning the flames, veering them closer to the frozen surfaces, at times even shoving them against the ice itself.

Within a few minutes the slope nearest to the fires began to shine. The sight wasn't dramatic at first—just a brightness on the ice where I'd seen dullness before. The wild orange light reflected there impressed me more than the incipient thaw that made the reflection possible in the first place. Yet the signs were obvious. The ice started sweating. When I approached the monument along one of its less flame-battered sides, even the briefest contact with the ice left my hand wet. Not long after that the whole pyramid began to release thin sheets of water which, however insubstantial one by one, combined to form a rivulet by the time they reached the pyramid's base. If anything, the ice melted so fast that the runoff put some of the fires in jeopardy: they streamed away from the pyramid faster than we could channel them, and more than once they swirled into one or two of the pyres and left them sputtering, hissing, billowing smoke.

The Heirs responded to each threat as it arose. When the flames dwindled, they brought more wood. When little creeks of runoff started quenching a fire, they shoved snow into channels and ducted the water off. When all this melted ice accumulated at the far edge of the gathering place and threatened to transform that corner into a lake, they poked a passage through the ice walls and drained all that water out onto the snowfield below.

The mountain monument soon began suffering from its closeness to all that fire. Its six faces grew uncharacteristically smooth as they started melting; then they developed odd textures, for the runoff carved little grooves that gradually deepened and widened into a network of channels; then the whole peak changed shape, since the fires on the windward side did more substantial damage than those on the leeward, until that face developed a conspicuous concavity from the flames' unceasing touch. The monument resembled Mt. Everest for a while: a big complex pyramid. Then it briefly started looking like the Matterhorn: more of a spire, with a nearly vertical front and acute angles where the adjacent cliffs met. Then it grew thinner and rougher—what the French call an *aiguille*, a needle—as the bonfires whittled it down still further.

All along the Masters watched, neither helping the lower-ranking Heirs who did all the work nor making any effort to stop them. Loftossotoi, especially, looked almost paralyzed by what he saw happening. The people under his command had in some sense run amok. The official members of the expedition, thousands of them, had overridden his authority and were now destroying the centerpiece to the Icemaster's own domain. The Veil suffered more and more damage as this rampage continued. Loftossotoi's own colleagues behaved as passively as he did—incapable of action, even of motion. As the mountain monument began to thaw, the Masters themselves seemed gradually to freeze.

The Icemaster wasn't the only person to watch this scene in bewilderment and fear. As the Heirs stoked the pyres and whipped up the flames, as they dragged forth big copper cauldrons to nestle in among the more sedate fires, as they melted snow and ice and set the water to boil, as they brought out clay pots to fill and then dashed their steaming contents against the dwindling monument—as they did all this, I couldn't help but feel some sort of anxiety as well. Somewhere inside that fast-eroding pile of ice, I told myself, there had better be something worth all the Heirs' efforts, something noble enough to justify not just their hard work that night but also the individual and collective hopes accumulated over the ages. If these people came away empty-handed, it wouldn't be the Icemaster who would have to do some fast talking.

I turned at one point to find Norroi standing next to me. I'd gotten so wrapped up in everything I saw that I'd almost forgotten him. "Where have you been?" I asked.

"Sometimes here," he said. "Sometimes elsewhere."

Ordinarily I would have bantered with him, would have asked his sense of what was happening. That night I didn't. I am the Man of Knowledge; I'm supposed to know. Was my hunch worth everyone's trouble? Did my dream hold some sort of truth within its chilly images? I had to believe it did. The alternative was too frightening to contemplate. Lacking the energy to talk, I simply stood beside the old man. I wish he could have answered my questions, but it didn't seem wise even to ask them.

The Tirno, as usual, said little. As the Heirs kept splashing the monument with hot water, he merely watched. Then quietly Norroi said, "What a cold night." He reached out toward the nearest fire to warm his knotty hands.

The monument still retained most of its height but had developed a frailty altogether different from its former appearance. It looked delicate rather than sturdy, insubstantial rather than solid, transparent rather than opaque. The whole pyramid had in fact deteriorated into a kind of vast honeycomb dripping with thin, clear honey. With every passing minute there was less of it, less to it.

Some of the Heirs—two or three women and a half-dozen men—soon stepped forth with hoes, planting-sticks, and other farming implements. Braving the flames that still whipped now and then toward the ice when the wind shifted, these peasants turned their tools against the pyramid and, with wild strokes, clawed at its damaged surfaces. Sheets of ice shattered like window panes. Chunks skittered down to the base. Chips and fragments flew in every direction. Water streamed out of hidden reservoirs. As these efforts began reducing the mountain monument even faster than before, still others among the Heirs rushed forth to join the task. Soon more than a score battered at what remained of the peak's base with hammers, axes, picks, and any other tools of their own trades, then with rocks, sticks, even other pieces of ice.

Heirs surged closer from all sides: shouting, shoving, clamoring for a chance to help wreck the mountain monument. The commotion started to alarm me.

I glanced around, unsure of what to do.

When I caught sight of Loftossotoi off to the right, the Icemaster saw me also, nodded, and smiled.

Should I have pressed forward, too? Or grabbed what might have been my last chance to flee?

Just then a mass of ice about halfway up the monument collapsed, clattering in fragments toward the base. Everyone around me panicked, staggered back, and fell all over one another. Innumerable chunks plummeted toward us. I saw several big fragments bound past, missing me by just a few feet, but nothing struck me except for some of the water spattering off the ice. Others fared much worse. People crumpled to the ground or got knocked flat. It happened so fast that everyone's first response was hesitation—this couldn't be happening!—then, as cries and moans welled up from those who had been struck down, the rest of us rushed forth.

Everyone struggled to pull the icy rubble off. Most of the pieces weren't much bigger than baseballs, but they were brittle and hard. Many of the Heirs who staggered up from the ground were bleeding from their hands, arms, and faces. Yet as we pulled them out, I could see that most had suffered relatively slight injuries: just cuts and bruises. Although some of these people cried out or wept, most of them looked more surprised than badly wounded. A few even laughed, as if what had happened were nothing more than a tasteless final trick that the monument had played on them.

At some point I noticed a group of Heirs hovering around a fallen figure. Whoever it was seemed badly hurt. I watched a while, unsure what to do, until I realized that the person lying there was Norroi. At once I rushed over.

The old man lay crumpled on his left side. He seemed to be unconscious. Some of the Heirs around him tried tugging him into a sitting position. Despite the Tirno's slight physique, their efforts met with only partial success; he kept slumping to the ground.

"What happened?" I asked. "What happened?"
The Heirs made way for me.

At once I sized up the situation. Blood welled
up from a long cut on the Tirno's scalp; a bloody
fist-sized fragment of ice lay an arm's-length from
his body.

I crouched. I eased my hand under his neck and
leaned over him to examine the wound better. As
I did so, the old man squeezed his eyes shut
tightly, then forced them open, like someone wakened too early from a nap. He looked up at me in
bewilderment.

I felt immensely relieved. "Norroi—don't scare
me like that."

"I should have ducked," he said. The Tirno
reached up to his head, touched the wound, pulled
back a bloody hand, and stared at his red fingers.

But a moment later I saw that his hand wasn't
what held Norroi's attention.

I looked up. Everyone around us had fallen silent. I eased back from the Tirno and looked
around.

Norroi, the Masters, and all the Heirs were
looking at what remained of the mountain monument. Not much of it remained but a pile of ice
fragments and, poking out of its center, a much
smaller pyramid than what we had just destroyed.
Unlike the ice mountain, this one was made of
stone: gray granite. It stood about ten feet tall.
Streaming wet and still crusted with ice, it nonetheless seemed relatively free of the massive layers that had encased it till just now.

"Get it loose," Loftossotoi commanded.

No one present would have needed his orders.
The Heirs nearest this stone object approached it
at once, chipping at the remaining layers with
their tools; the Masters themselves drew close to
watch.

Within fifteen or twenty minutes they had freed

it almost entirely. What stood before us resembled nothing so much as the Culling Stones—those mountain monuments rising from all other cities within the Mountain Land—only smaller. I saw one other difference right away. This stone pyramid revealed a triangle of lines etched into its surface parallel and close to its outer edges. Although I'd never seen anything similar, I knew at once that it was a door. It was about nine feet long on each side and equilateral in shape. Black rope forming complex knots bound the corners to a hole bored into the stone at their adjacent angles. The door itself revealed Rixtir symbols of an unfamiliar sort: blocky and crude. The overall effect was of a barrier simultaneously prohibiting our passage and daring us to attempt it.

"Open it," I said in Rixtir.

At once three of the Masters' attendants began struggling with the knots. Two of them knelt to untie the lower corners; a third mounted a little bench to work on the apex. None of them made much progress at first, for the knots were stiff from age and still coated with ice. None of the servants spoke while they worked, but everyone present could have sensed their frustration. The Masters themselves watched without comment, revealing neither anxiety nor dread. Yet I could detect some sort of excitement: the occasional glance from one to another; subtle motions of fingers touching to make the Upward-to-the-Summit gesture; a barely audible murmur of what could only have been prayer. It's a good thing they were patient, too, for the knots were just the start. Even as the ropes came apart, the attendants couldn't get the door open. The wood, having absorbed moisture over so many years, had expanded enough to lodge tightly in the doorway. It wouldn't budge. At last the men resorted to using their shoulders and feet and, with a series of concerted jolts and kicks, literally shoved the door in like a stubborn cork prodded into a wine bottle. The great triangular plug split into three separate pieces that the Heirs then carried out one by one.

Firelight angled down a wide stone staircase. All that shoving and pounding had loosed so much dust that we couldn't see much at first other than the swirling pall itself. Loftossotoi descended; at his signal, two attendants joined him. The rest of us waited, uncertain. When the Icemaster came up again, he spoke a few words that I couldn't follow, but their import was plain: we were to follow. I would go first. Then the Masters. Then a scattering of Adepts. Then Norroi, supported on both sides by some attendants. Then more Adepts.

The staircase led me down into a subterranean vault whose walls widened along the same angles as those of the pyramid above: the visible monument was merely the entrance to a more substantial room below. I couldn't see much initially, for the lamps seemed to bring in shadows rather than light. But as more people entered, each with a lamp, the room grew brighter; and as Loftossotoi directed the attendants to stand in a wide circle around the Masters, we saw more and more clearly what the room contained.

It was a kind of armory: not of weapons, but of something else. Gear. Mountaineering gear. Gear of sorts I'd never seen before. Every wall held racks of staffs, pikes, axes, hatchets, and hammers, many of each kind, each separated from the others, each in perfect order. Huge baskets of other implements—awl-like devices, knives, and tools I couldn't even recognize—stood waist-high on the ground before each rack. Other baskets overflowed with rope. Puzzled, I stepped forward to examine them; when I reached forth to pull some out, I touched a fibrous substance different from any I could recall. This wasn't the Rixtir rope

I'd seen elsewhere: ceremonial rope, ritual rope. This was real rope. I held a length, let it dangle, then tugged it with both hands. It seemed both delicate and powerful. I set it back in the basket when I noticed everyone else watching me. But there was no sense of dismay or prohibition in their gaze: simply interest in my response. I walked over to another basket and picked up one of the hatchets. It was considerably smaller than a modern ice-axe; its shaft was shorter, too, and its tip angled more steeply. I couldn't identify the alloy: darker than bronze but not as black as iron. A quick glance suggested that it hadn't been hammered into shape, but cast. I hefted it once or twice. Nicely balanced. What use its maker intended for it, I couldn't tell. For ice? Stone? All I knew is that it resembled nothing I'd ever seen in the Mountain Land or anywhere else. Intrigued and shaken, I set this tool back in its basket. Then, while the others watched, I walked from one basket to another, from one rack to the next, hefting and testing each of these implements in turn.

How many people would this room equip for a climb? Four hundred? Five? And for what kind of climb?

"How long have these things been here?" I asked.

No response.

"Who made them?"

Again no response.

I grew uneasy. My questions settled like the dust that coated everything around us.

Then a soft voice said, "The Founders."

It was Norroi who spoke. Braced by his attendants, the old man looked scarcely able to stay on his feet, yet he spoke as calmly as ever.

"The Founders made all this?"

"The Founders—and the Mountain-Drawn of

their own time. Everything has been here since they made them.''

"And you *knew*?" I asked. "Knew all along?"

"I did not know," answered Norroi. "I merely—"

"Why didn't you tell me?"

"I did. Or tried to."

I pondered the situation for a while: if what Norroi said was true, all this gear had lain entombed for almost four hundred years.

Then Loftossotoi spoke: "We should have known. We were fools not to know. But surely this ignorance—even my own ignorance—was the Founders' will. It was not wrong for these things to lie here undiscovered. It was not foolish for the Mountain-Drawn to wait all this time for you to discover them. Waiting has served its own purpose.''

Ignoring him, I reached over to one of the racks again and picked up an ice-hatchet. It felt heavy and strong, altogether a different device from anything the Heirs had ever shown me. I hefted it, felt its power. What ice could withstand its force?

"Well, then," I said. "Enough of waiting."

With those words, I climbed the steps out of that armory and walked out to the gathering place and the legion of Heirs waiting there. They fell silent when they saw me.

I raised the ice-hatchet in my right hand, shook it, and shouted, "Upward to the Summit!"

Their deafening cry came back at once:

"Upward to the Summit!"

[Jesse O'Keefe, journal entry, dated the Twenty-eighth Day of the First Moon-span, Sundecline (January 8, 1922).]

* * *

So the Rixtirra have been sitting on a cache of mountaineering gear for nearly four centuries. Maybe longer: who knows when it was made? But it's been here all along, a hidden stash of real equipment that may well allow them to do what they've wanted from the start but have been forbidden and unable to do.

How many people have known about this stuff? None, it seems. Given what's at stake, would even the Masters have feigned ignorance? Or is it one of their little secrets? A way for them to find out what *I* know?

And what will this stash really make possible? From what I saw, it's real equipment—real ropes, tools, clothing, and hardware of a sort that people could use to climb a real mountain—all of it a far cry from the sacramental trinkets I've seen throughout my stay in the High Realm. I couldn't examine anything closely or at length, but it looked pretty convincing. More than just convincing: impressive. I've never seen anything even remotely like it anywhere. The materials were substantial, the craftsmanship sophisticated, the designs remarkable. Some of the clothes looked as warm and durable as anything I've ever seen. The ropes were supple and strong. The fittings on the climbing tools had been crafted from alloys unlike any elsewhere in the Mountain Land. Yet what are the sources of all this stuff? Why did the Mountain-Drawn lose their capacity to make these kinds of equipment and resort to using sacred gewgaws instead? Perhaps more important: if properly outfitted with this stockpile, what would a Rixtir force be able to accomplish? How many people could set out to find the Mountain? To climb it? To reach the top?

I can't answer these questions. I'm still too stunned by what I saw to ponder them fully. All I know is that I've been shown the artifacts of an ancient indigenous technology. The Rixtirra's predecessors invented this stuff, made it, and stored it. The contemporary Rixtirra have not only lost the knowledge of the old technology, they aren't even clear about what to do with what they've found.

Where does that leave me?

Showing them.

[Jesse O'Keefe, journal entry, dated the Fourth Day of the Second Moon-span, Sundecline (January 12, 1922).]

The Mountain Stone has revealed the way.

Of course, from the start this miniature of the peak has indicated our ultimate goal; given a little time, it will no doubt reveal the path from base to summit. But how to reach the base? That's the question.

The Mountain Stone hasn't solved all our problems; still, it's at least giving us the means to solve them. Whatever else, it has given us a better chance than the Masters ever did. We have the tools now—the *matériel* to get us started. Whether we find our way, I have no idea. What I know is that we can at least try.

So here's the plan:

We'll find Forster Beckwith and his Umbrage lackeys. We'll follow them into the Inner Realm. We'll let their use of the Diadem lead not only their expedition, but ours as well, to the Mountain. And by some means we'll neutralize them, end their pretentions to the climb, and proceed ourselves to the Summit.

The Heirs are ready, eager, almost desperate to begin. I've already given the Masters my command to get started.

* * *

Norroi appears to be less badly hurt than I first thought. His scalp wound is serious, yet the Heirs have bandaged it with a poultice to stanch the old man's bleeding. Norroi himself seems a bit dazed but otherwise unhurt. Loftossotoi convinced him to rest a while—no mean feat with the Tirno.

So as nearly as I can tell, nothing argues against proceeding.

Tonight we'll be off.

[Jesse O'Keefe, journal entry, dated the Fifth Day of the Second Moon-span, Sundecline (January 13, 1922).]

This afternoon, as the Heirs mobilized to abandon the Veil—a few thousand people having already left, hundreds more getting ready—I prepared my own gear and engaged in some last-minute planning with the Masters. Right after nightfall Norroi, Loftossotoi, and I will set off as well, cross the snowfield, and catch up with the others.

I waited alone for a long time, watching the sunset's molten hues permeate the ice, the glacier ignited by the fire beyond. Except for the sun's slow descent, little moved around me. The place was still. Of course, the Veil has always had a strange mood about it, at once tumultuous and calm, its frozen state overwhelming virtually all activity; even so, seeing the place nearly deserted soon unnerved me. I set off to find whoever else was around.

The sequence of events that brought me to Loftossotoi's room is irrelevant. What matters is that I arrived there, and that the room was empty. My intentions were good: I meant only to find him.

Once there, however, I couldn't help but glance around. I'd never seen a Master's room without a whole coterie of Heirs present. Curiosity got the best of me.

Clothes rolled up and tied with leather thongs . . . Climbing gear in a pack . . . Sacramental objects of some sort lined up next to a box . . . Documents (whether religious or secular, I have no idea) rolled up in scrolls . . .

These last drew my attention at once. Except for the letters I'd intercepted from Aeslu last summer—letters I mistook initially for prayer scrolls—I've never seen more than a few scraps of Rixtir writing. Did the Masters write differently from anyone else?

Something else caught my eye. One of these scrolls was paper. Not cloth, as the Mountain-Drawn use: paper.

Without hesitation I picked up the scroll, slid off its restraining band, unfurled it, and read.

Seems this gal is some sort of princess. What kind, exactly, I'm hard put to tell you. I tend to get my princesses all mixed up. She's daughter of the moon—or maybe that's granddaughter of the moon, Mom and Pop themselves being the celestial offspring, Sonnol and Lissal. Got that? You figure it out. In any case, she gets a lot of attention here, even from people who don't care for her personally. The local myth has it that Aeslu will be the bride of whomever proves himself son of the sun—or is that grandson of sunny, son of the sun—at which point the happy couple will go off to a honeymoon atop the highest peak of 'em all . . .

The words struck hard—words in *English*.

For a while I was prime suitor for the lady's hand. I really had her bowled over. She knew it—knew it in her heart, her bones, her loins. She is the moon, I am the sun, and by our own melded light we would find the long-lost peak and climb it to the top. Why not? As I said, what matters isn't the truth so much as what the people here take it to be. If they wanted to declare me the sun incarnate, I won't quibble. Fine and dandy. It beats what I've gotten stuck doing at F. F. Beckwith & Sons.

By now I raced through the pages I held.

. . . addle-brained doughboy . . . Jesse O'Keefe . . . chap had caught a few too many whiffs of mustard gas . . . had decided he was the long-awaited lover for the moon-child . . . managed to cast aspersions on my character . . . I lost my cool and made a few false moves. Then this Jesse fellow overstepped himself, too; his fortunes took a rapid decline . . . About the girl, though: we crossed paths not long ago.

About the girl, though: we crossed paths not long ago.

Aeslu is alive. *Aeslu is alive!*

And the Masters know it.

How long have they known? Days? Weeks? The exact length doesn't really matter. What matters is that they've known—and that they've kept their knowledge from me.

I just don't understand. How could they do this? Never mind that I love her; that's a private matter. But she is, after all, the Moon's Stead—my partner in precisely the quest that the Heirs consider most important. It makes no sense that they should keep me from her, keep me ignorant of her survival and wellbeing.

Unless, of course, there's some other factor.

"We crossed paths not long ago." She's with Forster. Captive. Or is she? Ah, maybe there's the
catch. She's not really captive. But that's impossible. She'd never voluntarily ally herself with that
parasite. She may be near him; she may be among
his co-conspirators; but she isn't *with* them. So
why are the Heirs so hush-hush about the whole
thing? Would they be candid with me if they knew
Aeslu was a fifth column among the Umbrage?
This could only work to our advantage. It would
simplify our task. Above all, it would boost my
spirits, delight me, and make our endeavors all
the more worthwhile.

What else do they know that I don't? What, for
that matter, does Aeslu know that she isn't telling?

Aeslu, Aeslu—I don't really care what the Heirs
know that they won't tell me. But of all people
why are *you* keeping me in the dark?

6

January 12, 1922

Hail, Father!

Bad news today.

A messenger reached our camp around noon,
having worked his way into our valley from
parts east. These fellows appear from time to
time; in itself, his arrival wasn't cause for
alarm. The scroll he gave me, however,
changed everything.

Since I can't make heads or tails out of the
Rixtirs' chicken-scratch, I handed the missive
to Aeslu. She read it slowly, then read it again.

I tried to guess at her response but couldn't make sense of her expression.

She turned to me. "Jassikki," said Aeslu, "is leading the Heirs toward the Inner Realm."

How should I have reacted? I couldn't think of anyone I wanted around less than Jesse O'Keefe, yet I couldn't really take his presence seriously. What threat, if any, did he present? Even with a horde of Heirs, he wouldn't be likely to muster much of a challenge against my fully outfitted Umbrages. Jesse himself didn't worry me.

It was someone else who gave me pause. I felt the same unease I'd felt when I heard Aeslu calling out to him in her sleep. A dream-cry like that tells the truth. What truth, though? And what would the present news evoke in her heart?

Aeslu had said nothing since she first finished reading the message still gripped in her hands. She looked more at ease than I would have expected. Then she said, "We must leave at once for the Mountain."

7

[Message from an anonymous Umbrage spy to Forster Beckwith at the Umbrage high camp; dated the Eighth Day of the Second Moon-span, Sundecline (January 17th, 1922).]

Upward to the Summit!

Led by Jassikki the Throw-Pall-of-Gist, an Heir forthsetting of at least eight hundred persons has left the Veil and is now on its way to the pass between Leqsiffaltho and Lorssa. Unobstructed, this group will cross over into Lorssa within about two days.

Reports from sources elsewhere indicate that smaller forthsettings have meanwhile crossed from Makb, Zua, Iqtiqqissi, and Qallitti into Leqsiffaltho. All indications are that Heirs alone comprise these forthsettings, excepting perhaps a few of our confederates who have infiltrated the Heirs but are unable to communicate with us at this time.

We are unable to confirm rumors that still other forthsettings have departed from T'taspa, Nakixxo, Rokba, and other valleys, all with intent to enter the Inner Realm.

Upward to the Summit!

[Marcelino Hondero Huamán, formerly Marsalai S'safta, interviewed September 8, 1970.]

That first night we spent among the Heirs in their forthsetting, some sort of commotion started up just as all of us were settling down to sleep. First, shouts I couldn't understand. Then loud questions in Rixtir. Then more shouts—the first voice—now in our own language.

My wife and I listened from where we lay in our tent. We didn't worry too much at first: we were among Heirs. The Masters would take care of everything. When the noise continued, though, we pushed off our blankets and eased out of our tent for a look.

Mind you, it was dark. Clouds covered the moon. But whoever was approaching brought lamps, and their yellow light flickered all around. By this light I saw what was happening.

A big man strode into our midst. He was much taller than most Mountain-Drawn and thinner, too.

He wore Masters' robes—robes of exquisite weave—yet I knew at once that he was a Lowlander. His pale skin . . . His light-colored hair . . . Had I ever seen a Lowlander? No. But I knew. I just knew.

Anyway, this man strode in rather than walked—entered the camp so fast that the Masters with him could scarcely keep up his pace. And he shouted at everyone, shouted Lowland words that I couldn't understand. Not that I needed to: his meaning was plain enough. He was angry—no, furious. About what, I have no idea. But his rage was impossible to ignore. He was so angry that he soon woke everyone. Those among us who were already awake left their tents at once; everyone else now woke and urgently asked what was happening.

This Lowlander reached the center of our camp. The Masters, surrounded by their Adepts, Aspirants, and guards, soon followed. He kept shouting. Not all at once, but in bursts, like rockfall. After a while I realized that some of his words were in our own language: not quite what I expected them to sound like, but our words all the same.

—Mountain— and the Moon's Stead— then let us find it—

He alone spoke. Some of the Masters stood close to him, and one or two spoke among themselves, but no one spoke to him or to members of the forthsetting itself. The Lowlander stood facing the Masters. For a few moments neither he nor they spoke at all, but they simply faced one another. Then the Lowlander started shouting again and gesturing in the direction we had taken all that previous day—toward the Inner Realm.

"What is the matter?" asked my wife beside me. She had been asleep just before this commotion started; now, having watched a while, she turned to me. "Why is he shouting?"

"I don't know," I told her. "I don't even know who he is."

A woman near us turned to speak. "He's the Man of Knowledge," she said.

I asked, "*This* is the Man of Knowledge?"

"The Man of Knowledge, the Man of Light, the Healer of Wounds," said the woman.

[Message from an anonymous Heir spy to Jassikki and the Masters of the Veil at their camp near the pass between Leqsiffaltho and Lorssa; dated the Tenth Day of the Second Moon-span, Sundecline (January 19th, 1922).]

Upward to the Summit!

We have located the Umbrage forthsetting. At least seven hundred infidels have hidden themselves at the lower reaches of an icefall along the Sunsetting side of the Inner Realm. Although difficult to detect within the shadows that comprise their habitual abode, these Umbrage could not fully escape the Sun's light that ultimately revealed them to us.

It appears in addition that other Umbrage keep arriving at this camp and joining the infidels. These new arrivals do not constitute forthsettings of their own; instead, they are bands of a few men and women making their way over the pass to join the rest. Their limited number should not inspire any false confidence, however, as the constant trickle has already accumulated into a large pool.

As to what these Umbrage intend as their next move, we are unable to determine with any confidence. It would seem foolhardy for them to enter the Inner Realm by a route as heavily protected as what they have chosen. But of course they are Umbrage, thus fools.

Upward to the Summit!

[Juana Méndez de Mariátegui, formerly Huna-tau Mantassi of Va'atafissorih, interviewed September 8, 1970.]

What would you have me tell you? How we sneaked out of Ye'affissorih? How we made it up the valley without mishap? How some of the Masters' Guards detected us on the far side of the pass to Mtoffli? How they chased us, cornered Ottai and Loruqtu, and captured them? How I myself evaded the Guards simply because my companions grasped the hopelessness of their own fate and relinquished themselves to the Heirs' yoke—though not without a struggle!—and thus gave me a chance to escape?

I wish I could claim that I reached the Umbrage forthsetting by virtue of cleverness, strength, stamina, or insight into the Heirs' harsh ways. In fact, I arrived at the goal simply because my companions sacrificed themselves and made my own flight possible. I didn't really flee into the Umbrage camp—I *fell*! Tripping about in my effort to evade the Heirs, I lost my footing, tumbled down the icefield, and reached its lower reaches so dizzy and sore that I couldn't stay upright on my feet. So much for my brilliant escape.

Yet I did, after all, escape. This is what mattered. This is all that mattered. In some ways it's all that has ever mattered during the course of four hundred Sun-spans: that a few Umbrage have somehow slipped beyond the Heirs' grasp and made their way to safety. Now I straggled like those before me and found myself among others on the ice.

The camp was big. It wasn't as big as I'd hoped—I somehow imagined half the population of the Mountain Land there—but it was big enough. All I remember is the sense of delight that all these people were *Umbrage*. They hated the Masters. They loathed their ranks, their rituals, their incantations. This was evident from the moment I set foot among them. Warriors had accosted me as I approached, and rightly so; once they had determined my allegiance, however, they simply brought me into their fold. As simple as that! No ceremonies, no rites of passage. Just all kinds of people gathering to welcome me. Men, women, children—everyone—coming forth, smiling, embracing me, helping me into their midst, shouting, singing, and cheering as if to honor some sort of great dignitary. Of course I was nothing of the kind. They had no idea who I was. Yet they welcomed me. All they care about was that they were Umbrage—and so was I.

They led me through a complicated series of trenches dug in the ice. Then, abruptly, I found myself on a flat part of the glacier. Tents surrounded me, tents that looked like the glacier itself. They weren't really what surprised me most, however. It wasn't the place, but the people. Two especially.

At the center of the Umbrage camp stood a man and a woman. Everyone within sight of them—some two or three hundred people—gazed in their direction. For good reason, too. The man looked like none I'd ever seen before. With skin the dawn's pink and hair the color of flames, he could only have been the Sun in human form. The woman was striking in her own way: calm as the Moon herself.

I knew at once who they were. I knew at once that my journey was over. I knew at once that this

sacred pair would lead me—would lead all of us—
to the Summit.

This is what struck me most of all: how they
gazed at each other, how they lavished their light
and warmth on each other, how they illuminated
everyone around them with their love.

8

19 January 1922

O Father!

Everything has worked out as I planned, yet
somehow I feel a dissatisfaction, a
restlessness, far out of keeping with the
successes I have attained. The Umbrages are
all ready. Our equipment is complete. The
weather has begun to clear. Even so I feel
displeased with the situation—gnawed at from
within by some sort of mental parasite I can't
identify, much less exterminate.

Fear? No, I'm eager to face whatever lies
ahead.

Fatigue? On the contrary, I can't wait to be
off.

Impatience? That comes closer but doesn't
tell the whole story.

What, then? I simply don't know.

Perhaps I've simply spent so much time among
these aborigines that I'm losing my clarity of
mind. Or perhaps it's Jesse O'Keefe's
reappearance on the scene. In some ways it
makes no difference. I command the entire
expedition's loyalty; the shell-shocked
anthropologist can't stop us now. Aeslu is right:

there's no reason to delay our departure even a few more days.

Surely what I say about loyalty holds true not just for the others, but for Aeslu as well. Precisely what does she think of me? What does she want? What will she accept? Aeslu's commitment to the expedition is sufficient. She'll come along; she'll do her part; she'll work as hard as anyone toward the common goal. Yet despite her presence at the heart of this endeavor, she still seems elsewhere. She dresses in modern attire, eats modern food, converses with me in a modern language, and increasingly behaves in a modern manner. She even looks modern now and seems to have renounced most of her ancient ways. Why, then, does she seem so impervious to me, as if she still lies frozen in a crust of superstition which, properly thawed, would bring her supple and eager into my arms?

I can't answer this question. It makes less sense to try, however, than to continue dissolving the accretions that encase her. Thus my continuing campaign.

My trusty phonograph has been its chief instrument. The other Rixtirs seem helpless before the power of its charms; surely Aeslu will succumb as well. Each night we have a little dance to which all are invited, and each night I coax Aeslu into joining me for a spin. Last night I played her Bessie Smith's "St. Louis Blues" and "Lost Your Head Blues." I played her Jelly Roll Morton's "Grandpa's Spells." I played her Louis Armstrong's "Struttin' with Some Barbeque," "Potato Head Blues," and "Hotter Than That." I played her all sorts of things—enough for her to get the idea. Not only did she dance: she listened. I know she listened. Listened and *heard.* How do I know? Because she smiled. Who knows at what, but she got it, she almost got it. The jazz tickled her fancy; it almost lit her fire. If only she could have heard Louis live at the Apollo! Even Aeslu couldn't have resisted; she would have leaped up and boogied. How the cool cats would have gawked at this Indian maiden among them! How the flappers would have dropped their downy jaws!

Just in case my music didn't do the trick, I intensified its effect with the proper beverages. I don't have much of my wine stocks left, but what little remains will serve good purposes. She likes the stuff—champagne especially. No wonder. At this altitude it might as well be a hundred proof. How she resists the bubbly's influence as well as she does, I have no idea; but she's not immune to its charms.

More than these sensual delights, what lures this young lass closer to me is, of course, nothing more and nothing less than what we've undertaken in the first place. Aeslu wants the mountain. She wants the summit. The pleasures available en route hold no sway over this woman; her only interest is the final event. Ultimately all Aeslu wants is to find and climb the mountain.

Which brings home my own task as well. I can have my cake and eat it, too. Winning Aeslu, I win the mountain. Winning the mountain, I win Aeslu.

How neat. How tidy.

We depart tomorrow.

PART FOUR

"Why are you letting me use all these documents?"
"Because you want them."
"No one else does?"
"None who would understand."
"What makes you think I will?"
"Because you must."

1

[Jesse O'Keefe, journal entry, dated the Seventh Day of the Second Moon-span, Sundecline (January 16, 1922).]

The clouds dissipated briefly this afternoon and, like a dustcloth whisked from a sculpture, revealed the Mountain beneath. At once all activity in our camp halted. Everyone fell silent. Children fled to their parents. Men and women stood staring. Even the Masters, who had begun a complex obeisance when the peak appeared, soon fumbled, ceased their incantations, and merely gazed at the sight before them.

I gazed, too. There was no alternative.

Great buttresses of granite force their way up from the hills and tilt to form the lower cliffs. Ridges push still higher, giving the middle region of the peak its jagged silhouette. The upper reaches curve toward the top, tilt abruptly both right and left, then round out to form a vast summit dome. Ice coats almost the entire mass: fluted curtains near the top, rumpled accumulations halfway down, jumbled icefalls where the great glaciers thicken and spread out into the valley that they themselves have carved over the millennia. The ultimate effect of all this rock and ice is of something simultaneously rising and falling. The granite massif shoves its way into the sky; its mantle of ice continually descends toward the earth.

I don't know if this is the biggest mountain. I can't believe it's bigger than Everest or other peaks in the Himalaya. It's hard to imagine that this peak is bigger than mountains in the Hindu Kush or the Karakoram—bigger even than Chimborazo, Huascarán, Aconcagua, or other great South American peaks.

I don't even care. All I know is that here, now, it is the only mountain. The lesser peaks around it hardly deserve the name. They are nothing more than the first steps to the tower, the porch before the house. I scarcely notice them as the Mountain draws my vision.

How it looms, how it splits the clouds, how it shoves its way from earth to heaven!

[Aeslu of Vmatta, *Chronicle of the Last Days*.]

Ever since my childhood I had heard of this gateway, of its significance in keeping intruders out, and of the Inner Realm itself: perfect, remote, accessible only to the right people at the right time. Now was the right time. Yet as we approached, I knew that my companions were anything but the right people. On the contrary, they were the wrong ones altogether. The Man of Darkness and the Umbrage: who but they should those battlements have risen to block? Who but they should the sentries have stood ready to rebuff? Although I had failed to stop Forssabekkit and his minions, surely the Heirs who marked the line between the Middle and the Inner Realms would succeed.

Yet the gateway turned out to be far less than what I had anticipated: not a great citadel, but little more than a waystation; not an aerie overlooking some nearly unscalable cliff, but a cluster of stone huts on a long, low ridge; not an outpost for innumerable troops, but a resting place for no more than a few squadrons. Even from below we could see the weakness of their defenses. I watched, uneasy, baffled that one of the most important places in the whole Mountain Land could be so vulnerable. How could the Founders have left the Inner Realm so meagerly protected?

So this is the great barrier, said Forssabekkit when we took up our positions along the ridge opposite. For a long time he gazed through his distancelooker at the pass and at the handful of people defending it. After a while he said, It's not much more impressive than the hamlets we've been passing through.

I wanted to discourage him in any way possible. The appearance is deceptive, I said. Perhaps the defenses lie within the cliff itself. The warriors must be hiding there.

He laughed. Let them hide, then!

How could I have stopped him? The more I pleaded, cajoled, or threatened, the more this Man of Ignorance would have suspected my intentions. I could only hope that the Heirs guarding the pass were more numerous, more alert, more able than they appeared.

The Umbrage at our backs grew more and more restless as Forssabekkit gazed through the valley's trench of air at the Heirs' outpost. He said nothing to acknowledge the urgency they felt. Then, without speaking further, he stood, scrambled over the outcropping of rocks that had protected us, and eased his way down the slope into the valley.

I hesitated at first, then followed. The Umbrage followed, too, hundreds of them, a trickle at first, then a rivulet, a stream, a river, a flood, until the entire hillside was awash in Umbrage. Down they flowed till they reached the valley floor; never hesitating, they waded across the real stream coursing through that valley; and they soon began their unnatural flow up the other side.

I wondered even at the time if the Heirs posted

above us could have repelled a smaller force. Even now I have no idea how many faced us. Thirty? Forty? No more than that. Commanding the high ground, they might well have held the heights against five or six times their number. They could have slung rocks and picked us off, one by one, as we came up the slope. They could have met us halfway and, jabbing at us with pikes or swinging at us with maces, could have beat us back. If all else failed, they could have shoved boulders down on us. Indeed, they did all these things and more, yet their tactics failed simply because the Umbrage forthsetting was so big. We numbered at least one thousand adults and almost half again that many children. Even before we worked our way up to their ramparts, I realized that the Masters (perhaps even the Founders long before them) had never imagined that so many people would push forth at once toward the Inner Realm. Perhaps they never really imagined that the Umbrage would swell like a multitude of raindrops into this torrent.

Here they were now. Scrambling, scampering, clawing their way up the hillside, Forssabekkit's legions followed him toward the pass. Some of the Umbrage could scarcely keep up with the big Lowlander; even so, they moved fast. Within a short while this crowd had climbed to within a few manlengths of the valley's rim.

Guards came forth to meet us. Three Masters, arms outstretched and hands open, led their procession. At least thirty warriors accompanied them. I saw all the weapons I had expected: slings, maces, pikes, clubs. The warriors fanned out, taking their battle stances.

The Master in front bellowed, Who are you, and why have you approached the Inner Realm?

I faltered, unable to speak.

Forssabekkit heard what the Master had said

but did not understand the words. He told me, Go ahead.

I forced myself to translate. Then at once I told the Master, I am Aeslu of Vmatta. We are on our way to climb the Mountain Made of Light.

By whose authority do you seek the Mountain?

By my own, I called back, for I am the Moon's Stead. With me is the Sun's Stead—the Man of Light, the Man of Knowledge, the Healer of Wounds.

Never mind that I almost gagged in saying what I said; I had to speak these words. I had to do whatever would please Forssabekkit while at the same time bringing down the Heirs' wrath upon us.

At that moment Forssabekkit asked, What's the deal?

I am telling them who we are.

He responded with even more contempt than I anticipated: What difference does it make? I'm not here to present credentials. Just tell him to let us pass.

I ignored him. If I could just signal the Masters! Already I could see some of the Umbrage fanning out on each side as they prepared to storm the stronghold. At the same time, I noticed some of the Masters' guards loading their slings, lowering their pikes, raising their maces—

The Master sensed how quickly the scene before him had deteriorated. In the name of the Sun and the Moon, he chanted, and by the authority of the Founders who brought their light to the Mountain-Drawn—

Let's get this over with, said Forssabekkit.

At once he stepped forth. The Umbrage followed.

A scattering of stones thumped down on the crowd. I heard screams and cries of pain. Just then the Heirs rushed us, their pikes lowered and maces swinging. More thuds and screams. Yet within a few eyeblinks the Umbrage had overwhelmed that pitiable squadron; the Heirs toppled backwards; the crowd surged over them; the warriors' own squeals and shouts faded into the roar of the Umbrage battle cry: Upward to the Summit!

The Masters turned and fled, yet almost at once they, too, fell beneath the flood of Umbrage swirling over them. After that, reaching the ridge itself took no effort at all.

A few of the Umbrage lingered at the rim. Gazing back or else into the next valley, these men, women, and children called out to one another in shrill, eager cries:

Upward to the Summit!

—to the Summit!

—the Summit!

Upward—!

So little room remained that the force of the people still working their way up pushed those already there onward against their will. No one really cared. We were all too excited, too eager, too pleased.

All but one.

[Jesse O'Keefe, journal entry, dated the Tenth Day of the Second Moon-span, Sundecline (January 19, 1922).]

Even a brief glance at the Mountain has jolted all the Heirs into a state of high alertness. It came into view for only a few minutes but long enough to intensify our desire to seek the goal. Everyone here is ready.

As am I.

Yet I can't help but feel uneasy over how events have taken shape. I'm eager to find the Mountain but can't shake a sense of alarm to be doing so as I am. I lead the Heirs but resent how the Masters have manipulated me. What else have they neglected to explain? What have they told me that isn't true? And of course I'm leading the Heirs alone. Aeslu ought to be here with me, but she isn't. Her absence gnaws at me; her presence among the Umbrage corrodes my confidence in what I'm doing. The *wrongness* of the situation at once drives me forward and makes me falter.

I can't tolerate a delay much longer. I need to know where Aeslu is. I need to find out what's happening, why I haven't heard from her, why she hasn't explained herself. Are the Masters aware of my anxiety? Are they aware of its source as well? I can't let them know what I'm feeling. Yet I can't suppress it, either—which only intensifies my anger over how they've kept me in the dark.

Much effort this morning to maintain order in our camp, which is in upheaval after the cold, the wind, and the unfamiliar circumstances kept hundreds of the ill-seasoned Heirs sleepless all night. Everyone is exhausted and unruly. Even overnight our ranks swelled from four thousand to nearly five. (This despite the Masters' insistence that late-comers have lost their chance.) People just kept showing up.

The question now is not just what to do but how to do it. Sneaking five thousand men, women, and children into the next valley won't be a trick we accomplish by sleight of hand. How, then? That remains to be seen.

Later.
After working all day to secure the camp—setting up a perimeter with sentries at regular intervals, establishing a network of messengers, and so forth—I returned to my tent. I needed to rest. Our

altitude isn't much higher than fifteen or sixteen thousand feet, but the long march yesterday has left me weary. I also needed time to think. Hence my retreat.

Someone greeted me as I entered: "Upward to the Summit."

It was Norroi.

"You!" I exclaimed. "I wasn't even sure you'd come along."

"Maybe I have," he said. "Maybe not." The Tirno eased himself to the floor, pulled off his cat-like cap, and set it on his knees. He looked weary—no, exhausted. His scalp wound lay hidden under a leafy poultice. I felt a twinge of pity for the old man. How had he withstood the rigors of this trip? Yet his sporadic disappearing act frustrated me all the same. I said, "I've been worried about you. You don't seem well."

"Maybe so. Maybe not."

"If you're able to manage, fine. Otherwise you should stay put. If you're coming with us, I need to count on you."

"Always," he told me. "That is what Tirnora do."

I couldn't restrain my exasperation. "Norroi, I need help—not a game of hide-and-seek."

He gestured vaguely with both hands. "Here I am."

I reached out to him brusquely and grabbed a shoulder with each hand. "Are you? Are you?" I asked, shaking him. "Are you really?" I shook him so hard that his head bobbed. I may as well have been shaking a scarecrow. "Because if you can't be more reliable—"

At some point I realized that the old man had gone limp in my hands. I wasn't just shaking him; I was supporting him. His eyes ceased focusing on me and strayed about in their sockets. Then he slumped forward into my arms. Norroi caught himself, but so weakly that I still had to hold him up.

Now a new wave of emotion hit me: remorse. I slung an arm around the Tirno and eased him back till he lay on the floor. "Norroi, I'm sorry. Are you all right?"

He stared up at me, then away. "I want to help you."

"All right, I believe you. Are you hurt?"

He shook his head.

"Norroi, listen to me: Aeslu is alive."

He nodded.

I stared at him, listening to the silence between us. "You know, *too*?"

Again he nodded.

"How long have you known?"

The Tirno shrugged. "A while."

"How long, damn it!"

"It makes no difference. What matters—"

"It makes all the difference in the world! And it's not the first time this has happened, either. First regarding Forster. Then the secret climbing gear. Now it turns out you've known about Aeslu as well."

The old man looked genuinely perplexed. He reached up to his head with one hand, braced the tangle of leaves strapped there, and retained the pose as if in pain.

When he said nothing, I went on: "If you knew she wasn't dead, why didn't you tell me?"

"I did not *know* she was alive. I thought it likely."

"*Likely!*"

"Likely, too, that the Umbrage had captured her."

"Wonderful—that makes it all just fine."

Before I could lose my temper, the Tirno stopped me with the bony finger he jabs into my chest at such times. It had no force but silenced me anyway. "I did not know if Aeslu was alive or dead. I hoped for the best and feared the worst. This much I knew: if she survived, then no doubt the Umbrage had found her. Perhaps Forssabekkit had, too. Either way, you were in no shape to help her. Someday soon you will help her. Not yet, though. How ready were you earlier? Ready to fight Forssabekkit? Fight the Umbrage? You would have been lost—and Aeslu lost with you."

"I just don't understand," I told him. "We're talking about Aeslu, right? Aeslu? The Moon's Stead? If I recall correctly, I'm involved somewhere in this situation. Something about being the Man of Knowledge, the Sun's Stead—her mate and partner in the quest for the Mountain? I can believe that the Masters would try keeping me in the dark—but I still can't believe *you* would."

"I never kept you in the dark," Norroi said.

"Ha! Then why didn't you tell me earlier?"

"Because I did not know."

"You just said you did."

"I said I thought it likely—"

"You still should have told me."

"The right time had not yet come. If you waited—"

"That's my whole point!" I shouted. "I shouldn't have to wait. I'm the Man of Knowledge, damn it! I make the decisions. But how can I if everyone holds back the most important information I need? Can't you grasp why this matters to me? Aeslu! I've thought about her and I've longed for her ever since what happened at the City of Rope. Night after night I've wondered how she died, whether she suffered or not. Was there something I could have done? Could I have saved her life? Now it turns out she's alive. Not just alive—captured by Forster Beckwith. Can't you see what that does to me?"

"I can. I do."

"No you don't. Not a bit—"

"I see you shouting and waving your hands—"

"—because otherwise you wouldn't have strung me along like this—"

"Jassikki—"

"—and wouldn't still be doing it."

"Jassikki—"

"Hear me out."

"Jassikki, please listen."

"No, *you* listen to *me*."

Norroi fell silent. I went on a while longer, but soon his silence cut me short. At last he said, "You are so angry you can scarcely hear my words. This is why I said nothing earlier. You would not have heard me. Even now you hear only your own anger. Is this how to rescue Aeslu? Or will you run right into whatever trap the Umbrage have set for you?"

"What trap?" I asked, watching him suspiciously.

"Who knows?"

"Just as I thought—you don't even know." My voice grew louder and louder as I spoke. "Why should I trust anything you tell me?"

He made a quick wave with one hand: brushing me away. "Perhaps I won't tell you anything," he said. "You never listen to me any more."

"What do you mean?"

"You are so angry you no longer think. Why do you imagine I have held off till now? Because you are about to ruin everything."

"Explain," I told him.

"Why should I explain? You will not listen."

"All right, then—I'll listen."

"You will not listen."

"Norroi—*explain*!"

Before he could continue, however, he raised a hand in his familiar warning. Norroi turned his right ear toward the tent's door and listened a moment. "Soon," he said. "Now help me up. People are coming."

I pulled the old man to his feet.

[Aeslu of Vmatta, *Chronicle of the Last Days*.]

I awoke on the Fifteenth Day of the Second Moon-span, Sundecline, to find the whole Umbrage camp engulfed in snow. Snow whirled down everywhere. The air was so thick that I could hardly see my own outstretched hand, much less the peaks, glaciers, ridges, or grasslands—even the tents around me.

At first this sight filled me with dread. Not since my attempted escape from Forssabekkit's camp in late Sunrebirth had I seen snowfall of such intensity. The wind drove snow against us so powerfully that it seemed less a blizzard than an avalanche. The whole Umbrage forthsetting seemed on the verge of being swept off the glacier into the valley below.

Then I realized my folly. What more could I have asked? What better than to have Forssabekkit and his minions thrown into disarray, perhaps even purged altogether, precisely as they set off to accomplish what I wanted them to fail at attempting? This storm was not a nemesis but an ally. No doubt the Sun and the Moon had created it—had exerted their will against the infidels and now prepared to end their unholy quest. So much the better if the wind and the snow conspired to sweep us all away! If nothing else, the storm would alarm even the Man of Ignorance enough to make him delay his departure. He would think twice about traveling in this kind of weather.

Yet when Forssabekkit came to my tent he said, We're leaving this afternoon.

I was dumbfounded. I asked, In a blizzard?

There's no alternative.

We shall perish—all of us!

That's a chance we'll take. Even so, I expect the storm to ease up by nightfall.

And if you are mistaken?

Then we'll take a drubbing.

You would risk everyone's lives?

The Man of Ignorance shrugged. Not everyone's.

His lack of concern appalled me. These people may have been Umbrage, but they were still Mountain-Drawn; they were human beings. Despite my contempt for them, despite even my hope that their forthsetting would collapse far from its goal, I could not simply wish them into oblivion. Would the Man of Ignorance play so freely with their well-being?

These are perfect conditions, he told me. No one can see us leave. No one would be stupid enough to try following. With wind like this, we'll leave no tracks.

What if the Umbrage refuse to go along with your plan?

Forssabekkit laughed at my question. Refuse to go along? They can hardly restrain themselves, they're so eager.

I grew desperate for reasons to delay our departure. But how, I asked, shall they pass the time till we leave?

The Man of Ignorance shrugged. Let them do whatever they want. Have them check their equipment, tell stories, count snowflakes.

But surely—

As for you and me, Forssabekkit continued, I have another sort of entertainment in mind.

I was too startled to reply.

He smiled. Once you've announced the plan, he told me, come back here to the tent. We'll crank up the old phonograph and dance the afternoon away.

[Jesse O'Keefe, journal entry, dated the Fourteenth Day of the Second Moon-span, Sundecline (January 23, 1922).]

Traveling in a heavy snowfall, we crossed over the pass into the Inner Realm this morning. We reached the lip of the next valley right around noon but held back before proceeding. The Heirs' outpost had been decimated: the battlements damaged, the ramparts breached, the hillside strewn with corpses. To make matters worse, the snow was coming down so hard by then that we couldn't proceed without risking the expedition's safety.

"Umbrage," was all that Loftossotoi said as we surveyed the devastation.

"The Man of Ignorance," added Marhaislu.

There was no reason to doubt their assumptions. The whole place wasn't just destroyed, it was defiled—the walls splashed with blood.

Loftossotoi urged immediate pursuit; Marhaislu counseled greater caution. "We must bury the dead," she told the Icemaster. "Besides"—and here she motioned toward the five or six thousand Heirs massed in the vale below—"we cannot risk going ahead in such weather."

As their only superior, I decided in the Stonemaster's favor. It seemed wise for strategic reasons to wait. I didn't want the already weary Heirs to expend all their energy right at the outset. No doubt this storm would slow down not only our own force, but the Umbrage as well. So we hunkered down to wait.

Later, as the morning slid toward afternoon, three of the Masters and I crept up to the fissured knife-edge to peer down on the other side. We couldn't see much: the whole valley was obliterated by the storm. The wind wasn't especially intense, but the air had turned opaque with snow. We couldn't hear much, either—just the hiss of all that ice against rock and, when the wind eased briefly, the distant rush of water streaming out of the glacier's low edge far below us.

None of the Masters spoke. I was not alone in finding this view a source of dread.

Then, without warning, something caught my attention.

Marhaislu said, "We must—" but I silenced her.

"What is it?" asked Loftossotoi.

I hushed him as well.

We peered again into the half-light.

Below, to the left, came a noise I couldn't identify but couldn't ignore: a more complex texture under the static of the storm.

"The Umbrage," I told them. "I can't tell you exactly where, but they're down there on the ice."

Loftossotoi's response verged on outrage: "On the ice? But how? The storm will devour them alive."

"Maybe so. Or maybe they just want us to think so. But I'm still sure that's where they are."

The wind shifted and intensified; the updraft from below nearly shoved us back. Wrapping our cloaks around us tighter, we forced ourselves to hold our ground. Within a few moments the storm had coated us white.

Then, abruptly, one of those lulls came that transform the sharpest blast into total calm. The wind's shriek died; the rush of water reached us once again.

Something else did, too.

Music.

At first I thought I was imagining it, but the

Masters turned to me at precisely that moment as if for an explanation.

Music. Unmistakably music.

To my bewilderment, I recognized it: Jelly Roll Morton's "Black Bottom Stomp."

[Aeslu of Vmatta, *Chronicle of the Last Days.*]

Forssabekkit was right. Snow provided the perfect conditions for his purposes. Just as I once slipped away from the Umbrage by cloaking myself in a blizzard, so also did the Umbrage now hide in the folds of billowing snow. Over a thousand men, women, and children packed up their camp, loaded it onto their backs, and trudged up the glacier. Not only did the storm hide us from anyone who might have been watching; the wind muffled our noise as well.

This is not to say that our departure was simple, easy, or safe. Sneaking more than a thousand people up and over the glacier would have proved difficult under any circumstances. The glacier was both long and steep. Finding our way, even on a clear day, would have been treacherous. What were the odds that we could cross over without losing half the Umbrage present?

I know nothing of odds. All I know is that I underestimated Forssabekkit in two ways at once.

First, his skill. The Man of Ignorance knew more about finding his way up the glacier than I had ever thought possible. Despite the blizzard, Forssabekkit went forth unrelentingly: he probed the snow underfoot with his long-handled Lowland ice hatchet, peered into the blast, even sniffed the wind to find a safe path. He led us upward quickly and without hesitation.

Second, I underestimated his indifference even to his own people. Where the Man of Ignorance

led, the Umbrage followed. They would happily
have jumped off the highest cliff if Forssabekkit
himself had done so first. Small wonder, then, that
the Umbrage staggered after him eagerly despite
the massive packs burdening them, despite the
ropes entangling them, despite the ice underfoot.
In the midst of that storm, we could not even see
the glacier that we strove to ascend; all we knew
was that it would be deadly to traverse. True, it
served as a ramp from the valley floor to the peaks
themselves. But what a treacherous ramp! Great
ice fissures crossed this expanse of ice from one
side to the other—fissures at least half a man-
length across; in some instances one, two, even
five or ten man-lengths wide; and each fissure
would plunge deep into the glacier below. In addition to the obvious cracks, others were partly or
completely hidden by layers of snow and ice—
cracks no more evident to us than camouflaged
hunters' pits are evident to beasts in the forest—
which waited hungrily to swallow each of us upon
the slightest misstep. Time after time I heard the
screams of Umbrage whose bad luck took them
into the glacier's jaws, or, worse yet, Umbrage
whose rope linked them to someone else whose
own fall took two, three, four, even a whole line
of others down with them.

The people, I blurted, trying to keep up with
Forssabekkit. What about the people—?

He scarcely turned to respond. What about
them?

Forssa—so many are perishing.

Now he slowed, stopped, turned to me. The blast
striking him head-on had left his whole body encased in snow. Ice crusted his face. Lumps of ice
clung to his beard. Little icicles dangled from his
mustache like fangs.

If they want the mountain, he told me, they have
to climb it. He gazed at me a long time without

any emotion visible on his features. Then he added, If they thought it would be easy or safe, they shouldn't have come at all.

[Jesse O'Keefe, journal entry, dated the Sixteenth Day of the Second Moon-span, Sundecline (January 25, 1922).]

The blizzard trapped us in our camp all yesterday. We could have attempted a raid on the Umbrage anyway, of course, but not without great hazard. Chasing Forster would have been risky under the best of circumstances; I couldn't tolerate the thought of endangering any Heirs' lives by facing two enemies instead of one. For this reason we just hunkered down, bided our time, and hoped for the best. Surely even Forster Beckwith wouldn't be so reckless as to pull up stakes in such harsh weather.

I was wrong. Well before dawn this morning, once we made it over the pass and crept up to the glacier, we saw no sign of the Umbrage. At first I attributed their absence to the sophisticated camouflage these people have mastered. Loftossotoi, Marhaislu, and I went ahead for a better look. Still no Umbrage. Again we drew closer. Again no sign. All we detected were some puzzling marks on the ice—spots, lines, stains—but no people or equipment.

The Umbrage are gone. How they managed to leave during the blizzard, I have no idea—still less where they went—but they're gone. The marks we noticed are nothing more than the remnants of their camp: a few broken tent poles jutting up through the new-fallen snow, some fragments of a packing crate, a length of rope. Otherwise the Umbrage camp had been abandoned. Not just abandoned: obliterated by the storm.

* * *

[Aeslu of Vmatta, *Chronicle of the Last Days*.]

Yet we worked our way up the glacier, into another valley, across its riverplain, and from there onto the next glacier. In this way we entered a labyrinth in which cliffs and glaciers were the walls, valleys the paths, and our wits the only hope for reaching our destination. We plodded onward. We stumbled deep into that uncertain land. We felt our way without clear pathsight of where we were or of what lay ahead. Turning right into a gorge, we took all day walking its length; we camped for the night; we proceeded all the next day; we found our way to a scarcely detectable pass at the high end; and we filed through a narrow notch at the top and descended into the next gorge. Then new cliffs hemmed us in. New peaks loomed over us. New passes allowed us into new valleys. There seemed no end of cliffs, peaks, passes, valleys.

Did the Diadem help or hinder? It was a map, of course—but a map of what? Did the pattern etched on its miniature mountains lead us toward our goal—or continually more distant from it?

Following the route that Forssabekkit detected among the Diadem stones (and that I myself saw there) reminded me of a game I used to play as a child. I have learned since then that even children in the Lowland play a game much like it: what we called pod-and-pebble. The game required four dry seedpods and a pebble. We inverted the pods on a piece of wood or smooth cloth, then placed the pebble beneath one of the pods. One child shuffled the pods while the other watched. Then the other children tried guessing which pod hid the pebble. Simple. Difficult. So also with the Diadem and our search for the Mountain. Surely one of the Diadem stones would reveal our way to the Mountain Made of Light, yet we played a game now with twenty-six pods instead of four. If the Man of Ignorance was mistaken, if the Diadem lay in disarray despite its tidy appearance, if we followed a route that deceived rather than informed us, then we would never reach the Mountain.

Which was, of course, precisely what I hoped would happen.

I told Forssabekkit, I have reason to believe that the Heirs are following us.

Following us? he asked. How do you know?

By the same means as always. Messengers arrive now and then—messengers who bring news from certain Umbrage hidden among the Heirs.

The Man of Ignorance listened without showing the least change of expression. Then he asked, How many Heirs?

That is uncertain. More than I thought possible. Hundreds at the very least, maybe thousands. After a moment's hesitation I added, We must stop them.

Now Forssabekkit smiled. Of course. The question is simply *how*.

Intent on disarming whatever distrust still festered within him, I said, We have what we need. Maces, slings, clubs—

That won't work, said Forssabekkit.

—hatchets, lances—

It won't work.

His response startled me.

He gestured dismissively with one hand, reached out for some of the mudlike food he fancies at such time, and only then continued. We may end up resorting to devices of that sort, he said. Certainly they've proved their usefulness on a small scale. But I don't think we're really quite so desperate as that—we'd expend too much effort to accomplish a limited end.

Limited? I asked. The Heirs are pursuing us, and you call destroying them a limited end?

I understand, said Forssabekkit, raising one hand as if to restrain me. Just think about how many are following us. Thousands, you say. Maybe more? We number slightly more than a thousand. What chance do we stand with odds like that?

I told him, Perhaps what you say makes sense.

Look at it from another angle, he went on. What would we sacrifice in fighting them even if we won? Sacrifice in terms of people, equipment, and time?

A surge of relief coursed through me. The ploy was working. I felt the pall of danger lift from my people.

No, said Forssabekkit, reaching again for his mud, breaking off a piece, putting it in his mouth, and savoring it. There must be a better way. A safer way.

I watched him closely. I saw no suspicion in his gaze—only amusement.

I trust the Heirs' incompetence. Let's just proceed. What chance is there, really, that they'll ever keep up with us?

[Jesse O'Keefe, journal entry, dated the Seventeenth Day of the Second Moon-span, Sundecline (January 26, 1922).]

Loftossotoi is bitter that we missed our chance. "If we had struck earlier," he said, "the Umbrage would not be on their way. They would no longer exist."

His confidence annoyed me. "When was the last time you staged a nighttime raid?"

"They are Umbrage, thus fools."

"Perhaps they are. But their leader isn't. I wouldn't want to fight him in the dark—or in a snowstorm."

"The moon will illuminate our path to victory. The sun will show us the way."

"Fine," I told him. "I still want the weather to our advantage."

Then there was the Tirno's reaction. Compared to the Icemaster, Norroi badgered me less but disturbed me more.

I should mention that over the past several days the old man has seemed increasingly out of sorts. He lacked his usual stamina in coming up the trail and, in fact, needed to be carried for the last several miles. Yesterday he waited out the storm like everyone else. But his state of mind—or lack of it—troubled me from the start. While the wind howled, Norroi howled back. I couldn't understand what he said but heard from Marhaislu that few of his words made sense.

Today, when the bulk of the Heirs' expedition caught up with the Masters and me, I tracked him down. He was asleep in his tent. Not really asleep: dozing. The Tirno, curled up on a pile of blankets, watched me enter his tent but made no effort to greet me.

"Upward to the Summit," I told him.

No response.

"Are you all right?"

Again no response.

I walked over to his bed, crouched, and placed my hand on the old man's head. Clammy and cold. His eyes followed my motions; he was clearly watching me; yet the mousy luster I'd always seen there had disappeared.

"I know you're not feeling well," I told him. "I wish I could do something to help you. Unfortunately there's nothing—" I couldn't finish. It took all of my strength of will simply to remain there.

Norroi then began to struggle—not fast, not with any sense of desperation, but still struggling—to remove something from his cloak. The motions were awkward; he seemed unable to use his right hand. After a while, though, he succeeded in making his left find what he wanted. The rootlike fingers grasped something, pulled it free, and thrust it toward me.

I reached over and took what he offered.

It was the Tirno's lodestone: the toy mountain that Norroi often played with, holding miniature metal figures closer and closer till the magnet's pull drew them against the little peak. Those figures were stuck to the mountain even then.

"It's yours," I said. "Please keep it." I put the little mountain back in his hands. I curled his fingers over it.

Norroi held it out to me again.

"Please," I told him, "I can't."

Once more he thrust the lodestone toward me.

Reluctantly I accepted what he offered.

Only then did he speak: *"Allez-vous en pic-nic?"*

[Aeslu of Vmatta, *Chronicle of the Last Days*.]

Through a tight, rubble-strewn canyon we walked, with great star-stone boulders lying everywhere and smaller rocks tumbling from the cliffs above even as we made our way from the low end to the high; then over the pass we crossed, glad to be out of such a treacherous place; and we descended eagerly into a wider valley. But our new sense of safety did little to please Forssabekkit, for the Mountain seemed no closer than before. We consulted the Diadem. We tried to determine what path its stones told us to take. We proceeded nonetheless without any clear idea of where to go.

This aimlessness pleased me if no one else. The more difficulty the Umbrage encountered, the less trouble the Heirs would have in following them. The worse luck the Umbrage experienced in finding the Mountain, the better the Heirs' chances.

Sometimes the Man of Ignorance proceeded with a forthrightness beyond anything I had imagined possible. It was not simply that he went ahead by force of will; it was what he *did* with his will.

One rainy day, the morning's early progress stopped short when we found a recent landslide blocking our path. Rocks, mud, and dirt had poured down a cliff to jam the narrow gulley we were passing through. The Umbrage forthsetting slowed and stopped as Forssabekkit and I considered the situation.

"We can always climb over," I told him. "The slide is messy, yet everyone among us can get across."

"Seems rather a waste of time, though," he replied.

"Perhaps we should try some other route," I suggested hopefully—anything to throw the Umbrage off course.

"That's not what I meant at all."

Before I could object, I saw that Forssabekkit had another plan. First he rummaged through his pack and removed some small rods with bits of yarn attached. Then, backtracking to where some of the Umbrage carried his Lowland things, he located the bundle containing what he sought: the tubes that he had once used to tear open the ground.

The mere sight of what he was doing caused a frenzy among the Umbrage. Just as I feared, the

Man of Ignorance set to work preparing his device and jamming it into the rubble ahead. The Umbrage watched eagerly, then backed off as far as they could without losing sight of what drew their attention. Forssabekkit lit the fire-yarn and walked calmly back to where the rest of us waited.

For a few eyeblinks the rubble stayed still. Just an eyeblink later, though, the entire heap rose into the air, swelled like a mushroom after too much rain, then sagged and thudded to the ground. What had been a formidable barrier now lay scattered harmlessly: stones that anyone—even a thousand Umbrage—could walk over almost without effort.

Of course Forssabekkit's stunt greatly impressed the Umbrage. Nothing pleased them more than the spectacle of rocks leaping skyward. Yet no matter how much they relished this sort of display, it did little to solve the real problem. We did not know where we were. We did not know where we were going. And we did not know how to get from one place to the other.

Don't the Diadem stones tell us anything more? asked Forssabekkit one day in a moment of exasperation. Don't they offer any hint how to get over this ridge?

I told him, None whatever. At least none I can determine.

What about this? he asked. He turned the Diadem upside-down, shifted the stones in his hands, and pointed to something etched on one of them.

It looked like this:

He asked, what does that say?

Nothing, I replied without lying, for I had no idea what those marks meant. I went on: This is not writing in any High Realm dialect I know.

I thought you understood all the local languages.

Not all—most. Only those that the Mountain-Drawn speak now.

There are older ones? Languages even more ancient than the rest?

So it seems, I told him.

The Man of Ignorance stared at me with an expression of puzzlement or dismay. Then he glanced around at the Umbrage awaiting our instructions and said, Never mind. We have no choice but to continue.

[Jesse O'Keefe, journal entry, dated the Eighteenth Day of the Second Moon-span, Sundecline (January 27, 1922).]

This morning, right after dawn, a young Heir showed up at my tent: one of Loftossotoi's attendants. He spoke briefly without so much as glancing in my direction, turning this way and that, like a schoolboy reciting a memorized poem: "The Ice-master requests that you visit Norroi the Tirno."

"Norroi?" I asked.

"Norroi the Tirno."

"Is he all right?"

"You are to visit him." He beckoned to me.

I all but panicked. Leaping up, I forced my way past the tent flaps. I would have sprinted anywhere the boy led me. His pace did, in fact, reveal some urgency as we made our way among the other tents.

"What has happened?" I asked, but the boy just led me through the camp without speaking fur-

ther. Other Heirs watched as we passed. No greet-
ings; no gestures of recognition. I felt more and
more alarmed as we proceeded.

I saw the same response from people gathered
outside the Tirno's tent: eyes averted as I approached.

Someone held the tent flap open for me. I
stooped and entered.

Norroi lay on his little floor bed half-lying, half-
sitting, propped up by the rolled alpaca blankets
that the Heirs use instead of pillows. In a western
setting his posture would have suggested a con-
valescent's readiness, even eagerness, for tea and
toast on a tray. He looked half-asleep, gazing
drowsily toward his feet. I couldn't get a clear
sense of his expression at first in that tent-filtered
light, but he appeared to be smiling.

"Norroi," I said.

No response.

I faltered, not wanting to disturb him if he were
still asleep. I watched a few moments. Better to
be on my way, perhaps; to leave him a note; not
to bother him now.

Even so I spoke again: "Norroi."

Still no response.

A tingle of fear rose through my bones just then.
"Norroi?"

I was in the tent alone with him; I pulled back
the flap and glanced about for the boy who had
brought me. At least two dozen Heirs had now
gathered around and stood watching.

I rushed into the tent again, knelt abruptly at
the Tirno's bedside, and clutched his arm.

Cold. As cold as if I'd grabbed an icicle.

What should I have done? Should I have clung
to him? Wept on his shoulder? Torn out my hair?
Cried out, wailed, begged his forgiveness? There
seemed no point in bothering.

What's done is done. For days I'd worried that

the wound he suffered when the Icemaster's mountain monument collapsed had done real damage. How could it not have, given Norroi's age? Yet he survived it a while, just as he'd survived so much already.

I reached out again to touch him. Still cold. What did I expect? The Tirno had vanished and reappeared so many times that I almost expected him to spring suddenly to life. As if to make entirely sure, I touched him yet again. Cold.

I stood there a while. Five minutes, ten, maybe longer.

Then I left his tent and walked back to my own.

[Aeslu of Vmatta, *Chronicle of the Last Days*.]

Late one afternoon—this was the Seventeenth Day of the Second Moon-span, Sundecline—I prepared to perform further acts of sabotage. My plan was to pour grease on Forssabekkit's best stockpile of rope, rendering it treacherous, even useless, and perhaps thus prompting Forssabekkit to delay his march toward the Mountain. This plan did not lack for risks. The greatest was that I might be caught outright. Few people had access to the Umbrage rope-stores; even if I escaped at the time, the Man of Ignorance might well suspect me as the saboteur. On the other hand, if I were to discover the sabotage myself . . .

As it so happened, most of the Umbrage had gathered a short distance up the glacier to watch Forssabekkit demonstrate his prowess with the Lowland ice-hatchet; the rest of the camp was empty except for a scattering of guards. These presented no obstacles: being the Moon's Stead, I went anywhere I wished. I proceeded through the camp till I reached the tent housing Forssabekkit's best ropes.

I was surprised to find it altogether unguarded.
The tent's flap was shut but untied. I lingered at
the door a moment, then pushed my way inside.

At once I realized why the guards were missing.
They were inside, a youth and a young woman,
huddled at the tent's far corner. They jolted back
as I entered, twisting to stare at me while at the
same time fumbling to rearrange their robes.
Fourteen or fifteen Sun-spans in age, they looked
up with expressions of nothing less than mortal
fear. The girl had gone white. The boy trembled.
They looked so terrified that I could only smile.
To think that I would punish them for their little
tryst!

Then I caught sight of something only half-
hidden beneath the girl's hem: the tassled end of
a piece of rope. Not Forssabekkit's rope, but sacred rope. Rope of the sort used to perform the
Sunsetting Obeisance.

I stared. Sunsetting Obeisance!

They stared, too, their eyes fixed on me till they
realized that my own gaze fell elsewhere; then they
glanced down to the object of my attention. At
once the girl started to weep.

Reaching down, I pulled back her gown.

Sacred stones, ropes, hooks: how long had it
been since I had seen these implements? Just the
sight of them filled me with longing. Now here
was a set in Umbrage hands!

I asked, Where did you get these?

Both the boy and the girl now began weeping.
The girl cradled her head with both hands; the
boy tensed up as if stricken. Please kill us now,
said the girl between sobs. Please kill us!

For a long time I could only stare at them. The
boy seemed incapable of meeting my gaze; the girl,
unable to avoid it. My temptation was to demand
the implements, even to reach down and take them
myself. Like a lover coveting mementos of her be-

loved, I craved these objects for what they evoked. Yet somehow, despite the intensity of the urge, I held off. Perhaps this was nothing more than the mere animal impulse to preserve myself. If anyone within the Umbrage camp saw me with these things—

Get rid of them, I told the youths, and I stormed out.

[Jesse O'Keefe, journal entry, dated the Eighteenth Day of the Second Moon-span, Sundecline (January 27, 1922).]

Loftossotoi questioned my decision. "We are the larger forthsetting," he argued. "We could fight them, stop them, overtake them. What are we waiting for?"

I pointed out that what appear to be our advantages count for little now. The Umbrage would have the high ground. Despite our numerical superiority, the odds might easily tilt in their favor. Besides, fighting on a glacier would be sheer suicide: the icefalls and crevasses would prove more treacherous than the deadliest minefield. Maneuvering would be difficult under the best of circumstances; under the worst, scores of our people would end up falling into the great cracks that open throughout the glacier's surface. "Trust me," I told him and the other Masters. "I've fought hopeless battles before—I feel no desire to do so again." Since they seemed unpersuaded, I went on: "We'll catch them by other means."

They went along with my plan, though uneasily. What matters is that they went along. What I didn't tell them, however, is that my reluctance had little to do with strategy. I simply feel too dazed to fight—too dazed even to move. All I can think about is Norroi, now gray and solid as the glacier in which the Heirs, after almost no ceremony deserving the name, entombed him.

[Aeslu of Vmatta, *Chronicle of the Last Days*.]

By the Twenty-sixth Day of the Second Moonspan, Sundecline, we had entered and left six valleys within the Inner Realm. Never once did we cross paths with any other people, least of all the Heirs, and never once did we see the slightest signs of them. Antlerbeasts leaped out of the brush and fled our approach. Scamperbeasts, fangbeasts, and wild woolbeasts appeared now and then, startled, but kept their distance. Birds of all kinds flew around—split-tails, poke-the-bills, bug-gulpers, tinies—and, far above, watching us from where they leaned on the wind, even a few flesh-beakbirds. But people? We saw none. The Masters who had guarded the entrances to this part of the Mountain Land since the Founders' time had succeeded far better than I had first thought in excluding everyone; it was hard to believe that women or men had ever set foot in the Inner Realm at all.

Thus unchallenged, we walked onward.

So where's the Mountain? asked Forssabekkit.

I wish I knew, I told him—a response that left me no need to lie.

The Man of Ignorance gazed ahead, considering the wall of slopes, cliffs, glaciers, and peaks that barred our view to the east. I could not imagine a more formidable barrier.

He said, Somewhere over there, and he motioned with one hand. Of course this massif blocks our view—but no doubt it's over there.

* * *

Several times each day we consulted the Diadem. We stared at it, examined it, passed it back and forth between us. It told us everything and nothing. Somewhere within a protective ring of peaks rose the Mountain Made of Light: that much we knew. But how to reach it? That question the Diadem seemed unable to answer.

Over a period just short of a Moon-span we had come nearly halfway around the great oval of peaks that the Inner Realm comprised. What if we curved all the way around? Would we end up right where we started—with nothing accomplished?

Surely there would be some way into the depths of this Inner Realm: into the heart of the heart. Where, though? And once we found it, how would we make our way in? The Diadem posed but did not answer these riddles.

Tell me again what this says, says Forssabekkit, pointing to some marks etched on one of the stones.

Nothing.

It must be something.

It says nothing. These are not words.

What are they, then?

I have no idea.

Of course I had my hunches, though none I wished to share with my enemies—least of all with the Man of Ignorance. For a long time I had suspected that these marks had served the Mountain-Drawn in generations past, not as explanations but as reminders of knowledge that those persons initiated into their meaning already possessed. That, or else they were riddles that anyone seeking the Mountain would be forced to solve. Either way they made no sense by means of the languages I understood. They told their tale, but its meaning escaped me altogether.

* * *

[Jesse O'Keefe, journal entry, dated the Twenty-second Day of the Second Moon-span, Sundecline (January 31, 1922).]

For two days I sat gazing out over the glacier without taking action. I kept telling Loftossotoi that my hesitance derived from a need to step carefully. My words weren't untrue; yet neither did they tell the truth. In fact, I just couldn't stop thinking about Norroi.

The Tirno is dead. The man who brought me here—indeed, who guided me through the Mountain Land in more ways than one—now lies frozen within an almost fathomless slab of ice. Never again will he prod me toward what I need to do. Never again will he tease me into whatever odd insight he thinks I should gain. Lacking the old man's guidance, I feel stunned—certainly far more so than I'd admit to the Masters.

Then, abruptly, my rage got the best of me. Should I let my grief for the old man bog me down? Never—not when Forster Beckwith shows every sign of proceeding so confidently. What sort of memorial would that provide Norroi? And what good is that sort of paralysis when Aeslu—who I thought was long dead, and who now has reappeared as if sprung to life again—now awaits me?

One other development spurred me on. The Heirs now believe that Forster has acquired the Diadem. How do they know? Loftossotoi believes that Forster's actions speak for themselves. If so, then he has the map to the goal we seek. Yet he lacks the Mountain Stone—which I possess—and thus he lacks the means of reaching our ultimate destination. Following him may well lead us to the starting point of our climb. How will we contend with Forster if both the Heirs and the Umbrage arrive at the Mountain's base? I have no idea. All I know is that we're better off deciding when the odds lean more heavily in our favor. Between now and then, the Umbrage will at least lead us to the Mountain.

And now by day the Umbrage leave, and we watch them go. We wait; we observe their efforts to deal with the terrain; we make our own preparations. Then by night, with the Umbrage well out of view, we follow literally in their footsteps. We may well have an easier time at night than they do in full daylight. The snow is firm underfoot as we proceed. The ice blocks and slabs piled all around us are frozen solid. The glacier glows under all but the faintest illumination: stars, moon, or whatever light leaks through the clouds on an overcast night. The whole expanse takes on a silvery sheen. The lips of the crevasses are a conspicuous blue-gray. The depths below are blacker than the inside of a stone. Even without the trail these Umbrage have left behind, it wouldn't be difficult to find our way through the maze of cracks—in fact, the task might be simpler than by day, when the glare overhead leaves the great expanses of snow and ice all but blinding. And with the Umbrage leading us, we can see every path their scouts have taken in their attempts to find a safe route over the glacier—where they nearly stepped into a crevasse, where they circumvented a suspicious depression in the snow, where they avoided a huge teetering pinnacle of ice that might have crushed some of our people without a moment's notice—and we can use the trench that a thousand Umbrage have pounded into the snow when at last they made their way up to the pass. The Umbrage are showing us how to reach the Mountain in more ways than one.

"How, then, shall we fight the Umbrage?" Loftossotoi asked several days and thirty or thirty-five miles later. "And shall we fight them now or later?"

"I don't know. I haven't decided yet."

The Icemaster watched me warily. "We will fight them, though."

"When the time is right."

Marhaislu the Stonemaster picked up where Loftossotoi had left off: "We Masters know that you fought in the Great War. We understand your weariness of fighting—"

"I know you do."

"But please remember: our enemies are the Umbrage."

"I know they are."

"Then we must fight them," Loftossotoi went on. "The question is how and when."

"I've never disagreed with you," I told them.

"You are the Man of Knowledge," said Marhaislu.

"You must tell us what can stop the Umbrage," said Loftossotoi.

I couldn't stand their nagging any longer. "Look," I told them. "I know all this. I'm not disagreeing with you. But since I'm the Man of Knowledge, I'm the one who decides, right? So how about leaving me alone till I let you know what we'll do?"

Loftossotoi, Marhaislu, and the others fell silent. They seemed less angry than puzzled.

Which is all for the best. I need to keep them guessing. I need to stall for time while I figure out what's next.

[Aeslu of Vmatta, *Chronicle of the Last Days.*]

Within the merest eyeblink of having caught those youths at Sunsetting Obeisance, I grasped the implications of their activities, but I took a long time accepting what I had grasped. Members of the Umbrage forthsetting were engaged in Heir rituals. Why did the discovery surprise me? For hundreds of Sun-spans the Umbrage had hidden among the Heirs. Should it seem so strange that a few Heirs might also hide among the Umbrage? Perhaps I was afraid to grasp the nature of what I had seen—afraid that things might not be what they seemed; might be more complex, more treacherous.

Were these children Heirs born of Umbrage parents? Were they Heir spies planted among the Umbrage? Were they Umbrage longing to be Heirs? Were they Umbrage only pretending to be Heirs?

No matter how hard I thought through the possibilities, I could not make sense of them. And if I remained uncertain about those two children, how could I have been sure about any others? For if two Heirs had joined the Umbrage, there might be others. Five, eight, twenty, a hundred . . . I had no way of knowing. Trying to find out would run a terrible risk. Yet I could not gamble on ignorance.

That day we made unusual progress. Descending from the glacier and entering a narrow valley, the Umbrage walked farther than they had gone during any one march since entering the Inner Realm. The terrain was flat, the weather gentle. Great cliffs of star-stone rose above us on either side; waterfalls descended from the unseen glaciers beyond; nothing blocked our path ahead. As before, we saw no inhabitants. The only denizens of this place were the scamperbeasts bounding among the boulders strewn everywhere and, far above, two fleshbeakbirds riding the wind. We saw no signs of a route that might take us over the cliffs to the Mountain, and Forssabekkit expressed frustration at our bafflement; even so, we made great progress.

I should mention that although most of the Umbrage traveled as a group, small parties of scouts and warriors preceded or followed the rest. This was the usual way to travel in the Mountain Land. The Umbrage, however, took it to an extreme. Some of the scouts went ahead almost a half-day's travel; they reported back to Forssabekkit and me each evening about what we could expect. Others lagged nearly as far back as the scouts went ahead: a cautionary measure in case Jassikki and the Heirs tried sneaking up on us. These tactics worried me. How much more difficult would they make it for anyone to thwart the Man of Ignorance? I was unsure but uneasy.

The advance and rear guards simplified my plans in one respect, however. They made it possible to explain why certain members of the Umbrage forthsetting might be heading back toward the pass precisely as everyone else went forward. This opportunity offered me my next chance.

That night, when the girl entered my tent, I looked up, then returned to writing.

You called for me, she said.

I kept her standing in the doorway for a long time. Then at last I said, Come forth.

She took the few paces that brought her before me. The Umbrage men and women now wear the same attire: Lowland-style leg garments, jackets, boots, and caps. Dressed in this manner, the girl before me looked like any of the other Umbrage. She was no more than fifteen Sun-spans in age, womanly in shape yet still childish in manner: shy, awkward, uneasy. Her mouth lacked any expression; her eyes showed an uncomfortable calm for someone in mortal danger.

I asked, What is your name?

Massoritu.

I see. And you come from which valley?

Vmatta.

Vmatta. Perhaps that explains it.

She knew better than to ask what I meant, but her gaze presented the question anyway.

Your persistent clinging to ignorance, I added.

The girl simply stared at me.

You know that anyone among us caught performing the Sunset Obeisance must die.

She nodded.

Why, then, have you done what will cost you your life?

Because I must.

I forced a laugh. Must die, certainly.

Not once did her expression waver. That is for you to decide, she said. I must do what I must do.

You must talk nonsense? Rave at the Sun and the Moon? Follow the whims of tyrants?

Ossonnal and Lissallo are not tyrants, she went on, and they will lead me not to darkness but to light. For they are the Sun's and the Moon's presence among us (she was now quoting directly from the Sunrising Obeisance), and in their company I will never fall into shadow.

Listening to Massoritu recite her prayer, I snorted in derision, but only to mask the shiver that passed through my body. How long a time had elapsed since I spoke the same words aloud? How long since I performed the rituals for which I now scolded this girl? My impulse was entirely the opposite of my actions: to thank her, to embrace her, to join her in saying the words I loved.

Stop this yammering, I told her. It serves no purpose.

Only to tell the truth.

No—lies. Nothing but lies.

She did not respond.

I continued: Tell me something. How many others of you are there? That is, here among the Umbrage?

She avoided my gaze. For the first time I saw a hint of panic on her face: not a gesture, just the momentary lapse of the calm that till just then had been her only expression. I can speak only for myself, she said.

And for at least one other—that boy with you then.

I speak only for myself.

Surely you know of others. Men, women, children—Are there many? Just a few?

Looking toward me but not at me, she said nothing.

You need not tell me who they are. Just how many.

No response.

I told her, Others among us have ways of making you talk. Why not tell me now and spare yourself what you would endure at less gentle hands?

Still no response.

For a long time I watched this girl, admiring her even as I berated her, wanting to console her even as I threatened her. Most of all I wanted to thank her for such stubbornness and clarity of mind; I envied her ability to act so plainly on her beliefs. Well, then, tell me this, I said after a while: What is your duty among the Umbrage?

Sometimes I am a guard, she told me, but most often I am a runner.

I see. A runner.

[Jesse O'Keefe, journal entry, dated the Twenty-seventh Day of the Second Moon-span, Sundecline (February 5, 1922).]

Maybe Norroi was right: I've pushed my luck. I'm jeopardizing precisely what I most hope to accomplish. Yet he acted as if Forster and the Umbrage are beside the point—as if they present no danger to the Heirs, to all the Mountain-Drawn, to the whole Mountain Land.

What's the right way to proceed? I can't afford the time to wonder. If the Tirno could have clarified the situation, I'd never have objected. Yet he couldn't—or didn't—so I simply have to proceed with the tasks at hand: to stop Forster Beckwith from reaching the Mountain first, and to find out whether Aeslu is a willing accomplice or merely his hostage.

I can't get my mind off her. I can't believe she'd tolerate that man's presence voluntarily, much less join forces with him. Yet I don't understand why she hasn't given some sort of sign, however subtle, about her true intentions. The High Realm is full of spies. It's true that the Umbrage have probably infiltrated the Heirs more fully than vice versa, yet I know that the Masters have agents among their enemies. Otherwise how would they have acquired his letters in the first place?

Aeslu's silence baffles me, worries me, grieves me.

[Aeslu of Vmatta, *Chronicle of the Last Days.*]

Three days of hard walking: three more days without any luck in crossing the barrier that Forssabekkit believed lay between us and the Mountain. Over riverplain; up grass slope; through thicket, bramble, and wood; up icefall and down boulderfield—crossing all these barriers we walked, day after day, without the least sign of a means to our goal. By the First Day of the Third Moon-span, Sundecline, everyone taking part in the Umbrage forthsetting was weary, discouraged, and irritable.

Then, late that morning, we stopped to rest near a brook. The valley widened there and appeared still wider because the clouds, having relented for the first time in days, left the whole landscape visible. We could see the cliffs both in the Sunrising and Sunsetting directions; we could see a side-canyon opening off to our right; we could see a snowfield angling upward at its far end; we could see a splintery ridge rising from the snowfield's upper edge. In some ways what we saw resembled everything we had seen day in, day out, since entering the Inner Realm. Snow, rock, ice . . . These were simply what made up the Mountain Land.

Yet almost at once something caught Forssabekkit's attention. Having stopped, he stood for a long time gazing off into the distance. Then he unbuckled his big Lowland pack and eased it to the ground. He gazed a while longer. Without speaking, the Man of Ignorance opened his pack's top flap, rummaged around, and removed his distance-looker. He peered through it, easing the tube this way and that, for a long time.

The Umbrage, no matter how accustomed to their leader's long silences, grew restless. Or was it eagerness they showed? Perhaps they somehow understood that the Man of Ignorance would soon determine their fate.

Where's the Diadem? asked Forssabekkit.

Though alarmed, I saw no way of averting a response. I lowered my pack, opened it, and removed the Diadem from its leather bag. I extended it to the Man of Ignorance on my flattened palms.

He examined it carefully: leaned this way and that to get a better look; prodded here and there with a finger; tipped one stone over to look at its base.

Just as I thought, he said.

I said nothing. Better to remain silent than to clarify his thoughts.

Forssabekkit handed me the distancelooker with three terse words: See for yourself.

Only with great force of will could I accept what he offered me. Of his many Lowland gadgets, I loathed this one more than all the others combined—this device that had showed the Moon I loved to be nothing but a ball of ice! Yet I took it. I held it to my face. I gazed through the deadly tube toward the canyon wall that caught its owner's fancy.

At once I understood what Forssabekkit had seen. Great splinters of star-stone rose from the ridge rising above the glacier. Not splinters: needles. One of them (plain for anyone to see) had an eye.

Do you see it? asked the Man of Ignorance, speaking loud and fast. That's what the marks on the Diadem are showing us. A needle and thread!

With those words he turned back toward the Umbrage behind us: a sinuous filament of people winding their way up the valley.

Forssabekkit said, That's the needle. We're the thread. So let's go thread the needle's eye.

[Jesse O'Keefe, journal entry, dated the Second Day of the Third Moon-span, Sundecline (February 9, 1922).]

Snow.

It made no difference to us at first—just a fluttering of flakes—and we continued up the valley. The higher we climbed, though, the thicker the snowfall came down, and it soon made proceeding difficult. The temperature fell fast. The wind picked up, too, shoving icy air through even the thickest garments we wore. Within a few minutes everyone was badly chilled. I conferred with Marhaislu, Loftossotoi, and the other Masters, all of whom agreed that we should stop.

There was no alternative but retreat. Once I

gave the word, Marhaislu sent the Adepts down the line; the whole great procession reversed itself and started down. We struggled for almost two hours to find a safe resting place.

Now the tents are pitched and everyone is hunkered down. By all appearances, we're safe.

But of course we're getting nowhere.

[Aeslu of Vmatta, *Chronicle of the Last Days*.]

Whether Massoritu could succeed at her difficult task, I had no idea; whether I myself would survive the consequences of her attempt, I knew still less; but this is the letter I gave the young runner to take Jassikki:

From Aeslu the Moon's Stead to Jassikki the Sun's Stead:

Upward to the Summit!

Forgive me, beloved, for my haste and brevity. Only now have I secured the means to send you this letter, and the means may not last. Thus of the infinity of things I wish you to know, I can write only these:

That I am among the Umbrage by my own will, but for a purpose far different from what anyone images;

That what appears my worst treason is my greatest loyalty;

That what seems my greatest hatred for you is my deepest love;

That Forssabekkit and the Umbrage plan to approach the Mountain not simply to climb it, but also to draw you and the Heirs into their trap;

That I will do everything in my power to thwart them.

If I could explain their precise intentions, I would do so. Yet Forssabekkit has not yet told me all the details of what will make the Umbrage quest possible. Either he still lacks a clear sense of what to do, or else he wishes to deprive me of that same clarity. Of this, however, I feel sure: the Umbrage will soon reach the Mountain Made of Light.

Do not follow them. Find some other entrance, no matter how laborious; force your way through by another approach; or, if you have no other choice, simply forego the temptation to proceed. For if you enter by whatever route Forssabekkit intends for his own forces, you are doomed, and the Heirs, the Mountain-Drawn, the entire Mountain Land are all doomed with you.

How is it possible, you wonder, that I can urge you to ignore the Man of Darkness even as he makes way straight for the Mountain? I urge you (no, plead with you) for this reason: Forssabekkit can merely reach the Mountain; he can never climb it. For even though he holds the Diadem in his own hands, he can arrive only at the start of his ascent, not at its culmination. To reach the Summit he will need the Mountain Stone. Yet he lacks it. Who has it? I have no idea. He suspects that you do. Perhaps you do; perhaps not. I hope with all my heart that you do. Either way, he wants to lure you, to trap you and your forces, then to decimate you in his search for the object that will let him realize his goal.

Thus I fear both for your safety and for the safety of the object which, if yours, will lead you to the Summit. Thus, too, I must forego what I want most in the world: to be with you.

Please understand. Haste will keep us apart, and perhaps forever. Patience will some day reunite us.

I am yours.

Upward to the Summit!

* * *

[Jesse O'Keefe, journal entry, dated the Fifth Day of the Third Moon-span, Sundecline (February 11, 1922).]

The storm has relented. The Heirs are safe. Yet somehow our survival is less astonishing than another event that has just taken place.

This afternoon a messenger arrived at our camp. In itself this wasn't a remarkable event; messengers show up all the time. Everyone noticed the arrival, however, because most messengers are boys—yet this one was a girl. She caught everyone's attention at once.

She also looked worse off than messengers usually do, even considering the terrain and the weather. What a battering: scratches, bruises, welts. Her raincloak hung in tatters from her body. Her hair looked muddy and tangled. One of her sandals had fallen off; the bare foot was swollen and bloody. She was clearly exhausted.

Of course, people rushed over to help once she entered our midst.

Loftossotoi reached out to receive the message.

The girl stammered something but kept clutching the scroll in her hands.

"Let me have it," said Loftossotoi.

Again the girl spoke; again she made no sense. She lost her footing and almost collapsed. Someone pulled off her wet raincloack and wrapped her in a dry blanket.

The Icemaster seemed on the verge of losing his temper—it was outright insolence to deny a Master that scroll—but then Marhaislu intervened, saying, "She asked for Jassikki."

Loftossotoi was not one to be dissuaded. Taking advantage of the messenger's weak state, he reached out to the girl, snatched the scroll from her hands, broke the seal, and pulled it open. The girl moaned in protest but couldn't pull away from the guards restraining her.

The Icemaster gazed at the scroll for a moment, then handed it abruptly to me. A quick glance revealed why the messenger intended it for my eyes alone: its words were in English.

"Take her away," I told the guards. "Give her food and a warm place to rest." To the girl herself I said, "Trust me. We'll take good care of you."

Some guards left with her, but everyone else remained. There must have been fifty people watching me as I read the scroll.

From Aeslu the Moon's Stead to Jassikki the Sun's Stead:

Upward to the Summit!

Forgive me, beloved, for my haste and brevity. Only now have I secured the means to send you this letter, and the means may not last. Thus of the infinity of things I wish you to know, I have time to explain these alone:

That my silence has been unwitting;

That I am among the Umbrage against my will;

That Forssabekkit the Man of Ignorance is my captor;

That he has not only stolen my freedom but is now stealing my ability to resist his malignant power;

That I am in grave danger, and with me all the Mountain Land as well;

That I plead with you for help in avoiding a fate that I dread more than my own death.

If I could explain precisely what Forssabekkit intends, I would do so. All I know is that by some means, and at a time that remains uncertain, he will soon reach the Mountain. My ignorance is ironic: I myself possess the Diadem. Yet despite my efforts to throw them off the path to our goal,

the Umbrage and their leader seem capable of
perceiving how and where to cross this final barrier to the Mountain itself. I have prayed to the
Sun and the Moon that I might tell you more, but
my prayers remain unanswered. Of this alone do
I feel sure: they will soon reach the Mountain.

Please follow them. Be careful but be swift. Any
delay will endanger not just my own life, but the
life of my people. You are the Man of Knowledge.
You are the Man of Light. You are the Healer of
Wounds. The Heirs, the Mountain-Drawn, the entire Mountain Land all depend upon you.

Please understand. Patience will keep us apart,
perhaps forever. Haste will reunite us.

I am yours.

Upward to the Summit!

[Aeslu of Vmatta, *Chronicle of the Last Days*.]

A full day's scramble up the glacier brought us
to the splintered ridge; a short while longer took
us up a cliff to the needle itself. Needle indeed! It
was a great tower of rock that rose almost straight
up to the eye at its upper reaches—an eye that the
Diadem hinted would lead to the Mountain Made
of Light.

I find it difficult to explain my emotions at
the time. Nothing drew me more than finding the
Mountain—my goal both as a member of the
Mountain-Drawn and as my people's leader—yet I
dreaded nothing more intensely than this same
event. Our arrival at the needle's eye might well
mean that we had found the Mountain, that we
would soon reach it, that we might some day climb
it. However, *we* included the Man of Ignorance
and the Umbrage. Victory itself would be defeat.

I did everything I could to forestall the next

move. Arguing that the Umbrage were too tired to continue, I told Forssabekkit to let them rest.

Rest? he inquired. Now? When we're almost there?

The next step will be difficult. They are depleted.

Just seeing the mountain will revive them.

But perhaps they will not even see it. The weather grows worse, and clouds will soon surround us.

What I said was true. For two days the sky had opened up; now it closed in again, darkened, and converged on the peaks. I said, At best the Umbrage will have their hopes raised, then dashed. At worst we may find ourselves caught on the cliff during a storm.

We have to take that chance, said Forssabekkit, and he prepared to set off again.

The Sun and the Moon intervened. No more than halfway up the rubble-slope to that needle, we found ourselves engulfed by snowfall. Not just a squall, either: a true blizzard. Within a short while we floundered. Even Forssabekkit thought better of his previous intentions.

Tell everyone to head back, he said. We'll pitch our tents on the glacier and wait out the storm.

[Jesse O'Keefe, journal entry, dated the Sixth Day of the Third Moon-span, Sundecline (February 13, 1922).]

Aeslu's letter has thrown me off balance. Almost everything I've feared has come to pass. At least Aeslu hasn't betrayed me—but the situation otherwise couldn't be much worse. Forster has her captive, the bastard! And he clearly plans to use Aeslu as a pawn in the game he's playing. I can only guess what forces he's exerting against her, and what he means to gain by doing so.

"He has not only stolen my freedom but is now stealing my ability to resist his malignant power"—that's what worries me most.

Whatever else, I have to move fast. I only hope I'm not too late already.

Shortly after noon I managed to track down Loftossotoi. I knew he was somewhere in the camp, but he seemed to be avoiding me. Small wonder: he'd known all along that Aeslu was alive, and he'd kept the news from me; now I knew— and I had proof. Whether he knew I'd spotted his chicanery or not was another matter, one I decided not to press just then. What difference does it make now, really, if he's been treating me like a puppet on a string? I don't really care so long as I get Aeslu back.

"Read this." I thrust Aeslu's letter at the Ice-master, who then stared at the scroll as if at Egyptian hieroglyphs. I realized at once that the writing there might as well have been just that.

"I do not read Lowland," he told me with an almost audible sniff.

"No? What a surprise." But I didn't press the issue. I simply explained about Aeslu, about her situation, about the risks if we didn't take action at once.

Loftossotoi handed the scroll back to me as if without much interest. "What if someone else wrote the letter?"

His words caught me short. "Someone else . . . ?" The thought had crossed my mind. Forster was capable of so many ruses, why not yet another? "But this is Aeslu's handwriting," I told him. "I've seen it before."

"You have seen her write your own language?"

"Well—no. But I've seen her writing."

"In *our* language?"

"I think I can recognize her script."

The Icemaster made no reply.

I faltered, then said, "You're suggesting that Forster Beckwith wrote this letter?"

Still no response.

"You're not being much help," I told him.

He simply stood there waiting for me to explain myself. It crossed my mind for a moment that Loftossotoi might have been unaware of Aeslu's survival after all—that because he can't read English, he's oblivious both to what Forster Beckwith wrote earlier and to what Aeslu herself has written now. But that seemed out of the question. The Icemaster had other means of verifying his suspicions one way or another. He'd kept them to himself before; no doubt he kept them to himself now as well.

"What you're getting at," I went on, "is that Forster may be setting a trap."

He nodded once.

"That's possible. What if you're wrong, though? What if this letter *is* from Aeslu? What if we hold off on trying to find her, trying to save her? Then what?"

"Then Aeslu will come to harm," said the Icemaster.

"You don't sound very upset about it."

Loftossotoi shot me a quick up-down glance: the closest he ever gets to anger. "I would not like the Moon's Stead to be hurt," he said. "But the Realm's safety is what worries me, not that of any one person in it."

Whether Aeslu's letter is genuine or not, we have one major question still unanswered: how will we confront the Umbrage?

It's impossible for me to believe that Forster Beckwith will relent simply because we show up.

He'll confront us, threaten us, fight us—do anything he can to destroy us. The man is totally devoid of scruples. Whatever intentions the Umbrage may have, Forster will fan the flames of their resentment, rage, and hatred. I can't imagine that the two sides won't come to blows.

Perhaps this has to happen. I dread the possibility, but maybe there's no way around it. Whether the Umbrage have it coming or not, I can't really judge. But Forster himself does. Of course, if he follows through on his current actions—if he reaches the Mountain and climbs it—then there will be no limit to the damage he'll do to the Mountain-Drawn. Perhaps it's time that push comes to shove.

The question remains: how? By all accounts I have at least twice as many people under my command as Forster does. The Heirs have some of the Masters' Guards among them—maybe two or three hundred. These men and women aren't highly trained soldiers; their weapons are fairly standard Bronze Age knives, maces, hatchets, and slings; their tactics will be limited on a stark and treacherous field of battle. Forster and the Umbrage will face the same limitations, of course, yet I don't find that sufficiently consoling to make me brazen.

I'd avoid a confrontation if I could. I'm just not sure it's possible. If it's going to happen, I need to make sure that Forster and the Umbrage never prevail.

[Aeslu of Vmatta, *Chronicle of the Last Days*.]

The Umbrage were astir. It was not simply that the harsh weather had eased and they now prepared to leave their encampment; they knew what they were leaving *for*. Everyone in the camp rushed about distributing supplies, stashing food, filling packs, discarding unneeded gear, and performing whatever other tasks each person had been allotted. The tents remained in place—they were, after all, our principle means of blending into our surroundings—but what went on inside and around them made the Umbrage camp a different place altogether.

Let's go, said Forssabekkit when he stopped by my tent, well aware that he needed no other words to explain our next actions.

As soon as possible, I responded.

He lingered, watching my own preparations.

I told him, I have waited for this day my whole life.

Good. So have I.

Then he came over, stood staring at me a long time, caressed me, took me in his arms, and held me in an embrace I could neither accept nor resist.

The climb, I told him. Everything must wait till the climb.

He relented, though irritably. All right, then. Till the climb.

Forssabekkit stepped over to the door and passed halfway through the flaps. Instead of leaving, however, he turned to me and spoke again: By the way, it seems that one of the guards caught a spy.

A spy?

I'm a bit foggy on the details. Hard to say if there's any real damage done. One of the top Umbrages said she'd take care of it.

A quiver of alarm passed over me. I asked, Take care of what?

I assume these people have their own methods of dispensing justice.

But surely you know that the punishment—

Let them go about their business, said Forssa-bekkit. We shouldn't intervene.

As soon as he left, I stepped out of my tent and stood outside watching the Umbrage around me. I noticed at once that many of them were heading downhill, slightly to my left, toward where the glacier flattened out against the rocky slope. I hesitated a moment, then followed.

—caught with it in her hands—

—Heir sympathies—

—threat to all of us—

What I heard from these people filled me with alarm. Impulsively I rushed forth toward their same goal. Then at once I restrained myself and proceeded as they did: quickly, steadily, as if to join some long-awaited festivity.

Where the glacier angled down to rough patches of ice and snow, a crowd had formed. Half of the entire forthsetting must have been there: men, women, children, all of them standing in a wide circle. I lingered at the edge of this circle, desperate to push my way in, yet relieved that all these bodies presented a barrier between myself and whomever stood on the other side. Then the people present started to back up, jeering and laughing, so that once the circle had expanded I stood among them.

Even the quickest glance revealed the center of everyone's attention. It was Massoritu.

I tried convincing myself that someone else stood there, that this girl merely resembled the one I knew, that my fear deluded me. Even so, it was Massoritu. Those fawn-eyes, that pouty mouth . . . When she turned to face her accusers, I could no longer deny the obvious.

A long moment passed. I heard no sound but the wind ruffling against the tundra. The girl herself said nothing. Then, abruptly, a voice: Shall we take all day?

The words had been spoken in Lowland; the speaker was Forssabekkit.

I soon realized that everyone here awaited a signal—my signal. All the people gazed in my direction. An eyeblink later Massoritu cast her gaze toward me and held it there. I gazed back, wanting to escape but helpless to do anything but stay. I saw neither hostility nor anger in her eyes, neither supplication nor hopefulness. She, too, waited. Yet the fixity of her gaze revealed more than mere resignation. Massoritu awaited more than the signal sealing her fate; she awaited it from my own lips. Would I speak the words? Would I call her fate down upon this girl? Watching, I sensed her doubt of my willingness to commit this betrayal. Her eyes still showed no anger, her mouth no expression at all; yet everything about her seemed a dare. Do it, her eyes said. Do it if you can.

I tried to speak but was mute. The words withered, shriveled, fell to dust inside my throat.

Forssabekkit spoke instead: *What are you waiting for!*

When a hawk, ready to pounce, traps a mouse in her deathly stare, the mouse stares back, helpless to flee. But is the hawk perhaps just as trapped, as helpless, in the mouse's stare?

I, too, waited. Massoritu could have spoken as easily as I, could have blurted what she knew about me, could have shouted to everyone all around her that I had used her as a messenger to convey intelligence to the Heirs, could have screamed that I wrote a letter to Jassikki himself. For longer than I could have imagined tolerating before that afternoon, I stood there and waited, wondered, dreaded that this young woman would speak before I myself did—yet somehow I longed to hear the words. How long did I wait? Long enough that I stooped to pick up two chunks of ice. Long enough that my hands throbbed from what they held. Long enough that the ice itself started melting and streamed forth from my fingers. Long enough that I realized at last that Massoritu would never speak, that even in a Moonspan's time she would never speak a syllable, that in some way she awaited the signal as eagerly as anyone among us. Long enough that by the time all this had happened, my hands were numb enough not to feel the ice I hurled beyond their grasp.

What I threw missed her: fell far short. But the Umbrage understood as plainly as if I had uttered the curse they expected. At once they unleashed their barrage.

Lumps and chunks of ice thudded around her. It seemed hard to believe that so many people could miss such an easy target, but at first nothing struck her. Some of the Umbrage even laughed at their own incompetence or taunted one another. Ice is an odd weapon. Uneven and slippery, it throws poorly. Perhaps the Umbrage simply needed a while to master the weapons they wielded.

Massoritu herself showed more bafflement than fear: what had happened bore no resemblance to what she had expected. She shifted abruptly, glancing about as the ice landed here and there. I saw no effort to evade what came her way. Standing with her arms folded and pulled tight against her little breasts, she looked like someone fighting off the morning chill instead of a crowd of executioners.

Then, as the Umbrage took up chunk after chunk from the ground, hurled each in turn, and stooped for more, some of them struck home. One of them grazed Massoritu's shoulder and spun away. Another hit her right leg. Another, a foot. Another, her left hand. Her back. Her other leg. Her leg again. Her left shoulder. Soon ice was hitting her more often than it missed, mostly little chunks, but hard; and with each blow Massoritu jolted one way, then another, reaching out to fend off the chunks, and let out a little grunt. Soon the missiles rained down against her so steadily that there was no relief in her being struck, and her grunts came so steadily that they turned into one long utterance. She staggered this way and that. She brought her hands up to protect herself from one blow but missed another five or ten coming with it. She jerked and jolted. She swung about to block whatever she could. But every motion was pointless; nothing she did could make a difference.

The Umbrage moved in. Grabbing ice from the ground, they battered Massoritu with fragments that had already struck her once, twice, three times. Blood streamed from her face and left great blotches on her robe. Her hands, limp and red, reached toward us in supplication. There was no mercy: only ice.

Many Moon-spans earlier, on a slope in Leqsif-faltho, I once cowered as stones the size of a man's fist struck down everyone around me, and I myself felt the fear then that this young woman now surely felt. But those missiles had hit everyone among us; whatever else I feared, it was not dying alone. That is what struck me hardest about Massoritu as I watched her jolted this way and that by the ice everyone else flung at her: the girl's solitude.

As she sank to her knees, as she clasped her head with both hands, as she slumped forward to protect her face from this strange hailstorm now raining down upon her, I heard what sounded at the time like nothing more than a twisted wail, but what since then has echoed to clarity within my mind: ". . . may the Sun's brilliance and the Moon's radiance combine to illuminate my soul forever."

Some of the men staggered forth carrying great slabs of ice which, raised above their heads, they brought down on her.

[Jesse O'Keefe, journal entry, dated the Seventh Day of the Third Moon-span, Sundecline (February 14, 1922).]

Either Aeslu (as it seems) is tipping me off.

Or else Forster Beckwith has forged the letter.

It's true I've never seen her English script—I don't even know if she can write in English—but this *looks* right. There's nothing forged about it. I can't believe that Forster could fake her handwriting no matter how hard he tried. Surely this letter is what it seems.

But there's one other possibility. What if Aeslu wrote this letter herself, but its contents are deceptive? What if it *is* a trap—one she's setting herself?

No: that's out of the question. I can't believe she'd betray me. Not after all we've been through. Not to gang up with Forster Beckwith, of all people. Not with him in charge of the Umbrage. Aeslu would die before she ever coaxed me into that hyena's lair. Especially with herself as bait.

Yet how can I know?

There's only one way to be sure.

[Aeslu of Vmatta, *Chronicle of the Last Days*.]

The day of Massoritu's death turned out bright and warm. The Umbrage went about their business: dismantling the camp, grazing the path-beasts, gathering grass, mending equipment. Older children played games: dashing about and pelting each other with snowballs. Mothers and babies sat basking in the Sun's warmth.

By late afternoon all the ice had melted. Massoritu's blood remained on the tundra grasses, but the weapons that killed her had disappeared.

If only my thoughts about her might have vanished so easily! That whole day I could think of only her gaze as the chunks of ice rained down upon her.

We killed the wrong person that day. Massoritu was not the traitor; the traitor was someone else altogether, someone I had never suspected, someone so close to my own view that I never even thought to suspect her.

[Jesse O'Keefe, journal entry, dated the Eighth Day of the Third Moon-span, Sundecline (February 15, 1922).]

A messenger arrives with news of Aeslu's approach. It seems impossible, yet as I rush from my tent I see her coming up the glacier toward our camp. I set out with the Heirs to meet her. I rush forth, she runs to me, we embrace, we cling to each other as if we will never let go. She is alive; she is with me again at last!

Then we are alone in my tent. We gaze at one another for a long time. Aeslu is beautiful, cloaked in her long black hair, the curves of her body full of promise beneath her robes. I am burning with desire. Reaching out, I untie her garments and let them fall to the floor. I take her in my arms.

But she is cold to my touch—cold as an axe-blade on a winter's day. I push her back. At once I see that her skin lacks its lovely brown hue; it is blue-white instead. I touch her breasts. Cold and hard. Hard as ice. I touch her hips: ice. Her thighs: ice. Her belly: ice. Aeslu has turned to ice. Yet she moves, she motions to me, she beckons invitingly.

Baffled, frightened, I am sure only of one thing. I am aflame with craving for her. Literally: for when I glance at my hands, they are glowing and pulsing like embers in a banked hearth. I rip off my tunic and find that my chest, too, is red-orange with fire. I tear off all my clothes. My feet, my legs, my belly and groin are all in flames.

I stammer something.

Aeslu laughs gently. "Are you surprised?" she asks. "I am the Moon's Stead, thus made of ice. You are the Sun's Stead, thus made of fire. Come to me." She opens her arms to me.

I hesitate, then embrace her. Aeslu's flesh sputters and sizzles against my own. I pick her up, carry her to the bed, settle her down on the blankets.

When she takes me and I enter her, we explode in a blinding flash of light, heat, and sparks—and I awake.

[Aeslu of Vmatta, *Chronicle of the Last Days*.]

I would like to have blamed Forssabekkit for what had happened—not just for a young woman's death at Umbrage hands, but also for everything else leading up to that death—and of course in some respects the Man of Ignorance was indeed at fault. Yet is a fish, tempted by bait on a hook, obliged to swallow? No doubt many fish convince themselves that they will eat the bait and spit out the hook, and thus end up snagged on their own delusions. Now I found myself caught in more ways than I had thought possible.

If it had been a matter only of appetites whetted, I would not have cared. But something else had changed, too; something harder to place and identify and even harder to describe. I felt something wither within me. What, precisely? At the time I had no idea, and none even now. All I can say is this: what I now knew filled my mind till it forced out what I had known before. I could no longer recall most of the prayers I had spoken all my life. What few of them I remembered I now spoke without full grasp of their significance. *May the Sun's brilliance and the Moon's radiance combine to illuminate my soul forever....* What did that mean? Whatever it meant, why did it matter? Once I knew; now I had forgotten. This grieved me. Yet precisely because of what I had forgotten I felt helpless to understand the reason for my grief.

All I knew was that I had forgotten how to worship the Sun and the Moon. I had forgotten how to love Ossonnal and Lissallo. I had forgotten how to believe that my worship and my love made any difference. I had forgotten how to care why forgetting mattered.

[Jesse O'Keefe, journal entry, dated the Ninth Day of the Third Moon-span, Sundecline (February 16, 1922).]

"If you want to stop the Umbrage," I told the Masters, "then let's stop them. Let's stop them so fast and hard they'll never know what happened."

Loftossotoi looked skeptical, as always. "You said it was not yet time."

"It wasn't—but now it is."

Marhaislu asked, "How will we do it?"

"By whatever means it takes."

"We have only the same weapons as before.

Weapons you said were insufficient against the Man of Ignorance."

"Let's use something else, then."

"A Lowland thing?"

I grew impatient with their interrogation. "I'm the Man of Knowledge. I reject the Lowland. I'll use what the Sun and Moon themselves bestow on the Mountain-Drawn to stop our enemy."

The Masters waited in silence.

"I need people to help me," I told the Masters.

"Whatever you want," said Marhaislu, "you will have."

[Aeslu of Vmatta, *Chronicle of the Last Days*.]

This is what frightened me most of all: that the losses I now suffered would not be mine alone. I was the Moon's Stead; what I did was in its own way a baited hook. Dangling myself before the Mountain-Drawn, whom I had caught? What chance did my people have for disengaging before I dragged us all to our doom? If I did not or could not disengage, what other choices lay before me?

Not long before (though it seemed a thousand Sun-spans past) a madwoman had screamed at me about the risks I ran in seeking the goal before me. I had ignored her. She was a crazy old hag, a vine-infested crone whose words I could scarcely follow, much less understand. That woman had turned out to be my mother. Now I myself was the Moon's Stead, which she had been at the time, and her words came back to me in a rush.

The Woman of the Wood had ranted at us—at Jassikki, Norroi, Forssabekkit, and me—when we set off to find the Hermit on his mountaintop. As we stumbled about the morning, she shouted, babbled, and screamed. We had worried at the time that the Woman would signal our whereabouts to whomever lurked in wait for us. We soon discovered that our fears were well-founded; we crossed paths with Varkoislu's band of Umbrage not long afterwards. Now, looking back on that time, it wasn't the Woman's noise that worried me. It was the words themselves.

You can seek the Mountain, she had told us. But do you imagine that the Mountain Made of Light is that and nothing more? The Mountain Made of Sun, the Mountain Made of Moon? A warm glow from which you never have to shield your eyes?

Recalling her words, I considered the Woman's utterances to be dares more than questions. Perhaps my state just then tinged these words with a sense of danger that the Woman herself never intended. Perhaps she was just a crazy old hag after all. Yet the more I remembered, the more uneasy I felt.

Ask whatever questions you want! she screamed. Dream whatever dreams! Hope whatever hopes! Let me warn you: it is not so simple.

My own doubts lent more and more credence to the Woman's words.

Once you see the Mountain you will wish you never cast eyes on it! You will stagger back, clutching at your face and praying the Sun has not blinded you for whatever remains of your scant days! You think that is the whole story? Then listen to me, you pitiable fools! The Mountain Made of Light is the Mountain Made of Shadow! The Mountain Made of Darkness! You do not believe me yet? Well, then—soon enough!

How soon, I wondered. Now?

Seek it and fail! Worse: seek it and find the opposite of what you wanted. *Then* you will come to your senses! You will understand that the Mountain Made of Light is the Mountain Made of Rain! The Mountain Made of Dust! The Mountain Made of Fire! Mountain Made of Song! Mountain Made of Clouds! Mountain Made of Blood! Mountain Made of Bone! Mountain Made of Paper! Mountain Made of Eyes! Mountain Made of Fog! Mountain Made of Flesh—

She had said nothing more (or at least we heard nothing) for we soon lost the Woman's shouts to the river noise. But I had heard enough. Though still baffled by what each word meant on its own, I now understood what they meant together—how they both dared me to do what I must do and cursed me for doing it.

2

19 February 1922

Hail, O noble father!

For weeks now we've navigated the back-alleys of the Andes; we've slogged across muddy bottomlands, forded rivers, strayed through boulder fields, scaled cliffs, skittered up glaciers, eased our way over passes, lowered ourselves into the next valley, and, reaching the other side, we've started the same sequence of ordeals yet again; in short, we've wandered about in a maze whose path we can scarcely imagine and whose goal may not exist. To what purpose? Ah, there's a good question! Of course the Rixtirs are confident that they know: to find the Mountain Made of Light. I've let their enthusiasms inspire me in turn, define my purposes, drive me on.

Yet I now wonder if my first assumptions— my assumptions from almost a year ago, when I first arrived in these mountains—was

perhaps more accurate than what I've relied
upon more recently. I've been duped. Worse
than duped: hoodwinked, bamboozled,
shanghaied. Not that the Rixtirs mean any
harm (at least the Umbrages don't) for they
seem far too simple to pull much wool over
my eyes. Yet their fundamental eagerness got
the best of me; their enthusiasm overwhelmed
my better judgment; their childlike trust
became a bacterium that infected my
otherwise strong powers of circumspection.
One party, especially, has deluded me more
than I ever thought possible.

I refer to Aeslu, the moon-child, the princess
whose presence here has served my purposes
so well. Or so I imagined. I noted some months
ago that you might well question (as I myself
did) the veracity of her claims of loyalty
toward me. I noted as well that I had
considered the possibility of expedience on her
part—and the possibility, too, of still darker
motives. Perhaps I should have been more
stringent than I was in my suspicions. It now
appears that the young lass constituted a fifth
column from the start.

A few days back, one of my lieutenants
intercepted a letter (a love letter, no less!) that
Aeslu had sent to my arch-rival hereabouts. I
refer to none other than Jesse O'Keefe, the ex-
doughboy I've mentioned, who, though
formerly content to putter on his aimless
anthropological errand, now bandies about in
local garb, poses as the long-awaited Man of
Knowledge, and calls himself Jassikki. What a
dreary surprise. It's bad enough that this chap
has reappeared on the scene; but to think that
Aeslu is in league with him (not to mention in
love)! I would have liked to see the letter as a
mistake—someone else's smear tactic against

the young lady, perhaps—but I can find no way around the facts when they appear before me in the most literal black and white. So I must face the reality of Aeslu's intentions. Far be it for me to end up hookwinked by a woman. . . . Somehow the impossible has come to pass.

Almost. I have, after all, intercepted the letter.

The question now is what to do in response. The Umbrages don't take kindly to this sort of disloyalty. Even a mere commoner met a grisly end some days ago: stoned, or rather iced, for the pecadillo of merely transporting the letter in question. Natives don't beat around the bush on these matters. Imagine the punishment likely when someone of far greater rank commits a far greater betrayal.

Of course, she has it coming.

Yet somehow I've balked. Why, exactly, I can't say. All I know is that I've balked.

I could have turned her over to the Umbrages for a little of their summary justice; I could have dispensed it myself. But I haven't. I haven't even indicated to anyone that Aeslu wrote and sent the letter. (The Umbrages, though capable of writing their own crude alphabet, are usually illiterate in modern languages, among them English, and thus know only that the messenger was en route to their enemy. They remain ignorant of the message itself.) I haven't even let on to Aeslu herself that I know what she's up to. All she knows is that her packet never made it out.

This is not to say, Dad, that I've been passive in response to these events. Quite the contrary. Why grant Jesse O'Keefe, of all people, the satisfaction of a straight story? No, I've made sure that the doughboy's rattled brain keeps rattling. Shortly after I learned of the

intercepted letter, I sent another messenger to
dispatch an epistle outwardly much like
Aeslu's to the good professor—an epistle that
will nevertheless prompt him to do precisely
the opposite of what he would have done if the
moon-child's words had reached him after all.
His efforts to pursue the Umbrage will keep
him busy; the fullness of time will deliver him
right into my hands.

The surrogate letter also buys me time as
well to decide Aeslu's own fate.

I can't believe she's done this to me. I
thought I'd swayed her, changed her,
transformed her. I thought I'd coaxed her out
of her benighted ways—not just her pointless
infatuation with Jesse O'Keefe, not just her
allegiance to the Heirs, but her commitment to
all the Rixtirs' gobbledegook. I thought I'd
helped her see the light.

What she doesn't understand is that she's
wasted on these people. The Rixtirs made
Aeslu a princess but still don't see what's
remarkable about her. They don't fully grasp
her beauty, her wits, her fire. She's more than
they bargained for. She's more than even *I*
bargained for. Yet at least I see what makes
her such a live wire. She's sharp, this Aeslu.
There's far more to her than I first thought.
Forget the moon-princess stuff; what matters
is more than that—her cleverness, her zeal,
her fighting spirit. You don't find women like
that at home. You would blanch at the
thought, Dad, but this gal has more to her than
a whole legion of your tycoon-cronies' well-
bred debutantes. What a relief to find someone
with a little spark: someone who knows what
she wants—something worth having, too—and

knows how to get it. Now if only I could
convince her that I'm what she wants as well.

I just don't understand why she hankers for
that little troublemaker when she might have
me instead.

And so I'm brooding a bit, deciding what to
do next.

Forster

3

[Marcelino Hondero Huamán, formerly Marsalai
S'safta, interviewed September 9, 1970.]

One afternoon the Man of Knowledge came to
the tent where some of us had been quartered. I
didn't know who it was at first. The Man of
Knowledge didn't usually deal with us directly; he
sent an Adept or an Aspirant to speak with us instead. For this reason I didn't react when I heard
voices outside the tent. Then someone said, "It's
him!" We rushed outside.

It was indeed the Man of Knowledge. *The Man
of Knowledge*. I was bewildered—no, terrified.
Why was he here, visiting *us*? We found out a moment later.

"Who among you," he asked, "will help lead the
Heirs against the Umbrage?"

No one spoke. No one stepped forward.

"Who will help destroy the Man of Ignorance?"

Still no response.

"This could be the last mission of your lives,"
the Man of Knowledge went on. "But I know you
will accept the challenge anyway. For I am asking

you to be among the first Heirs to push past the Umbrage camp and start our climb of the Mountain Made of Light."

No one leapt forth to volunteer.

He went on: "Why should you accept the danger? Because I depend on you. I myself will lead the raid."

I could scarcely believe what I heard. Raids were for pathscouts and warriors—not for the man who led us. Scouts would make the way safe for warriors; warriors would make the way safe for Masters; and Masters would make the way safe for Jassikki himself. It made no sense for him to go first.

"Who will protect the Man of Knowledge when he takes the Umbrage by surprise? Who will help him fight the Man of Ignorance?"

Three people stepped forward: two men and a woman. Even as I contemplated Jassikki's words, two more women stepped forward.

"The time has come for knowledge to banish ignorance," he told us, "and for light to vanquish darkness. Who will join me?"

I could no longer refuse. This was the Guide who would lead us to the Mountain and upward to the Summit!

I, too, stepped forth.

[Juana Méndez de Mariátegui, formerly Hunatau Mantassi of Va'atafissorih, interviewed September 9, 1970.]

One afternoon something seemed different. Something in the air. Maybe the air itself. We were about ten days into the Third Moon-span, Sundecline, so the wet season was ending. Within another Moon-span we would see the Sun again in all his glory, but not yet. Still, something was dif-

ferent. During Sunrebirth the clouds had pressed
down upon us night and day, with almost no letup
in the rain; now we could tell the storms apart,
and they came later each day. That afternoon we
could smell the rain coming and hurried about in
expectation of the downpour. Clouds rolled about
overhead, parted around the peaks, shifted,
poured down the valley. We heard the rumble of
distant avalanches but no thunder. We kept working. More clouds descended from between the
peaks: avalanches of clouds. But no rain. The rain
never came.

Then I saw someone—a young pathbeast
herder—looking off toward the far end of the valley. Just looking. I turned to see what he saw—
and I saw it myself.

In and among the clouds rose the Mountain. The
Mountain I'd never seen, but recognized at once.
It filled half the sky! It seemed to *be* the sky, for
it loomed over us, dwarfing the ice, rocks, land,
rivers, everything. The other mountains scarcely
deserved the name: little more than footstools set
before the great wall itself. But calling it a wall
does no justice to the sight. Stone and ice made
up this mountain, but not stone and ice alone. The
light! Imagine the aftermath of a rainstorm—how
the clouds part, how the Sun shines through, how
the great beams splay outward to form a pyramid
of light—and this will begin to reveal what we
saw. I blinked, I squinted, I shielded my eyes, so
dazzling was the Mountain. It was impossible to
watch yet impossible not to watch.

A cry went up around me: others among the
Umbrage who saw what I did. Catching sight of
the Mountain, people called out to one another.
Each made some sort of utterance in fear, delight,
surprise, alarm, or exaltation. Some beckoned to
their fellows. Some pointed. Some fell to their
knees. Some wept or shrieked or laughed. Some

fainted. Some cowered on the ground. Some danced. And as the word went out, more and more of the Umbrage dropped what they were doing, emerged from their tents, looked up, saw what everyone else had already seen, called out, and stared as helplessly as the rest of us.

PART FIVE

"Can you explain this to me?" asked Esperanza Martínez. *"I do not know your language."*

"Perhaps it's not just the language," I told her.

22 February 1922

Pater Noster,

This will be my last letter for a while. Not that it makes much difference: I won't be sending it and you won't be receiving it. Yet for reasons I find hard to articulate, I feel a continuing obligation to explain myself. Don't get me wrong, Dad. I don't mean explain in the sense of justify. As you may have noticed, I gave up justifying myself in your eyes long ago. Rather, I mean a desire to set the record straight. Not that I care what you think—don't kid yourself.

Let me start by reminding you of some events now years past.

When I returned home from Yale, you agreed that a *wanderjahr* would do me no harm and might (in your words) "serve as a kind of spiritual purgative." I took issue with the implications inherent in your metaphor but agreed that a year's travel in Europe might well get something out of my system. Indeed it did. That trip purged me of the most noxious psychic infestations, the most poisonous emotional toxins, the most debilitating intellectual parasites, which, for as long as I could remember—verily, for as long as I had been alive—had been devouring me from the inside out: the Beckwith mystique; the concomitant family obsessions with propriety, social position, and Duty; the

pursuit of money at the expense of everything
else. Of course you arranged for me to take
the usual Grand Tour, replete with visits to
the right families, the right museums, the right
concert halls, the right tourist sites. Were you
surprised that I did everything wrong? That I
visited no families, no museums, no concert
halls, no tourist sites? That I spent little time
in the cities at all, and then only enough to
consort with precisely the debauched
aristocrats whom you warned me to avoid at
all costs? That I fled to the countryside
instead—first to Wales, then to the Pyrenees,
at last to the Alps—and spent virtually the
whole year eating in fourth-rate inns, sleeping
in shepherds' huts, and scrambling among the
crags? That the first year gave way to a
second? That the second year gave way to a
third? That the third year led me not just to
semi-civilized areas of Europe, but to
Afghanistan and the Karakoram? No, you were
not surprised. Neither were you surprised
when I claimed that these travels, far from
being the waste of time and slide into
indolence that you considered them, had in
fact proved to be precisely the spiritual
purgative that you had so urgently prescribed
in the first place.

But you were angry. Father, you were angry.
Hardly for the first time; certainly, however,
with an intensity that I found surprising
despite what I knew of you. By what right did
I go gallavanting halfway around the world
(and at your expense) for no purpose more
substantial than to wander the treacherous
labyrinths of Swiss glaciers? By what right did
I expend not just time but incalculable energy
surmounting the deadliest obstacles that
nature might raise before me? By what right

did I regard this athletic vagabondage not merely as valuable in its own right but as *preparation* for efforts of still greater foolishness and irresponsibility? Your telegrams all but smouldered when I read them. Your letters, having somehow survived their transit to me without reducing themselves to ashes, rustled in my hands as if on the verge of spontaneous combustion. But despite the remoteness of my farflung camps, you reached me. You made your feelings known. You demanded an explanation, a proper accounting of myself.

And I gave it.

That, Father, was when you threatened to cut me off. I hesitate to use the word "disown." Despite the sheer abundance of all your worldly goods, I suspect that even you would admit that your sons, whatever else, are something other than mere chattel. Nevertheless, you made your intentions clear. I should quit the precincts of my indolence or remain there at my own expense.

You still imagine that I came home because your threat weighed too heavily upon me. I'll admit that it was a considerable millstone—heavier, in fact, than the full expedition packs I've carried on my own back at altitudes of 20,000 feet or so—but not heavier than I could have tolerated. No, I returned to Europe, then to England, then to New York, for other reasons. Perhaps you can guess which. Something about the Kaiser. Something about a festering disagreement between the Germans and the French. Something about— But you grasp my implications. Not that I felt personally in danger. On the contrary, I knew that President Wilson, whatever his shortcomings, would keep America out of the fight, and that an American of my age and background had little to fear from a European war of the sort that appeared imminent. Hearing what little news we received in Afghanistan about the possible outbreak of hostilities on the Continent did little to alarm me. You would be surprised, Father, by how slight even the world's greatest calamities appear when viewed from the summit of any mountain worthy of the name. Even once you cut the rope I dangled from (so to speak) and I started home, it occurred to me that waiting out the war in Switzerland might have its charms. The Swiss know better than to entangle themselves in these internecine squabbles. More to the point, observing the battle from a lofty alpine seat would have its charms. It would put things in their proper perspective.

Yet I returned. Precisely why, I still find difficult to explain. No doubt the impulse to draw close to one's own kin in times of danger has something to do with it. Perhaps on some level I feared for my own safety despite what in retrospect now seems wise about a possible return to Switzerland. Think what you will: my voyage back to America wasn't what you construed it to be.

Of course war broke out shortly thereafter. F. F. Beckwith & Sons ended up indispensible to the British effort, and, in the long run, the family's munitions works proved crucial as well to successful American participation. And as the need for our products grew, as our factories expanded to meet the need, as the demands of running the family empire demanded more and more of your time, energy, and ingenuity, you exerted continually greater force against me to do what needed to be done, what in all honesty I wanted to do, and what ultimately seemed beyond my ability: to accept your challenge that I become a captain of industry; that I lead my troops of factory workers into the breech; that I honor my family, my father, and myself.

Can you believe me that I tried? Can you believe me that regardless of what you consider my habitual sloth and dereliction of duty, I wanted to perform the task in such a manner as to do the family justice? Father, I tried. I did everything within my power to follow your directives, to learn the workings of the factory, to manage the subordinates assigned to me—in short, to contribute whatever skills I had to offer. My failure does not bespeak indifference or contempt. No matter how convinced you are that all Beckwith blood runs hot with a zeal for business, I know that something else courses through my veins.

But confessions of ineptitude are not my intention now. I have already apologized; I have already asked your forgiveness. Never mind that you felt no reason either to accept the apology or to forgive me. The battle is on, you said; that was no time for weakness, whether paternal or filial. Our whole civilization was at stake. If I could not fulfill the special duty that was our lot, then perhaps I should try by other means.

Here, too, I tried. Volunteering for the officer's corps seemed more than just a gesture, did it not? More than one family— even of our exalted station—has acquitted itself through a son's willingness to serve in the American Expeditionary Force. I would be a liar to claim that I did so without trepidation. Despite my comments about the petty nature of these conflicts as viewed from the mountaintops, I'd seen enough of Europe to imagine the ensuing debacle. By 1918 I had no illusions. I knew what I'd be facing if I ended up Over There. Even so, I volunteered— and eagerly.

What a surprise to find myself rejected. For reasons of physique? I am six feet four inches tall; I weigh two hundred and twenty pounds. For reasons of intelligence? Despite my lack of application (as you sometimes accurately identify what you otherwise misname my sloth) I graduated from Yale with honors in three years instead of four. For reasons of indolence? I have climbed more mountains than all but a handful of men in America. For what reason, then? What explains that I should volunteer my services to my country and find myself rejected? Could it have something to do with my name? With my family? With our wealth?

Thus as the war skidded toward its arbitrary end, you reassured me that more fitting tasks awaited me, that past mistakes could be corrected. Why not (you suggested) join Stuart in Peru? The tutelage of an older brother would do me a world of good. The mines at Tingo María might prove the ideal place to learn a little responsibility. Other Beckwith endeavors—the rubber plantations near Pucallpa, the fertilizer operations off Pisco— would provide some variety to my education in commerce. Not only that: time spent profitably in Peru might even allow for occasional moderate indulgence in the alpine sports which had proved so harmful to my character when pursued in excess.

Need I recapitulate what happened next?

Father, I can spare you the details. You know all too well.

Our family owns tin and silver mines, chemical plants, armament factories, farms, a whole fleet of cargo ships—more companies than you can count. You could have let me look after something that would have inspired me; that would have made me want to please you. It needn't have been extravagant: one of the smaller manufacturing plants, perhaps. Photographic cameras? Rubber boots? Bonbons? You could have let me manage the railroad from Lima to Huancayo. You could have. You didn't. What did you give me instead? The fertilizer business. The guano operations. F. F. Beckwith & Sons has the lease on all those islands off Pisco. I realize that mining the stuff is profitable. For a million years the birds have roosted on the rocks out there, stupid seagulls with nothing better to do than sit there in flocks the size of Cincinnati and add their two cents' worth to a godforsaken landscape. I realize that it adds up. The situation isn't just what it seems; the stuff is worth half its weight in gold. No wonder we have a small army of *cholos* scraping guano off the rocks and loading it into sacks. As you continually reminded me, those islands are one of our most profitable operations. True. And you turned them over to me.

But don't you understand what you did? You put me in charge of shit. Not railroads, not explosives, not industrial chemicals, not even chocolate. You put me in charge of shit.

Why, you ask (or at least you would ask if you were reading this letter) have I exhumed these long-dead events, some of them now almost ten years gone? Why have I dug up our worst misunderstandings, resentments, and points of contention? Why have I refused to let them lie buried where they belong?

For this reason, Father: precisely because I want to show you how dead they are, how dessicated, how well on their way to becoming dust. You argue that I protest too much. How can I claim that these events are dead when they loiter so persistently within the memory? Ah, but that's no argument against their deathly state. Allow me to illuminate all these other recollections with yet another.

Not long ago you took time off from your many endeavors to visit me in Peru. You sailed from New York to Panama, from there to Lima and, disembarking from your ship at Callao, traveled by smaller boat down the coast to Pisco. There you inquired into the state of my work on the fertilizer operation, toured the guano islands, and offered whatever advice I might accept to make both my efforts and their outcome more satisfactory. You expressed concern over my state of mind. Neither then nor now do I doubt the honesty of your expression; even so, I knew (and know) that you were as concerned about the fertilizer trade as you were about your youngest son's happiness. When you dispatched me to Pisco with marching papers to take over the operation, you knew as much as anyone about the desolation of that outpost on the coastal desert. Were you really surprised that a sleepy fishing village flanked by equatorial waters on one side and arid rubble on the other provided a less than hospitable climate for a young man's emotional health? Even so, your comments focused on the foreman's statistics that guano shipments had decreased by almost two percent since the previous year.

Remember our picnic? Having ridden in a motor-launch to the islands—those great wave-battered, slime-streaked outcroppings—we then set off for Pisco and some refreshments at the compound. But I had already spoken with the pilot and, claiming to relay your own instructions, had asked him to head for Paracas rather than the bay. Paracas! There are few sights more sobering than a city whose inhabitants have abandoned it more than a thousand years earlier. You yourself had brought this culture to my attention as a boy: I recall the gold ornaments in your collection. But I suspect that you hadn't seen the place itself despite your many visits to Pisco. Thus my decision to take you there.

"What place is this?" you asked when we finished walking the short distance from the shore, over some dunes, to the site itself.

"Paracas," I replied.

"This is Paracas?"

We stared out over the desert. At first we seemed to be looking at nothing at all: more dunes, hummocks of sandy rock, occasional tufts of grass. Then our eyes adjusted to the contours and detected something more regular, more suggestive of artifice.

"Small wonder," you said. "It simply indicates the fate of cultures that lack an adequate industrial base."

By then Armando and the boy had brought our basket, two folding chairs, and a collapsible umbrella. They began to set things up.

You looked at me in astonishment. "What is the meaning of this?"

"I thought we might have a little *déjeuner sur l'herbe*."

"You can't be serious."

"Quite serious. And quite hungry."

You were, too, and ultimately hunger won out over your sense of propriety. We sat. We ate. Josefina had prepared a passable imitation of *vichissoise*; her watercress sandwiches had somehow survived the heat; the wine was Chilean but more than potable. Armando aquitted himself well as a butler despite his true calling as a fisherman. Food and drink calmed you, and me as well. The deracinating equatorial sun beat down all around but spared us where we slouched beneath our canopy.

Then, at some point, as you gazed out over the desert, as you noticed irregularities in the otherwise uniform grainy texture of the sand, you asked, "What are all those stick-like things?"

"Bones," I replied.

"I beg your pardon?"

"Bones."

You looked at me aghast. "Animal bones?"

"Human."

You stood, Father, abruptly left the circumference of shade that surrounded us, and stalked eight or ten paces into the yellow-white furnace beyond. Looking this way and that, you then stalked back to where I remained sitting.

"Forster, for God's sake," you blurted, "this is a *cemetery*!"

"Technically it's a necropolis—'city of the dead.' This is where the Paracas culture buried everyone."

I then discoursed at some length about how so many bones happened to be lying out in the open. Over the course of their thousand-year history, the people of Paracas placed their dead in the fetal position within woven bags, then interred them in burial mounds. The dry air dessicated the corpses: mummified them. Thousands of these cadavers—perhaps hundreds of thousands—remained in shallow graves scattered over mile after mile of the coastal desert. Only in recent years had anyone thought to disinter them.

Archaeologists from Lima were considering a project to excavate the area, though funds were limited. Men from nearby towns had also begun digging with another, less lofty purpose in mind: treaure-hunting.

You looked at me with a shocked expression. "People are plundering the graves?"

"Of course. That's how you got your jewelry."

"I obtained these items from a reputable antiquarian," you protested.

"And where did *he* obtain them?" I asked in return.

"I see your point. I suppose it's a perfect instance of finders-keepers."

I pulled out some gold ornaments from my pocket just then and held them out to you. "That's how I see it."

At about that time your crude discomfort with the situation smelted itself into pure anger. "You mean to tell me that despite how badly things are going at the plant, you've spent time out here fishing trinkets out of graves? You've diverted your attention from the matter at hand to prowl about like a common grave-robber?"

"It's not what you think."

"What is it, then?"

"A project in its own right."

"Project!"

"Dad, listen to me."

"I've listened well enough. What more could you possibly tell me?"

"Let me explain and I'll tell you."

You stood, signaled to Armando, and stepped aside as he and the boy began to dismantle our improvised gazebo. I waited in hopes that you would signal as plainly to me what I should do. No signal came: not a word, not a smile, not a hint that I might at least explain myself.

"How do you suppose all these bones got here?" I ventured. "It's not because someone took them out one by one. Most of the burial sacs had lain here for half a millennium before the Europeans even showed up in South America. They'd lie here another thousand years if no one bothered them."

"So now you've decided to bother them?"

"To harvest them. Not the bones—their trappings. Jewelry, funerary objects, things like that. And I've done it efficiently."

You looked at me with a gaze of amusement and contempt. *"Efficiently?"*

Another discourse: how some of the locals had grown impatient with random plunder of the necropolis and had devised a more productive technique. They would fasten a stick of dynamite onto the end of a long pole and jam the pole deep into a burial mound, or *huaca*. Once detonated, the dynamite would blow up the *huaca*, launch its long-dead tenants skyward, and rain bones, dessicated flesh, fragments of pottery, shreds of cloth, and other, more precious items over the surrounding area. It was then a simple matter for the *huaqueros* (as they called themselves) to pick over the windfall and gather whatever met their fancy. But it seemed a pity to let these men have their run of the place. Why let their furtive efforts make a shambles of an ancient archaeological site?

"So you stopped them?" you asked.

"No—I hired them. We're cleaning up the mounds at a rate of about ten or twelve daily."

I could remind you of your reaction to this exchange, Dad, but I'm sure you need no reminding. You were outraged. What intrigued me then, however, and intrigues me now, is that your anger struck not at what I had done, but at what I had failed to do: not at my plundering a pre-Columbian burial site, but at my neglecting the guano project near Pisco.

Yet I mention this story—our visit, our boat ride, our picnic, our argument—less to trot out another fight than to press upon you the image of Paracas. Almost a hundred square miles of human bones lie exposed on that desert. Once we stood among them, the skeletons and fragments of skeletons are unavoidable; we saw them everywhere we turned. Yet they are nothing. Exposed to the sun and wind, they will be gone in a trice. Yet something valuable rested in their midst: fine goldwork nestled among dessicated hulks of parchment.

Thus it is when I extract a few insights from the memories of what has happened between us in the past.

One other question you would ask me (again, assuming that you were able to read this letter in the first place) is this: Did the events at Paracas lead to my present situation?

The answer is both yes and no.

After you left Pisco, I had no intention of abandoning my post. This is not to say that I felt pleased with what had transpired between us during your visit, or that your directives to "run a tighter ship" had inspired me toward new heights of managerial excellence; but in truth I had no inclination, much less a plan, to flee the desert. I communicated once or twice with Stuart at Tingo María, in part to sound him out on the outcome of your stay, and I may even have considered the possibility of a quick trip to the mines to talk things over with him further. But Stuart is so clearly a chip off the old block that any fraternal discussions in the near future would most likely resemble paternal ones in the recent past. I may be imcompetent, but I'm not a fool. I'd had enough trouble to last me a while. Thus (and this may surprise you) I decided simply to stay put a while, to settle down, to see what happened.

It was, however, the guano islands themselves that prompted me to seek loftier realms. Sometimes the ridiculous engenders the sublime.

A few days after you left, I made one of my weekly visits to the islands to check up on the operations. It was entirely routine—the boat ride out, the dicey docking procedure in rough seas, the climb up rickety ladders onto the main island itself, the brief interchange with the foreman, the *cholo* laborers' sullen stares, the descent and departure. What these visits accomplish, exactly, I have always found incomprehensible. But this one was different. Altogether different. Not the visit itself: its aftermath.

It was March. Late winter on the coast meant the rainy season in the mountains. Ordinarily I wouldn't have thought much about the season, much less the weather, since the Peruvian coast is nothing if not consistent in its dreariness. But that day the seemingly eternal overcast had dissipated, the sky turned perfect blue, and I could see not only Pisco, Paracas, Nazca, and other towns along the coast, but the desert stretching west and, beyond, barren foothills rising toward the east.

Even you, Father, will understand what crossed my mind. On a day like that I could see the Andes as clearly as one sees the Manhattan skyline from the piers at Hoboken. And in an instant nothing appealed to me more than the prospect of that view.

"Set your course due west," I told Armando.

"*Patrón*, you mean due east."

"If I'd meant east I would have said so."

Though reluctantly, Armando took our little motor-launch out to sea—beyond the islands, beyond sight even of the desert—until we gained enough distance from the continent to see its full height against the eastern horizon.

Surely even someone with such a practical mind as your own, Father, can grasp the impact of the sight before me. One *cordillera* of the Andes parallels the coast only fifty miles inland; another runs alongside the first just a few dozen miles beyond. The resulting walls of mountains rose before me bigger than anything I'd ever seen. Imagine a castle whose breadth extends from one edge of the horizon to the other. Imagine its towers, parapets, spires, domes jutting so far into the sky that the clouds part around them. Imagine the spindrift flying bannerlike from their summits. Imagine the realm over which the lord of such a castle would hold sway. Imagine this, Father—even a little—and you will begin to grasp how Paracas led to my current state of affairs, why leaving the operation at Pisco came to seem necessary (no: inevitable), and what prompted me to do what I have done in the months since then.

So here's the rub.

My past several letters have explained what I've done here but not what it means. What it means, Dad, is that whatever fiascos devolved from my efforts in the past, the present is something else altogether. Do you understand what I'm telling you? Probably not. You think I'm wasting my time. You think I'm wasting *your* time. I suspect you would hesitate to admit even that I'm doing anything at all. No doubt you'd rather sit enthroned in your office directing chits to craven subordinates than go out and *do* something. And this is, in fact, what I'm doing—doing far beyond the reaches of your imagination.

Long ago, Dad, you gave me one of your periodic lectures, in this case a diatribe against my inability to accomplish anything worthy of our heritage. "Are you a Beckwith simply for lack of some other name?" you asked, scarcely able to keep your voice from wavering. "Or are you willing to honor those who preceded you?"

Well, here's my response. I'll confess I'm not in charge of a department, a division, a plant, a company, a corporation. Things are a little different out here in the bush. But this hardly means that I have failed to accomplish anything. Quite the contrary: I have staged a coup worthier of Gordon in the Sudan, of Clive in India, of Cortez in Mexico, than of any fourth-rate industrialist who has built his little castle on alternate layers of chocolate, guano, and high explosives.

Can you grasp what I'm saying? I'm living like a king out here. Better than a king, really:

like a god. And not for nothing. For in a short while the Rixtirs—all these people who wait on me, bring me whatever I want, and listen to my every word as if to an oracle—these Rixtirs will (and this is what's truly remarkable) help me to accomplish something far greater than any of the feats you admire and hold so dear.

What about Aeslu? I hear you asking with the inevitable tut-tut scarcely masked behind a veneer of paternal concern. Never mind that she has proved herself a wolf in lamb's clothing. Within a short while even Aeslu, no matter how smitten with Jesse O'Keefe, will see the light as we reach the mountain of her heart's desire. How can she fail to notice that I, not Jesse, am leading her to the goal? That I, not Jesse, am capable of making the climb itself? That I, not Jesse, will guide her to the summit? In fact she won't fail at all. That mountain is what Aeslu wants most in the world; thus my delivering the goods will sway this poor benighted lass more than she imagines possible.

This is why I've made no effort to call her down on the treachery of that letter. This is why I've tolerated what now seems an unbroken string of lies. It's not that she doesn't crave the doughboy. Perhaps she really does. It's that she doesn't understand how quickly her craving will vanish, a mere bubble in the wind, once we reach the mountain.

Which we will in a trice.

Somewhat later.

We've now come even closer to our destination than I thought possible this morning. I've outdone myself.

After an early start—well before dawn—I led the Umbrages off the glacier and up the ridge to what we thought was our final barrier. This was a granite cliff perhaps two or three hundred feet high, a steep wall culminating in several splintery formations. Anyone casting eyes on them would have thought at once of needles. The Rixtirs are no exception. Needles they were: great narrow shafts of rock. One of them took the name rather more literally than the rest, however, having a fissure at the top that presented an almost perfectly proportioned eye. Clever, these people. The needle's eye. Even you, Father, would have grasped the implications of what I then proceeded to do.

I'll spare you the details. It was a difficult climb. The face turned out to be nearly vertical (as I'd expected) but also less rough than I'd hoped—not ridged or cracked enough to provide enough hand and footholds. I worked my way up with far more trouble than I would ever have anticipated. Some of the trouble was inherent in the rock face; some I caused myself. Of course, a slip would have been fatal, and even a few iron pitons would have provided more than a modicum of safety, but I passed up the opportunity in favor of wowing the natives. Even the Umbrages—by far the best climbers in the area—are so rudimentary in their technique that I wanted my ascent to leave them speechless. It seemed important to confirm my stature in their eyes. Besides, I wanted to save as much ironmongery as possible for later, when I'll really need it. I confined myself to placing one solid spike at the top for later use. A necessary ploy—but nearly disastrous more than once when the holds I trusted gave way and left me dangling. Luckily I managed to catch myself.

Nothing quite like plummeting to my death to compromise my status in the Umbrages' eyes!

The top—if that's the proper term—was what I anticipated. By some fluke of geology that great shaft of granite had split at its highest reaches; two blocks of stone had slid sideways in opposite directions until stopped by parallel shafts on either side; a third block had toppled onto the first two, capping them and creating what appeared at a distance to be the needle's eye. The fissure itself was about ten feet wide at the base and perhaps twenty feet tall. Some needle. Some eye. Bits of granite debris and a grit-studded snowdrift had accumulated there—nothing that complicated my setting up a good anchor for the Umbrages' use when they followed me up. Of course I could have merely thrown down the rope and signaled to them; they are sufficiently adept at least to figure out the rest. Here, too, I thought the proper effect was important. I anchored the line, tested it, then slung the rope around my body in the proper way, backed off the edge, and rappeled down to where everyone else waited. Umbrages thrive on that sort of display.

After that it was quick work to send them all on their way. I went up again to anchor two more lines and keep an eye on things. Aeslu stayed below to translate my shouted commands to her people. Up they went, three at a time, most of them doing pretty well. A few balked, but not many. This was, after all, what the whole race had been awaiting for an unseemly long time span. To think that these people had restrained themselves nearly four hundred years from doing what I've pulled off in little more than six months!

Of course there wasn't room up there for everyone. The Umbrage expedition numbers a thousand people, maybe more; that little belfry couldn't have housed more than a few dozen safely. Either the ascent had to stop or the descent had to begin on the opposite side. In some ways there wasn't much reason to linger. We'd all hoped for a fine view, of course, but the weather hadn't deigned to comply. The usual dense cloud cover lay over everything in sight. For a while these clouds actually settled onto the spire we'd climbed, shrouding us in gray. This soon lifted but still left us no sense of our surroundings.

A pity. The Rixtirs would have given anything for a glimpse of their peak. Aeslu, especially, was all but dying for it.

"No luck with the scenery?" I asked her as she gazed off to the east.

"It is there," she said. "I know it."

She was probably right. No matter how little we could see, what we heard was something else altogether. Now and then great splitting noises reached us from beyond the cloudy void, with arrhythmic rumbles following for a long time after. This part of the world is plagued with avalanches, of course; all of the big Andean peaks send great masses of rock and ice flying almost continuously. The sound of rockfall didn't promise that the peak producing it was the much-touted Mountain Made of Light. Yet the thunder we heard was impressive: bigger, louder, more frequent, and originating from higher up than what I might have expected otherwise.

Anyway, there wasn't much to see, and Aeslu knew it. Even so she insisted on staying up there with me as I helped the Umbrage up into the vestibule of sorts that we now occupied, then down the other side.

"The other side" was a shorter drop: a brief

rappel onto what appeared to be a relatively harmless snowfield. I saw no evident crevasses; its angle seemed consistent with an unbroken surface. I couldn't have asked for anything much more convenient. If nothing else, this would allow us a safe place to camp and regain our bearings.

Aeslu remained at my side throughout the whole process of hoisting and lowering the Umbrages. In itself this was a good sign. Then, once we two were alone and prepared to make our own descent, she turned to me. "What about Jassikki?" she asked.

"What about him?" I responded without even looking in her direction at first.

When I looked, though, I could see that my seeming diffidence put her off. "Are we not going to stop his own passage?"

"Of course not."

By now she was baffled. She couldn't constrain her bewilderment. "But he is Jassikki. He leads the Heirs."

"True," I said as I slung the rope around my legs, back, and shoulders. "Very true." Almost at once I backed off the edge and descended.

There was no point in telling her what I had in mind—not after Aeslu herself had kept me in the dark so long about her own intentions. Nothing appealed to me less than having Jesse O'Keefe around for this final phase of the hunt. Who knows what sort of nuisance he could still make of himself? Yet he did, after all, still have the Mountain Stone in his possession. No matter how confident I felt of climbing the mountain without the help that an overrated paperweight might provide, I didn't feel like taking chances. What if it truly turned out to be the *sine qua non* to the climb itself?

More than once this thought had crossed my mind: to barter Aeslu for the stone. If Jesse wanted his lush native maiden, let him have her. The price would be the stone itself. Aeslu herself might go along quite eagerly with the bargain; she would get her doughboy after all. Meanwhile, I could proceed to what mattered most. A tidy deal.

Ultimately this arrangement made no sense. Jesse had no right either to the mountain or to the maiden; I felt no obligation to forego either one. Why not have both? The letter I sent him a while back—with Aeslu's signature, of course, to make it more persuasive—should serve as an adequate invitation. And the sentries I've posted up at the needle's eye should prove the perfect welcoming committee. Surely the much-coveted Mountain Stone will fall right into my lap.

A few last lines.

Having grown a bit stiff writing at length, I stepped out of my tent briefly to stretch and to catch a breath of fresh air.

I ended up with rather more than that.

Some time ago I mentioned that this is the wet season—rainy in the valleys, snowy up here on the ice—and, in fact, few days have passed without a storm of one sort or another. Most of our glacial camps have left us vulnerable to flurries, abrupt storms, even blizzards. These at once complicate and simplify our lives: complicate because of the mess and discomfort they impose; simplify because of the effortless camouflage they allow. Our present camp has been no exception. Ever since threading our way through the so-called Needle's Eye, we have

been under siege by alternate barrages of rain,
sleet, and snow. This has served our
purposes—not just for hiding us from
whatever pesky Heirs may be lurking about as
we prepare for the next step, but also, in the
restless meantime, for writing the occasional
anti-paternal diatribe. Even so, the rough
weather wears thin. Time's a-wasting.
Admittedly I'd like to size up the terrain
before we proceed further.

   I just got my chance. Leaving my tent, I stood
beyond the door a few minutes. I nodded to the
guards, chatted with them to the degree
possible, and watched some of the other
Umbrages go about their business. I then
stepped away. They have no concept of personal
privacy; it's not hard to feel hemmed in among
them. It felt good to back off and get a little
distance.

   Something else made a difference, too,
something I couldn't identify at first. The light
shifted. No: intensified. It grew more complex.
I realized just then that the overcast had
loosed its grip on the sky and had begun
dissipating, so that a single mass of gray
quickly became individual clouds. The process
happened with bewildering speed. It almost
appeared as if a great head of steam were
simply boiling away.

   What remained was the mountain. I say *the*
because I felt no doubt over which. I'd not
seen anything like it in this part of the world—
or anywhere else, for that matter. In contour it
bears more than a passing resemblance to
other Andean peaks: a massive parabola frayed
by millennia of wind, snowfall, and erosion. Its
scale, however, is almost Himalayan. Granite
has thrust upward to form a single dome at
least 22,000 feet in altitude. Glacial ice has

then coated this dome over the eons to augment its already vast dimensions. Innumerable avalanches have whetted each ridge into a deadly blade, and faults in the underlying stone have exposed cliffs that to the present day probably unleash cataclysmic rockfalls. It's a splendid, terrifying sight.

Of course I was observing from so close that I couldn't get a good sense of detail, yet I could see enough to know that this peak has been worth the wait. How is it that no one has found it yet? Who knows! Who cares! It really makes no difference.

All that matters is that I've found it. Now I'll climb it. It's here, it's magnificent, it's mine—a peak indeed worthy of the name Mt. Beckwith.

PART SIX

PART SIX

We sat in a dimly lit room. A single lightbulb dangled from the ceiling, its filament pulsing slightly to the rhythm of a decrepit generator. A few bugs orbited the bulb. Below, Juana Méndez de Mariátegui, Marcelino Hondero Huamán, and Esperanaza Martínez sipped Ovaltine and nibbled some crackers that Juana's thirtyish granddaughter had served us. For a long time no one spoke.

[Juana Méndez de Mariátegui, formerly Hunatau Mantassi of Va'atafissorih, interviewed September 10, 1970.]

I should have been happy that night, and in some ways I was. The next day we would set off to climb the Mountain! How long had I dreamed of this event? How long had all the Mountain-Drawn before me dreamed, too? I could scarcely believe what was happening. Best of all, the Umbrage, not the Heirs, would be making the climb. Dawn could not come soon enough.

So I worked hard to prepare my equipment; I helped some of the others get ready, too; and I lingered with them outside our tents to sing Umbrage songs—anything to pass the time more quickly.

Let hailstones fall, let snow come swirling;
Let Lowlanders swarm through the whole High
    Realm.
Let the Masters rail and the Heirs run in dread—
The Umbrage have reached the Mountain Made
    of Light!

Somehow it wasn't enough. No matter how delighted I felt to be setting off, I felt some other emotion as well. Some kind of puzzlement. Some kind of uncertainty. I couldn't even place what it was. All I knew was that as we built our fires, danced around them, sang our songs, and watched the sparks fly upward, I hoped that the man and the woman leading us knew what they were doing.

[Aeslu of Vmatta, *Chronicle of the Last Days.*]

I would have used Jassikki's own knife, of course, if I could have done so. That would have given Forssabekkit a dose of the same medicine he once gave my mother: the exact same medicine from the exact same source. It would also have given Jassikki a role in administering the cure, however indirect, though my hand alone would perform the surgery. But this was impossible. Jassikki's knife lay far away, lost somewhere in the grass near the Leqsiffaltho wood. Some other instrument would have to suffice. Ultimately it made no difference. Anything would do—anything that could remove the tumor growing in the flesh of the Mountain Land.

I speak of medicine, of surgery, of cures. Yet in preparing to do the deed, I felt less like a flesh-healer than a patient, as though I, not Forssabekkit, would fall under the knife. My head spun at the thought of what I was about to do—or would fail to do. My chest heaved for breath. My legs trembled so hard that they nearly failed me altogether. Why was I so afraid? All I intended was to do what needed doing—and not for myself, but for all the Mountain-Drawn.

If anything, I felt worse than a patient does before the healer's ministrations. What would happen in just a short while seemed more than a fleshly cure. It was a rite, a purgation of something terrible from our midst. I have heard that long ago (even longer ago than the white bearded slavemasters' arrival in the Mountain Land) the tribes dwelling here sacrificed human beings now and then in the belief that their offering would calm the angry gods they worshipped. I dreaded even the thought that such savagery had existed before the Mountain-Drawn perceived the true gods who protect and nurture us. Yet no doubt such sacrifices still occur. Perhaps from time to time they must. Thus in bracing myself for a tryst with Forssabekkit, I was well aware that one would now take place—though whether I would be the priest or the victim, I had no idea.

This is how I prepared.

First, I dressed in the robe that Umbrage weavers had contrived at Forssabekkit's bidding. What strange attire! Despite its length, this garment left me feeling more exposed than clothed, for its fabric was loose in weave and did little to cover my arms, back, shoulders, and upper chest. Yet if the Man of Ignorance found such garb enticing, I would wear it.

Next I put up my hair in the manner that Forssabekkit's flatbooks suggested: great swirls accumulating on my head. Here again I felt astonished by the awkwardness of Lowland ways; but if hair became the web necessary to catch my prey, hair would be the thread I spun. If nothing else, my hair now provided the perfect hiding place for my stinger.

Then I set the Diadem on my head. Symbol of the land I loved, gift of the Founders who taught my people who they are, this crown surely protected me from the dark forces I would soon confront.

Or would it? I wavered. I faltered in securing the Diadem to my hair. There was still time . . .

Perhaps I should do something else, try some other gambit. I could find some of the Heirs who, like Massoritu, were hidden among the Umbrage amassed here on the ice. I could rouse them into mutiny against the infidels. If that failed, I could dissuade the Umbrage themselves. I could convince Forrsabekkit of his foolishness and depravity. I could—

It was hopeless. Nothing would turn back the Man of Ignorance but the forces of knowledge. Nothing would dispel his darkness but light. Lacking help from Jassikki, from the Masters, and from the Heirs, I had no choice but to do alone what needed to be done.

Then another impulse coursed through me: the urge to flee. No matter how little time remained to fight off Forssabekkit, surely there was still time to spare at least my own life. I could leave the camp. I could stumble off the ice to safety. I could seek refuge in the valley below. I could make at least an attempt to escape. If I succeeded, then perhaps I might reach the Heirs and (if they had already grasped the danger facing them) might lead their forthsetting in one last thrust against the Umbrage. And if I failed—well, then I would fail. I would be no worse off than when I first attempted to flee the Umbrage camp nearly five Moon-spans earlier.

At once I threw off this foolishness. Not that I would inevitably have failed to get away: the Umbrage seemed so busy with their preparations that I might have eluded them. Something else convinced me to go ahead. Jassikki. I owed him this act. I would end Forssabekkit's quest. Would this thwart the Umbrage as well? I had no idea. But I had to gamble at least on stopping the Man of Ignorance.

This is why I finished my preparations and, sealing my own fate as well as Forssabekkit's, took up a knife from the utensils left in my tent. It was little more than an eating knife: a short, wide Sunset-metal blade with a thick wooden handle. Compared to the Lowlanders' knives it seemed a paltry thing. Jassikki's knife had not been much bigger but (as my mother had found out) it was far sharper. Forssabekkit's own knives put this one to shame. Any of those I had seen—glass-shiny and harder than any metal I had ever touched—could have cut this little blade in two. Yet what were my other choices? I saw no alternative but to use whatever fell into my hands.

Besides, the knife would not be my only weapon. Forssabekkit's own craving for me would ultimately seal his fate.

[Marcelino Hondero Huamán, formerly Marsalai S'safta, interviewed September 10, 1970.]

Getting to the Umbrage camp was difficult—much more so than I'd expected—but it wasn't just the terrain that caused the difficulty. It was also the task of getting so many people over the terrain at night.

At first I'd thought the Man of Knowledge wanted nothing more than to sneak a raiding party into the Umbrage camp. Once we set off, though, I realized that this raiding party (which was what I'd volunteered to join) was only the advance guard. Everyone else was coming, too: the Masters' Guards, at least fifty or sixty of them; several large squadrons of warriors; and—following all the rest—the whole forthsetting of Heirs. At some point I realized that this was it. We were on our way at last—on our way to the Mountain Made of Light.

First we approached the pass: scrambled up a rubble-heap of rocks that lay piled against the cliff, then waited at the cliff's base for a long time. We could have gone over, but we didn't. We just waited.

It was the Man of Knowledge who told us what to do, of course, though several Masters were along as well. I didn't really care who gave us orders. All I wanted was to get down to business. Under orders from the Man of Knowledge, I'd brought several of my slings—and I couldn't wait to use them.

Somewhere ahead I could hear the sounds of people starting to climb—thuds, scraping sounds, hard breathing. Bits of gravel sifted down on us. I kept feeling the urge to look up and figure out what was happening, but the rain of grit forced me to turn away. In the dark there wasn't much to see anyway.

The wind whipped up. Within a short while I was shivering.

"Now," I heard someone say on my left. By his accent I knew the Man of Knowledge was the speaker.

One of the Guards nudged me then. I got up and groped my way along the ridge to where others from our group had clustered. Two voices—Masters', I think—soon gave us the orders to follow. I couldn't hear everything, but it sounded as if we would soon be heading up.

At about that time I started hearing a terrible commotion overhead. I couldn't see a thing in the dark. Somewhere above and to my left I heard two or three shouts, then silence. All of us waiting there froze. I had no idea how many people were around me—perhaps ten or twenty right close by, a hundred scattered on the rubble-heap, hundreds more waiting farther below. Yet despite the numbers, they were all silent. Not one person spoke, called out, coughed, or made any other sound. Even the children fell entirely quiet. Somehow everyone understood what was at stake. Or perhaps people were simply listening to the muffled noises that reached us from above.

Suddenly I heard a sound like nothing I'd ever heard before. It wasn't a scream—it was a drawn-out groan that started out faint and grew louder, moving quickly from right overhead to some-where below and behind me. It ended with a crunch like that of someone dropping a bag full of kindling on the ground. At once another noise started: a loud, shrill scream that lasted just an instant before stopping abruptly.

After that, silence.

I expected more noise. Nothing happened.

Was I scared? Of course. But before I could think much about what was happening, someone nudged me in the dark. "Get ready," said a voice. Just then I felt a hand shove a rope against me. The same voice continued: "Tie yourself onto this and prepare to climb." I tied myself to the rope. I waited. I felt a tug. Then the rope nearly pulled me off my feet. Before I knew it, I was on my way upward. I did half the work; whoever pulled that rope did the rest.

First up the cliff. Then through a hole at the top: sort of a tunnel through the rock. Lots of people crouched up there—Guards, Masters, and the Man of Knowledge himself—whom I saw by just the faintest light. I saw some bodies, too, but couldn't see whether they were our people or the others. I didn't have time to wonder: the Masters were already telling me what to do.

Then I went down again, dangling on the rope, to the other side. Descending the cliff wasn't what frightened me most; it was descending in the dark. I had no idea where I was till I landed with a jolt. I toppled over. When I braced myself for the fall, my hands touched hard snow: I'd reached another gla-cier.

Once more people had joined us, the Masters split the advance guard into two groups. Then they divided the equipment and sent us in opposite di-rections. All of this happened in the dark. I'd like to say that we managed everything quickly and easily, but I'd be lying if I did. We stumbled all over each other. We couldn't see. I could only hope that the Man of Knowledge knew where we were and how to get closer to the Umbrage without being spotted. All I knew at the time is that we weren't the sneaky band of marauders I'd imagined.

I'd never been on ice before. Not ice like that: a great floor of ice beneath my feet. It dizzied me to stand on solid ground feeling so precarious. In the dark, yet. By now it wasn't altogether black—some sort of strange glow hovered in the valley. Whether this came from the clouds or from the ice, I couldn't tell. But this glow made it possible, at least, to make our way toward the Umbrage.

The camp itself gave off light, too. The Umbrage had torches or lamps among their tents, and the flames lit up little pockets of the larger camp. How they expected to hide from us with so many lamps lit, I have no idea. Maybe they thought we were too stupid to find them. Maybe they *wanted* us to find them. Maybe the lamps and their light were a kind of dare. I didn't like what this might have meant, but I couldn't worry just then. It was difficult enough just finding my way without falling into the ice-fissures that started appearing underfoot as we neared the Umbrage camp.

We had already disconnected ourselves from the ropes we'd been using earlier. Now we spread out, half-crouched, creeping up on the Umbrage from two or three sides at once, just like a pack of foxes converging on their prey. I understood the Masters' strategy then: other squadrons of the advance guard would be converging on the camp from other angles.

And the rest? Where were the rest of the Heirs? I couldn't see them in the dark. . . . I only hoped that the Man of Knowledge knew what he was doing.

Someone whispered in the dark. "Down! Sentries!"

We all crouched. Where the ice had buckled or bulged, we could find some protection.

I saw shadowy figures ahead: two or three people who appeared to be Mountain-Drawn yet wore Lowland attire: what I now know are pants, jackets, boots, and gloves—but what looked at the time like garments for men from the spirit world. So this is what the Umbrage had become! They were not Mountain-Drawn anymore—just Lowlanders!

Before I could even think about how we would deal with them, five other shapes appeared abruptly from the right and left, pounced on the Umbrage, and knocked them down. A few blows with a mace silenced each one before he could cry out. The Masters then stripped the Umbrage of their Lowland clothes, put them on, and proceeded farther while the rest of us followed from a short distance behind.

We kept going like this without mishap. At each step we ambushed more Umbrage, quashed their resistance, and pressed deeper into their camp. Only once did the Umbrage get away with more than the slightest outcry; but when some of their fellows came running, we were ready for them. Within a short time we had all clothed ourselves like the Umbrage in their Lowland attire. This is how we managed to walk right up to their camp without resistance.

I must tell you, though, that we didn't enter the camp itself just then. I don't know why. Having come that far, we might have gone anywhere we wished. Of course, getting out of there would have been difficult—someone would have found us out soon enough. But just as we'd lingered earlier at the valley's edge, now we lingered at the edge of where most of the tents clustered. And just as earlier we'd waited and watched, now we did the same.

The Man of Knowledge found a ridge of ice rising like a wall from the glacier itself. Working himself partway up, he peered down onto the Umbrage beyond. Some of the Masters went up there with him. I didn't—I was just a slinger. But as nearly as I could tell, I saw what they saw, too.

This: tents arrayed in wider and wider circles, each larger circle protecting the smaller circles within. At the center of the labyrinth rose the tallest, biggest tent of all, a mountain-shaped tent surrounded by all the lesser peak-tents. Among all these various tents wandered a scattering of Umbrage, mostly guards, but others, too, whose roles I couldn't begin to imagine.

As I say, we watched. How long? I couldn't say. I didn't think in clock-time, as I do now—it could have been a few hours or half the night. Certainly more than just an hour. Long enough that I grew cold and weary. What did Jassikki want here? How could he justify coming all this distance, and at such great hazard to the hundreds of men and women who accompanied him, just to stare at the Umbrage from a distance?

But of course he was the Man of Knowledge. I was only a slinger. Even the Masters did nothing to question the Man of Knowledge. Who was I to wonder?

We just watched.

And waited.

And, after a while, we saw what Jassikki seemed to be waiting for.

A woman left one tent and walked over to another. A woman attired like none I'd ever seen before. A woman dressed in dewdrops, spiderwebs, or snowflakes. The garment she wore scarcely covered her body—I could see her arms, her shoulders, and legs well above her knees—yet it seemed to move over her as sunlight sparkles on a lake. Something on her head sparkled most of all: even in the light of the Umbrage lamps it shot needles of light in every direction.

We were all transfixed. I had never seen this woman, had only heard of her, yet understood who she was. Of course everyone among us did as well.

As the Man of Knowledge himself did, too.

He had begun to argue with one of the Masters. Watching the sight before us, Jassikki had spoken loudly—far more loudly than any of us had till then—and that Master had spoken back. Several of the others hushed them. Their disagreement continued. I have no idea what they said, but even in my ignorance I couldn't miss Jassikki's astonishment and the Master's attempt to quench it.

While we watched, that woman waited briefly outside the largest of the tents. Several men stood around it—sentries. We couldn't hear them well. We could see their gestures, though: clearly some sort of disagreement. One sentry in particular spent a long time talking with the woman. The other moved around her while the chief among them argued with her.

Then, surprising all of them, a man emerged from the tent. He surprised us, too. His size—I'd never seen anyone bigger. But something else, something beyond his size, a sense of power that seemed evident in his every gesture, told me that we now stood watching the Man of Ignorance, whom all Heirs had learned to hate.

The Moon's Stead (for we knew as well that this woman was the Moon's Stead) spoke to that huge Lowlander for a moment. Then, even as we watched, he took her in his arms, embraced her in full view of the guards around them, and stepped back into his tent with her, one arm draped across her back and resting on her waist.

Jassikki spoke only one word—again, in Lowland—but none of us present with him needed it translated into our own language.

[Aeslu of Vmatta, *Chronicle of the Last Days.*]

His tent was heavily guarded, of course; it always was. The tents surrounding Forssabekkit's own were little more than armories, with Umbrage warriors rotating into them at intervals. The sight that night was even more imposing than usual: men everywhere, some wielding maces and hatchets, others holding torches whose flames multiplied the weapons into a legion of deadly shadows. On nearing the place, I realized that those weapons were precisely what would soon gash my flesh and break my bones even if my mission proved successful.

As I approached, several of the six or eight guards around the tent itself watched me with a wariness more appropriate to the situation than they could have imagined. One especially (a small-eyed fangbeast of a man from Qallitti) stared with obvious derision. Did he somehow grasp my intentions? Or did he dislike me simply because the Qallittira have always disliked everyone from Vmatta? I gambled that this sentiment, not something more personal, was the truth. I walked forth to the tent. I stopped before that same guard whom I dreaded most.

I am here to see the Man of Knowledge, I said.

The answer came quickly: He is asleep.

That makes no difference.

He asked not to be disturbed.

Let me pass.

Resolute, the guards simply stood there. Stood —and did one thing more. They stared. For no matter how well-trained these Umbrage, their eyes were unruly as they beheld me in a garment as slight as what draped my flesh. These guards seemed to have been stunned, almost mind-darkened, by my appearance. Their reaction both amused and frightened me, as if I wielded a power beyond what I could control. Yet I suspected even at the time that the odd robe was what convinced these guards to let me pass. What doubt could they have felt about my purpose there?

One last flicker of suspicion crossed the chief guard's face, however. Standing before me, he motioned for several of his fellows to step in back of me with their lamps. Firelight rippled around me; I could see my silhouette overlapped five, six, seven times on Forssabekkit's tent. No one spoke. The head guard simply stared, his flesh-hungry gaze examining me. As when the setting Sun casts its beams sideways, revealing a woman's form within the robe she wears, so also did the guards' lamplight reveal my contours through the thin fabric clothing me. The guard suppressed a smile. He raised one hand to shield his eyes. He stepped a single pace to one side, then one to the other. How he longed to touch me: all, of course, under the guise of protecting Forssabekkit. He knew better than to try. He saw nothing he could hold against me, no weapon of any sort, for the guards' lamps were helpless to penetrate the bulk of my hair.

Go ahead, then, he told me.

The other guards dispersed to their posts around the tent; the head guard pulled back the flap; I stepped forward.

At precisely that moment, Forssabekkit emerged. He stared at me for little more than an eye-blink, then smiled. He reached out to me and (despite the guards not two or three paces distant) took me in his arms. I was startled yet again by the man's size. How could I ever prevail against someone of such immense strength? Yet I could see no alternative but to try.

Aeslu.

I had to come here, I told him.

You said you shouldn't.

I had to. I felt it was time.

He put an arm around me and eased me into his lair.

At first I could not see what lay within. A single lamp burned there. Its flame was feeble. My eyes soon grew accustomed to the darklight, however; I saw Forssabekkit's Lowland pack, other bulky masses of his mountain gear, and, in the far corner, his special sleeping blankets. The bed lay neatly pulled open as if awaiting us.

Once inside the tent, he stared at me for a long time. Then he forced himself into a kneeling stance on the bed, reached out to me with both hands, and pulled me down to him. I knelt before him. He ran his hands up my arms, over my shoulders, then down again. He grasped me by the waist. The gown, he said.

I put it on for you.

So I see.

Do you like it?

I always have. It's the next best thing to fireflies. With those words he pulled me close again, embraced me in his huge arms, and forced his mouth against mine.

Now, I thought, *now!*

But his left arm blocked my right; I found myself helpless to move at all. What little force I could muster, my own revulsion depleted. The Man of Ignorance!

Then Forssabekkit himself pulled back. Is this really safe? he asked. You sounded so adamant before. As if all hell would break loose—

We must. *Now.*

He gazed at me a while, unsmiling.

To my dismay I shivered.

Well, he said, I'd hate to keep you waiting.

With those words he slung one arm around my back and, still kneeling, eased me backwards onto the low bed; with only one more motion he leaned toward the bed as well and shifted his body onto me. His weight knocked my breath away. I cried out once in astonishment and pain. Groping for his shoulders, I tried to shove him back but succeeded no better than if struggling to push off a massive stone. I gasped out his name.

His mouth silenced mine. I tried to speak but failed. I could scarcely breathe. His lips and tongue gagged me, choked me. He thought he was making love with me, but he was wrong. All I could think about was an avalanche, ice and rock descending, a great mass smothering me.

His right hand clutched at me, caressed me with an abruptness just short of desperation. He tore at my gown. He pulled it up toward my waist—

I would have shouted but could not. I would have groaned, moaned, squealed but did not. As much as I dreaded what this Man of Ignorance was doing, I dreaded the guards' interruption even more.

I tried raising my right hand above me. I tried reaching the bundle of my hair. The knife, the knife— My fingertips touched the handle, but I could not seem to grasp it. My own efforts pushed it deeper.

Forssabekkit now eased back, then brought his weight to bear against me even harder than before. I felt so afraid that I ceased to struggle against him. This could not be happening. A strange, haunting cry emanated from my throat— so strange that it seemed to come from somewhere else.

It took me a long time to realize that it *did* come

from elsewhere. This was someone else's cry, not mine at all.

I heard shouts outside.

Within an eyeblink the guards would burst in, I realized. But for what purpose? To rescue me—or the Man of Ignorance?

No one entered.

More shouts: some at a distance, some close by. Forssabekkit relented for an instant, pulled away, glanced toward the doorway.

Then loud shouts, all very close, in the Common Dialect. The clank of men grabbing hatchets from their racks. Many footsteps.

Then I heard the first words I could understand: Heirs! Heirs coming up the ice!

Forssabekkit gazed at me as if having just wakened from a dream. He asked, What's happening?

I did not need to feign astonishment when I answered him: We are under attack.

[Juana Méndez de Mariátegui, formerly Hunatau Mantassi of Va'atafissorih, interviewed September 10, 1970.]

When did it start? I can't tell you exactly, but at some point I heard a ruckus off to one edge of our camp. Shouts. Shrill whistling noises. More shouts. At first I didn't pay much attention. There had been lots of noise that night; all the Umbrage were feeling tense, eager, giddy, and restless from the time we first made camp; celebrations had started early and continued ever since; people danced and sang. This new noise wasn't anything we hadn't heard already. Yet it continued. More shouts, then a couple of screams. All at once the whole camp erupted into commotion.

I remember looking toward the people with me. The dim yellow lamplight made them hard to see, but I could tell they were afraid. Then, before we could make even the slightest move, men came crashing in among our tents.

A woman shouted, "Heirs!"—and she was right. Even the bad light didn't prevent me from seeing their battle-masks: fox, deer, snake, puma. Before we could strike out against them, though, they struck first. Their ice-hatchets seemed to be everywhere. My companions fell at once. I toppled back, too, when a warrior's blade came down against me, but I dropped so fast that it did no damage. I lay there—played dead. Fear came over me so fast and strong that I couldn't have moved even if I'd tried. The best I could do was to keep my eyes open as the Heirs ran wild through the camp, slashed at any Umbrage they found, and fought everyone who managed to reach a hatchet, a mace, a sling, or anything else to fight off the invaders. If nothing else, I'd at least witness whatever atrocity the Heirs would commit against the Umbrage.

Fear soon gave way to rage. Rather, my fear soon fed my rage. For all too long the Umbrage had tolerated what the Heirs did to us; now, at the very threshold of our freedom, they would return to enslave us yet again.

This is why I forced myself up to fight. This is why I grabbed any weapon I could find—a hatchet, a stick, a piece of jagged ice—and used it as best I could. I make no claims to my skill as a warrior. I'd never fought before; I've never fought since then. Yet I fought and fought well. More than one Heir lost his chance to reach the Mountain because of what I did that night.

[Aeslu of Vmatta, *Chronicle of the Last Days.*]

If I could explain all the events that followed, I would do so—how so many of the Mountain-Drawn came to grief, and why—yet such an account lies beyond my abilities, for I never witnessed what took place at the Mountain's base. No one did. These events occurred almost entirely in darkness. The Moon emerged now and then from behind dense clouds but never long or brightly enough even to let me gain my bearings, much less to observe the calamity taking shape on the glacier. Indeed, the Moon was little more than a sliver of ice hung pointlessly in the sky: she failed to rescue us; she cast only a little light on the commotion below; she made only the slightest difference to what transpired during the long, cold, fearful night that the Mountain-Drawn endured.

Most of what I know I learned afterwards:

That the Heirs, led first by Jassikki, then by the Masters under his command, sneaked up to the Umbrage camp, overwhelmed the guards stationed at its lower edge and right flank, then probed upward into its center;

That Jassikki and a small squadron of warriors invaded the camp as an advance guard and, once detected, called in the much greater legion of Heirs who waited nearby;

That the Umbrage faltered in their early response to this invasion, then fought back with great energy and resolve, soon throwing the Heirs into disarray;

That each side struggled to overwhelm the other without any clear sense of who was who, where they were, or what surrounded them;

That Heirs and Umbrage alike did as much damage to themselves as to each other;

That as the battle raged—as slingers flung ice lumps blindly into the dark, as mace-wielders swung right and left, as hatchet-wielders hacked at one another, at other enemies, at anything that moved, at the very shadows—in short, as warriors on both sides fought more and more desperately, both sides collapsed into panic; men, women, and children raced every which way; and more people than anyone could count fell victim not just to each others' weapons but to the hazards gaping all around them on the glacier.

What I knew at the time, however, was something altogether less clear.

Even as I first told Forssabekkit of the attack, the first stones had begun thudding around us. I heard screams, shouts, and noises of Umbrage warriors falling into formation. Through the tent's walls I saw lamp-cast shadows flickering, shifting, intermingling. A great bulk fell outside to my left, nearly toppling the whole tent. More shouts. A high-pitched noise: the condor-bone whistle ordering counterattack. Then the sound of a hundred people in full flight.

I realized at once that only the Heirs could have triggered all this chaos. I knew in my heart that Jassikki had arrived. I rejoiced at what was happening.

At the same time, I panicked. The Heirs' attack was still an attack. The chunks of ice and stone crashing into the Umbrage camp were as deadly as if anyone else had hurled them. I feared for my life.

Something else frightened me: Forssabekkit. I feared the man himself and feared being caught here with him.

Well, he said, Let's be on our way.

Whether quenched by accident or on purpose, all the lamps outside went out just then. We stood in darkness.

I reached into my hair and, with a single tug, withdrew my knife. I stood less than half a man-length from the Man of Ignorance. I raised the weapon. I waited.

He spoke again, now much louder: Come on—time's a-wasting.

Where are you going? I asked as calmly as possible.

To my surprise he laughed. Going? Of all people, *you* should know.

But the Heirs—

Forget the Heirs. Forget the Umbrages. Let them settle their old squabble and be done with it.

My own bewilderment kept me in check. Did this man really intend not just to abandon the Umbrage but to try climbing the Mountain alone?

He answered my question before I could ask it. I never thought these Umbrages were much more reliable than the Heirs anyway, said Forssabekkit. Who could imagine taking this many people up the peak? Some of them, maybe—ten or twelve—but not this *horde*. Besides, I can't afford to get bogged down in a tribal tiff. If the Heirs and the Umbrages want to have it out, so much the better. They'll keep each other busy while I attend to other matters.

I could scarcely speak. You never— From the start you never planned to take anyone—

The shadowy mass before me shifted. That's not true, he said. I've always figured on a team effort. Big groups never suit my purpose. A smaller team is better.

At that moment I felt him reach out to me in the dark.

Isn't that how the story goes? A team of two? A man, he said, and a—

Just then something smashed into the tent, toppled it, and took us down with it. I was jolted more than hurt: knocked breathless. At once a great scramble began, arms and legs flailing, people shoving themselves free, a knee or foot slamming into my back, a great bulk pinning my left arm. I pulled free and rolled to one side. Everywhere I heard the sounds of metal brought down against flesh and bone, of men grunting in pain, of cloth tearing as who knows how many people tried to escape the tent now shrouding us. Then another weight fell onto me, this time against my legs, heavier even than before. I scarcely managed to kick free. Yet the tent still trapped me. I grappled with its folds. Remembering my knife, I slashed at the cloth, poked my head through, and wriggled out onto the ice. The abrupt collision with someone knocked the knife from my hands—but at least I was free.

I could not see much better outside. Heavy clouds lay banked above. As in a burned-out hearth, the whole sky looked ashen except for the glow from one faint ember of Moon. The glacier around me was so dark that it may as well not have existed; the same for the people on it.

They existed, however, and I could never have thought otherwise. All around me I heard the noises of battle—the cries of the warriors, the clank of their weapons, the screams of the wounded. How did they manage to fight? How did they know where to strike? How did they tell friend from foe? I have learned in many Sun-spans since that night, of course, how little both the Heirs and the Umbrage understood of what they were doing; they simply groped their way toward one another and struck out in the dark. Unsure how to fight, they fought anyway. Unsure whom to kill, they killed anyone. In a single night these two sides spent the rage hoarded throughout the course of nearly four hundred Sun-spans.

Wandering, stumbling, dodging people as they, too, staggered about on the ice, I felt so stunned by what was happening around me that I lost track of what to do. I was the Moon's Stead. The Mountain-Drawn were my people. Perhaps I should have cried out, rallied the Heirs, gained

control of the situation. Yet my sense of failure—
of having gambled on how to stop Forssabekkit
and having lost—made it difficult to do anything
at all. Somewhere on that glacier the Man of Ignorance even now worked his way up toward the
Mountain. Everything I had struggled to attain
had come to nothing.

The Mountain . . . I had almost forgotten about
the Mountain. Looking up the glacier I could see
it looming; or rather, I could *not* see it looming,
and precisely this absence revealed the presence,
for the Mountain appeared simply as a darker
dark than the darkness everywhere else, a great
curve missing from the mottled gray cloud-sky.
Was this heap of shadow truly the goal I sought?
Was it my people's destination? Cold, exhausted,
and afraid, I found it hard to remember what had
drawn me forth so urgently to the Mountain in the
first place.

It struck me then that all I wanted was to be
with Jassikki. Not with Jassikki the Man of
Knowledge or Jassikki the Sun's Stead—just Jassikki. Just that odd Lowlander who, having
strayed into the Mountain Land, had been kind,
curious, and gentle; who had done so much, however reluctantly at first, to help the Mountain-
Drawn; who had loved me. All I wanted was the
comfort of his presence.

How to find him, though. . . . In the dark, among
the furious legions, on a vast glacier, I had little
chance of locating this one person. Shouting was
out of the question: even if I made myself heard
past the din of battle, I would more likely reveal
my own position than locate Jassikki's. Finding
Jassikki presented its own risks: how the Umbrage would revel in knowing just where he stood!
No, I had to restrain my own craving for his company. I had to stay patient, proceed carefully, and
find him by another means.

What I decided was to remove myself from the fracas and, waiting till dawn, see if I could find my beloved under less treacherous circumstances. This course of action, too, offered a share of risks, but I could not quite contemplate them yet. Better to wait. Better to face them only as they occurred.

Thus I worked my way to the right, leaving the Umbrage camp and the forces clashing there, and I fled that central part of the glacier toward the relative safety of its outer edge. Fled! I can hardly write the word without laughing. I moved like a sleepwalker. My world was a dream. Crawling, groping, grasping, I felt my way ahead as if newly blind. Only three features of my surroundings gave any help: the glacier's uphill slant; the battle noises; and, now and then, the glimmer of Moonlight. Of these, the first two offered more help than the third. Keeping the slope on my left headed me off toward where the glacier met one of the cliffs channeling it down the Mountain. Keeping the din at my back confirmed my course. As for the Moon, it provided so little light that I ceased to rely on it.

Gradually the battle noise diminished. Whether this occurred because the fight began subsiding or simply because I gained more distance from it, I had no idea. All I knew is that I soon heard less of the human commotion and more of the wind sputtering against the ice-fissures in its descent from the Mountain.

At one point, as I hurried across the first level place I had encountered so far, I saw the textures of shadow change before me, and, abruptly fearful, I stopped short. I crouched. I got down on all fours and eased ahead with both hands flat on the ice. With my right I then reached ahead, groping. The ice stopped at a low ridge. Beyond that, nothing. I lay flat and reached forth again. I pulled myself up far enough that I could poke my head over the edge. I could still see nothing, but some sort of deep cold welled up from below. I reached to my right, found a chunk of ice, and grabbed it. I tossed it over the edge. For a long time I heard nothing. At last (after I had almost given up on hearing any sound at all) a clacking noise reached me, then another, then another, another, another, each fainter than the one before.

Fear rushed through me then, fear so intense that I dug my fingers into the packed snow at the pit's edge as if an irresistible force might suck me in. Yet fear of falling was not all that overwhelmed me; it was fear of moving, of taking the least step, of making the smallest effort in any way whatsoever. Everything else had come to nothing, so why should a new attempt fare any better? The Heirs and the Umbrage would tear one another to shreds; the Mountain Land would cease to be; Forssabekkit would attempt to climb (and perhaps succeed in climbing) the Mountain Made of Light. It seemed pointless to resist. My struggle was over; I had failed.

For this reason I stayed right there by the ice-fissure. I wrapped my cloak tight around me. I pulled my legs up close, grasped my shins, shoved my face hard into my knees. I had a long wait ahead of me. It made no difference. If the cold took me, I no longer cared. If I survived, then I would face the morning when it came.

[Marcelino Hondero Huamán, formerly Marsa-lai S'safta, interviewed September 10, 1970.]

I was not badly hurt. An Umbrage warrior had struck me with his mace, but the blow had only glanced off the side of my head and raised little more than a welt. I'd fallen, too, when I tripped over some bodies on the ice. I felt sore and tired. I was angry. Still, others had fared much worse than I. At least my slinging arm was safe—not injured at all.

I was scared—no, terrified—but that didn't matter. I was on the Mountain. All I cared about was doing what I could for the Mountain-Drawn, the Heirs, the Masters, and the Man of Knowledge.

We didn't know much about what had happened that night. We couldn't see more than a short distance in the dark. We couldn't venture out from our position because of so many ice-fissures gaping everywhere. We couldn't even risk signaling others among the Heirs—who knows how many Umbrage still lurked nearby? All we could do was wait.

I learned two things at the time, however.

First, the Heirs, being more numerous, had routed the Umbrage. We hadn't defeated them—but their camp was ours. Tents, packs, food, rope, and all sorts of other mountaincraft supplies lay everywhere. The sheer quantity surprised us. By lamplight, too, we saw things that even the Masters found astonishing. Lowland things. Big boxes. Piles of tools. Bottles, gadgets, strange kinds of food. All this stuff lay right there at the base of the Mountain. Everyone among the Heirs felt shock and dismay at how close the Man of Ignorance had got to reaching the Summit.

I learned something else as well. Once the battle subsided, the Man of Knowledge started arguing with the Masters. I don't know what they were upset about—I didn't even hear all of it—but it went something like this:

"—and I'll go after him." (That was Jassikki who spoke.)

"Madness!" shouted Loftossotoi the Icemaster.

"No, it's not—but letting him go would be."

Then Marhaislu the Stonemaster said, "Of

course we'd like to catch him, but we can't risk you."

The Man of Knowledge sounded furious. *"You* can't risk *me*? You have the audacity to say *you* can't risk *me*?"

"What I meant—"

"Let me decide who risks what, all right?"

"But you are the Man of Knowledge."

"That's the whole point, isn't it? I'm the Man of Knowledge. I'm the one who decides what happens here—so do what I tell you."

They went on like this for a long while—long enough to alarm those of us nearby at the time. The argument grew worse as it continued. Jassikki shouted till he grew hoarse. No one seemed willing to give in. At some point I realized that the Masters might have been arguing just to delay whatever the Man of Knowledge intended to do. But it didn't work.

Not long before dawn, Jassikki cut them short, started rummaging around in the packs of Lowland things scattered everywhere about, and removed a black object looking somewhat like a small log. To my surprise, light came out of one end. Light! He didn't seem the least bit surprised, though, and soon set off up the glacier, following the beam he cast ahead.

[Aeslu of Vmatta, *Chronicle of the Last Days.*]

When dawn finally arrived and I roused from my frigid stupor, I found myself looking out onto a scene even worse than what I had anticipated. My immediate situation was the least of it: a chasm that not only opened before me, but to my right as well, with a porch-like slab of ice jutting out over the edge so precariously that even a few more steps would have tipped it and sent me tum-

bling into the void. What horrified me more was
the view down the slope. People and equipment
lay strewn over the ice. Bodies, clothes, packs,
footgear, ice-hatchets, and countless other items
dotted that entire middle portion of the glacier.
Puddles of fabric accumulated where tents had
collapsed. Dead pathbeasts crouched or slumped
where they had fallen. Bundles, boxes, and bags
of food had scattered their contents all over. Entangling all the rest—bodies, gear, food, animals,
everything—were great lengths of rope, both of
Lowland kinds and of others, too; kinds that
looked different from what Lowlanders made but
that did not resemble any I could recall having
seen before.

Most of this scene was motionless. Now and
then, however, I saw something or someone move:
a fleck of color shifting as a wounded man or
woman tried to stagger upright on the ice.

What I heard horrified me still more than what
I saw. I should explain that the glacier was anything but silent, for the wind ruffled almost con-
stantly against the ice, and the rumble of small
avalanches reached us now and then from the
Mountain above. When the wind relented, however, I heard another sound. At first I mistook it
for the wind itself: a deep, complex warbling, as
if a multitude of separate wind-cries, wind-
screams, wind-moans, and wind-pleas had been
woven into a cloth of lamentation. Soon I realized
that I heard something other than the wind.

Not everyone was dead or wounded. The longer
I gazed down the glacier, the more I saw survivors
who seemed to be relatively unhurt. Of course I
could not determine as much as I would have liked
from my vantage; I watched from too high and too
far to one side. Still, I could see enough to confirm
my first impression. Some people crouched behind packs, bundles, or piles of equipment. Some

huddled in holes they had found or dug in the snow. Others stood now and then, surveying the scene much as I myself did. A few wandered about on the ice, stumbling and straying, either indifferent to their state or oblivious to it.

At some point I noticed that many people were gazing across the glacier. I turned at once to face the same way.

The Mountain rose before us. Great shafts of sunlight angled off both the right and left ridges into the now cloudless sky, which shone with such intensity that the Mountain itself appeared to emanate all that light; yet the Mountain, still caught in its own shadow, showed up largely without detail. It was at once unavoidable and hard to see. Precisely because I now observed the Mountain from so short a distance, I could not see it well. It filled half the sky yet seemed vague, the bulk less substantial than its mere outline, a wall of mottled gray. Staring upward, I tried to make sense of what I saw but without success. The sight stunned me back into the daze from which I had just emerged.

How long did I take to realize that not just the Mountain but also something below it (something on the glacier itself) had caught everyone's attention? Something above the Umbrage camp. Something in motion.

Two small figures walked in careful, roundabout steps on the ice. One wore light-colored attire of a sort I soon recognized as Lowland mountain garb. The other wore robes characteristic of the Mountain-Drawn but of a radiant hue I had never seen before. One man was huge, the other man smaller. I watched them a long time before I accepted what I had known from the start: these were Forssabekkit and Jassikki.

The two Lowlanders stalked each other on the ice. I found it difficult to determine who was the hunter and who the prey, for each man appeared simultaneously to seek and to flee the other. Great fissures crisscrossing the ice created a labyrinth that they struggled to work their way through, complicating the hunt and rendering it all the more treacherous. In a sense each of them had two opponents: the other and the glacier surrounding them. Thus Forssabekkit approached Jassikki in a long sequence of steps, and Jassikki backed off, glancing about desperately to avoid toppling backwards into one of the mouths agape all around him; then, having worked his way into a relatively open area, Jassikki rushed up the slope, angled to the left, and swung around from the rear; Forssabekkit in turn emerged from the constricted passage, sprinted uphill, and soon flanked his pursuer. Time after time the pursuer became the pursued only to become the pursuer once again. They circled each other with relentless patience.

At one point Forssabekkit trapped Jassikki where two fissures ran almost parallel, so that the Man of Knowledge ended up walking on a vast wall of ice between two chasms. The Man of Ignorance considered his quarry from the entrance to the long, narrow trap he had set; he then proceeded slowly along the top of that same wall. I watched in terror: where the two fissures angled together and joined, the ice-wall ended. Jassikki stood at its far end. He had no way out. Forssabekkit walked toward him with careful steps, his long Lowland ice-hatchet held ready in both hands. Jassikki glanced about like a cornered beast. Then, calming himself, he stepped forth to meet his nemesis.

I dreaded what would follow. The Man of Ignorance was much bigger than Jassikki, and his hatchet was far longer; no doubt Forssabekkit would swing at my beloved with great ease and deadly force. At the same time, Jassikki's smaller size made him more agile; he might gain some advantage in such a narrow place. Yet whatever the strengths that each man brought to bear against the other, I could not believe that Jassikki could prevail under the circumstances.

Jassikki then fooled Forssabekkit. Having approached the Man of Ignorance to a distance of about five or six manlengths, he suddenly turned, sprinted, and leaped the gap between the ice-wall and the other side. This wide leap scarcely took him to safety: he landed with only one foot on the edge opposite. Yet he fell face-down against the broad curved lip, both feet skittering against the dense snow and showering bits and pieces into the depths. Then Jassikki dug his ice-hatchet in hard enough to catch himself, and, struggling hard, he managed to scramble up and pull himself out. He retreated at once. Within a few moments it was Jassikki who moved about freely on the glacier's surface, while Forssabekkit stood nearly trapped on that knife-blade of ice. Thus the Man of Ignorance now took his own turn to flee, escaping by the same route that had led him there; the two men resumed their game of pursuing one another.

Over the many Sun-spans since those events took place, I have often wondered why those of us who observed their occurrence did nothing else but watch. Hundreds of Umbrage and perhaps thousands of Heirs passed what felt like an eternity simply observing the savage dance that unfolded before our eyes. It seems odd now that no one intervened.

What I keep reminding myself is that the struggle between Jassikki and Forssabekkit was in some ways the pivotal event of our history. The Man of Knowledge battling the Man of Ignorance: this is what we watched. The weight of half a thousand Sun-spans came to rest on these men's shoulders. Should we have been surprised to find ourselves watching? To find ourselves incapable of anything else but watching? None among us, I believe, saw any alternative.

Something else restrained us. Many among both the Heirs and the Umbrage had suffered injuries, whether trivial or serious, during the night. Even the least injured among us had stumbled repeatedly in the dark; had scraped, bruised, or cut our hands; had tripped over ropes, bundles of equipment, mountaincraft tools, or other supplies; had collided with other members of the Mountain-Drawn, whether friend or enemy, in our panic and confusion. The worst injured had fallen into fissures and now lay broken, chilled, and dying at the bottom of an icy grave. Everyone else now huddled on the glacier watching whatever we could tolerate of a conflict that all of us both dreaded and welcomed. It seemed impossible that it had finally come to pass: too frightening to contemplate, too powerful, too significant, too substantial to imagine. Yet even as we waited, chilled and aching on the ice, the fight itself unfolded before us.

Forssabekkit had succeeded in catching up while Jassikki worked his way across a series of cracks in the ice. The gaps were narrow enough to jump, but doing so required finding the best place to cross, leaping hard, and taking care not to stumble forward into the next. The Man of Knowledge made good progress. Yet the Man of Ignorance was so much taller, and his legs were so much longer, that he made up the distance between them with far less effort than Jassikki had expended. Within a few eyeblinks Jassikki had no choice but to face his opponent yet again.

Each man held his ice-hatchet and prepared to fight. Forssabekkit swung first—a great downward arc. Jassikki ducked, narrowly avoiding a blow to the head. Caught off balance by his own strike, Forssabekkit leaned hard to the left. At once Jassikki lashed out. His hatchet, too, missed its mark. Forssabekkit then took advantage of his opponent's vulnerability and, with a strong upswing, hit Jassikki hard against his left shoulder. The Man of Knowledge recoiled, staggering sideways from the blow's force. He did not fall: the Man of Ignorance had landed only the shaft of his hatchet, not the blade, against the Man of Knowledge. Jassikki stumbled toward one of the waiting ice-fissures. Just as I thought all was lost, however, he kicked out from the near side of the gap, shoved himself clear to the other side, and fell to the flat surface beyond.

At this point I could no longer tolerate what I saw happening. Rather, I could no longer remain in the state of mind-numbness that had afflicted me before the two Lowlanders' duel had begun. I shook off my panic and dread; I roused my body from its stupor; I forced myself out of my hiding place and back onto the glacier.

Let the Man of Knowledge fight the Man of Ignorance, I could have told myself, for this is what Ossonnal and Lissallo long ago told us would take place. But why should the Man of Knowledge struggle alone? I was the Moon's Stead, thus destined to union with him; and if that union meant standing united in battle, so be it.

But of course these thoughts were not really what coursed through my mind. Never mind that Jassikki was the Man of Knowledge. Never mind that he was the Sun's Stead. Jassikki was the man I loved.

As I approached the combatants, I realized that two courses of action lay before me. One was to sneak up on Forssabekkit and attack him unawares while he confronted his opponent. The other was to join Jassikki and fight our nemesis at his side. Each plan offered its own hazards and advantages. In some ways the first made more sense: the Man of Ignorance would find battling an assailant on each side more difficult than battling two face-to-face.

Ultimately I decided instead to join Jassikki—but not because of any considerations I might have weighed. Rather, I simply found any further separation intolerable. During the course of half a Sun-span I had been away from him and had, in fact, spent all my time with our greatest enemy. Perhaps I would have served Jassikki better by approaching Forssabekkit from behind, then distracting him or delivering the death-blow myself. Yet this was not what I did. I went to Jassikki instead. I wanted to be with him whether we won or lost—whether we lived or died.

Crossing the ice was more difficult than I expected. I quickly understood why the Lowlanders' duel had become such a complex dance of approach and retreat. The glacier's surface that far up turned out to be still more uneven than that farther down the slope: a vast gray-blue plain broken by a nearly limitless sequence of cracks, a few of them shallow and narrow enough that I could hop right over, most of them big enough that I had to find a path around them, and some so wide and deep that, when I peered over the edge to see what confronted me, I could not see all the way to the bottom. The most ingenious of trappers could never have set such a formidable array of pits for his prey; indeed, I felt like a helpless animal, doomed if I made the slightest misstep. Within a short while I despaired of reaching Jassikki at all.

Something else unnerved me. Inside some of those trenches lay men, women, and children who had chanced to stumble in during the previous night. Most were dead: I could see their bodies, twisted and motionless, down where the ice walls converged. Yet some remained alive in the white jaws clenched around them. Some, lost in a daze of pain, moaned without awareness of anyone there to listen. A few roused as I worked my way far above them, and, catching sight of me, they reached out, flailed, wept, screamed, or shouted, pleading for help. Were they Heirs or Umbrage? I could not tell. Perhaps it made no difference. They were all Mountain-Drawn—all people who had sought the Mountain only to find it in a way none had anticipated. Their fate frightened me, sickened me. Within a short while they would all be dead. Even under less drastic circumstances I could have done little to help them; now I could do nothing at all. If I stopped or even hesitated, all would be lost. All I could do now was join Jassikki in confronting the Man of Ignorance.

Slowly, cautiously, I worked my way across the ice. The light helped: by then the Sun had risen high enough to slant into the valley, and his beams cast the whole glacier into relief. The smooth places lay dazzling white before me; the fissures brimmed with shadow. By avoiding the dark pits and trenches, I could find a path more safely. I knew that layers of snow might hide treacherous jaws capable of devouring me in an instant, yet even the slightly sunken spots that marked them appeared more obvious than they would have earlier or later in the day, and I could proceed more confidently than I would have otherwise. I clambered across a low gray wall thrust upward from below; I eased down a path between two narrow cracks in the ice; I crossed a snowbridge over a chasm so deep that, when I glanced down, I saw only the shadows pooling there. Within a short while I neared the two Lowlanders on that precarious battleground.

They were speaking to each other, or rather

shouting, the words loud but as broken as the ice all around us:

—hopeless—

—don't kid yourself—

—you really—

—never!

By this time they stood less than a few manlengths apart, but two ice-fissures, rather than distance alone, separated them. Yet neither of the cracks looked so wide that one man or the other could not have jumped it. Whoever crossed first, though, would have allowed his opponent the advantages of a firmer stance and at least the first strike; thus the men traded insults rather than blows, each stalling for time, as they decided what to do next.

No doubt Forssabekkit saw me approach. I was in full view, and nothing about my garb or the light overhead would have hidden my form against the glacier's backdrop. Yet he did not acknowledge me at all: gave no sign of shock, alarm, or delight—no glance whatever. Even as he matched Jassikki's maneuvers with his own, easing forward or back, shifting a few paces to the left, then back to the right again, Forssabekkit acted as if oblivious to my presence. Yet this obliviousness itself revealed what he assumed about my intentions. He thought I was sneaking up on Jassikki to harm him. The Man of Ignorance thought I was helping him defeat the Man of Knowledge. His presumption infuriated me. I wanted to shout, Here I am—not your ally but your enemy! Yet I kept silent. The longer Forssabekkit maintained his illusions, the greater his surprise when he faced two opponents instead of one.

Soon I was just a few manlengths behind Jassikki. I intended to signal him at the last moment, then move in close to present a united front against the Man of Ignorance. I hesitated because

Jassikki moved about so wildly and shouted so loudly that he would not have heard me; I would only have tipped off Forssabekkit. Holding back, I watched and waited. Jassikki seemed totally attentive to his foe. I could not see his face, but his body looked tense and alert, like those of animals preparing for a fight to the death.

Then, without warning, he turned. He looked my way. He swung around to stare straight at me.

His expression was completely different from what I had expected—completely different from anything I could have imagined. Far from showing delight, it was full of fury. His brow tightened, his eyes narrowed, his mouth constricted. He stared at me like that for an eyeblink, then shouted, *You!* That one word hit hard as a stone. If only that was all he flung. Jassikki hurled himself toward me, his ice-hatchet raised, and brought the blade down at once.

Somehow I twisted away fast enough to avoid the direct blow. The hatchet struck, but just glancing against me. I felt the blade rip through my robe and skitter down my arm. The pain hurt less than my bewilderment at his actions. Then Jassikki himself, thrown off balance, slammed into me. We toppled together and fell onto the ice. He was on top of me; we flailed about; I struggled; he struck me hard; I could not escape. I called his name once, twice, three times. He was somewhere else, someone else, possessed by his own rage. When I managed to pull away and fling myself to one side, he swung out at me so wildly that I realized for the first time how Jassikki, not Forssabekkit, would be my doom.

Oddly, the Man of Ignorance himself cut the knot of my dilemma. I was unaware of his precise actions at the time but grasped their consequence: Forssabekkit took advantage of the situation and, leaping the two ice-fissures between us, came crashing down in our midst. The force of his body colliding with mine knocked me clear of Jassikki. I skidded over the ice. Somehow I was aware of the edge: a great crack gaped not a half-manlength distant. With great effort I managed to force myself up and backward. By this time the two men grappled just short of the brink, Forssabekkit pressing his ice-hatchet sideways with both hands against Jassikki's throat, Jassikki trying with all his might to shove back the shaft.

The sight appalled me. What appalled me more, however, was Jassikki's expression. He fought off his assailant but gazed toward me with frightened, angry eyes: eyes that accused me, tried me, and found me guilty. Yet again my best intentions had gone awry; what I had striven hardest to prevent, I had brought about instead.

An ice-hatchet lay near the men. I felt a double jolt at the sight: not just that it lay in reach; also that it looked so strange. I had never seen anything like this thing yet recognized it as something other than a Lowland tool. With a braided leather handle and a finely engraved black metal head, this hatchet resembled those that my own people made yet differed from them as well. It was not a tool that served ceremonial purposes; it was a tool that *did things*. It looked strong, powerful, dangerous. It was something one could use for cutting steps on a glacier, for picking one's way up an ice-cliff—or for killing an enemy. Not that I dwelled on what I saw or its implications: everything I thought passed in an eyeblink. What I saw and thought simply clarified the course of action I would have taken by some other means.

I reached down for the ice-hatchet. I took it up. I raised it high in my right hand. I brought it down as hard as I could against the Man of Ignorance.

Forssabekkit moved at the same instant I struck, yet the hatchet hit home anyway. The black metal blade glanced off the back of his head, thudded into his right shoulder, and tumbled out of my grasp. At that same instant, the Man of Ignorance released his grip on the Lowland ice-hatchet now on the verge of crushing Jassikki's throat and, with a reflex that even a man as strong as he was could not suppress, he reached up with both hands to brace his skull. He crouched, fighting off mind-darkness. He said nothing; his voice released only a slow stutter.

Jassikki, too, struggled to pull himself back from the infinite brink that Forssabekkit's hatchet had shoved him toward. With one hand he clutched at his throat; with the other he pushed back the wooden stave that now lay harmlessly across him. Coughing and retching, Jassikki flopped over, eased onto his hands and knees, and forced himself upright.

I can no longer recall every emotion that coursed through me just then, but most of all I felt astonishment. I could not believe what I had done—could not believe what my actions had accomplished. However clumsily, I had saved the Man of Knowledge and fought back the Man of Ignorance. Yet I was not alone in my astonishment. Jassikki stared at me with unwavering eyes even as he staggered about trying to regain his breath; Forssabekkit, still clasping the sides of his head, swung about to observe me through whatever squint the pain allowed him. As if neither could quite believe how quickly and totally these events had turned, both men sized me up. Whose side are you on? their eyes asked. Whose side are you *really* on?

I was unarmed. My knife lay far below on the glacier, where I had lost it the night before. Forssabekkit's ice-hatchet lay near Jassikki, Jassikki's near Forssabekkit. My only weapon was surprise.

Without planning to do what I did next, I rushed

them: ran forth, screaming, and flung myself on
the Man of Ignorance. The force of my body striking his knocked him down again. At once I felt
myself flung aside as he struck back. Then another bulk collided with me when Jassikki hurled
himself into the fight. A bolt of pain shot through
my bones. I could feel myself spun sideways, one
arm wrenched halfway around my back and
caught beneath it. I could hear shouts but could
not make sense of them. I toppled face-forward,
my left brow, eye, and cheek shoved hard into the
ice. Somehow I writhed free of the tangle and
found myself half a manlength from the Lowlanders.

They forced themselves up again. Crouching,
trembling, panting for breath, the two men shifted
back and forth, each trying to gain the advantage.
Neither had a weapon in hand. The ice-hatchets
now lay to my right. Both men stood beside the
wider of two fissures nearby, so that even a single
false move or well-aimed blow would send either
tumbling into the depths. Yet neither took the next
step; they just kept dancing their angry little
dance, and both kept glancing my way, well aware
that I alone could break their deadlock.

When I eased toward Jassikki's ice-hatchet, the
Man of Ignorance called out to me: Stay out of
this!

No words could have enraged me more. As if I
were the intruder! As if I belonged neither with
Jassikki nor with the Mountain-Drawn!

With a few quick steps I reached the ice-hatchet.
I picked it up and prepared to toss it toward Jassikki. Then at once I faltered. If I missed or even
struck him, I would give Forssabekkit the upper
hand. Even if Jassikki caught the weapon, catching it would distract him long enough for the Man
of Ignorance to strike. My efforts would not help
Jassikki—I would doom him instead.

This is why I resumed the attack myself: raised the hatchet, sprinted toward Forssabekkit, and brought it down just as I slammed into him. The impact threw us both off balance.

Now Jassikki could move in for the kill.

Yet at once I knew something was wrong. The big Lowlander jolted his own weight against me and flung me hard against Jassikki. Thrown to the ground, Jassikki and I skidded down some kind of slope. I clutched for something—anything—felt nothing but the rough snow rushing beneath me, felt one last jolt against my back and, glimpsing the blue-gray depths below, plummeted into the void.

[Juana Méndez de Mariátegui, formerly Hunatau Mantassi of Va'atafissorih, interviewed September 10, 1970.]

After the battle that night I hid in a heap of corpses. I wanted to flee but didn't. I had no idea where I was—whether among Heirs or Umbrage—and the cold seemed even deadlier than our foe. Despite my revulsion I thought I'd better stay where I was. This is what the Heirs did to me: reduced me to someone who sought comfort from the fading warmth of dead bodies.

Morning came, however, and with it the realization that I was safe. Several hundred Umbrage had escaped the Heirs' attack and fled across the glacier's width. Their escape wasn't altogether successful: many had suffered terrible fates in the dark. Yet others managed at least to gain some distance from the invaders. I was among them. Without knowing just where to go, I'd somehow stumbled in the opposite direction from the greatest number of Heirs and had gained at least a little distance from them. This is not to say that the

Heirs no longer presented any threat. On the contrary, I could see hundreds of them lingering in the place that had so recently been our camp. But they made no move to come after us. Did they hold off out of mercy? Not a chance. Even at the time I thought it more probable that they needed time simply to lick their own wounds.

As I reached the other Umbrage survivors, I took pleasure in thinking that we had done to the Heirs something like what they did to us. We would rest, regroup, and have it out with them again. Or perhaps we would simply head up toward the Mountain. That was it: we wouldn't even bother with the Heirs. Let them claim whatever victory they imagined! Let them revel in our flight! Meanwhile, we would simply be on our way. Forssabekkit would lead us to the Summit.

Yet I found the Umbrage sullen, dazed, almost motionless. I don't mean the injured: I'm speaking of people who escaped almost entirely unhurt. Even so they simply stood there and stared up at the glacier's slope.

"What happened?" I asked the first of the Umbrage I encountered.

They looked at me as if not understanding the question.

I walked into their midst. Two men and a woman glanced my way, then resumed their reverie.

"What are we waiting for?" I asked them.

No one answered.

I looked around. There must have been two hundred people there. Most of them looked capable of continuing the climb. Some even had equipment— packs, ropes, tools. Yet none made even the least effort to move.

On impulse I asked, "Where is Forssabekkit?"

A young woman gestured at the Mountain. She

didn't point toward any one place, but almost at once I saw what she meant.

Some distance above us on the ice was a small figure. I couldn't tell much about him, but I could see that he was alone.

"Forssabekkit went up to fight Jassikki," said the young woman. "He won. Yet he never came down for the rest of us. He just set off for the Mountain."

"By himself?"

"He left us here—abandoned us."

"That's impossible."

"See for yourself."

There must have been some sort of mistake. Forssabekkit wouldn't have left without us. Not after everything the Umbrage had been through. Not after everything we'd been through with him, *for* him. It didn't make sense.

"He's finding the way for us," said one of the Umbrage.

"He's waiting for the right time to have us join him," said another.

"He's preparing to fight the Heirs again," said yet another.

We couldn't figure it out. None of us. All we knew was that Forssabekkit had left without us, and he showed no sign of returning.

That was when we got up and followed him. We took what little remained of our belongings—a few coils of rope, some bags of food, five or ten ice-hatchets, some clothing. We just grabbed what we could and started up.

Never mind that the Heirs stirred at the sight of our departure. Never mind that they, too, started preparing to leave. Let them come after us! Let them do whatever they wanted!

Forssabekkit must have been testing us. That was it. He was testing us to make sure that we sufficiently longed for his guidance.

On our way up we sang one of the Umbrage anthems:

> The wind will never chill us!
> The sleet will never cut us!
> The night will never trap us!
> We will find the Founders' refuge
> On the Mountain Made of Light!

[Aeslu of Vmatta, *Chronicle of the Last Days*.]

At first I had no idea how long I had been lying down there in the ice. Any length of time might have passed: an eyeblink, a day, a Moon-span, a Sun-span, the rest of time. . . . Trapped not just in the ice but also in the deepest mind-darkness, I knew nothing of what was happening around me. I have learned since then that my oblivion lasted little more than half a morning. The Moon and Sun protected me; any longer within the icy tomb and I would have died. Yet when I first made my way back from darkness to light, I did not feel like a swimmer groping her way to the surface after an unexpected spill into a lake; I felt instead like a fish who, caught on a fisher's line, finds herself dragged upward against her will. The closer I came to awareness, the more I dreaded my arrival.

My back, neck, arms, hands, everything hurt. Pain and cold smashed down on me like blocks of ice. I could scarcely imagine so much pain in the world, much less all of it descending on me at once. I tried turning away as if to evade it. There was no escape. Pain seeped into every fiber of my flesh. Pain *was* my flesh.

At some point I became aware of my effort to

avoid an intense light striking me head-on. I opened my eyes, then recoiled at once from the glare. Something white-hot stabbed straight through my face into my brain. No matter how hard I tried to turn away, it found me and seared into me. I looked again. It was the Sun, I realized, beckoning to me from the far end of a white hallway. Then I saw that the hallway was nothing of the kind: it was a trench. A trench made of ice. A trench I was observing not from the side, but from the bottom. Bit by bit I understood that I lay at the bottom of an ice-fissure.

The events that had put me there now rushed in like the light itself.

With great effort I managed to sit.

I find it hard even now to describe the sight before me. I was indeed in an ice-fissure. I was not, however, at the bottom. As if a large stone had toppled from one of two walls and had lodged in the narrow alleyway between them, a block of ice lay bridging the gap between the two sides of a chasm. The block was immense—two full man-lengths across. Its top surface rested almost that same distance below the ice-fissure's lip. I had fallen that far. Was it any wonder, then, that my body ached all over? Was it any wonder that I had lain oblivious to my surroundings for so long? Yet the harm I had suffered was not what surprised me; rather, I felt astonished that the harm had been no worse. On each side the alleyway of ice extended till its curve blocked my view. When I pulled myself over to the edge, I peered into a fissure so deep that even the dazzle of light overhead diminished to a chilly blue glow.

Yet even this sight startled me less than one other. Something moved to one side. Bracing myself against the ice, forcing myself to turn despite the pain pounding at my head and back, I swung around.

Before me, right there on the ice, sat Jassikki.

He watched me but did not speak.

I told myself, This is Jassikki. This is the man I love. This is my partner on the quest we have undertaken. Yet even as I spoke those silent words, I stared at the sight before me—stared despite having seen him earlier, when we had battled Forssabekkit on the ice. Everything during the fight had happened so fast that I had never fully grasped what I saw. Now I gazed at him in bewilderment.

This was Jassikki, yet he looked nothing like the man I knew. His beard was gone. His hair was tied back in the manner of our own men. His attire was no longer of the Lowland sort but was instead a robe of fine wool interwoven with so much Sunmetal thread that the whole garment shimmered even down there in the ice-fissure. Everything about his appearance told me what I had long hoped and suspected: that the Heirs had proclaimed Jassikki the Sun's Stead, the Man of Knowledge. Even his battered state (for he had suffered many bruises and small cuts on the hands and face) did not contradict the sense of authority that his attire bestowed on him. But to see him dressed like that! He looked just like a Mountain-Drawn.

At once his stare struck me full force. My Lowland attire—this is what caught his attention. The thin robe that Forssabekkit had made for me—I felt vulnerable and strange. With great effort I eased forward, crouched, and tried to stand.

He said, Don't even come near me.

Please understand—

I understand all to well.

What you imagine is not what truly—

Why should I imagine when I can look at you and know the whole story? he asked. See for yourself! Forssa's flapper! Decked out for a night on the town! And if I had any doubts, there you were right at his tent!

For a long time I could not even speak. The burden of too many events weighed down on me; the constraint of too many misunderstandings choked me. Then at last my voice gushed forth: I wanted only to defeat him! I did everything possible to stop him! I tried to kill him! Why else would I attack him on the ice? Not you—him!

Jassikki made no response. He watched and listened but neither spoke nor moved. It occurred to me that he might have suffered at least the same sorts of injuries that I myself did; he might even have struck his head hard enough to harm his judgment. Yet he stared with such a slow, clear gaze! Whatever stunned him was less what he suffered than what he now held against me. Never mind that I had struggled for half a Moon-span to defeat our common enemy; having failed, I found it hard to fend off the accusation that Jassikki's harsh stare presented.

I began to weep.

Then, against my own inclination, I made myself stop. Think what you will, I told him as I forced myself up from the ice. Believe anything you want. Question my loyalty, dismiss my efforts, mock my desire to bring down the man we both hate. No matter what you say, you can only start to imagine what I have attempted in your honor.

Why should I believe you? he asked, almost shouting.

Because it is true.

And why should I believe it's true?

Because I love you.

You love me! Wonderful! I suppose that's why you leaped right into his arms. Jassikki's eyes examined me, searched me, took me apart, and put me back together again.

If you will not believe me, I told him, then all is lost. The Heirs are doomed, the Umbrage will prevail, and Forssabekkit will reach the Summit.

Jassikki said, Even Forssa can't get there alone.

What do you know about what he can or cannot do? I asked. All along I have been watching him, learning of his weaknesses, and deciding how to stop him. Dismiss what I know if you want—but at your own peril. He is both more dangerous than you imagine and far less so.

Well, he went on, far be it from me to quibble with you when—

Listen to me! I shouted.

To my surprise, he fell silent. He looked at me without sympathy, but at least he listened.

He brought something powerful, I told Jassikki. Some kind of fire.

My words changed his expression. Fire? What do you mean, *fire*?

A special kind of fire.

Jassikki seemed not to understand. Although he waited patiently, I could sense his bafflement.

Special fire. Sticks full of fire.

Matches? he asked. Little sticks that make a flame?

No, bigger. Red. Thick as a root.

Jassikki still watched without comprehending. With each effort his frustration grew more and more obvious. I saw less anger in his gaze now— only a thwarted eagerness to grasp what I was trying to explain. I felt foolish, stupid, heavy beneath the weight of my own ignorance.

Were they flares? he asked. Bright red lights?

These words made no sense to me. When I shook my head in the Lowland manner, telling him no, I could feel his puzzlement deepen.

Then I tried another approach. He stuck them in the ground, I said, recalling when the Umbrage watched Forssabekkit tear open the earth and gather the special dirt. He lit a piece of yarn attached to the tubes, then waited. The rocks leaped into the air and fell again like hailstones.

Another change came over Jassikki's face just then. I saw no sudden shift in his expression, no dramatic difference in his eyes, in his mouth, or in any other feature. Rather, his awareness changed. Jassikki stared as if I were the only sight and my words the only sound.

He blew something up? asked Jassikki, his voice growing loud again. The rocks flew all over?

It was terrible, I said. Terrible.

There was a big noise?

Worse than thunder. I thought it was the end of—

God damn the bastard!

It was now my turn not to understand.

I didn't think even Forssa would stoop that low.

I gestured in puzzlement.

Dine-a-mite—

Please explain, I told him.

He spelled the word for me: *dynamite.* But how could it make sense to you? he exclaimed, grasping his head at each side as if to keep it from splitting. It's an explosive, a bomb—not much different from what soldiers used during the War. He'll tear the place apart. He'll kill us and everyone else.

I listened a while, then said, No.

Jassikki looked at me, perplexed. What do you mean, *No*? I just told you—

He will not do that.

His expression changed again—now to a mix of pity and exasperation. You just don't understand, he said. You can't even imagine what it's like. The bastard is going to rip the entire Mountain Land—

I *do* understand.

You don't, believe me.

I saw what he did with my own eyes.

But you can't understand what he'll do, said Jassikki.

I can.

Now Jassikki grew annoyed. Aeslu, he's got dynamite. That makes no sense to you because—

What I want to explain—

He'll kill us all!

Jas—

Listen to me—

No, *you* listen, I told him suddenly, losing my temper. I want you to understand.

Dynamite, for God's sake!

He no longer has it.

You said he brought it, said Jassikki.

He did. He did before, I went on, but no longer.

Faltering, he showed that same alertness as before. He asked, Who does, then?

We do.

The Heirs?

Your forthsetting routed the Umbrage and overtook their camp. Those who escaped fled to one side of the glacier.

He said, I don't understand how you know this.

I watched from higher up. I saw everything while you and Forssabekkit hunted each other.

Now Jassikki exhaled abruptly in weariness and anger. Instead of looking up at me again, however, he glanced about at our surroundings.

Then let's just get out of here, he said. What are we waiting for!

I said, Together—

He turned my way then, watching carefully. He said nothing.

What choice have you got? I asked.

One wall of the ice-fissure rose at our backs. When Jassikki stood, I could see that the wall was at least half again his height. It was steep but not vertical. If we could somehow manage to work our way up to the lip . . .

Let me give you a boost, he said, though the sound of his own words brought a shadow over his gaze.

I told him, Trust me or not as you prefer. If you do not trust me, then we shall both perish right here. If you trust me and I betray you, then I shall escape and you shall perish. But if you trust me and I honor you, then we shall both escape and face the Man of Ignorance together. Will you gamble, or do you wish simply to die?

Jassikki looked at me a long time. If only he could have understood how that hesitance hurt more than all the pains wracking me!

Then he set his shoulder against the ice, laced the fingers of both hands together, and made a foothold for me from his own flesh and bones.

I worked my way over to him. I wanted to embrace him but did not. Our escape itself would grant the embrace I craved.

Setting my left foot in his cupped hands, I grasped Jassikki's shoulders and boosted myself upward. I wavered dangerously but kept my balance. Jassikki grunted from the effort of sustaining my weight; even so, his hands held. I reached out to the wall with my right hand to keep steady. The ice felt cold and far smoother than I expected. If it offered no more resilience above than below, I would never be able to claw my way out. Again I wavered, nearly falling, before Jassikki shifted to counteract the sway. I steadied myself.

Ready?

I think so.

Now step onto my shoulders.

I have nothing to hold!

Lean into the wall. I'll brace you.

Doing as he said, I raised my right foot to his left shoulder, set it there as firmly as I could, then reached up to the wall with my right hand while maintaining my balance with my left hand against

Jassikki's head. I faltered a moment, then said,
Now.

Jassikki jolted slightly as I made my move. For
an eyeblink or so afterwards, I teetered: he was
standing too close to the wall. He stepped back
slightly, though, and I managed to stay upright.
Cautiously I set my left foot on his right shoulder.

By then I stood just a little taller than the ice-
wall itself; I could peer over the top. But the surface beyond slanted upward, so that everything
ahead lay out of view. Still, I was almost out. All
I needed now was to get a grip on something to
pull myself up. If the surface before me was snow,
then I might succeed. If it was ice, however—all
would be lost.

I reached up as slowly as possible. Even the
weight of my arms swinging outward nearly threw
me off balance.

Jassikki's voice reached me from below: —careful!

Calling back seemed too risky. Instead I kept
reaching forth. My elbows came to rest on the
edge; my forearms extended; my hands crept
across the gray-white surface before me.

Its sheen warned me that it was ice.

I curved my fingers into claws and plunged them
downward. Snow. Dense snow. When I dug my
hands in, they held.

I could have called back to Jassikki but chose
otherwise, for the effort of leaning backwards
might have thrown me off balance. Instead, I
groped for the strongest possible handhold; shifting my weight forward, I tried boosting myself up.
The effort was even more difficult than I had expected. My knees kept skittering against the wall.
Twice my hands lost their grip in the snow. No
matter how hard I tried, I could not seem to take
hold of the surface ahead. I struggled time after

time. Soon I felt so fatigued that I nearly lost my grip altogether.

Then, just as I expected to fall, I felt something raising me from below. Jassikki must have eased the heel of his right hand beneath my left foot, for I soon found that shifting my weight to that side let me pull myself half a hand-length higher. With a great push I managed to claw my way beyond the first two handholds. I then got a grip on some deeper snow and, with a desperate pull, dragged my torso up over the edge. From there I found it easy to swing one knee up and drag my whole body out.

I lay there heaving for breath longer than I would have liked. From below I could hear Jassikki calling up to me. Even calling back was beyond my ability.

When I turned around, I saw him standing in the middle of the ice-block that had saved us from the depths.

I glanced around.

The glacier slanted down toward what remained of the Umbrage camp. Many small figures moved about directly below; others had clustered off to the right. Across the glacier I saw a few more people, though whether Umbrage or Heirs I could not determine. All around I saw nothing but ice and ice-fissures—no people, no equipment, nothing.

Is there any rope close by? asked Jassikki.

Nothing, I replied. No hatchets, either.

He stared up at me.

I said, Let me find help.

Of course.

We did not say goodbye. There was no time to lose.

[Marcelino Hondero Huamán, formerly Marsa-lai S'safta, interviewed September 10, 1970.]

* * *

You can imagine my surprise, though, when Jassikki called for me the afternoon following the big battle. Jassikki and someone else. A woman. I didn't recognize her at first. She was one of us—one of the Mountain-Drawn—but wearing Lowland attire. At some point I remembered her from the night before: the woman who had visited the Man of Ignorance at his tent. Yet here she was again with the Man of Knowledge!

Both of them looked terrible: scratched, bruised, smeared with blood. Neither could walk well without help from the Adepts who had brought them back to camp from the glacier. What had happened to them up there? What were they about to do next? It wasn't my place to understand these events. I was just a slinger from the village of Panli. All that concerned me was what I could do for those I served.

"We have heard of your deeds," the Moon's Stead told me. "We have heard of your prowess as a slinger."

"That is my duty," I replied.

"You do it well."

"All I do is honor the Sun and the Moon."

The Moon's Stead then spoke to the Man of Knowledge—the Sun's Stead himself—in a language I couldn't understand. They talked briefly as the Masters watched. Then to me again: "Would you honor them again with more deeds?"

"In any way I can."

"Difficult deeds?"

I nodded.

"Dangerous deeds?"

Again I nodded.

At a signal from the Man of Knowledge, two Adepts came forth carrying a box of light-colored wood. I recognized it as a Lowland thing but knew nothing about it otherwise. The same was true when the Moon's Stead reached over and removed some red objects from the box. They looked like something I'd seen when some Zuara passed through Panli: a smooth staff for pounding meat. Somehow I knew they were nothing like that ... They looked waxy and smelled funny. I saw strange black marks on their sides.

Then the Sun's Stead asked, "Would these work in your sling?"

His question puzzled me. "Work ... ?"

"Would you be able to throw them? Hurl them?"

I reached out for the stick, grasped it, hefted it. "I could sling it far enough," I told them, "but it will tumble in flight."

"That makes no difference," he responded. "Just so long as you reach your target."

"I will do everything possible to sling them right."

"Good. We're counting on you to stop the Umbrage. The Umbrage—and the Man of Ignorance himself."

"Let me do what I can."

"Even at peril of your own life?"

"Anything to serve the Sun and the Moon," I said.

[Aeslu of Vmatta, *Chronicle of the Last Days*.]

It took me longer than I would have liked to descend from the glacier, but the delay served me well; by the time I reached the Umbrage camp, the Heirs had overtaken it completely. For this reason Loftossotoi, Marhaislu, and a throng of weary but jubilant Heirs made quick work in rescuing Jassikki from the ice-fissure. Our haste was fortunate: the Man of Ignorance had already set off for the Mountain followed by a band of Umbrage. Even as we prepared our equipment, we could see a scattering of small, dark figures moving slowly up the ice.

Thus we did not tarry in reaching the place where the glacier, having risen gradually more than halfway to the Mountain's cliffs, now angled steeply upward—precisely that place where the ice, having been a flat surface that countless fissures slashed back and forth into a deadly maze, now became still deadlier.

At the time I found it difficult to grasp how our surroundings might have ended up even more treacherous than they were already. I should not have been surprised. Like all glaciers, this one was a vast, slow river—a river flowing with blocks and fragments of ice instead of water. During our brief time at the Mountain's base, I had heard it move when great rumbles welled up now and then from below, and I had felt it move when the ice shuddered beneath my feet. It was in motion as fully as any stream; the motions simply took place more slowly and violently. Rivers flow smoothly on the level but churn and boil down a slope: this holds true whether the flow is water or ice. Thus the Mountain's glacier, though relatively flat on its lower slopes, turned into a jumble where it descended from the cliffs. Innumerable blocks of ice teetered on one another in a massive but precarious heap. Slabs of ice jutted out from the rest. Smaller chunks lay heaped among everything else. Like a vast frozen waterfall, this whole mass angled steeply above us.

Yet Forssabekkit, followed at some distance by a band of Umbrage, proceeded upward as if oblivious to the dangers all around. Oblivious—or indifferent. They scrambled up a pile of fairly small chunks to a slab that angled to their left. From there the Man of Ignorance boosted himself into the narrow gap between two chest-high blocks wedged against each other. One of them abruptly tilted with a low grinding noise; the Man of Ignorance lost his balance for an eyeblink; then he caught himself, shifted his weight, eased his way up the gap, and climbed onto the block. No sooner had he reached safety, however, than the other block shifted again, closing the gap from which Forssabekkit had only just emerged.

This is madness, said Marhaislu. We shall all be killed!

I could hardly dispute the Stonemaster's words. The whole great pile of ice seemed ready to collapse at any moment.

Loftossotoi said, Stop him by some other means—

What other means? asked Jassikki. You'll never catch him.

The sight before us made his point clear. Forssabekkit and the Umbrage with him were already too far ahead for us to overcome their lead.

Jassikki asked, Where is the slinger?

Marhaislu gestured to a man—short and broad-shouldered, like all good slingers—who had come along with the ten or twenty Heirs in our group. He looked fearful but resolute. With him were a woman whose pathpack held a load of Forssabekkit's doomsticks and, to her left but keeping a little distance, a man with a lighted torch.

Forssa! Give up! shouted Jassikki. Just give up!

Two or three of the Umbrage with him looked back at us briefly, then proceeded upward.

The Man of Ignorance had vanished somewhere beyond the top of that block. Jassikki and I looked up toward where we had seen him last.

Just then Forssabekkit reappeared, now gazing down at us from his roost. He stared for a while only to disappear again. Jassikki and I faltered at first, then started up after him.

The ice became more and more difficult to climb. I had grown accustomed to ice over the past several Moon-spans, had learned to walk on ice in its many textures, had mastered the rudiments of using the Lowland ice-hatchet and footclaws, had

developed the intermingling of caution and reck-
lessness needed to move about on the ice. Yet my
surroundings just then bore no resemblance to
anything I had experienced before. It was not just
that these slabs and pillars of ice tilted every
which way, nor that they created a stairway whose
steps frequently stood taller than I myself did.
Rather, what alarmed me was that the stairway
crumbled beneath me even as I climbed it. Jassikki, the Heirs, and I seemed on the verge of
bringing the icefall down upon us with every step.

Off to the left! shouted Marhaislu as we started
up. Some of you go that way, the rest go this way.
We have to spread our weight.

Jassikki headed to the right.

I want to be with you, I protested.

No—too dangerous. We can't stay too close together.

As if to prove the point, the slab beneath him
shifted just then, sinking at least a full armlength.
Jassikki almost lost his balance but regained it when
the slab settled again. He then stepped off carefully
onto the block against it and, anchoring the point of
his ice-hatchet, pulled himself to safety.

We proceeded upward—Jassikki on the right, I
myself on the left, each of us flanked by five or six
Heirs. Within a short while I felt breathless and
weak. Never in my life had I felt so exhausted. The
effort of taking each step, of pulling myself upward, was the least of it; what sapped me was the
constant uncertainty as the blocks of ice beneath
me groaned and creaked under my weight. I could
scarcely believe that any of us would gain another
few manlengths, much less enough distance to
overtake the Man of Ignorance. And if we reached
him, what then? What sort of battle could we fight
where the very ground beneath us shifted without
the least warning?

Jassikki must have sensed my desperation, for at about that time he called out to me: Keep going—he can't be far ahead.

Jassikki—

Just keep going!

I pushed myself harder; I hooked my hatchet over the edge of the next ice-block and pulled myself upward; I kicked hard to drive my footclaws in securely; I strove without pause for the place where the steepness seemed to relent. If we could just reach that rim, I told myself, we could stop Forssabekkit . . .

Just then the Man of Ignorance shoved a great block of ice toward us. It must have been half a manlength long and almost as thick—big enough to split two or three of the other blocks in its path and jolt the rest. It shook the whole heap we were clinging to. With a loud crunching noise it sank into the pile, upended a slab, shoved some other blocks aside, and slid toward us. Jassikki flung himself to his right as it approached. Marhaislu scrambled to her left. I could not see Loftossotoi, but I heard his shout. The others leaped or clawed their way to safety. Then a long pillar tilted on its end, teetered briefly, and fell in my direction. I clawed my way up another block and barely missed being crushed by the first. Yet within a few eyeblinks everything in motion came to rest; Jassikki and I found ourselves almost exactly where we had been.

God damn you! shouted Jassikki, and he started up at once after the Man of Ignorance.

I looked back at the great broken staircase we had ascended. Below, where the fallen block had come to rest, I saw the edge of Loftossotoi's robe protruding from underneath.

* * *

[Juana Méndez de Mariátegui, formerly Huna-tau Mantassi of Va'atafissorih, interviewed September 10, 1970.]

What can I tell you? We Umbrage chased after Forssabekkit as fast as possible; some perished, falling into the crevasses that lay open everywhere on the surface of that glacier; others—more skillful or just luckier—managed to work our way higher on the ice. Yet the man we sought offered us no help. He glanced back at us now and then, he saw us, he watched us carefully, yet he proceeded as if indifferent to our fate.

We called out to him. We pleaded with him. We begged him to help us.

There was no answer to our cries—unless it was simply the sight of him ahead, always ahead, with his back to us.

But someone else paid us more attention. From the start of our scramble up the ice, I'd noticed some of the Heirs coming up after us. Others among the Umbrage saw them, too. They were not only Heirs: some were Masters. And if I wasn't mistaken, two of them were a man and a woman whom the Masters treated with great deference. Could they have been the Sun's and Moon's Steads? Of course, now I know that they were, but at the time I knew nothing of the kind. All I knew was that a pack of Heirs had started chasing us. And though they never caught up with us, they didn't need to.

How can I explain what happened next? How can I make sense of what they did to us?

Let me try. Let me—

No, maybe I shouldn't.

Maybe I can't.

[Aeslu of Vmatta, *Chronicle of the Last Days.*]

We found it easy to outflank the Umbrage. The ice-boulders they rolled down on us did great damage, killing six Heirs and wounding at least that many, yet we made our way up the glacier much faster than they did: the boulders themselves made us desperate to accomplish our task. Too, the Umbrage themselves moved so erratically, so awkwardly, so devoid of energy or spirit that they were far less challenging enemies than before. The Man of Ignorance went ahead without paying his followers the least attention. At times it almost appeared as if their leader intended not so much to lead them as to flee from them.

Arriving on the ridge allowed us a full view of the Umbrage and their progress. We gazed over a sunken area and prepared our onslaught. I dreaded what was about to happen, yet I welcomed it all the same. Forssabekkit had brought a dangerous fire to the Mountain Land; now he would feel some of its heat. His dynamite—what Marhaislu called doomsticks—would do the work. A slinger named Marsalai would provide the means of delivery.

All right, said Jassikki as he placed a doomstick in the pouch of Marsalai's sling. Move fast once I light it. If you don't, we'll all be killed.

Marsalai remained calm despite this warning. He spoke not a word; he just accepted what Jassikki gave him and took his stance.

All the while Forssabekkit and the Umbrage proceeded laboriously up the ice.

Jassikki accepted the torch from Marhaislu, touched it to the doomstick, and said, Now do it—now! *Now!*

The slinger hesitated. Having seen the damage that those red tubes could do, I felt weak with fear at the sight of sparks flying off it. But Marsalai whirled his sling around and around till at last his strange projectile rose, curved overhead, and dropped toward the ice.

We watched it fall. Soon it diminished to little more than a red speck dwarfed by the great expanse of white. Below us the Umbrage, too, stopped to watch.

A flash of light followed almost at once. Knowing what would follow, I covered my ears instinctively; the thunderclap caught everyone else by surprise.

I suspect that none of us had seen where the doomstick landed till just then, but at that moment we knew. A white plume blossomed over the glacier. Chunks of ice rose into the air, sank, and rained down on the fleeing Umbrage below. Just as these small pieces came to rest, however, two big ice-blocks disengaged from the slope and, loosening other blocks as they fell, tumbled toward the Umbrage. Even as we watched these slabs crushed at least five people.

At this sight Marhaislu and the Heirs shouted in exaltation: Death to the Umbrage!

Again, said Jassikki. With that word he handed another doomstick to the slinger. Do it again—only this time bring it right down on Forssa.

I spoke his name but did not respond.

Marsalai loaded his sling; Jassikki lit its deadly cargo; the weapon whirled; the doomstick rose and fell.

When the thunder struck, the ice tumbled forth—so much at once that it seemed liquid instead of solid, a great wave splashing down the mountainside—and it swept away another ten or twenty of the men and women scrambling to escape.

Again a cheer went up among the Heirs:

Death to the Umbrage!

Death to Forssabekkit!

Death to Forssabekkit and the Umbrage! Jassikki then handed another doomstick to the slinger, waited for him to set it properly in his sling, and set it alight with the torch. Everyone stood back. The slinger began to whirl his sling; he released the missile with an abrupt snap; the doomstick sailed off toward its targets.

The flash of light followed almost at once, then the thunderclap an eyeblink later.

Two pillars of ice toppled as I watched, began to roll, and soon started more ice-blocks in motion than I could count. The Umbrage, panic-stricken, seemed unable to move. They simply watched. Then, already too late, they fell all over themselves trying to flee. The icy rubble descended over them before any could reach safety.

Death to Forssabekkit and the Umbrage!

Fewer than five or six Umbrage remained. None of them looked our way. Like mice scampering to flee a brushfire, they simply fled. Ahead of the rest, at least as desperate but higher and less awkward in his motions, was the Man of Ignorance.

Now again, said Jassikki as he handed another doomstick to the slinger. Try harder. Can't you bring it down any closer to him? At this rate he'll be halfway up before—

I told him, *Stop.*

As if unaware of my words, Jassikki waited for the slinger to set the red tube in his sling. He said, Hurry—

Stop! I told him again. This is enough!

We've almost got him. We've almost got the son of a bitch—

Let him go.

He turned to me now. What did you say?

Let him go. The Man of Ignorance is doomed.

Not yet he isn't! shouted Jassikki.

How far can he get without equipment? I asked. Without food? Without cold-weather clothes?

Who knows? Let's not take chances.

Please—no more.

Now Jassikki gazed right at me. You *want* him to escape, don't you?

I want us all to escape.

Even as I spoke, a rumble reached us from somewhere on the Mountain.

I gestured uneasily and said, The doomsticks will destroy us—

We can't let him go. You can't, either, unless you've lied to me about your intentions all along. He paused a moment, then asked, Have you?

I faltered, then fell silent.

While I watched, the slinger held the doomstick close to Jassikki, who then lit its yarn with his torch. All right, he said, Let's get this over with.

Again the whirling; again the high arc of the doomstick toward the Umbrage fleeing it.

The flash of light came before the doomstick struck the ice. At once the thunderclap followed— this time far louder than before.

Was I relieved or pleased? Not that I wanted the Umbrage to escape; I simply wanted to be done with all this killing. Let Forssabekkit and his minions flee. Let them try climbing the Mountain. How could they last more than a day or two? Let the Mountain determine who reached the Summit—or else died trying.

The Heirs cried out again: Death to the Umbrage!

Death to Forssabekkit and the Umbrage!

I motioned for them to be silent.

Death to Forssabekkit!

Something had changed. At first I was unsure precisely what. A sound hit me: dull, distant. I could not tell what was happening. I remember glancing toward Jassikki, who looked back with a quizzical expression, as if to say, So: here we are.

By this time some of the Heirs had begun pointing to a place far above us on the Mountain. A white plume rose from that place and grew larger even as we watched. The plume itself looked harmless at first, little more than the spindrift that rises from any peak in a high wind; then it doubled in size, tripled, and with every passing moment augmented its height and width. Yet no matter how alarming its changes during those few eyeblinks, I realized that the plume itself was not what should have frightened us; it was something else, something for which the plume served merely as a messenger. For the plume was indeed nothing but snow whipped up into the air. What truly frightened me lay at the plume's root: an avalanche whose crest now swept down the Mountain toward us. Ice, rock, and snow churned together into a great beast that devoured everything in its path.

At once everyone began to flee. Heading this way and that, all the Mountain-Drawn stumbled off, slamming into one another and tripping over the glacier underfoot, for the whole Mountain had begun to shake. Staying upright grew difficult, then almost impossible, as the avalanche rattled the already treacherous ground beneath us. I saw Heirs and Umbrage slip about, screaming, as they lost their footing. I saw others sprint as if to safety, heading sideways across the ice, only to plunge at once into a crevasse. I ran, too; fell, got up, ran again; fell once more; struggled to avoid the lip of an ice-fissure; fell again; forced myself up; slammed at once into a pair of Umbrage skidding down the slope; scarcely disentangled myself from the rope that linked them before they slid, screaming, over the edge of another fissure; and ran harder than I had ever run before when I saw a nearly unbroken expanse of hard-packed snow ahead.

By then what lay underfoot was not the only danger. A trickle of ice-bits hissed a few manlengths to my left, and a few chunks spun after, cracking into bits and knocking loose more ice as they fell. More chunks followed. Then still more. This is it, I thought. Within a few eyeblinks the avalanche would come and crush us all. Yet when I glanced backward to look—

for no matter how afraid I felt, no matter how much I wanted to run away, my curiosity got the best of me—I saw that the avalanche was still approaching. Even at such a distance, its force had begun to shake the whole Mountain.

Four boulders that would have been immovable to a hundred men struck the slope ahead of me, plummeted into the jumble of rocks pushing out of the ice right there, splashed fragments of stone in all directions, and wrenched themselves end over end as they bounded into the valley. The smell hit me a few seconds later: thick as the odor of burning bone. I faltered, stopped short by the sight but also by the smell. I almost started to gag. I crouched, crying. As if my hands might somehow protect me from what would soon come crashing down, I held them over my head. *May the Sun's light illuminate my life forever,* I prayed. *May the Moon's glow bring radiance to my soul.*

The smell stung my nostrils. The roar of all those rocks and slabs of ice clashing together blasted my ears. The dust and grit they unleashed into the air shrouded my eyes. Yet even as I felt myself overwhelmed by the smell, the sound, and the sight of what was happening, still more rubble came down. I wanted nothing more than to hide, yet I forced myself to watch, to see what we had brought upon ourselves, as the avalanche itself arrived; and I saw a great wave arch before me, striking down any Heirs or Umbrage who struggled to outrun it; and the noise increased into the loudest that I had ever heard—vast, random, lacking any detail; and when the slabs of star-stone had spun away into the valley, when the last fragments had vanished, when the tide of snow and ice had spread out like water, when the final patter of snow and gravel had diminished, the surrounding silence was more massive than the Mountain itself.

The two old women and the old man sat without moving. Marcelino Huamán, his eyes vague with cataracts, gazed toward the wall but seemed to be looking at something far away.

At last I asked, "How many of the Mountain-Drawn survived?"

"None," answered Esperanza at once.

I couldn't quite suppress my suprise at this answer. "You did, at least."

Before Esperanza could respond, Juana Méndez de Mariátegui said, "There must have been twenty or more. People who ran away. People who ran toward the sides of the glacier and somehow escaped the avalanche. That's what I did."

"There weren't that many," interrupted Marcelino. "Maybe twelve. Everyone else got swept away."

"How did you escape?" I asked him.

"I didn't."

Their evasiveness began to frustrate me. "Clearly you did."

"I didn't. Not by my own efforts, anyway. I was rescued." There was an odd tone to these words; I couldn't tell if he was boasting or apologizing.

"Rescued by whom?"

Marcelino Huamán smiled. With only two or three teeth left in his mouth, his smile was at once charming and ugly. "By her." He nodded toward Juana de Mariátegui.

"You?" I asked. "You—an Umbrage—rescued this Heir?"

The fat old woman smiled shyly. "If I'd known

*he was one of them, I wouldn't have bothered. I
just saw this body half-buried under muddy snow.
I pulled him out. Then it was too late—he was
alive. I couldn't just stick him back in, could I?"*

Everyone laughed.

*Everyone but me. "How did you get down from
the glacier?"*

*Marcelino shrugged. "I don't remember. I was
half-dead, I think."*

*"He was not!" said Esperanza abruptly. "I saw
him. Both of them. A number of us managed to get
away."*

"Heirs and Umbrage alike?"

"Mostly Heirs. A few Umbrage, though."

*"How did you tolerate one another after all
that?"*

*"We had no choice. There was some fighting, of
course—the whole Mountain Land was in an up-
roar. Mostly those of us who escaped the avalanche were too tired and sick and hurt to care."*

*All three of them fell silent for a while. From
somewhere outside we heard two radios wafting
music our way from different stations: one playing
an Indian song called "Mambo de Machahuay," the
other playing some cuts from the Beatles'* Abbey
Road.

*I asked, "What about Jassikki? What about Aeslu
and Forster? Did they survive, too? Did they get
away?"*

*Their responses couldn't have been more non-
existent if I'd never asked my questions. Both
women and the man simply sat there. The only answer came from the open window.*

Once there was a way to get back homeward.
Once there was a way to get back home.
Sleep, pretty darling, do not cry—
And I will sing a lullaby.

Later, as Esperanza and I walked back to the bus stop, I asked her, "Why did you say that none of the Mountain-Drawn survived?"

"Because they didn't. We didn't."

"Yet here you are right beside me."

People watched as we passed: a young gringo and an ancient Indian woman. A few of the boys we crossed paths with laughed when they saw us.

"Once I was Issapalasai of Mtoffli," she said. "Now I am Esperanza Martínez. Once I was a Keeper of Records. Now I am a scrubber of floors. Once I was a First-order Adept of the Heirs to Ossonnal and Lissallo, Founders of the Mountain Land. Now I am just another Lowlander."

She held out both hands as if checking for rain. She went on: "No, there were no survivors."